SHADOWS STRIKE

"You're perfect," Heather declared, and cringed when it emerged almost as an accusation.

Ethan grinned. "And you're not?"

"No, I'm not," she said. "Trust me when I say I'm aware of every single one of my flaws because my damned telepathy allowed me to hear past boyfriends mentally catalog them."

All levity fled his handsome, perfect features. "I don't understand. What flaws? I don't see any."

"You will when I'm naked," she muttered, cursing the insecurity instilled in her by the men of her past.

He considered her thoughtfully. "How attached are you to those clothes?"

Heather blinked. "Not very. Why?"

He blurred.

Heather felt a tug and looked down. Her mouth fell open. "Holy crap!" She was completely naked.

Ethan laughed. "One of the perks of being immortal."

She reached for the covers.

Ethan captured her hand and brought it to his lips, stopping her. "Don't. Let me see you."

She swallowed. "What about you? You're still semi-clothed."

Rolling off the bed, he stood beside it, blurred, then stilled, as bare as she was.

Wow. Ethan could easily grace the pages of one of those hunky guy calendars. His body was perfectly sculpted, thick with muscle. And he was very aroused.

She swallowed.

"Now," he said, his voice lowering to a purr as he knelt on the bed beside her, "let me see if I can find all of these flaws the imbeciles you dated in the past thought they saw. Lie back."

Books by Dianne Duvall

DARKNESS DAWNS

NIGHT REIGNS

PHANTOM SHADOWS

"In Still Darkness" in PREDATORY
(with Alexandra Ivy, Nina Bangs, and Hannah Jayne)

DARKNESS RISES

NIGHT UNBOUND

"Phantom Embrace" in ON THE HUNT
(with Alexandra Ivy, Rebecca Zanetti, and Hannah Jayne)

SHADOWS STRIKE

Published by Kensington Publishing Corporation

SHADOWS
STRIKE

DIANNE DUVALL

ZEBRA BOOKS
KENSINGTON PUBLISHING CORP.
http://www.kensingtonbooks.com

ZEBRA BOOKS are published by

Kensington Publishing Corp.
119 West 40th Street
New York, NY 10018

All Kensington titles, imprints and distributed lines are available at special quantity discounts for bulk purchases for sales promotion, premiums, fund-raising, educational or institutional use.

Special book excerpts or customized printings can also be created to fit specific needs. For details, write or phone the office of the Kensington Sales Manager. Attn.: Sales Department. Kensington Publishing Corp., 119 West 40th Street, New York, NY 10018. Phone: 1-800-221-2647.

Zebra and the Z logo Reg. U.S. Pat. & TM Off.

First Printing: September 2015
ISBN-13: 978-1-4201-2982-3
ISBN-10: 1-4201-2982-1

eISBN-13: 978-1-4201-2983-0
eISBN-10: 1-4201-2983-X

10 9 8 7 6 5 4 3 2 1

Printed in the United States of America

Chapter One

Fog stole across the ground and curled cool fingers around Heather Lane's ankles. Shivering, she pried her gaze away from the eBook on the tablet in her lap and studied her surroundings.

Tall, dark, hulking trees surrounded the small clearing in a cylinder of dense foliage her eyes couldn't penetrate. A full moon had set about an hour ago, leaving behind blackness and twinkling stars occasionally obscured by wispy clouds. Slouched in her comfy tailgating chair, Heather glanced at her watch. 5:43. The sky would soon begin to brighten with dawn. Until then, lawn lights encircled her like a fairy ring, providing ample illumination.

It was so peaceful here, the quiet and dark beauty loosening the knots stress tended to lodge in her shoulders.

She dropped her gaze to her tablet once more.

A faint rustling sound distracted her.

"Please let that be birds or squirrels up, foraging about early," she murmured.

Unable to locate the culprit, she lifted her feet and propped them on the portable footstool that matched her chair. She really didn't want to encounter any less-cute members of the rodent family. Or snakes. But if she did, she might as well make it harder for them to skitter or slither up her pants leg.

A breeze whipped the fog into a mild frenzy, carrying with it a noise that seemed out of place amongst the chirping of crickets, croaking of frogs, and scuttling of squirrels.

Please, let it be squirrels.

Heather tilted her head to one side, listening.

Seconds later she heard it again.

Was that . . . voices?

Setting her tablet aside, she sat up straighter and lowered her feet to the ground.

A faint shout floated on the night. Then another. And another. Words indiscernible.

Her eyes fixing on the forest to the west, Heather tucked her tablet into the backpack beside her chair.

Branches snapped in the distance, the pops and cracks increasing in volume as if some huge creature barreled through the forest toward her.

Heart hammering in her chest, she slipped her hand deeper into the backpack and curled her fingers around the grip of the Walther PPQ 9mm she kept hidden there.

Thuds. Curses. Grunts. Branches still crackling. Foliage rustling.

She rose, withdrawing the weapon. What the hell was coming?

Dark figures burst from the trees on her left.

At first, she couldn't determine what the hell she was seeing. Even with the lawn lights aiding her, it looked almost as though a blurry tornado had spiraled into the clearing. Then . . .

Her eyes flew wide as the tempest's movement slowed.

Men. Seven of them. With eyes that glowed brighter than the stars above.

As they noticed the lawn lights, half of them paused to examine their surroundings.

Eyes that glowed *and* long, glinting fangs that didn't look like the cheap plastic store-bought fangs she saw each year on Halloween. These looked real.

The other half of the men fought some foe dressed all in black, circling him like hyenas and darting in to strike whenever they saw an opening.

The vibrant blue gaze of one of the males who had gone still latched onto Heather. His lips stretched into a sneering smile.

Oh crap.

Raising the 9mm, Heather aimed it at him, hoping she wouldn't have to pull the trigger.

Red liquid splattered one side of the sneering man's face.

She swallowed. Was that blood?

Two men fell limply to the ground behind him.

Yeah. That was blood.

The figure in black stilled and looked her way. He was well over six feet tall with broad shoulders encased in a long, black coat. Large hands clutched gleaming sais that dripped crimson liquid. His handsome face—bracketed by short, wavy, black hair—might as well have been carved from stone. Dark brows. An angular jaw shadowed with stubble. Luminescent amber eyes that caught and held hers as his lips parted, revealing fangs that rivaled those of his opponents.

"What the hell are you waiting for?" he growled. "Shoot them!"

He sprang back into motion. Blood sprayed as two more . . . vampires? . . . fell beneath his blades.

Ignoring his fallen comrades, the sneering vampire took a step toward Heather. Then another. Then shot forward in a blur.

Heather stumbled backward and fired her weapon.

Brah! Brah! Brah! Brah!

Beep! Beep! Beep! Beep!

Heather jerked awake. Heart racing, she glanced over at her alarm clock and threw a hand out to hit the button. 5:00.

When the annoying beeps ended, she slumped back against the covers and waited for her heart to stop slamming against her ribs.

Frustration pummeled her.

She would *never* feel rested as long as she kept battling freaking vampires in her sleep!

Tossing back the covers, she stomped into the bathroom to brush her teeth. Seriously, who dreamed about vampires?

Heather zipped through her morning ablutions.

She didn't even read vampire novels or watch vampire movies, yet almost every night she had the same damned dream.

Fifteen minutes later, clad in a comfy black jogging suit, she tied her sneakers, looped her backpack over one shoulder, grabbed her tailgating chair, and headed out onto the back deck. Cool air washed over her as she strode toward the handful of steps that led down to the backyard. A bucket full of bright solar-powered lawn lights awaited her at their base. Snagging the handle, she tromped toward the trees that bordered the back of the property.

The dream had begun haunting her about a year earlier.

A whole year of the same dream over and over again, never varying.

A year of that hot, dark, and dangerous vampire clad all in black ordering her to shoot the other vampires.

Vampires, for crap sake!

Grumbling beneath her breath, she trudged through the trees that thickened into forest, letting the lawn lights show her the way.

Discovering the reason behind the dream had become an obsession. She had to find some logical explanation for it, because the roommate she'd had in college—a psychology major who had psychoanalyzed everyone she had met *and* their pets—had thought the recurring dream a symptom of some mental illness when Heather had asked her about it.

"Mental illness, my ass," Heather griped as, minutes later, she stepped into a clearing.

Stepped into *the* clearing. The one from her dream.

Heather still couldn't believe she had found it. She hadn't even thought it real, had assumed it a fictional manifestation of she-didn't-know-what in her dream. She might not have *ever* found it if she hadn't finally located a house farther away from town that she'd wanted to rent and had just happened upon the clearing while scanning satellite maps for nearby waterways that—in heavy rains—might flood the rental property. (She had lost almost everything she'd owned in a flood once. She wouldn't do it again.)

She had no idea who owned the property that bordered the small parcel she had rented, unwilling to buy in the current housing market until she was sure she wanted to make North Carolina her home. Or if *anyone* owned it. But as soon as Heather had signed the lease and moved into her new home, she had begun to visit the nearby clearing in hopes of finding . . .

Well, she didn't know what. Something to explain why she kept dreaming about the place. And once she had begun visiting the clearing, the battle scene that continued to replay itself over and over again in her dreams had—in rare instances—been supplanted by surprisingly erotic dreams about the vampire in black. Dreams of his hands roving her body as his lips devoured hers, his bright amber eyes full of passion and possession.

She swallowed. Yeah. She needed to get to the bottom of the damned dreams.

Dropping her backpack near the center of the clearing, Heather set up her chair and the footstool that came with it.

At least no one had bedeviled her about trespassing. Yet.

She created her fairy ring of lawn lights and set the bucket aside. Fog stroked her ankles as she surveyed the peaceful meadow. Stars sparkled above her like diamonds. The moon, however, had already sought its bed.

Satisfied with the lights, she sank down into the chair and retrieved her tablet from her backpack.

The recurring dream of fighting vampires in this clearing might not be a sign of mental illness, but she wondered if coming out here before dawn every damned morning might be.

What the hell was she thinking?

Ethan rolled down the window of his Rimac Concept One and embraced the remainder of the night as he sped toward David's place.

His own home had been too quiet of late. Lisette, the woman with whom Ethan had been smitten for the past century, had married a year or so ago and spent all of her time with her husband Zach . . . something that still grated a bit. And Ethan's mortal Second, Ed, had a new lady love with whom he spent a great deal of time.

Without Lisette or Ed, Ethan's only company at home was silence.

David's house, on the other hand, always bustled with activity. Love. Laughter. Mischief. Mayhem. Life was never boring at the incredibly powerful elder Immortal Guardian's home. Ethan was never lonely at David's home.

So, yet again, Ethan found himself speeding toward it as dawn approached.

The metallic scent of blood assaulted his nose, riding on the breeze that buffeted him.

Hitting the brakes, Ethan brought the car to a halt on the road's dirt shoulder and cut the engine. The quiet of the country-side enfolded him as he stepped from the vehicle and drew in a deep breath.

His lips curled. Vampires. He couldn't tell how many. The

vamps' scents were nearly indiscernible beneath the blood of their recent victims, which no doubt coated them liberally.

Ethan's acute hearing picked up the vampires vying to see who could brag the loudest about the atrocities they had committed as they had drained their victims of blood.

Reaching into the car, Ethan retrieved his sais from the passenger seat and closed the door. Long strides carried him swiftly across the street and into the trees beyond.

The night sky would soon begin to lighten with daybreak. Ethan wanted to be comfortably ensconced in David's place before then, so, putting on a burst of preternatural speed, he raced after the vampires.

He made no effort to conceal his approach, just tore through the forest. Let the vamps wonder what the hell was coming. Let them fear the predator who hunted them as their victims had feared the vampires.

Ethan slowed when he saw them.

Seven. Hell. He hadn't expected that many.

Seven would be a challenge.

Seven could be a problem.

"Immortal Guardian," one managed to snarl a second before Ethan struck.

Having only been transformed a hundred years ago, give or take, Ethan was only slightly faster and stronger than the vampires. But his thoughts remained clear, unclouded by the insanity that plagued the latter, and he had been trained by a master swordswoman. Most vampires, on the other hand, were former college students who had been turned after getting drunk or high at a party and becoming easy prey. So most had spent their free time in sedentary pursuits, screwing around on the Internet and playing video games, before they had been transformed.

Their lack of combat training evened the playing field a bit. For every wound the vampires inflicted, Ethan inflicted four. His sais swept their flashy Bowie knives aside, tore clothing, and parted flesh. Cries of pain, coupled with roars of fury, abounded as they crashed through the underbrush. One vampire sank to his knees, but stumbled back up again.

Ethan swore. Remaining in constant motion, he drew blood from every opponent.

Light glimmered through the trees up ahead as he swept a weapon from a vampire's bloody hand and pressed forward.

Now what? he wondered as it grew brighter.

Heather glanced at her watch. 5:43. About this time in the dream, vampires would burst into the clearing and freak her the hell out. As usual, she'd give it a few more minutes, then pack everything up and—

A faint rustling sound intruded upon the night.

Her heart gave a little leap.

"It's just a squirrel," she murmured. But . . . it was 5:43. In the dream, she always heard a rustling sound at 5:43.

She eyed the trees to the west with trepidation.

A breeze ruffled her bangs and scattered the fog at her feet as the first voice reached her.

Her heart began to ram against her rib cage as a faint shout followed. Then another. And another. Words indiscernible.

Heather's hands began to shake as she shoved her tablet into her backpack and drew out her Walther PPQ 9mm.

Branches and twigs snapped and crackled as something plowed through the trees toward her.

Oh shit. This wasn't really going to happen, was it?

Thuds, curses, and grunts increased in volume. Foliage rustled.

Rising, Heather backed away, raised her 9mm, and aimed it at the shadowed evergreens. Chest level. Her finger near the trigger. Ready to squeeze it at a moment's notice.

Dark figures burst from the trees.

As in the dream, she could see little more than a blurry

tornado of motion, spinning across the meadow, knocking over a couple of her lawn lights.

Fear consumed her. Adrenaline surged through her veins. Her breath shortened as she eased back another step.

The tempest's movement slowed. Seven men swam into focus with blood-soaked clothing, glinting fangs, and eyes that glowed blue or green or silver. Seven men who bore the exact same features as the vampires in her dream. Seven men with fingers curled around the hilts of big-ass knives with which they seemed intent upon slaying the eighth.

And the eighth . . .

Garbed all in black, he stood nearly a head taller than the rest. His short, black hair was mussed. His face and clothing, like theirs, bore streaks of blood. His chest rose and fell with rapid breaths that emerged from lips parted to reveal fangs as he swung deadly sais at his opponents.

One of the blue-eyed vampires took a step toward Heather, drawing her wide-eyed gaze. A sneering smile that chilled her blood stretched his thin lips.

Two of his companions fell to the ground behind him.

The man in black looked her way. Glowing amber eyes locked with hers. "What the hell are you waiting for?" he growled. "Shoot them!"

He sprang back into motion, attacking two more.

Ignoring his fallen comrades, the sneering vampire took a step toward Heather. Then another. Then blurred as he shot forward.

Heather stumbled backward and fired her weapon.

Brah! Brah! Brah! Brah!

The vampire stumbled to a halt, four holes now decorating his torso, but he didn't go down. Fury and pain contorted his sneering features.

"The arteries!" the handsome, amber-eyed warrior shouted. "Hit the major arteries!"

Too terrified to ignore him, she fired again, hitting the

sneering vampire in the carotid and femoral arteries. When another vampire raced toward her, she shot his blurry form several times in the chest until he slowed and she could see him better, then sent a bullet through *his* carotid artery.

Both vampires fell to the ground as a third vampire sped toward her.

Heather fired her Walther again.

Brah! Brah! Brah! Brah! Click. Click. Click.

Shit! She was out of bullets.

The vampire was but a breath away when something swept between them and knocked her down.

Heather hit the ground hard. Dirt and weeds abraded her hands and elbows. A flurry of motion erupted a few feet from her face.

Grabbing the 9mm she had dropped, she scrabbled away and dove for her backpack.

More grunts and thuds and hisses sounded behind her as she upended the pack and rifled through the contents in search of her spare magazine.

There!

Grabbing it, she ejected the empty magazine and shoved the full one home.

"It's okay," a deep voice spoke behind her.

Advancing the first bullet into the chamber, she spun around, sat on her butt, and aimed the weapon up at . . . the vampire clad in black.

Bending over, he braced hands that still clasped sais on his knees and nodded toward the corpses on the ground at his feet. Beneath her horrified gaze, the bodies began to shrivel up like mummies. "It's okay," he repeated. "It's over." Crimson liquid speckled his handsome face. His clothing glistened with damp patches.

Heather adjusted her aim, sighting his carotid artery down the barrel. But her hands shook so violently now that she doubted she could even hit the trees behind him.

He started to straighten, but halted mid-motion and emitted a grunt of pain. Sheathing one of his sais, he reached behind him to feel his back, then swore. His nostrils flared as he drew in a deep breath and clenched his befanged teeth together. He made an odd, jerky movement with his hidden arm, then brought his hand back into view, now clutching a short knife.

Heather stared. Had he just pulled that thing out of his back?

He slung it at one of the deteriorating vampires. "Asshole." Sheathing his other sai, he pressed a hand to his side and limped toward her. "I'm sorry I knocked you down. Are you okay?"

"Stop!" she blurted. "Don't come any closer."

His steps halted. He squinted down at her. Frowning, he reached into his coat.

Heather touched her finger to the trigger. "Keep your hands where I can see them."

He froze. In slow, incremental movements, he raised the hand he had pressed to his side and held it bloody-palm-out toward her. "Easy," he crooned. When he withdrew his other hand from his coat, he held up a white handkerchief. "I just need to wipe my eyes. Blood keeps dripping into them and blurring my vision."

When he seemed to wait for a response, she gave a jerky nod. "Go ahead."

Heather scrambled to her feet while he wiped his eyes, turning the pristine cloth red. She hadn't realized until then that a deep gash marred his forehead. Blood did indeed trail down over his dark eyebrows into his eyes.

As soon as he cleared his vision, the dark warrior from her dreams narrowed glowing amber eyes at her.

"Forgive me," Ethan said, realizing he had made a mistake. "I thought you were Nichole."

The woman before him appeared to be in her midtwenties and bore the same height—about five foot five or six—and slender build of Sean's Second, Nichole. The woman's hair was about the right length—halfway down her back. She was garbed all in black. Although, now that he could see her better, he noted that she wore a slim-fitting jogging suit rather than the black T-shirt and cargo pants Seconds tended to prefer. Instead of black combat boots, colorful sneakers encased her small feet.

"You can lower your weapon," he told her. Was he so coated in blood that she couldn't identify him? "I'm Ethan. I'm immortal, not vampire. Are you . . . ?" He tried to think of any Seconds in the area whom he hadn't met. "Are you Aidan's Second? Or Alleck's?" He couldn't remember if their Seconds were male or female.

The woman didn't respond, just stared back at him with wide, brown eyes so light they almost appeared golden. She was pretty. Fresh-faced and makeup-free like the girls of his youth. Pale skin lightly dusted with freckles, a pert nose, and lovely lips.

Her aim never wavered.

Unease trickled through him. "You *are* a Second, aren't you?"

She inched backward, her gaze darting around the clearing as though seeking some avenue of escape.

Ah hell. "At least tell me you work for the network," he damned near begged.

She muttered something beneath her breath. Something about a dream.

He frowned. Maybe she had hit her head when she had fallen. "Are you all right?" he asked as he raked his gaze over her. "Are you injured?" He hadn't thought any of the vampires had touched her, but he *had* been distracted. If one had bitten her, it would explain her being less than lucid. The glands that formed above the fangs of vampires and immortals during their transformation released a chemical similar to GHB under the pressure of a bite.

But this woman didn't seem drugged. She didn't appear acquiescent. She didn't look as though she were about to pass out. She looked alert. Very much so.

She just seemed a little . . . off.

"Miss? Are you injured?" he prompted again and took a careful step toward her.

"Who are you?" she demanded, tightening her hold on the semiautomatic until her knuckles turned white. "*What* are you? What are *they*?" She nodded at the vampires, who would soon be no more than piles of clothing once the virus that infected them devoured them from the inside out in a last, desperate bid to live.

"Please lower your weapon," Ethan said, infusing his voice with as much calm and reassurance as he could. "I won't hurt you."

A laugh of disbelief escaped her before she bit her lip, brow puckering.

Hell. As much as her hands shook, she'd shoot him eventually if he didn't take the gun away from her. Unwilling to lose more blood than he already had, Ethan leapt forward in a burst of preternatural speed and yanked the weapon from her hands.

Gasping, she stumbled backward, then turned to run.

Ethan reached the trees first and turned to face her.

She stopped short. Backed away.

"I'm not going to hurt you," he repeated, voice soft. He could hear her heart pounding in her chest, as hard and fast as the hooves of a galloping horse.

Again biting her lip, she looked around, took in the piles of clothing where the vampires had fallen . . . and seemed to come to some decision.

Turning her back on him, she crossed to the nearest lawn light, bent, and yanked it out of the ground. She went to the next, bent, and yanked it out of the ground, then continued on to the next and the next until she had gathered every single one of them.

Puzzled, Ethan watched her. "What are you doing?"

Offering no response, she dropped the lights into a bucket he hadn't noticed and started folding up her chair.

"Miss?"

"Heather," she said as she knelt and started shoving the belongings scattered on the ground back into her pack. "My name is Heather, not that it matters." As soon as she finished, she glanced up and opened her mouth—to ask for her gun back, he suspected—but apparently thought better of it and zipped the pack closed.

Rising, she looped it over her shoulder, grabbed the chair with one hand, the bucket with the other, and started toward him.

Ethan tucked her 9mm into one of the many inner pockets of his coat, then showed her his empty hands so she wouldn't fear he would shoot her.

Such precaution proved unnecessary. Heather walked right past him and plunged into the trees.

"What are you doing?" When she didn't answer, Ethan followed. "Heather? What are you doing? Where are you going?" He tried not to notice the sway of her shapely hips as she moved forward in smooth strides, but it had been a long damn time since he had had sex and this woman's body, hugged so snugly by her soft jogging suit, made him want to strip her bare and—

"I'm going home," she announced.

Ethan's eyebrows flew up. "I beg your pardon?"

"I'm going home!" she practically shouted. "I'm going home. I'm going to bed. And I'm going to wait for the damned alarm clock to wake me up."

She really thought this was a dream?

"I don't know why it didn't wake me up this time. It

always wakes me up at the same point in the dream. Every freaking time. Right after I look down and see that it's 5:43. All hell breaks loose. I fire my gun. And the alarm wakes me up." She shook her head, her wavy, brown hair swinging into motion and sweeping across her back. "Maybe there was a power outage. I can't remember the last time I changed the backup batteries in that thing. Or maybe the damned thing just crapped out on me. I don't know."

"The clock?" he asked, trying to follow her words.

"Yes. I don't know why the alarm didn't go off this time, but it didn't, and I need to wake up. I *really* need to wake up."

"This isn't a dream, Heather. You aren't asleep."

The trees thinned.

Heather exited them, leading him into a backyard that had recently been mown. "Yes, I am."

"No, you aren't," he insisted, thinking this the most bizarre conversation he'd had in recent memory. Beyond the lawn, a quaint little frame house painted pale yellow stared back at him over a slightly warped back deck.

Dropping the bucket, Heather spun to face him. "I didn't know it was real!"

Ethan stopped short, nearly bumping into her. "What?" She smelled good, too. And standing this close to her, towering over her the way he did, gave him a tantalizing glimpse of her cleavage.

What the hell was wrong with him?

"I didn't know it was real, okay?" She motioned to the meadow on the other side of the trees. "I knew the clearing was real. I knew *that* much. But I didn't know *you* were real. I didn't know *they* . . . the freaking vampires . . . were real. I thought you were all symbolic or something. I mean, who the hell knew vampires really existed? And I didn't know I was going to kill two of them. Or that you would slice and dice the others right in front of me. Or that they would shrivel up and . . . and . . . and . . ." Words seemed to fail her. "The dream never went that far because the damned alarm always woke me up!"

She combed her fingers through her hair in an agitated gesture. Noticing that her hand shook, she rubbed it on her pants leg as if the tremors could be removed like dirt. "I just . . . I need for this to not be real," Heather finished, turning pleading eyes up to his.

"I'm sorry," he said, fighting an absurd urge to wrap his arms around her, draw her close, and tell her that this *was* all a dream, that everything would be okay. "But it *is* real."

Heather stared up at him for several seemingly endless minutes. "Your fangs are gone," she mentioned, her voice soft and low now.

He nodded.

"Your eyes are still glowing."

Because he was attracted to her and, evidently, had lost all control over his body. Not that he could tell her that. "It takes a little longer for their color to return to normal."

A bird twittered nearby as the sky began to lighten.

"What did you say your name was?" Heather asked.

"Ethan."

Another lengthy silence followed.

Oddly, he didn't mind it. Didn't feel awkward. Just concerned for her.

"This is real, Ethan?"

"Yes."

She drew in a deep breath and let it out slowly. "Then thank you for saving my life."

Chapter Two

Heather willed her hands to stop shaking as Ethan raised his eyebrows. "What?"

"That third vampire would have killed me if you hadn't taken him out."

He smiled, flashing straight, white teeth. "Well, I couldn't have defeated seven vampires without your aid, so why don't we call it even?"

He *had* suffered some pretty atrocious wounds.

She eyed his bloody and battered form. "Are you okay?"

He nodded. But she noticed he couldn't straighten all the way.

"Are you sure?" she asked. "Because you look like hell. Not that I know what you look like without all of the blood and gore."

He started to laugh, but cut it off with a pained grunt. "Honestly, I've been better." He motioned to the house behind her. "Is this your home?"

She nodded. "Sort of. I'm renting it."

"We have a lot we need to discuss, Heather. Would you like to do it inside?"

She noticed his eyes kept going to the brightening sky. "Oh. Right. The whole vampire sunlight thing."

He opened his mouth, closed it, then smiled. "Right. We'll get to that. First, I need to ask a favor of you."

She shrugged, his easy manner finally unwinding her nerves and aiding her pulse in slowing. "Ask it."

"Would you wait here for just a moment? I need to retrieve my car."

"Oh." Why did it seem weird that a vampire would drive a car? Too many cheesy movies in which she had seen vampires turn into bats and fly away, perhaps? "Okay."

"Please don't make any phone calls while I'm gone," he added.

Who the hell would she call? Anyone would think she had cracked if she called them, said she had been swept up into a battle between vampires, then proudly displayed a clearing with empty clothing scattered about on the ground. "Okay."

Ethan tilted his head slightly. "I'll hear you if you do."

It was a warning, albeit a very kindly delivered one.

"I won't make any calls."

Nodding, he backed away. Then his form blurred and shot away into the forest.

Heather stood there, numbness seeping into her that could not be blamed on the cool breeze.

Was this what it felt like to go into shock?

The mind that had raced with various and assorted freak-outs only moments ago now slowed to a standstill, as if trying to process everything she had seen and done in the past few minutes had overloaded its circuits.

Gravel crunched as a car pulled into her driveway.

She frowned. That couldn't be Ethan. He hadn't even been gone a full minute.

Leaving her bucket of lights where she had dropped it, Heather headed for the house, walked around the side toward the front, and stared at the vehicle parked behind her little compact car.

The sleek red and black sports car looked as if it could fly and fairly oozed money. Every man she had ever dated would have drooled and instantly declared it his dream car. Even the damned rims were cool, and Heather *never* noticed crap like that.

The driver's door swung open. Ethan stepped out.

The car was so low to the ground that she didn't think it even came up to his waist. How the hell did he fold his— what?—six-foot-four-inch frame into it?

Closing the door, he strode toward her. A limp marred what might have normally been a smooth, graceful gait.

"Now I *know* this is real," she told him with resignation.

"Why?"

She motioned to his car. "Because I've never seen anything like that before, so it wouldn't make sense for it to appear in one of my dreams."

Nodding, he reached toward her.

Heather's breath caught as butterflies erupted in her belly in anticipation of his touch.

What the hell?

Tucking his long fingers under her backpack strap, he drew it down and off her arm, then looped it over his own shoulder. He motioned to the house. "Shall we?"

Her tongue inexplicably tied, she turned toward the house and headed up the steps to the front porch.

Ethan kept pace with her, his hand lightly brushing her lower back as if she were a date he escorted home.

Her fingers fumbled a little when she tugged the keys from her pocket and unlocked the door.

He didn't wait for an invitation the way vampires in movies often did. He just entered on her heels. Even standing a bit hunched over, he had to duck to enter.

Heather closed the door behind him and watched him set her backpack down.

He gripped the lapels of his long, black coat. Struggling to shrug it off his shoulders, he winced and issued a soft grunt of pain.

Heather closed the distance between them and brushed his hands aside. "Let me do it." She could feel his gaze as she eased his coat—sticky with blood—over his shoulders and drew it down his arms.

Touching those broad shoulders—shoulders she had seen bared and bunching as he moved over her in the erotic dreams—drove home again that he was real.

He sighed. "Thank you."

Nodding, she hung the coat on one of the hooks by the door. Sheesh. The thing was heavy, and she soon discovered why. Numerous bladed weapons were tucked into sheaths in the coat's lining. As was her 9mm, which she opted not to retrieve for the moment.

Quiet embraced them as she turned to face him.

Heather had been born with the ability to read others' thoughts, so she rarely experienced complete quiet like this in another's presence.

"This is weird," she said.

Ethan laughed and winced once more. "Yes, it is."

"I'm having a little trouble processing it all."

"I don't blame you."

Heather stared up at him. She was alone with a tall, dark, and dangerous vampire. What the hell should she do?

She motioned to the sofa. "Would you like to sit down?" Pure habit, she supposed, prompted the offer. Her parents had worked diligently to instill good manners in her.

He followed her gaze. "Do you have an old towel or a sheet or something I can cover the cushions with so I won't stain them?"

Heather amended her earlier thought: She was alone with a tall, dark, and dangerous vampire who was polite enough to want to avoid staining her furniture. "Sure. Do you . . . want to wash up first?"

He glanced at the curtains covering the nearest window. "Really? You wouldn't mind?"

"No." She doubted theirs would be a short conversation. Once she jump-started her brain, she would have little trouble coming up with questions for him.

He opened the front door. "Excellent. I'll be right back."

Damn, the man could move fast. He flew out the door, then returned almost swifter than it took her to realize he'd left.

She eyed the small duffel bag he carried. "That had better not contain duct tape, rope, and a scalpel."

He grinned. "I'm not a serial killer, Heather. This is just my first aid kit."

"Oh." His kit didn't include blood, did it? *Gross*.

"Where's your bathroom?"

She pointed to a hallway just off the living room. "First door on the right."

"Thanks. I'll just be a minute," he promised and disappeared into the bathroom, closing the door behind him.

Heather took two steps toward the kitchen, intending to wash her own hands, then halted. Was that her shower turning on?

When the telltale squeak of her shower faucets repeated, she looked toward the bathroom. She had thought he had just meant to wash the blood off his face and hands, not take a shower. That didn't seem odd to him? Showering in a complete stranger's home?

It sure as hell seemed odd to her.

The water turned off.

She frowned. Not even a full minute had passed, so he couldn't have taken a shower. It must've been the sink. She hadn't realized the sink's faucet squeaked, too.

She started toward the kitchen once more.

The bathroom door opened.

Ethan strode out, carrying his duffel bag.

Heather's mouth fell open. It *had* been the shower.

Ethan's skin no longer bore ruby stains. His short, black hair was wet and slicked back from a face Heather found even more handsome than she had anticipated. Heavy stubble dusted a strong jaw. His straight nose fit his face perfectly. Dark brows hovered above pretty brown eyes that no longer glowed with that peculiar iridescence.

The clothing that adorned his large form was fresh and clean, if a little rumpled. A tight, black T-shirt clung to broad shoulders, a muscular chest, and biceps the size of freaking bowling balls. The man worked out. His black cargo pants hugged a narrow waist and thighs that also bulged with muscle.

When she finally managed to drag her gaze back up to his face, she felt her heart turn over at the boyish grin he sent her.

"Thank you. That feels much better."

Heather couldn't find her voice. Her heart began to pound erratically in her chest as images from those erotic dreams bombarded her. Damn it. They had been few and far between. Why had they affected her as much as the nearly nightly battle scene dreams?

Ethan's smile slipped. "Heather?" Dropping his bag, he approached her with care. "Are you okay?"

She forced herself to nod. "Yes, it's just . . . been a rough morning."

"For both of us," he agreed. Only a few feet away now, he drew in a deep breath and frowned. "You're hurt."

"What?"

"You're hurt. I smell blood. And not vampire blood." His gaze swept her form. Stepping closer, he took her hands in his and turned them palms-up so he could study them.

Heather dragged her gaze away from him and glanced down, surprised to see several scratches on her hands. She must have scraped them on rocks or sticks when Ethan and the vampire had knocked her down. Though the cuts weren't deep, they had managed to birth a few beads of blood.

She looked up at Ethan.

A faint amber glow entered his eyes. Was he drawn by the blood?

She cleared her throat. "If you start licking my hands, I'm going to totally lose it."

He laughed—a deep rumble that warmed her insides and demanded she smile in return. Then his grin twisted into a grimace of pain. "Don't make me laugh."

"Sorry."

He raised her hands and pressed them back toward her shoulders so he could see the underside of her forearms. "Your elbows are scraped, too. Do you have any first aid stuff, or do you want to use some of mine?"

"They'll be fine if I just wash them."

"You should put some alcohol on them. I know it'll burn like hell, but it will help keep the cuts from getting infected."

She tried to protest again, but soon found herself squeezed into her bathroom with him. Ethan positioned her hands over the sink. Turning on the water, he soaped up his large hands, then shocked Heather by gently sliding them over her hands and up her arms to her elbows.

Her heart again pounded in her chest.

"I'm sorry," he said. "I know it stings."

"I'm fine," she whispered. How could he smell so good when he wasn't wearing any cologne?

He rinsed the soap off them both, then patted her skin dry and bent to draw a bottle of rubbing alcohol from the bag she hadn't realized he had brought with them. Opening the small closet behind him, he drew out a small, clean hand towel.

Heather secretly cringed at the huge box of tampons that sat front and center on the shelf above the towels.

Ethan didn't seem to notice it, though.

Hell, he was a vampire. He might not even know what they were for.

Pouring some alcohol on the towel, he looked down at her and raised his eyebrows.

Gritting her teeth, she nodded.

Fire flashed through her hands and up her arms when he applied the towel to her scrapes.

Tossing the towel aside, he bent his head and blew on the throbbing cuts.

Even his warm breath on her skin made her pulse race.

"Better?" he asked, his face close to hers.

"Yes, thank you."

Straightening, he took her hands in his own and held them. "How did I do?"

She raised her eyebrows. "What?"

"I only recently started learning first aid. You're the first person I've tended. So . . . how did I do?"

What was it about him that kept making her want to smile? "You did well."

He grinned that heart-stopping grin of his. "Excellent." Raising her hands, he pressed a quick kiss to the back of each, then released them and grabbed his bag.

While she stood there, stunned, her skin tingling from the touch of his soft lips, he motioned for her to precede him out of the bathroom.

Heather led him back into the den.

"Shall we sit?" he asked.

The fact that he was so sweet and polite only made the situation seem more surreal. A *kind* vampire with exceptional manners who was learning to administer first aid to humans in need?

"This is so weird," she repeated as she sat on the sofa.

Again he laughed, then grimaced. "I thought I told you not to make me laugh." He seated himself beside her, a few feet away. Swiveling to face her, he propped an ankle on the opposite knee and draped his muscled arm across the back of the sofa.

Damn, he looked good.

He's a vampire, Heather! Get a grip!

"Why were you fighting those vampires?" she asked. As that odd numbness finally wore off, question after question flooded her mind. "They looked like they were trying to kill you."

"They were."

"Why?" *Was it a territorial thing?* she wondered.

"Because I was hunting them."

She stared at him. "*You* were hunting vampires?"

"Yes." His face sobered. "Those vampires were insane, Heather. They preyed upon humans, torturing them and killing them at will. I couldn't allow that."

There were good vampires and bad vampires?

Not too surprising, she supposed. There were good humans and bad humans, after all.

"Why did they shrivel up like that?"

"That's what happens to vampires when they die."

She eyed him with disquiet. "So . . . that's what would happen to you if you died?"

"Yes."

"That's messed up."

He shrugged. "Every living thing decomposes when it dies. We just decompose a little faster."

A *lot* faster. Too fast to even bury. "Will more vampires come looking for the ones we killed?"

A look of unease swept over his handsome features. "I can't rule it out." He glanced at the curtain-cloaked windows, then met her gaze. "It would be best if I stayed until sunrise. I'd like to be here to protect you in case more of their ilk should follow their friends to the clearing and trace our scents here."

Crap. "Should I be worried?" she asked, fear resurfacing.

He shook his head. "Vampires can't bear any level of sun exposure, so you'll be safe during the day. And it's supposed to rain this evening. That will wash away our scents. If you can stand having me around that long, I'll stay until then to ensure your safety."

She said nothing.

"Heather?"

"I'm sorry. This is just a lot to take in. I went from believing vampires only existed in my dreams, fiction, and folklore, to helping one vampire defeat seven others, and am now being asked if one can spend the day with me."

He tilted his head to one side. "You mentioned something earlier about a dream. I thought you were just in shock at the time. Are you saying you dream about vampires?"

She studied him. "You're on the up-and-up, right? I mean, fangs and glowing eyes aside, you seem like a nice guy." He could have killed her several times over by now if he had been anything else.

"I am. You can trust me, Heather. I won't let anyone hurt you."

She hesitated, *wanting* to trust him, but . . .

"If I were like the ones we destroyed earlier, I would have already tortured and killed you by now," he added, his words mirroring her thoughts.

He didn't pull any punches, did he?

And both knew he spoke the truth. It was why she hadn't fought his coming inside. She had seen his incredible speed and strength. Had known windows and doors would've proven no deterrent to someone that powerful. Yet he had *suggested* they speak inside.

And she had wanted to understand those dreams. What better way than by asking the star of them?

Heather drew in a deep breath. "I don't dream about vampires in general. I dream about the vampires we fought together this morning." She met his curious gaze. "I dream about *you*, Ethan."

* * *

Ethan blinked. "You dream about me?"

How the hell was that possible? They hadn't even met until half an hour ago.

"Yes."

"So when you were ranting about wanting to wake up earlier . . ."

"I thought that what happened this morning was another dream."

He frowned.

"I know it sounds crazy," she said with a sigh, "but I've had the same vivid dream almost every night for a year now. I'm sitting in a clearing." She pointed in the direction of the meadow in which the melee had taken place. "*That* clearing. I'm surrounded by lawn lights. I'm reading an eBook. I look at my watch. It says 5:43. I hear a rustling sound. A breeze stirs the fog that creeps across the ground. I hear distant voices, followed by what sounds like a large animal barreling through the forest toward me. I grab my gun. You and seven vampires—the same seven vampires you fought this morning—burst into the clearing. I freeze. You tell me to shoot them. I fire my weapon. Then the alarm wakes me up."

Understanding dawned. "You thought your alarm had malfunctioned."

"Yes. At least, I hoped it had."

"You have the same dream every night?"

"*Almost* every night," she corrected.

"Nothing in it ever changes?"

"Nothing."

He smiled. "You must be a *gifted one*."

Her brow furrowed. "I'm sorry. A what?"

"A *gifted one*. A human born with special abilities other humans don't possess."

She blanched. "W-why would you think I was different from other humans?"

"You clearly have precognitive abilities. Your dream foretold the future."

She relaxed a little. "No. I'm not . . . I don't have precognitive abilities."

"Sure you do. The dream told you you'd meet me."

"But that's never happened before. If I were precognitive or whatever, wouldn't I have been like that all my life? Wouldn't I have had other dreams that predicted the future?"

He lost his smile. "This has never happened before?"

"No."

Puzzled, he pondered that. *Gifted ones* were born with their abilities and began using them at a very early age. They didn't just suddenly gain abilities in their twenties. "If you aren't a precog, why did you look so uneasy when I suggested you were different from other humans?" He heard her heart begin to pound as a spark of fear entered her lovely brown eyes. "Do you possess *other* gifts or abilities?"

She remained silent.

"It's okay, Heather," he assured her. "You can tell me. I'm different, too."

Her lips twitched. "The fangs, glowing eyes, and super speed kinda clued me in to that."

Ethan laughed, ignoring the pain that shot through his back. He *really* liked this woman. "I was different before my transformation."

Heather studied him. "Are you saying *you* are a—what was it—a *gifted one*?"

"Yes."

"What are your abilities?"

"I just have one, which I'm afraid is pretty boring."

"Somehow I doubt that."

He sent her a wry smile. "I have what you might call a photographic memory, raised to the nth power."

She frowned. "You remember everything you read?"

"Everything I read, see, hear, smell, touch, and taste. I remember every detail of every minute I've ever lived."

She stared, her expression saying, *Really? That's it?*

Ethan grinned. "I told you. Boring as hell, right?"

"No," she very kindly lied. "Not at all."

"What's the earliest memory you can dredge up?" he asked.

She thought about it for a moment. "My granddad giving me a puppy when I was three or four."

"Where were you?"

"I think we were in the living room of my grandparents' home."

"What shirt was he wearing?"

She raised her eyebrows. "I don't know. I think something light."

"Was it day or night?"

"I don't know that either."

Ethan nodded. "Most peoples' earliest memories are like that. Most start around the same age, too. Now ask me what *my* earliest memory is?"

"What's your earliest memory?" she parroted.

"The day I was born."

Heather regarded him with obvious disbelief.

"I remember the midwife who delivered me," Ethan told her. "The floral pattern on the dress she wore. The sweat stains under her arms and between her breasts. It was hot as hell that day and the house had no air-conditioning." He saw it all as clearly as a video. "A mix of gray and blond hairs had escaped her chignon and clung damply to the edges of her face. I remember my father bursting into the room, drawn by my crying. His shirtsleeves were rolled up to his elbows, and he looked both scared and elated at the same time. I remember my older brothers peeking into the room while my dad took me from the midwife and presented me to my mother. And I remember feeling an instant connection to my mother, remember the fear draining away when she took me in her arms and kissed the top of my head."

Heather said nothing.

He smiled, accustomed to the response. "You don't believe me." He liked that she would rather say nothing than admit she thought he was full of crap and hurt his feelings.

She had a kind heart.

"When we were in the clearing," he said, "you dumped the contents of your bag onto the ground when you were looking for your spare magazine."

She nodded.

Ethan proceeded to list every single item in her backpack.

Her eyes widened.

He told her how many lawn lights she had used, told her how many speckles of blood adorned her shoes.

She looked down. Counted. Confirmed he was correct.

"I asked you where you were going when you left the clearing," he went on. "You said, 'I'm going home. I'm going home. I'm going to bed. And I'm going to wait for the damned alarm clock to wake me up. I don't know why it didn't wake me up this time. It *always* wakes me up at the same point in the dream. Every freaking time. Right after I look down and see that it's 5:43. All hell breaks loose. I fire my gun. And the alarm wakes me up. Maybe there was a power outage. I can't remember the last time I changed the backup batteries in that thing. Or maybe the damned thing just crapped out on me. I don't know.'"

"Wow," she said. "I really rambled on like that? I sound crazy."

He shook his head. "Those vampires were crazy. You were just rattled." He went on to tell her how many feet they had walked before they had entered her backyard. How many steps led up to her back deck. How many steps led up to her front porch. How many boards composed the floor of her porch. How many tiles made up her bathroom floor. "I'd recite everything you have in your bathroom closet, but I honestly don't know what half of that stuff is."

A moment of silence passed.

Rising, Heather crossed to the bathroom and disappeared inside it. Several minutes passed before she leaned out and stared at him with wide eyes.

"Was I right about the tiles in the floor?" he asked.

"Yes."

"Do you want to know how many tiles are in your shower?"

She nodded.

He told her.

She ducked back into the bathroom. Several minutes passed. She exited, returned to the sofa, and sank down beside him. "You were right."

He smiled. "Do you want to count the boards on your front porch? I could tell you how many shingles are on your roof, if you'd like."

"No thanks. You've blown my mind enough."

"If I *really* wanted to blow your mind, I'd tell you how many pieces of gravel are in your driveway."

"Seriously?"

He nodded. "I told you. Photographic to the nth power. I remember every detail of every minute I've ever lived with exceptional clarity." Occasionally he wished like hell he could forget some of it. He had amassed a lot of memories in just over a century. He enjoyed being able to recall the good times so clearly. But the bad times . . .

He had watched helplessly as a friend had been decapitated last year and would give almost anything to be able to erase that from his memory.

"What did you call us?" she asked, voice tentative. "I mean, people who have special abilities."

"*Gifted ones.*" He gave her a moment, then leaned forward and took her hand, careful to avoid touching the scratches. Another spark of attraction zipped through him at the contact.

He'd been fighting it ever since he had torn his gaze away from her swaying hips earlier. Something about her just tempted the hell out of him. "What gift have you been hiding?"

Her fingers tightened around his. "You won't believe me," she said.

"Try me." He sent her an encouraging smile. He knew how hard it was to talk about such things.

"I can read minds."

"You're a telepath?"

"Yes."

"I'm guessing you can't read my mind."

She bit her lip. "No, I can't. But I really *am* telepathic."

"I believe you. I know other telepaths who can't read my mind even though they can read almost everyone else's. Apparently I have a very hard head," he said with a grin, hoping the furrow in her brow would smooth.

Her expression turned doubtful. "You know other telepaths?" Did she think he mocked her?

"Several actually. Only the most powerful of them can read my mind. And it's so difficult that, when they do, it makes my nose bleed and hurts like hell." Fucking Zach had damned near brought Ethan to his knees, trying to read his mind.

"Not being able to read your mind was one of the reasons I thought I was dreaming earlier. I could never read your mind in the dreams. And I've never encountered anyone in real life whose mind I couldn't read."

"There are others out there who are hard to read, we're just very rare," he assured her.

She leaned forward, hope and fear mingling in her wide eyes. "Are you bullshitting me, Ethan? Because—"

"No. I'm telling you the truth." He frowned. "You've really never had any other prophetic dreams?"

"None."

Maybe she was like Sarah. Sarah hadn't known her dreams foretold the truth until Seth had told her. But Sarah's dreams were riddled with symbols. Events didn't unfold in them exactly as they would in reality.

Heather's dream had shown her vividly and precisely what was to come.

"That's a puzzle," he admitted.

She nodded.

He drew his thumb across the back of her hand. Her skin was so soft.

He heard her heartbeat pick up again. "Are you afraid of me, Heather?"

"No. Not really. Why?"

"Your heartbeat keeps picking up whenever I'm near you or when I touch you."

Color flooded her cheeks.

"It's okay. I won't be hurt if you are. Considering how we met—"

"I'm not afraid of you."

Ethan studied her. If she wasn't afraid of him . . .

She groaned. "This is so embarrassing. You're going to think I'm a total loon."

"I assure you I won't."

She bit her lip. "You must know you're good-looking. I mean, women probably throw themselves at you wherever you go."

"You're attracted to me?" he asked with some astonishment . . . and a *lot* of interest. This night—or morning—was taking an unexpected and wholly welcome turn.

She covered her eyes with her free hand. "Yes."

"Good." When she peeked through her fingers at him, he smiled. "I'm *incredibly* attracted to *you*."

She lowered her hand. "You're just saying that to be nice."

"No, I'm not. Why do you think my eyes keep glowing? I assume my eyes are glowing faintly?"

"Yes."

"They're doing that because I want you."

She remained quiet for a moment. "They were glowing when you fought the other vampires. Somehow I doubt you wanted *them*."

He laughed, pain again streaking through his back. "I was furious. My eyes glow whenever I'm gripped by strong emotion. Anger. Pain. Grief. Lust. The stronger the emotion, the brighter they glow."

She was quiet for a moment.

"Does it frighten you or make you uneasy when they glow?" he asked tentatively.

"No." Her eyes locked with his. "I think they're pretty when they glow."

Now *his* heart began to thud against his ribs.

"I know I sound like a broken record," she murmured, still staring into his eyes, "but this is so weird."

He grinned. "It *is* weird. Here I thought I'd dispatch a few vampires, then head over to a friend's house to stave off the loneliness that's been plaguing me of late, and instead, I get to spend the day with you." He narrowed his eyes. "I *do* get to spend the day with you, don't I?"

She smiled. "Yes."

He winked. "I'm going to tell myself it's because you enjoy my charming company instead of it being because you're afraid more vampires might show up."

She laughed, and seemed to relax for the first time. "And if I admit that it's for both reasons?"

Something warm unfurled in his chest as he gave her hand a squeeze. "Then I'd say my day just got a hell of a lot brighter."

Chapter Three

"Can I bum a smoke?"

Nick Altomari looked over at his friend. "Where are yours?"

"I promised Cindy I'd stop smokin' before the baby's born."

Releasing his hold on the M16 looped over his shoulder, Nick removed the pack he always carried from a pocket and held it out to Weston.

Wes drew out a cigarette, lit it up, and took a long, satisfied drag.

Smiling, Nick shook his head, pocketed the pack, and returned his attention to the forest his perch high in the southwest guard tower overlooked. A full moon cloaked by clouds cast dim blue light on the dense trees and thick tropical foliage. Hidden behind the jungle, the ocean lapped at a narrow shore and joined the other night sounds.

A tall, thick cement wall surrounded the small military base Nick guarded. Beyond it stood two chain-link fences, positioned several yards apart, that were woven with razor wire. The bare ground between them had been covered with thick sand none could cross safely without guidance. Any who tried would die when their foot inevitably found one of the many land mines buried within it. Beyond that, a wide swath of foliage had been cut down so no one could approach the "beach" without gaining notice and being challenged.

"Check it out." Wes pulled a white envelope from his back pocket, opened it, and withdrew a photo.

Nick leaned over to study it.

Weston's wife, Cindy, was seated on a tattered sofa, the waist of her pants nudged down to expose a huge, pale belly, her shirt pulled up to just beneath her breasts.

Nick grinned. "She looks like she swallowed a beach ball." Of all the guys bunking at the army base, Nick was closest to Wes. Though Nick was a few years older, they had known each other and been friends since basic training. Wes was twenty-one, Cindy twenty. A bit young to start a family, Nick thought, but he said nothing. "How far along is she?"

"Eight months."

Nick regarded her big belly and arched a brow. "Are you sure she isn't carrying twins?"

Wes grinned. "We're sure. The doctor warned us early on that the baby might be big like her daddy."

Nick shook his head. "What the hell are *you* going to do with a little girl?"

"Chase off all her boyfriends when she's old enough to date."

Both men laughed.

Weston carefully tucked the picture away. "Last time I talked to her, Cindy kept cryin' about bein' fat and ugly."

"Really? I think she looks cute."

"Me, too." He frowned. "Wait. Cute how? Cute like 'I'd do her' cute?"

Nick snorted. "Damn, you're a jealous man."

Wes sighed. "I know. I just can't stand the idea of any other man even *lookin'* at her. And with her bein' thousands of miles away . . ." He frowned. "Sometimes I worry she might find someone else."

"Get serious. Cindy loves you." But Nick knew it wasn't

just jealousy that precipitated his friend's pensive expression. "Only four months and a wake-up till you're outta here."

Weston nodded, staring out at the dark jungle. "It kills me that I won't be there when my daughter's born."

Nick could understand that. He clapped Weston on the back. "Have your sister videotape it so you can have all the gory details."

He grimaced. "I don't know how many gory details I want."

Amiable silence claimed them.

Nick glanced at his watch. Two more hours, then he could turn in. "I think I might have a pregnant woman fetish," he mused. "Is that a thing? Is there a pregnant woman fetish?"

Wes laughed. "I don't know. Why would you think that?"

"Some of the other guys have flashed pics of their pregnant wives or girlfriends and, unlike you, complained about how fat they were, saying they hoped the weight would fall off as soon as the baby was born." He shrugged. "I always think the women look hot."

Still smiling, Wes shook his head. "I'd say you were strange, but I don't think Cindy has ever looked hotter than she does now. Maybe we're *both* strange."

A cry sounded in the distance.

Straightening, Nick scowled and peered in the direction of the ocean. "What was that?"

"I don't know." Wes squinted. "Was it a bird?"

"I don't think so."

Another cry.

Foliage far in the distance—barely discernible in the darkness—began to jerk and sway.

"What the hell?" Nick muttered.

Trees shook and bent. Foliage rustled and bounced.

"What is it?" Weston asked, face anxious.

"I don't know. But it's coming this way." Nick touched his earpiece. "Hit the lights. We've got incoming."

Stadium lights, so bright they hurt Nick's eyes, flashed on, lighting up the "beach" and the trees on all sides of the base.

A wide swath of forest rippled with movement that grew closer and closer with every breath. Eerie growls or snarls or *something* deep and ugly swelled as whatever the hell it was approached.

Nick's hands tightened on his weapon as images from every dinosaur and big-ass monster movie he had ever seen flashed through his head.

"What the fuck is it?" Weston hissed, his voice high with fear. "A fuckin' T. rex?"

"I know, right?" Nick tried and failed to keep his voice light.

A buzzing whir sounded behind them. Nick risked glancing over his shoulder and saw remote-controlled fifty caliber automatic weapons rise atop the roof of the main structure.

"Attention," a voice blared from the speakers on the wall. "You are trespassing on property of the United States of America." The entire island—not just the base—fell under the army's jurisdiction. "This military installation is off-limits to all civilians and unauthorized personnel. Deadly force has been authorized. Trespassers will be shot. Stop where you are and leave, or approach slowly with your hands in the air and identify yourself."

"If you *have* hands," Weston muttered.

Nick nodded, his heart pounding as the message repeated.

Unless they were plowing through the forest in large, exceedingly fast machines capable of knocking down trees as they went, whatever approached wasn't human.

The . . . thing or things . . . were almost to the tree line when Nick heard a male voice speak low in his earpiece.

"Light 'em up, boys."

Fire shot from the muzzles of the rooftop weapons as

big-ass bullets tore through the jungle beyond the makeshift beach.

That ought to do it, Nick thought with some relief.

Foliage began to topple beneath the barrage, so powerful were the mini-missiles.

"Yeah!" Weston cheered. "That's what I'm talkin' 'bout!"

Nick didn't celebrate.

The growls and tree jostling didn't cease. They increased.

Glass shattered above Nick's head.

Wincing, he ducked back as the stadium lights above went dark and glass fell past his post in shards. More glass shattered down the way as *all* the lights were targeted. The stadium lights, the floodlights on the walls, those above the front gates, and every other light that was visible from the jungle burst into sharp confetti.

The base plunged into darkness.

Explosions lit up the night as something unseen breached the first chain-link fence and attempted to cross the "beach."

Nick and Wes both lunged for the drawer that contained the night-vision monoculars.

Nick yanked it open. "Here." Glancing up, he held out a monocular to his friend.

Something large and dark struck Wes, driving him backward.

Dropping the monocular, Nick turned and raised his weapon. As his eyes adjusted to the darkness, faint moonlight allowed him to find Wes down on the floor, his head lying two feet from his body.

"Fuck!" Nick looked around wildly, turning this way and that, searching for whatever had attacked. It was so damned dark.

Screams erupted in the next tower. Then the next. Down on the ground.

Nick backed toward the drawer, his heart slamming against his ribs.

Nothing moved.

Taking a huge chance, he released his weapon with one hand long enough to grab the other monocular from the drawer.

His hand shook as he attached it to his scope. Even over the screams, the gunfire, and those growls, his breath sounded loud in his ears.

Securing his hold on his weapon, he raised the scope to his eye and peered through it.

Ice sliced through his veins.

"Shit!" Nick squeezed the trigger as he stumbled backward.

Ethan downed the glass of tea Heather had offered him, wishing he had thought to bring a couple bags of blood with him. As he glanced around the room, taking in the half dozen or so framed photos, unease trickled through him. "Heather, who is the man in the photographs? The one in the uniform?"

She glanced at the pictures hanging on one wall. "My father."

"He's in the military?"

"Yes. He's in the army."

And there were a hell of a lot of shiny things on his uniform. "He's an officer?"

She nodded "A general."

Oh shit. This was bad. This was *so* bad. The Immortal Guardians had just fought several huge battles with mercenaries who had discovered the existence of vampires and immortals. The bastards had wanted to use the virus that infected both parties to create an army of supersoldiers they could hire out to the highest bidder. The military could *not* be allowed to learn the truth or they would likely follow a similar path.

"Are *you* in the army?" he asked, fearing her answer. She was damned good with a gun. When he had ordered her to hit the main arteries, she had done so with her next shot.

"No. We traveled around so much when I was a little girl that I swore I'd find an occupation that would allow me to put down roots and stay in one place."

That was a relief. "What occupation did you choose?"

Her face scrunched up. "Do you want my *public* profession or my *secret* profession?"

Intrigued, he chose "Both."

She sighed. "I read minds for a living. But everyone *thinks* I read facial expressions."

"I'm not following you."

"I call myself a FACS specialist, someone who studies the facial action coding system."

The facial action what? "Still not following you."

"The facial action coding system categorizes the physical expression of emotion through minor contractions or relaxations of one or more muscles in the face. I've gained a reputation for being so accurate that I'm often called in by local law enforcement and sometimes by the military and . . . certain agencies . . . to observe interrogations and interviews and tell them whether or not the suspect or criminal being questioned is telling the truth. Those who call me in think I'm reading microexpressions."

"But you're really reading thoughts."

"Yes."

Law enforcement. Military. Certain agencies. Hell. After everything that had happened during the past few years, Seth—the leader of the Immortal Guardians—would have Ethan's ass if he didn't call the network in on this. And Chris Reordon, head of the East Coast division of the human network that aided immortals, would go ballistic if he found out Ethan had let someone with Heather's connections retain knowledge of vampires' existence without Chris's ensuring she would keep the information to herself.

"Are you and your father close?" he asked.

"Yes. Why? What's wrong? You look worried all of a sudden."

Inwardly, he swore. She had been honest with him. He wouldn't feel right about being less than honest with her. "I *am* worried," he admitted.

"Why?"

"We've worked very hard to keep our existence hidden from humans."

"You and the other vampires?"

Again he swore silently. He didn't want to lie to her. She really *had* saved his ass earlier, taking out a couple of the vampires so he would only have to defeat five rather than seven. And she had revealed more about herself than she had cared to at his request.

But life had grown incredibly dangerous for immortals of late. So many enemies had risen up against them. Both vampire *and* human. Until he gained some assurances that she wouldn't tell her father or any of her other contacts, he couldn't explain the differences between vampires and immortals. He couldn't even tell her that he *was* an immortal.

"Yes." Technically, he didn't lie. Vampires didn't want humans to know about them either, especially after rumors of recent events had circulated the globe.

"Are you afraid I'll tell someone?"

"Yes."

She shook her head. "Who would believe me?"

"Your father might, if the two of you are close."

She considered that for a moment. "I think Dad would worry that I'd suffered a mental breakdown or something if I started babbling about vampires."

Five years ago, Ethan would have agreed. Now . . . not so much. "You haven't told him about the dreams?"

"No. I won't tell him about this, either. As I said, he'd only worry about me."

"Would you be willing to sign a confidentiality agreement, vowing not to tell anyone what you learned tonight or what I'm prepared to tell you?"

She stared at him. "Seriously?"

"Yyyyyeah," he said with some regret.

"There are vampire lawyers?" she asked incredulously.

Several lawyer/bloodsucker jokes sprang to mind, but Ethan opted to keep them to himself. "Not vampire. Human. The humans who work with us—"

"Humans work with you?" She seemed more taken aback by that than by the lawyers.

He nodded. "And they're very protective of us. The powers that be will have my ass if I don't let the humans talk to you so they can be assured of your silence."

She pulled her hand from his grasp. "Be assured of my silence how? By making me disappear? Because you look like you think they're going to—"

"No," he hastened to correct her. "They won't harm you. They'll just talk to you and ask you to sign a confidentiality agreement. That's all. I'll be with you the whole time." Holding her hand, if she would let him. And he would kick Reordon's ass if Chris upset her.

A full minute ticked past.

"Do I have any choice in this?" she asked, her pretty face grim.

"Not really. But I promise, Heather, no harm will come to you. You're a *gifted one*. These confidentiality agreements aren't just meant to protect us. They're meant to protect you and other *gifted ones*, too. Once you understand all that being a *gifted one* entails, you'll likely conclude that hiding what you are has been the wisest decision you've ever made."

She studied him for several long minutes. "Okay, I'll sign.

Now tell me what you meant by that. Why are *gifted ones* so special?"

It didn't surprise him that she would wish to know that first. Being different and not understanding why sucked. "*Gifted ones* are men and women like you and me who were born with gifts ordinary humans don't possess. Those gifts are a result of extremely advanced DNA."

Her brows drew down. "How advanced?"

"Every human has forty-six DNA memo groups that provide the blueprints for his or her existence. According to our researchers, *gifted ones* have seven thousand."

She stared at him, unblinking. "Seven *thousand*?"

"Yes."

"And everyone else has forty-six?"

"*Humans* have forty-six."

"If *they're* human, then what the hell are *gifted ones*?"

"We don't know the source of our advanced DNA. We just know—or rather we've learned, over the millennia—that it's best to conceal knowledge of our differences from the general public."

"What do you think would happen if humans found out?"

"In the past, they slew those whom they discovered were different. Today they would dissect you, experiment upon you, and seek to duplicate and exploit your gifts for monetary gain . . . *if* they didn't kill you outright."

She gave him a slow nod. "Yeah. That's pretty much what my dad told me."

"So he knows you're telepathic?"

"Of course."

"And he's never told the men he works with?"

"The army? No. He tells them the same thing I do, that I'm a FACS specialist."

That was good. That was *very* good, and should help ease Reordon's concerns regarding the military.

She pursed her tempting lips. "This might be a good time for me to admit I've used my gift for my *own* monetary gain."

"How so?" Judging by her current modest lodgings, she wasn't wealthy.

"I paid my way through college with money I acquired gambling."

He fought a smile. He knew many telepathic immortals, Lisette included, who had gambled their way to an impressive fortune.

"But I always chose the guys I fleeced carefully," she hurried to add. "They were all either assholes or bored multimillionaires or billionaires who wouldn't miss it. Or both. With a few freaks thrown in."

Ethan laughed. "Good for you. I admit I've done the same."

"You're telepathic, too?"

"No. It's the photographic memory thing."

"Counting cards?"

He nodded. "And everyone really *does* have a tell. When you remember every second of everything you see, you identify those quickly and can guess—"

"If your opponent is bluffing."

"Exactly."

"I don't feel so bad now."

He winked. "I *never* felt bad."

Her lips quirked up in a smile as her brown eyes lit with amusement. "So . . . any other revelations you'd care to make while I'm sitting down?"

"Actually, yes," he said. "I'm not a vampire. I'm an immortal."

She studied him a long moment. "This is going to be one of those days, isn't it?"

Again he laughed and wished his damned back didn't hurt so much when he did. "The traits humans have long associated with vampires—fangs, superior speed and strength, enhanced senses, photosensitivity, greater regenerative capabilities, and a need for blood—are a result of a very rare symbiotic virus. Vampires are humans who have been infected with it. Immortals are *gifted ones* who have been infected with it. In humans, the virus causes progressive brain damage that drives them insane. With *gifted ones*, however, our advanced DNA protects us from the brain damage, as well as some of the other, more corrosive aspects of the virus."

"So no insanity?"

"No insanity."

"Lucky you."

"Absolutely. Immortals live longer. We're stronger. We're faster. The older an immortal is, the greater his speed and strength, and the more sunlight he can tolerate. Older immortals also possess stronger and more varied gifts, because their bloodlines have been diluted less by ordinary human DNA over the millennia. So we spend our nights and—on very rare occasions—days hunting and slaying psychotic vampires who prey upon humans."

"Wow."

He frowned, unsure what had spawned the solitary word. "Wow what?"

"Wow. Those humans who work with you and keep your existence a secret must *really* be hard-core. With a *lot* of connections. How the hell have they managed to keep all of this a secret? Especially today, when everyone and their brother has a cell phone that can record video and instantly upload it to the Internet? Someone must have seen *something* by now."

He shrugged. "As you said, they're hard-core and have connections."

"I'm guessing anyone who tries to renege on that confidentiality agreement you want me to sign tends to meet a swift, untimely end."

"Honestly, I have no idea what the network does to those who attempt to betray us. I haven't had much hands-on contact with the network until recently. But, again, you have nothing to worry about, Heather. Once they learn you're a *gifted one*, they'll want to protect you the way they do us. I know I already said this, but you *really* don't want anyone to find out about your advanced DNA. Now more than ever."

His cell phone chirped. Ethan drew the phone out of his back pocket and saw that it was Ed, his Second. "I'm sorry. I have to take this."

She nodded.

"Yeah?" he answered.

"Are you at David's?" Ed asked in his gruff voice.

"No. I'm"—he glanced at Heather—"at a friend's."

She watched him curiously.

"What friend's?"

Ethan didn't want to go into detail and sought some way to avoid it.

Heather caught his attention. "Do you want me to give you some privacy?" she asked, voice low.

"Was that a woman?" Ed asked with an astonishment that grated on Ethan's nerves.

Ethan mouthed *No* to Heather and rose. "Yes," he answered Ed.

"Hot damn! You're finally getting laid," came Ed's jovial response.

Ethan lowered his voice. "It isn't like that."

"It had *better* be like that. You've been celibate for decades. That shit isn't natural."

Ethan turned his back to Heather. "It hasn't been *that* long, damn it." Hell, Lisette had just broken things off with him a year ago, not that Ed knew anything about that. "Did you call just to piss me off or did you want something?"

"I called to find out where you are. The sun is rising and your ass tends to fry in it when you're stuck outside. I wanted to make sure you were settled somewhere safe for the day."

Ethan sighed. "I'm safe."

"You suffer any injuries tonight?"

"A few," he admitted. His Second's job was to keep tabs on him and keep him safe. He wouldn't begrudge the man his ability to do so.

"Do you need blood?"

"No, I'm good." An overstatement, but he didn't want Ed to rush to his damned rescue. "Just sit tight. I'll talk to you later."

"If you say so. Have fun. And do *everything* I wouldn't do," he added, laughter in his voice.

Ethan ended the call and turned back to Heather.

She raised her eyebrows. "Was that your girlfriend?"

He shook his head. "My Second."

"Second what? Second wife?"

He grinned. "No, Ed is my Second, or human guard. My Renfield, if you will." Most movie buffs were well-acquainted with the fictional character Renfield, who had been Dracula's human assistant in films for almost a century.

"So . . . he keeps you safe during the day?"

"Yes."

"You really can't go out in daylight?"

"Correct."

She studied him. "Please don't take this the wrong way, but . . . are you bullshitting me, Ethan? I really want to believe you, but it's all so . . ."

"Weird?" he suggested, using her word.

"Yes."

He smiled and held a hand out to her. "Come here."

After the slightest hesitation, she rose, circled the sofa, and placed her small hand in his.

Damned if that didn't make him feel all warm and fuzzy inside.

Ethan led her over to the window that wasn't shaded by the front porch's roof. Releasing her hand, he raised the blinds halfway, then held his hand in the bright morning sunlight that flowed inside. His skin swiftly began to pinken with a sunburn that deepened and darkened to an angry red before blisters began to form. He gritted his teeth as pain rose.

"Stop!" Pushing him back, Heather hastily lowered the blinds.

Ethan's hand burned as though he had just rested it upon a hot stove.

Heather carefully took it in both of her own and inspected it. Her brow furrowing, she raised her gaze to his. "You didn't have to do that."

"I've been asking you to believe a hell of a lot, Heather. Most of it on faith. This was something I could prove to you with ease so you wouldn't be left doubting."

When she looked down at his stinging hand, her hair flowed forward and shielded part of her face from him.

Ethan reached out with his free hand and brushed the hair back, tucking it behind her ear.

Her breath caught.

Fingers tingling from the brief contact, he struggled to suppress the urge to bury them in the silky brown tresses and draw her closer. "I want you to feel safe with me," he murmured. "I want you to feel comfortable with me."

"I do," she whispered. "I probably shouldn't, but I do." She glanced at his hand. "Does it hurt?"

His lips quirked wryly. "Not as much as my back."

"Where the vampire stabbed you?"

He nodded.

"Is there anything I can do? Would you like me to take a look at it?"

He hadn't been able to do much with it on his own beyond splashing some alcohol on it and clumsily dabbing it with a towel. "I'd appreciate that. Thank you."

Smiling, she led him over to her kitchen's breakfast nook

and motioned for him to sit in one of the two chairs at her small table.

Ethan pulled it out, swung it around to face him, and sat down, straddling it.

"Take your shirt off," she ordered.

He drew his long-sleeved T-shirt over his head and draped it over the chair's back. When he looked at Heather, he found her staring at his chest.

Was that admiration in her gaze? Or was she checking out his wounds?

Heather glanced up. A pink flush mounted her cheeks as she moved to stand behind him.

Admiration. That was promising.

She hissed in a breath.

"Is it that bad?" he asked over his shoulder.

"Well, it isn't bleeding, but . . . yeah. It looks pretty bad."

Mortified that Ethan had caught her ogling his chest, Heather stared at his broad back.

Sooooo much muscle, which rippled as he folded his arms over the back of the chair and leaned forward.

The ragged edges of the deep puncture wound the vampire's knife had carved gaped a little, revealing damaged muscle she didn't examine too closely, afraid she might see bone if she did. Had Ethan been human, the wound would no doubt still be bleeding profusely.

"Do you have any butterfly closures?" she asked.

He nodded. "In my bag."

Heather retrieved his duffel bag and returned to his side. "Anything you don't want me to see in here?"

"No. You might want to avoid touching the clothing, though. It's probably still sticky with blood."

Kneeling down, she unzipped the bag and peered inside. Wadded-up bloody clothing, some spare blades, and first aid supplies. Nothing that would raise red flags. No naked selfies, freaky porn, severed body parts, or anything else alarming.

"Do you want me to pour some rubbing alcohol over it?" she asked, rising with the butterfly closures in her hand.

"Yes, please. I splashed some on it earlier, but did a pretty half-assed job."

He made no sound when Heather saturated a cloth she retrieved from the bathroom with alcohol and held it to the wound. He was so tall, she didn't even have to bend down when she leaned in close and blew on the stinging flesh.

Ethan tensed and rested his forehead on his arms.

Regretting the pain she must be causing him, Heather carefully pinched the edges together and secured them with butterfly closures. She taped a gauze bandage over everything, then rested a hand on his warm shoulder.

Weren't vampires . . . or immortals . . . supposed to be cold?

"How's that?" she asked, shifting to his side so she could see his face.

He raised his head. "Thank you."

She swallowed. "Your eyes are glowing." A beautiful, vibrant amber. "Is it from the pain?"

He gave his head a slow shake. "It's from your touch," he rumbled, his voice deep and husky. "I like the feel of your hands on me, your warm breath on my skin."

Her heart kicked into high gear again, slamming against her rib cage.

Ethan took the hand she had rested on his shoulder and raised it to his lips. "Don't be afraid," he murmured and drew her toward him.

She nodded, pulse racing as his gaze dropped to her lips. When she licked them nervously, his eyes brightened.

Releasing her hand, he wrapped his free arm around her

waist and urged her closer until she was pressed up against the back of the chair he faced.

With him seated, Heather could look into his mystical eyes without having to tilt her head way back.

His lips brushed hers. Featherlight. Sparking excitement and a desire for deeper contact.

"I am so drawn to you," he murmured and kissed her again, lingering this time.

Heather leaned into the back of the chair and dared to touch his tongue with her own. Shocks of pleasure darted through her like little sparks of lightning.

His arm tightened a moment before he released her lips. Those brilliant amber eyes met hers. "What are you thinking?"

"I'm questioning my sanity."

"Damn."

"Why?"

"Because I want to kiss you again, but I don't want to frighten you."

She gave him a slow nod. "Okay."

Disappointment darkened his features.

"Then *I'll* kiss *you* this time," she decreed. Cupping his strong, stubbled jaw in her hands, she captured his lips with her own.

He tasted so good. *Too* good. Too tempting by far. As tempting as he had in those damned erotic dreams she couldn't forget.

And the man knew how to kiss, how to stroke and tease until her body went up in flames. She had never in her life been so aroused by the simple touching of lips to lips, tongue to tongue.

Both moaned when she broke the kiss.

She pressed her forehead to his. "You don't know how confusing this is for me."

"I can hazard a guess."

Leaning back, she studied his ruggedly handsome features, drew her thumbs across his budding beard, and sobered. "I just met you," she told him, "but I've seen you in my dreams almost every night for a year. It makes you feel . . . familiar to me. As if we've lived next door to each other for a year, seen each other every morning when we stepped outside to fetch the newspaper, smiled and waved and retreated inside three hundred and sixty-five times, never speaking until you suddenly decided to round the hedges that separated our properties, introduce yourself, and ask me if I'd like to have a cup of coffee with you."

"I wish that *were* how we had met," he replied.

"But it isn't. I *don't* know you. Not really."

His lips tilted up at the corners. "And I wouldn't have waited a year to ask you over for coffee."

She smiled. He was such a likable guy. Why had they had to meet under such screwed-up circumstances?

Dropping her hands, she stepped back with more reluctance than she cared to admit.

His arms fell away. "Thank you again for tending my wound."

"You're welcome." She rubbed her hands up and down her thighs. "Now what do we do?"

He loosed a long sigh and looked as disappointed that the moment was over as she was. "I'll call the network and see if we can't take care of the confidentiality agreement now so you can go on with your normal life."

If going on with her normal life meant he would walk out of it and never return, it seemed to have lost some of its appeal. She didn't *want* Ethan to leave, not if she would never see him again. He really did feel familiar to her. And she liked him, damn it. He was charming and funny with old-fashioned manners, a body that made her want to tear his clothes off, and . . .

He didn't care that she was different.

She rather liked that he was different, too. Liked that she

couldn't read his thoughts. Her damned telepathy had destroyed every relationship she'd ever had, robbing her of the ability to form anything remotely long-term.

Everyone had dark thoughts on occasion. Hell, she had bitchy thoughts herself, sometimes wondering where the hell they had sprung from, and had been glad she hadn't spoken them aloud. Her boyfriends had lacked that luxury. She had heard them all. Every nasty thought produced by stress, or lack of sleep, or jealousy, or just having had a bad day.

It was hard to forget those. Hard to brush them off once she'd heard them. Her telepathy had shut down every budding relationship she had ever begun before anything permanent could evolve.

Not hearing Ethan's thoughts was a relief. Not knowing if he thought she was a total basket case or thought her ass was too big or thought she was weak because she had shaken like a leaf in gale force winds when faced with possible death.

For once, she didn't have to give herself a migraine trying to tune out someone else's thoughts.

And, again, she *liked* him.

It would be a shame to never see him again.

Chapter Four

Rising, Ethan retrieved his cell phone and dialed Chris at network headquarters.

"Reordon," Chris answered.

"It's Ethan." Ethan gave him an abbreviated rundown of his morning, letting Chris know that a mortal woman had come to his aid in battle and he needed to bring her to the network to sign a confidentiality agreement.

"We can't do it here," Chris said, surprising him. "We're on lockdown. No one enters or leaves until the situation stabilizes."

Ethan scowled. "What happened?" Had network headquarters been attacked again?

The last time such had happened, the network had been so damaged by the barrage of mercenaries' missiles, grenades, and more that they had had to abandon the site for a new one.

"One of the vampires had a psychotic break. Some men were injured and tensions are running high."

Ethan's stomach sank. "Which vampire?" Cliff had been infected the longest. He had also become a true friend and ally of the Immortal Guardians. All of them dreaded the day the madness he fought tooth and nail would prevail.

"I'll give you the details later. Where are you? At the woman's place?"

"Yes."

"What's her name?"

"Heather Lane."

"Heather Lane?" Chris repeated, his voice lightening with interest. "Daughter of General Milton Lane?"

"Yes," Ethan responded, waiting for Chris to flip his lid.

"She's a *gifted one*."

Ethan's eyebrows rose. "How did you know that?"

"I definitely want to talk with her," Chris said, ignoring the question. "Give me ten minutes to take care of a few things here, then I'll be on my way. Can you confirm her address for me?"

Ethan dictated her address.

"Good. That's the one we have on file. I'll see you in a few."

Ethan stared at his phone when Chris ended the call.

"Everything okay?" Heather asked.

He had no idea. "Change of plans. There was a problem at network headquarters, so we'll have to do it here. Is that okay?"

"I guess so. Although, to be honest, I don't know how comfortable I am with your friends knowing where I live."

He didn't tell her that, judging by Chris's response, they knew a hell of a lot more about her than that. "No one will harm you, Heather," he vowed. "They would have to go through me first."

She smiled.

"What?"

She gave him a titillating once-over. "You're hot when you're all tough and protective."

He grinned. "Stop tempting me. Chris is on his way, so I need to keep my head."

She winked. And damned if it didn't make him want to toss his phone, lock the door, and bend her over the sofa.

"Your eyes are glowing again."

"I know, damn it."

She laughed.

Trying without success to dampen his libido, Ethan dialed Lisette's number.

"*Oui?*" she answered on the third ring, voice groggy from sleep.

"Hey. Did I wake you?" he asked.

"Yes, but that's okay." She yawned. "What's up?"

"I was having the best dream," Zach muttered in the background.

As always, imagining the elder immortal in bed with Lisette irritated Ethan. Until his gaze slid to Heather, who watched him with open curiosity, her lips still curled in a playful smile.

Ethan's irritation fell away. "I need a favor," he told the French immortal.

"Okay."

That was the great thing about Lisette. Whenever he needed her, she was there.

"Seth made it clear that we're supposed to abide by Chris's wishes and let him speak to any mortal we want to bring into the fold."

"You want to bring a mortal into the fold?" Lisette asked, sounding more alert. "Is it a mortal *woman*, by any chance?"

"Yes." Ethan decided to let her draw her own conclusions. "Seth said we could be present when Chris talks to her and recommended a telepath be present as well to make things go more smoothly. Would you do it?"

"I'd be happy to."

"There's a catch. Chris wants to do it now."

She chuckled. "Freaked out a little, did he?"

"I couldn't tell if it was that or if he was stressing. Something went down at the network earlier."

"What happened?" she asked, all levity fleeing. "Does he need us?"

"No. One of the vampires had a psychotic break."

"Oh no! Not Cliff," she pleaded. The young, courageous vamp had grown on them all.

"I don't know. Chris will tell us when he gets here. Do you think Zach could pop you on over here?"

"No," Zach grumbled in the background. "Zach wants to get back to dreaming about making love with his wife on a sunny beach. On second thought . . . screw that. I'm going to make love with her here in our bed. Hang up, love."

Ethan heard a thump.

"Behave," Lisette admonished with a laugh. "And get up. We're going. I want to meet Ethan's mortal girlfriend."

"Ethan has a girlfriend?" Zach asked.

He didn't have to sound so damned surprised. Or was he relieved? Zach knew Lisette and Ethan used to be lovers and didn't even *try* to hide the fact that he loathed Ethan for it.

When Ethan had been turned by vampires a century or so ago, Seth—the leader of the Immortal Guardians—had taken him to Lisette to be trained. Ethan had instantly been smitten with the fierce, female immortal and had become even more so once he had coaxed her into his bed. Alas, Lisette had not loved him in return, so they had transitioned into what his Second called *friends with benefits*. It had been a comfortable relationship that had staved off the loneliness for decades until Lisette had fallen hard for Zach last year.

"So, are we a go?" Ethan asked, not bothering to correct Lisette's assumption that Heather was his girlfriend.

"Yes."

"Thank you." Glancing at Heather, he swiveled away and lowered his voice. "And tell Zach to put some damned clothes on and to tuck his you-know-what away."

Lisette laughed. "I will. I'll call you when we're ready."

Pocketing the phone, Ethan turned back to Heather.

She arched a brow. "What is it you want him to tuck away?"

He laughed. "Not what you're thinking. Let's just . . . save that for another day." Until Chris and Lisette confirmed what Ethan already sensed—that Heather was worthy of their trust—he thought it best not to mention the fact that Zach rarely wore shirts because they interfered with his big-ass wings. Wings he could tuck away or make vanish at will.

"If you say so," she drawled. "Was that your Second again?"

"No. That was Lisette, one of the telepaths I told you about. She'll be coming here to do the same thing you do in your work. She'll assure Chris you aren't bullshitting him when he talks with you."

Her look turned uneasy. "She's immortal?"

"Yes."

"And she's going to read my mind?"

"Yes. I'm sorry. I know it's an intrusion. But it's the fastest way to get Chris out of our hair. An interview with him"—he opted not to use the word *interrogation*—"would take hours otherwise until we convinced him you could be trusted." And Ethan would've likely become so angered by whatever intimidation tactics Chris would've used that Ethan would've hurt the man and earned Seth's wrath.

"As often as I've read others' minds, I guess I shouldn't balk." She sighed. "All right."

Ethan studied her for a moment. "You look nervous."

"I am."

Closing the distance between them, he took her hand. "Don't be. I'll be with you the whole time."

"Thank you."

Damn, she appealed to him. "May I ask you a question?"

"Sure." Heather was almost a foot shorter than Ethan and seemed so fragile. So very mortal. It terrified him a little to recall her standing with him against seven vampires earlier. "Why did you welcome me into your home?"

She raised her eyebrows. "Temporary insanity?"

He flashed her a quick grin. "No, seriously." Even though he had done his damnedest to convince Heather that he wouldn't harm her, it still surprised him that she hadn't continued to run away from him.

"You defeated seven vampires," she said.

"With your help."

She rolled her eyes. "I wasn't that much help. You clearly were the strongest and most skilled fighter in the bunch." Hard not to preen a bit over that declaration. "And I figured, if you had wanted to kill me or harm me, you would have done so in the clearing."

"You had a weapon with a full mag trained on me in the clearing."

"But my hands were shaking so badly that I didn't have a hope in hell of hitting one of your major arteries. I would have only gotten one—maybe two—shots off before you jumped into hyperspeed and disarmed me."

"I *did* disarm you."

"After trying to talk me down." Shrugging, she offered him a smile. "As you pointed out earlier, you could have easily killed me on the spot. Or you could have forced me into your car and whisked me away. Or you could have forced me into my house. Instead, you politely asked me if I'd like to discuss matters inside. And you trusted me enough to confirm that vampire folklore had gotten it right with regard to your not being able to withstand exposure to sunlight. You revealed a weakness to me. A vulnerability. It made me feel . . . not safe exactly, but saf*er*." She studied him. "Your eyes are glowing again."

"You're beautiful, you're smart, you think quickly in a crisis, *and* you kick ass. Do you have any idea what a desirous combination that is?"

"Since I could say the same about you, yes."

He grinned. "You're bold, too? Be still, my heart."

The phone rang before she could respond.

Still holding her hand, Ethan answered. "Yeah?"

Zach and Lisette appeared three feet away.

Heather jumped and emitted a little shriek of surprise. Tilting her head way back, she gaped up at Zach's six-foot-ten-inch glowering form, then sidled up to Ethan.

Releasing her hand, Ethan wrapped an arm around her and glared at the elder immortal. "You could have given us a little warning first."

Zach arched a brow. "I did. I called." He curled an arm around Lisette's waist and drew her closer as if to remind Ethan of his claim on her.

Lisette smiled and offered her hand to Heather. "Hello. I'm Lisette."

Heather shook it. "Heather."

Lisette patted Zach's chest. "This is my husband, Zach."

Heather eyed the two of them, her face full of curiosity. "You're both immortal?"

"Yes," Lisette answered.

"How did you . . . ? I mean, you just . . . appeared out of nowhere."

"I can teleport," Zach told her.

Heather turned wide eyes on Ethan. "Can *you* do that?"

"No," Ethan confessed, hoping she wouldn't be too disappointed. "Remember I told you we all have different gifts? Well, that's one of his."

"*One* of his?"

"Yes. Zach is an elder, so he has several gifts. I only have the one."

"Oh."

Silence fell as they all studied one another.

Lisette's curious gaze kept darting back and forth between Ethan and Heather as if she were already sizing them up for wedding finery.

"I don't think you want to do that," Zach drawled, his dark gaze zeroing in on Heather.

"Do what?" Ethan asked, frowning.

"Read my mind. There are things up there you *really* don't want to see."

Great. Way to make her feel more comfortable, asshole, Ethan thought dourly.

Lisette's lovely face lit up. "You're telepathic?" She turned bright eyes on Ethan. "She's a *gifted one*!" *She can be transformed,* she whispered in Ethan's mind with glee.

Ethan shook his head, unable to tell her she was getting ahead of herself. He hadn't been exaggerating when he had told Heather telepaths like Lisette couldn't read his mind. She could *send* thoughts his way, but couldn't *receive* them.

Awkward silence engulfed them.

Ethan wasn't sure he liked the way Heather was studying Zach.

Zach's lips twitched. "It isn't what you're thinking," he told Heather, who blushed.

"What?" Ethan asked.

Zach nodded to the mortal in their midst. "She's still wondering what you wanted me to tuck away."

Lisette and Ethan both laughed.

Heather did, too.

Even Zach finally allowed himself a smile.

The tension eased.

Heather motioned to the sofa. "Would you like to sit down while we wait?"

"What exactly are we waiting for?" Zach asked.

"Chris Reordon," Ethan told him.

"He's at the network?"

"Probably. He said he had to wrap some things up there before he left."

"I'll go get him." Leaning down, Zach pressed a quick kiss to his wife's lips, stepped away from her, and vanished.

"That is so cool," Heather declared.

Ethan silently agreed and again bemoaned the fact that he had been born with such a boring gift.

"My brother can teleport, too," Lisette informed her with a smile. "I admit I've always envied him that gift. It seems much more fun than constantly being bombarded with others' thoughts."

Heather smiled. "I agree."

"And few can defeat him in battle."

"I imagine so. Hard to defeat someone who's there one second and gone the next."

"Precisely."

Zach abruptly reappeared, his black T-shirt peppered with holes and glistening with blood. Leaning forward, he braced his hands on his knees as blood trailed from his lips and dappled the floor.

Heather gasped.

Lisette did, too, and leapt to Zach's side, wrapping an arm around him. "Zach! What happened? Are you all right?"

Zach released a growl of fury, then straightened, his eyes glowing golden.

Ethan rested a hand on Heather's hip and eased her behind him.

"Did you neglect to tell me something, Ethan?" Zach snarled.

Ethan took in the bullet holes. "Oh. Right. The, uh . . . the network's on lockdown."

Lisette sent Ethan a reproving look.

"What?" he said. "I told you one of the vampires had had a psychotic break. How did you *think* Chris would react?"

Lisette went to work, unbuttoning Zach's shirt. "I take it someone was injured?"

"Several someones, apparently. Chris didn't go into details. He just said everyone is on edge and he doesn't want anyone in or out until tensions ease."

"Thank you," Zach sneered, "for the heads-up."

Well, hell. Ethan had been just a *tad* distracted.

As Lisette untucked Zach's shirt and parted it, little chunks of metal fell to the floor.

"What are those?" Heather asked. Prying Ethan's hand from her hip (he hadn't even realized he still gripped her), she stepped up beside him.

"The bullets that didn't pass through me," Zach gritted. His chest and abs, leanly muscled, bore a dozen or more holes that wept blood.

"Heather," Lisette said, "do you have a towel or something I can use to clean his wounds?"

"Of course." Heather hurried to the bathroom.

Zach continued to fling visual daggers Ethan's way.

"Look," Ethan said, preternaturally soft so Heather wouldn't hear him, "I know what you're thinking and I *didn't* neglect to warn you on purpose. I didn't set you up, Zach, because I'm jealous. What Lisette and I had is over. We're just friends and I'm fine with that." The truth in that statement startled him. He really *was* fine with it. "I was distracted." His gaze drifted past Zach and Lisette to the bathroom doorway. "Incredibly, temptingly distracted."

"You're smitten with her," Lisette pronounced with a sly smile.

Ethan didn't bother to deny it. "Yeah, I am."

Heather hurried back into the room and offered Lisette two towels. "I brought a wet one and a dry one. Can I do anything else?"

Lisette took the towels. "No, thank you."

Heather returned to Ethan's side while Lisette used the wet towel to wipe away the blood that stained Zach's skin. The wounds beneath sealed themselves and healed as they watched.

Zach was thousands of years old and almost as powerful as Seth, the Immortal Guardians' leader. That came with serious perks.

"That's amazing," Heather breathed, eyes wide.

A tinny version of the R.E.M. tune "It's the End of the World as We Know It" suddenly filled the room.

Zach pulled a cell phone from his back pocket and answered. "What?"

"Zach, was that you just now?" Chris asked on the other end.

Ethan's heightened senses allowed him to hear both sides of the conversation.

"Yes."

Chris swore. "Sorry about that. We're on lockdown and everyone around here is a little trigger-happy today."

"No problem. Shall we try this again?"

"Yes. Were you coming to take me to Miss Lane's house?"

"Yes."

"Then skip the lobby and just teleport directly to my private office this time."

"I'm on my way."

As soon as Lisette finished swiping his chest with the dry towel, Zach dropped a kiss on her lips and vanished.

Heather looked up at Ethan. "You live in a fascinating world."

He fought the urge to tell her that she could, too, if she chose to do so.

The incredibly tall, handsome, and scary elder immortal returned with another man.

Heather studied the latter. Dark blond hair he appeared to have finger-combed a few too many times stopped short of meeting his collar. Discerning blue eyes catalogued everyone and everything in the room as he gave her home a quick survey. Standing just short of six feet tall, he had broad shoulders and a lean build like Zach. Neither, she noted, packed as much muscle as Ethan did.

The fingers of one of the new man's hands clutched the

handle of a worn, soft leather briefcase. "Heather Lane?" he asked, those blue eyes locking on hers.

"Yes."

Striding forward, he held out his free hand. "Chris Reordon. It's a pleasure to meet you."

Heather shook his hand. "Nice to meet you, too," she returned with caution.

"What happened at the network?" Lisette asked. "Ethan said a vampire had a psychotic break. Was it . . . was it Cliff?"

His shoulders slumping wearily, Chris nodded and turned to the others. "Yeah."

Low curses all around.

Heather wondered who this vampire Cliff was and why they all seemed so heartbroken by the news. Weren't vampires supposed to be the bad guys?

"What happened?" Ethan asked.

"I don't know. We're still trying to piece it together. But, shortly after sunrise, Dr. Whetsman apparently said something that set Cliff off."

"Dumb fuck," Zach muttered darkly.

Ethan nodded. "I hate that prick."

"I do, too," Chris admitted, "but he's a fucking genius. So we need him. Anyway, Cliff just . . . lost it. I've never seen him like that before." He rubbed a hand across the back of his neck as though stress had tightened the muscles there. "He broke one of Whetsman's arms, his hip, and looked like he was doing his damnedest to rip Whetsman's head from his shoulders when the guards opened fire."

"Was Whetsman hit?" Zach asked with what sounded to Heather like hope. She couldn't quite place his accent, but it almost sounded British.

"No. My guys are excellent marksmen."

"Damn," all three immortals exclaimed.

"Whetsman made a run for it, though," Chris continued.

"Cliff followed and made it all the way to the damned lobby before blood loss and the tranquilizer brought him down."

Lisette bit her lip. "Did Cliff . . . Is he . . . ?"

"No."

Everyone breathed a sigh of relief.

"But he won't wake up for hours. It took double the usual dose to knock him out."

Ethan whistled. "I'm surprised that didn't kill him. Is Linda with him?"

"No. She left just before it happened and we haven't been able to reach her."

Zach's eyebrows lowered. "What about Bastien and Melanie? Are they with him?"

"No. I couldn't find Seth to teleport them over and didn't want Richart to teleport them in case Bastien did something rash. So I figured I'd wait and tell them when the sun sets."

Zach shook his head. "Seth is in Mozambique. And Bastien and Melanie will want to know now. I'll tell them and take them to him."

Lisette caught his arm. "Heal Ethan first. I can sense his pain and I'm not even an empath."

Heather snapped her head toward Ethan. She had been so distracted that she hadn't realized he was slumping a little more to one side. "Ethan?"

"I'm fine," he insisted, sending her another of those smiles that made her heart race.

Sighing, Zach crossed to Ethan and flattened a hand on Ethan's chest.

Within seconds, Ethan's shoulders straightened and his face regained some color.

"Thank you," Ethan said when Zach broke the contact.

Zach gave him an abrupt nod and disappeared.

"He healed your wounds?" Heather asked.

Ethan nodded.

"All of them?"

"Yes."

"Just like that?"

"Yes."

"Can I see?"

Smiling, he grabbed the hem of his shirt and pulled it up to his armpits, revealing a torso—front and back—that now bore no wounds.

Heather stared. "That's incredible."

Chris looked at Lisette and cocked a brow as Ethan lowered his shirt. "So when did the two immortal black sheep suddenly become best buddies?"

Lisette laughed. "Zach and Bastien both have dark pasts, couldn't care less who likes them or who doesn't, and share an appalling lack of concern over pissing off Seth. How could they *not* gravitate toward each other?"

Shaking his head, Chris turned back to Heather. "I'm sorry. I shouldn't be away from the network long, so . . ." He motioned to the sofa. "Shall we get down to business?"

She nodded, relaxing a little when Ethan took her hand in his and linked their fingers. In short order, Heather found herself seated on the sofa between Ethan and the lovely French immortal.

Chris grabbed the chair Ethan had vacated and positioned it on the opposite side of the coffee table. Seating himself in it, he faced them. "I understand you helped Ethan defeat some vampires this morning, Heather. Thank you for that."

Heather shrugged. "Honestly, I don't think I helped him all that much."

"She did," Ethan countered.

Chris removed some papers from his briefcase and flipped through them. "I assume Ethan has explained that you're a *gifted one*e and what that means?"

"Yes. He said my DNA is advanced."

"*Very* advanced," Chris said. "Fortunately none of your doctors have caught on to that fact thus far." He set the papers on the coffee table and met her gaze. "You didn't come to my attention until you moved to North Carolina a couple of years ago."

He had known about her before today? "What happened then?" she asked warily.

"I was sent your file from the West Coast division of the network. We've known about you and have been watching over you since your birth."

She looked at Ethan. "That's a little creepy."

"I know it seems so," Lisette interjected, "but had you suffered an ailment or injury that brought your differences to light, the network would have been prepared to protect you."

Heather considered her words and those Ethan had spoken earlier, but still found it disturbing to know someone had been tracking her movements all these years.

Chris leaned back in his chair. "We do the same for all *gifted ones* who come to our attention. But I admit I've been watching you more closely than the others. Because of your unique connections . . ."

She arched a brow. "I assume you're talking about my father?"

"Your father," he confirmed, "as well as your connections with various law enforcement and . . . *other* . . . agencies. The fact that you've managed to make a career for yourself doing what you do without revealing your gift impressed the hell out of me. It's shown me you're smart. You're a swift thinker. And you're good at keeping secrets."

Beside her, Ethan tensed. "You had better not be going where I think you are with this."

Chris's eyes never left Heather. "I could use someone like you on my team."

"Chris!" Ethan barked, sitting forward.

"I'd like you to consider working for the network," Chris continued, undeterred.

"Hell no!" Ethan growled, his face darkening.

Heather glanced up at Lisette, unsure what to make of this.

The Frenchwoman's brow furrowed as she watched the two.

Chris—calm, cool, and collected—looked to Ethan. "It's not your decision to make."

When Ethan opened his mouth, Heather hurried to speak. "I'm not sure what you're asking me."

Ethan scowled down at her, radiating fury. "He wants you to become one of his informants."

"Okay. But what does that mean exactly?" And why was Ethan so against it?

"It means," Chris explained, "you would continue to do what you're doing now. You would just keep your eyes, ears, and mind open while doing it, and let me know if anything unusual comes up. Anything that might be related to vampires or immortals and the virus that infects them. Or anything related to *gifted ones*."

Kind of vague. But it didn't seem all that difficult. Hell, she had been working with law enforcement agencies and the military for several years now and had heard nothing of the sort. What were the chances she would now?

Chris removed a small spiral notebook from an inner pocket of his jacket, along with a stubby number two pencil. He scribbled something down on the top sheet of paper, then tore it out of the notebook and handed it to Heather. "This would be your annual salary."

Heather looked down at the piece of paper and felt her eyes widen. "Wow. That's a lot of zeroes." She looked up at Ethan. "Why don't you want me to do it?"

"Tell her," Ethan ordered Chris, his eyes clinging to hers.

From the corner of her eye, she saw Chris lean forward and brace his elbows on his knees. "There *is* an element of danger," he said. "Of risk. It's actually one of the reasons I haven't approached you with this before now."

Ethan shot Chris a disbelieving look. "An *element* of danger?"

Chris ignored him. "Until recently, my contacts primarily aided us in keeping vampires, immortals, and *gifted ones* a secret. They kept their ears peeled for whispers that someone may have seen or heard something, then let us know—if they did—so we could take care of it. But problems have arisen during the past few years that have changed that. My contacts now have to keep an eye out for any indication that the agencies or military outfits they work for have learned of the virus and its potential use as a weapon—"

"A weapon?" Heather interrupted. "What kind of weapon?"

Lisette answered her. "The kind that can produce a race of supersoldiers that cannot be defeated by traditional armies and weapons."

Oh shit.

"Exactly," Ethan said, reading her expression.

"It's made things trickier," Chris said. "The stakes are higher."

"Tell her what happened to your last group of informants," Ethan bit out.

Chris's lips tightened.

Heather looked back and forth between them. "What happened to them?"

Ethan's eyes once more locked on hers. "They were tortured and killed, their spouses and children killed alongside them, by our enemies."

Her heart began to slam against her ribs.

Ethan's look softened, as did his voice. "It isn't worth it, Heather. You've already risked your life once to help me. I don't want you to risk it again."

"She *wouldn't* be," Chris insisted. "Not necessarily. Because of her gift, she wouldn't have to do any physical snooping, wouldn't have to dip into classified files or sneak into areas of the building she wasn't supposed to access and disrupt satellite feeds or take keyhole surveillance photos for us. She's telepathic. All she would have to do is listen to the thoughts of the men and women around her. That's it. Nothing more. Then, if she heard something about vampires or immortals or *gifted ones*, she could give me a call from an encrypted, untraceable phone once she gets home."

Lisette covered Heather's other hand. "I agree with Ethan. It's too risky."

"No one would know she'd heard anything," Chris insisted. "No one would even know she was reading their thoughts—"

"The Other would know," Lisette interrupted.

The air suddenly grew heavy.

"The Other would know," Lisette repeated, "if his destructive desires took him to one of the agencies she works for. He would know it as soon as he looked into her thoughts, perhaps as soon as she walked into the room."

Heather studied the somber expressions of her companions. "The other what?"

"That's classified," Chris said, spearing Ethan with a meaningful look. "And it will *remain* classified even after she signs the confidentiality agreement until I say otherwise."

Ethan responded with a stiff nod.

Heather thought it odd that a human would give orders to two powerful immortal beings. The fact that Ethan and Lisette obeyed seemed even odder.

Lisette patted her hand. "Chris keeps us safe. We bow to his wishes because we trust his judgment."

Ethan sighed, his expression losing much of the anger that had tightened it. "We spend our nights hunting. We don't have time to learn all of the new technology that constantly inundates society. Don't know what threats it may pose. Can't anticipate the problems it will spawn. Chris does that for us. He and the other mortals who work for the network are the reason society still knows nothing about us. They've proven to be invaluable allies over the millennia, helping us defeat

our enemies with a minimum of losses. Chris may be a pain
in our asses . . ."

Chris grunted.

"But he gets the job done. Whatever we need, he finds a
way to provide, even when it seems impossible."

"Then why don't you trust him when he says my becoming an informant wouldn't be dangerous?" Heather asked,
thinking of all those zeroes.

"He didn't say it wouldn't be dangerous," Ethan clarified.
"He said it may not be as dangerous for you as it is for some
of his other informants. But you could still easily be killed."
He sent Chris an accusing glare.

"I don't like it any more than you do," Chris gritted. "But
we need access to information that only informants can
provide. I've worked for the network for a long damned time
and have never *once* encountered a human or *gifted one* who
could tap into as many resources for us as Heather can."
When Ethan opened his mouth to rebut, Chris held up a hand.
"Do you think this is easy for me, asking someone to do
something I know is dangerous? Something that may,
somewhere down the line, result in her death? Do you think
building a new network of informants is a breeze after losing
every one of my former contacts? Not a single day has passed
since we found them down in those stinking, reeking cells,
with the fucking flies buzzing around their corpses, the
mothers still clutching . . ." He clamped his lips shut and
looked away. A muscle in his jaw tightened.

What the hell had he seen? Heather wondered. He
looked . . . haunted.

Chris rubbed his eyes, appearing weary all of a sudden.
"She doesn't have to do it." He looked at Heather. "You don't
have to do it. I just had to ask. It's my job." He shuffled the
papers around on the coffee table. "It's what I fucking do."

Lisette and Ethan shared a somber look.

"Here." Chris pushed several pieces of paper that had been

stapled together toward her, then offered her a pen. "Print your name in the space provided, then sign and date it. Initial it in the places I've highlighted. Feel free to read it first. We're just asking you to guarantee your silence regarding all knowledge of *gifted ones*, immortals, vampires, and the virus that infects the latter. Both the knowledge you possess now and that which you will learn throughout your association with us."

Heather flipped through it. "What happens if I violate the agreement?"

"Since you're a *gifted one*, I'll just have Seth bury your memories of all of this."

"And if I weren't a *gifted one*?" she couldn't help but ask.

Silence was his answer.

Chapter Five

Bastien.

Bastien's eyes flew open. Beside him, Melanie slumbered peacefully, her soft body curled up against his. *Seth?*

No. Zach.

Bastien frowned. *Where are you?*

In your living room.

Anger rose. He did *not* like unexpected visitors invading his home.

I mean you and Dr. Lipton no harm, Zach said in his head.

Though the other immortals remained leery of Zach, still accepting his presence in their midst with caution and wariness, Bastien had come to view him as something of a kindred spirit. Both men had begun their association with the Immortal Guardians as the immortals' enemies. And both could've easily walked away were it not for the women they loved.

Or at least that *used* to be the case. Much to his surprise, Bastien had actually begun to form bonds with some of the other immortals.

Nevertheless, Bastien did *not* like Zach rambling around in his head. *Stay out of my head, elder*, he groused. Carefully untangling his limbs from his wife's, he slipped from the bed.

Melanie smoothed a hand over the sheets, reaching for him. "Where are you going?"

"Zach is here," he told her softly as he donned a pair of pants.

Raising her head, she frowned up at him through the tangles of her long, brown hair. "What? Why?"

"I don't know. He's waiting for me in the living room."

Throwing back the covers, she rose. "I'm going with you."

Bastien bit back a groan as she crossed to the wardrobe and pulled a robe on over her beautiful bare body. He wanted to tell her to stay in bed so he could hurry back and spend the next few hours exploring those lovely curves, but knew Zach didn't pay surprise visits unless something was wrong.

Melanie dragged her fingers through her hair a few times, then gave him a nod.

Taking her hand, Bastien headed for the living room.

Zach waited for them in darkness.

Bastien flicked on the overhead light, wincing at the brightness of it.

For once, the mysterious elder immortal's upper body was covered in a black shirt, his wings tucked away in whatever magical way he had of making them disappear. His shirt was far from pristine, however. It bore numerous bullet holes and glistened with blood. Zach's expression, as he nodded a greeting to them, was grim.

Though Bastien was over six feet tall, he still had to look up at the elder. "What's up?"

"There's been an incident at the network."

Bastien stiffened. Dread coursed through him.

Melanie's hand tightened around his.

"Cliff had a psychotic break," Zach informed them.

Bastien swore. "When?"

"Around dawn."

It must have happened shortly after Bastien and Melanie had left. "How bad was it?"

"Bad. Several humans were injured. The network is on lockdown. And the tension level there is about a fifty on a scale of one to ten."

"Is Cliff okay?" Melanie asked, the same fear Bastien felt in her voice.

Cliff was the last remaining member of the vampire army Bastien had raised to take down the Immortal Guardians several years ago. Cliff and two others had wisely surrendered during the last big battle in which Bastien had been captured. The other two, Vince and Joe, had long since succumbed to the madness spawned by the virus that infected them. Cliff continued to fight it, however, and was like a brother to Bastien. To Melanie, too, since she'd been working with Cliff at the network, looking for a way to either prevent or cure the madness vampires suffered.

Hell, Seth had even given Bastien permission to take Cliff hunting with him, so Cliff would have an outlet for the rage and violent impulses that bombarded him.

"Cliff was shot multiple times," Zach said. "And it took twice the usual dose of the sedative to knock him out."

"But he's alive?" Melanie pressed. "He wasn't . . . ?"

"He's alive," Zach confirmed. "Just unconscious." He shifted, a hint of awkwardness stealing into his posture. "I thought the two of you would want to know. If you want to see him, I can teleport you to him so you won't have to wait until the sun sets."

Bastien nodded. "Thank you. I would appreciate that."

"Yes," Melanie added. "Thank you, Zach."

Bastien motioned to Zach's bloody shirt. "Were you there when it happened?"

Zach shook his head. "I made the mistake of teleporting to network headquarters without calling ahead first. Everyone is on edge, and the guards all have itchy trigger fingers."

"Do you need blood?" Bastien asked.

"No, I'm fine."

"Then give us a minute to dress and we'll be ready to go." Bastien offered him his hand. "Again, thank you, Zach."

Zach shook it. "You came to *my* aid," he said, referring to the time Bastien had bandaged his wounds after Zach had been tortured by the Others. "Now I come to yours."

Bastien nodded. Zach was a powerful ally to have . . . and was a hell of a lot more likable than some of the other immortals.

Zach smiled. "I'll take that as a compliment."

Shaking his head, Bastien wrapped an arm around Melanie and headed back to their bedroom to dress. "Stay out of my head, elder."

Zach stood in the same spot in which Bastien and Melanie had left him when the couple returned to the living room, holding hands like teenagers. Now that Zach had found Lisette, he could understand the need immortal couples had to constantly touch each other.

Bastien wore the traditional hunting garb of an immortal: black pants and a black shirt that wouldn't show bloodstains as easily as other colors, heavy black combat boots, and a long, black coat that likely concealed numerous blades. Melanie wore snug-fitting blue jeans, a pale blue TAR HEELS T-shirt, and black-and-white Chuck Taylor canvas high-top sneakers.

Zach drew his cell phone from a back pocket and dialed.

"Yes?" a male voice answered.

"Todd, it's Zach."

"What can I do for you, sir?" Todd asked.

Zach wasn't sure where exactly Todd fell in network security's grand scheme of things, but knew Todd was the highest-ranking human guard on the fifth subterranean floor at network headquarters. Sublevel five could only be accessed by those with the highest levels of security clearance. On it, one would find the lab in which Melanie and her colleagues studied the virus, Melanie's office, the infirmary, a break room, several apartments that housed vampires, and a few holding rooms.

"I'm about to teleport Bastien and Dr. Lipton in. Tell your men to take their fingers off the triggers."

"Yes, sir. Where can we expect you to appear?"

"Just in front of the elevators."

"One moment." Todd's voice quieted as though he pressed the phone to his chest to speak to the human guards around him. "Stand down. We have three immortals incoming."

"Which ones?" someone asked.

"Zach, Dr. Lipton, and Bastien."

Curses erupted over the last name.

Bastien's lips twisted in a dark smile.

Frowning up at him, Melanie elbowed him in the side. "Behave."

Amusement filtered through Zach.

Bastien had few friends at the network. None could forget the violence the immortal black sheep had spawned there— not to mention the broken bones—on some of his earlier visits.

"Okay," Todd said into the phone. "We're ready."

Zach pocketed his cell. "Shall we go?"

Faces full of dread, both nodded.

Zach touched their shoulders.

The room around them darkened and fell away, replaced by the bright white hallway in sublevel five.

Zach lowered his hands.

At least two dozen guards congregated around the desk near the elevators. All were heavily armed with automatic weapons. A handful also carried tranquilizer guns that could loose darts filled with the only sedative that would affect a vampire or an immortal.

More guards lined the hallway.

"Where is he?" Melanie blurted, her face full of worry. "The infirmary?"

"No, ma'am." Todd started down the long hallway with them. "We thought it would be safer all around to chain him up in one of the holding rooms."

Bastien swore.

"But Zach said he's been sedated," Melanie protested. "Surely the infirmary—"

"You didn't see him, Doc." Both Todd's face and voice carried regret. "He was . . . crazed. Like Joe used to be toward the end."

Melanie bit her lip.

"And fast." Todd shook his head. "I've never seen Cliff move so fast. He moved and fought like an Immortal Guardian."

Zach cut Bastien a look, knowing the former vampire leader had secretly bestowed upon Cliff the same weapons training all immortals received when they transformed.

"What happened?" Melanie prodded. "What set him off?"

"Dr. Whetsman. I don't know what he said, but Cliff went berserk and wanted to kill his ass. Damned near succeeded, too. We held him off with gunfire while Whetsman ran. I even tranqued Cliff once, but he still got past us and made it all the way up the stairs to the ground floor. If one of the guards up above hadn't managed to tranq him a second time, Cliff would've either torn Whetsman apart or followed him out into the sun."

Bastien muttered several slurs against Whetsman.

"What did Whetsman say to him?" Melanie asked.

"We don't know. He's out cold. Cliff broke his arm, his hip, and gave him one hell of a concussion. The other docs think he may be brain damaged."

Zach frowned. "Seth hasn't been by to heal him?"

Todd shook his head. "Seth said he's tied up in Mozambique and will be by later to do it." As they stopped in front of a heavy steel door, Todd lowered his voice. "I think Seth is pissed at Whetsman for triggering the break. Cliff has fought long and hard to keep the madness at bay. And you know what a dick Whetsman can be."

All nodded.

Zach had once heard Chris say Whetsman wasn't a prick, he was a *brilliant* prick whose input on their viral research, unfortunately, had been so valuable to the network that it made overlooking his dickish nature imperative.

When Todd reached for a set of key cards attached to his belt, Zach waved him away and held his hand over the electronic lock. A loud *clunk* sounded, then the door—as heavy and thick as that on a bank vault—swung open.

The room beyond was small. Several feet of concrete coated the heavy steel walls, ceiling, and floor. A cot, the only furniture present, rested opposite the door with thick titanium chains embedded in the wall above it.

Cliff slept on the cot, his wrists and ankles manacled.

Melanie looked around. "Where's Linda? She isn't sitting with him?"

Dr. Linda Machen, Zach knew, was one of the other doctors at the network. The *only* one, aside from Melanie, who was comfortable working hands-on with the vampires.

"She left just before it happened and isn't answering her phone," Todd told her.

Frowning, Melanie strode forward and seated herself on the cot at Cliff's hip. "Did you try her at Alleck's?"

Zach's eyebrows flew up. "Alleck's?" Alleck was a German immortal Seth had been teleporting in on occasion to compare notes on the virus with Melanie. Zach had only met him once, but had found the immortal to be shy and soft-spoken.

"Yes." Melanie leaned forward to press a palm to Cliff's brown, stubbled cheek. "She's sort of dating him."

"Linda is dating Alleck?" Bastien questioned with disbelief.

Todd looked equally shocked.

"Yes." Melanie peeled back one of Cliff's eyelids. Curled her fingers around one of Cliff's wrists. Paused. Then combed her fingers through his sticky dreadlocks, searching for the wounds beneath the blood. "Couldn't you have at least cleaned him up?"

Todd shifted restively. "He injured a lot of guards, ma'am. By the time we brought him down, some were ready to hurl him out into the sun . . . and probably would have if Mr. Reordon hadn't stopped them."

Bastien moved forward and stared down at the young vampire. "I don't understand. He was fine when we went hunting earlier."

Melanie looked up at him. "Did he say or do *anything* to make you think he was struggling?"

"No. I mean, he told me a long time ago that it was harder to keep his violent impulses in check when he was around Whetsman, but he's held it together thus far. And hunting provides him with an outlet for the violence. He *always* seems calmer after we hunt. Tonight was no exception."

Melanie drew up the vampire's T-shirt, exposing smooth, brown, leanly muscled skin riddled with bullet holes. "You didn't even give him blood?" she demanded.

Todd shrugged. "As I said, we haven't been able to reach Dr. Machen. And none of the other medical personnel will go near him. They're too afraid of him."

"Stuart?" Bastien said suddenly.

"Yeah?" Zach heard a vampire answer from one of the apartments down the hallway.

"Did you hear what happened?"

"No," the vampire answered. "I was asleep until the gun-shots sounded."

"What about the rest of you?" Bastien asked.

The other five vampires housed at the network all responded in the negative. All had been asleep until the guards had started firing.

Melanie rose. "Can we move him to the infirmary?"

"You'll have to ask Mr. Reordon," Todd offered apologet-ically.

"Bastien, talk to Chris," she ordered. "I'm going to get Cliff some blood."

Bastien took out his cell phone and dialed Chris, who was still at Heather's home.

"Reordon," Zach heard Chris answer.

"It's Bastien. I'm at the network with Zach and Melanie. We're moving Cliff to the infirmary." Bastien hung up.

Zach laughed.

The British immortal's grave expression lightened ever so slightly. "You want to help me with these chains?" Bastien asked as he leaned over the bed.

Zach waved a hand.

The wrist cuffs and ankle cuffs sprang open.

Bastien lifted the young vampire into his arms and headed for the door.

Todd followed them out into the hallway. "Well, I'll leave you to it. Let me know if you need anything. And if all three of you intend to leave, please tell me ahead of time so we can restrain Cliff again. I have no idea what his mental state will be when he awakens and I'd rather avoid a repeat of what happened earlier."

"Of course," Zach agreed.

Todd hesitated. "I like Cliff, you know. He's a good guy. And I know he can't control what's happening to him. I felt like shit, ordering the men to shoot him, but . . ."

Zach nodded. "We understand. And I know Reordon wasn't the only one who prevented those with hotter heads from surrendering Cliff to the sun. You're a good man, Todd."

"Thank you, sir." Spinning on his heel, Todd strode down the hallway, his boots thudding on the professional-grade linoleum floor.

In the infirmary, Bastien lowered Cliff onto one of the hospital beds. "Can you read Cliff's mind, Zach, and tell us what went down?"

"I'll try." Zach frowned as he combed through the young vampire's thoughts. The sedative muddled things and made it more difficult than it ordinarily would've been. Sort of like trying to understand the point of a long-winded tale spun by a sloppy-drunk man with slurred speech. "All I can discern is that he thought Whetsman meant to harm Linda. Either that or he thought Whetsman had killed her. It's all jumbled up in there."

Melanie approached, carrying several bags of blood, and began to set up an IV for Cliff.

Bastien helped her. "Where *is* Whetsman?"

Tight-lipped, she motioned behind him. "Over there. I saw him when I came in."

Farther down, a curtain had been pulled closed around a bed.

Melanie met her husband's gaze. "I should try to reach Linda."

Bastien nodded. "I'm sure she'd want to know. Zach, would you see what you can find in Whetsman's thoughts? Cliff hasn't exhibited any of the paranoia that struck Joe when the madness took him. I want to know what Whetsman said to trigger Cliff's break and make him think Linda was in danger."

Zach crossed to Whetsman's bed and yanked the curtain back. The paunchy doctor slept soundly, thanks to the morphine drip or whatever other pain-relieving drug was steadily trickling into his veins. He looked like shit, though. Lots of bruises. Casts. Bandages on his head.

Seth must have been pissed to postpone healing the human.

As Zach delved into the injured doctor's thoughts and sifted back through what had happened, he heard Melanie dial Linda's number on her cell.

Barely discernible through all of the cement and steel and layers of earth above them, a phone rang somewhere outside.

"Oh shit." Zach turned to face the others.

Bastien and Melanie looked over at him, Melanie holding her cell phone to her ear.

The phone outside the building rang again in tandem with the one coming over the line on Melanie's cell.

"Cliff was right," Zach told them. "Whetsman shot Linda. He left her bleeding in the backseat of his car." He pointed to Melanie's phone. "Keep calling that number."

Before they could react, he teleported to the network's parking lot. Blinding sunlight struck as Zach appeared just outside the network's bland front door. But, like Seth, Zach remained unaffected by the sun's harsh rays.

"Code nine! Code nine!" he heard Todd shout over an intercom inside. "Immortals are on the move! All guards stand down and let them pass unharmed!"

Row after row of cars filled the parking lot.

The ringtone on Linda's phone led Zach to a shiny black SUV parked under a tree down near the end of one of the first rows of cars. Just as he had seen in Whetsman's thoughts, Linda lay crumpled on the backseat.

Zach gripped the handle of one of the back doors and yanked it off the vehicle.

A car alarm immediately began to whine an annoying complaint.

"We have a situation in the parking lot!" another voice in the building shouted.

"Stand down!" Todd barked. "I repeat, stand down! We have a code nine! Immortals are on the move, inside *and* outside the building! Lower your weapons and let them pass unharmed!"

Heat and the scent of blood blasted Zach as he leaned into the SUV.

He heard Bastien struggle with Melanie somewhere inside the building, trying to keep her from running out into the sunlight after Zach.

A heartbeat—faint, unsteady—met Zach's ears. "She's alive," he announced, knowing the other immortals would be able to hear him, even over the alarm.

Melanie began to sob.

Zach eased Linda onto her back and rested a palm on her bloody stomach. Warmth rose in his chest and flowed down his arm, through his hand, and into Linda's body. The ugly wound, which would've proven fatal had Zach not arrived when he had, closed and healed beneath his touch.

"I'm bringing her in," he announced and gently lifted the mortal into his arms. "Meet me in the infirmary." Easing back out of the SUV, he adjusted his hold on Linda and teleported to the infirmary.

Bastien and Melanie burst through the doorway.

"It's okay," he told them as he lowered Linda onto the hospital bed next to Cliff's. "I healed her wounds. If you give her blood and liquids, she should be fine."

Taking Linda's hand in both of her own, Melanie looked up at him with tearstained cheeks. "Thank you, Zach."

Bastien stepped up beside her and glowered down at her. "Don't you *ever* pull that shit again!" he bellowed.

"She's like a sister to me," Melanie tried to explain.

"I don't care if she's your fucking twin! You don't rush out into sunlight without donning your protective suit!"

"It wouldn't have killed me," she protested. "It would have just—"

"Burned you, then blistered you, then barbecued your ass, and would have hurt like hell while it did! It would have felt like your skin was being seared in a frying pan over a high flame. Zach is immune to sunlight and was already handling things. Next time use your fucking head!"

Melanie stiffened.

Zach saw the storm rolling in and, for some reason (Lisette's influence, no doubt) tried to dispel it. "He's right," he told Melanie, his own voice calm. "I was handling the situation. The sunlight *would've* harmed you. And it would've harmed Bastien far more when he raced after you in an attempt to protect you had you made it outside. You may be fairly newly transformed, but you were transformed by Roland, a nearly millennium-old immortal, and possess his strength. Bastien is only a couple of centuries old. By the time you had begun to pinken with a burn, Bastien would've already blistered while trying to protect you."

Regret and self-condemnation filled her features as she looked up at her husband. "I'm sorry. You're right. I didn't think. I just . . . reacted."

Sighing, he drew her into a tight hug. "I'm sorry I shouted. I didn't mean to be harsh, sweetheart. I just can't bear the thought of you being hurt." He rested his cheek on her hair and closed his eyes. "And . . ."

"And you're worried about Cliff," she finished for him. "I know. I am, too." Her face resting on Bastien's chest, Melanie looked to Zach. "Why would Whetsman shoot Linda? I know they don't like each other, but—"

"*No one* likes Whetsman," Bastien grumbled, rocking her back and forth in his arms as if he still needed to reassure himself she was unharmed.

"But trying to kill her . . ."

Zach eyed them grimly. "Linda caught him smuggling out vials of the sedative."

Bastien's eyes flew open. "What? Why the hell would he do that?"

Zach shook his head. "I'll have to dig deeper into his thoughts to find the answer to that and can't do it without Seth's permission, because it could cause damage."

Melanie gently pried herself from Bastien's tight hold and started setting up an IV drip for Linda. "Shouldn't we call Seth?"

Seth, Zach knew, was busy following a lead, hoping to find Gershom, the Other who plotted against . . . well, the entire world. They'd had so few leads. He didn't think it wise to interrupt the Immortal Guardians' leader. "Don't worry." Zach nodded to Whetsman. "He won't be going anywhere soon. Seth can deal with him upon his return."

Ethan stared down at Heather. The two stood in her living room, shrouded in silence after Zach had returned and tele-ported Chris and Lisette away. Ethan couldn't read Heather's expression, but thought it somewhere between shell-shocked and just plain weary.

"I'm sorry," he said.

Her eyebrows rose. "For what?"

He dragged a hand down his face, fatigue sifting through him.

He should have asked Zach or Chris to bring him some blood. Losing quite a bit had left him weak, even though Zach had healed his wounds. Ethan thought it would be rude to crash out on Heather's sofa and sink into a deep healing sleep. Plus he would much rather spend time with her while he had the chance. The best thing he could do for her, after all, would be to never see her again after today so she wouldn't be

tempted to take that damned job Chris had offered her and
end up getting killed.

Fucking Chris.

Ethan knew Chris was just doing what he always did—
compiling every possible resource he could to aid immortals
in their quest to protect humanity—but Heather was one
resource Ethan didn't want Chris to exploit.

"Sorry for what?" Heather prodded again.

"I feel like I dragged you into all of this," he told her.

Her expression lightened. "*I* was the one who camped out
in the clearing every morning, hoping I'd see or find something that would explain the dreams. Hoping I'd find *you*, I
guess."

Ethan stared at her. "You camped out in the clearing every
night?"

"Only for a half hour or so before dawn, around the time
the dreams took place."

"Holy hell." Closing the distance between them, he drew
her into a hug.

"What's wrong?" She slid her arms around his waist and
rested her head against his chest.

"Those vampires were headed straight for you. If I hadn't
driven past when I did and smelled them, they would have
found you and . . ." He didn't even want to think about the
atrocities they would have committed as they killed her.

"Geez. With everything that's happened, I didn't even
think of that."

"Don't camp out in the clearing anymore unless the sun
is up," he urged her.

"I thought you said you didn't think more vampires would
follow."

He shook his head. "It's unlikely, but . . ." He sighed. "I
have the most absurd urge to ask you to promise me you
won't go out after dark anymore."

"Um . . ."

"I know. It's totally unreasonable. I just . . ."

She leaned back to look up at him. "You said your enemies killed Chris's former contacts. Your enemies were vampires?"

"No." With great reluctance, Ethan released his hold on her and coaxed her into sitting beside him on the sofa once more. "They were mercenaries."

"Human mercenaries? As in private military companies?"

"Yes. Not long ago, a small mercenary outfit got their hands on the vampiric virus and thought it would be a great idea to use it to create an army of supersoldiers they could hire out to the highest bidder."

She mulled that over silently while she twisted to face him on the sofa, curling her legs up on the cushions so her knees brushed his hip. "That army would be worth a fortune."

"Yes, it would."

"If it weren't for the madness that would infect the soldiers, my dad would be interested in contracting that army."

"I'm sure he would. But the leaders of the mercenary group didn't care that their soldiers would be driven insane. They considered them all expendable and intended to kill them off after a year, then rotate in new recruits."

"Wow. What total assholes."

He laughed. "Very much so. Long story short, the smaller mercenary group's actions led to a larger mercenary group procuring the virus and . . . well . . . Have you ever heard of Shadow River?"

"Yes. My dad mentioned them several times. They were a very elite private military group that was slated to receive some hefty government contracts until a group of their own men . . . blew up . . ." Her eyes widened. "Holy crap! That was *you*?" she asked incredulously. "You blew up their entire compound?"

"I, my immortal brethren, and Chris's network soldiers blew it up."

"It was, like, four or five thousand acres!"

"Yes."

"Every structure was leveled!"

"Yes."

"The casualty list was—"

"I know."

Sliding her legs off the cushions, she placed some distance between them. Her look turned uneasy. "That's a lot of dead men, Ethan. A lot of dead *humans*."

"Dead humans and dead vampires," he corrected.

"What?"

"Shadow River infected a third of their soldiers with the virus."

Her lips parted.

"The vampire mercenaries alternated their time between training for battle, preying upon humans, and hunting Immortal Guardians."

"Why would they hunt you?"

"The higher-ups at Shadow River knew they would have to kill off their soldiers a year after infecting them in order to avoid the soldiers descending into madness. An uncontrollable army, after all, is of no use to anyone."

She nodded.

"When the mercenary leaders discovered that immortals don't suffer the insanity vampires do, they wanted to get their hands on a few of us so they could study us, dissect us, and determine the whys of it."

"They didn't know about your DNA?"

"No. They just knew we were different."

She remained quiet for a long time. "The slaughter at that compound was all my dad—and everyone else I encountered who was either military or law enforcement—talked about for weeks."

"We couldn't afford to leave any survivors. Doing so in the past came back and burned us in a bad way."

"But there *were* survivors. A dozen men—"

"Those were Chris's men, posing as mercenaries. And there were losses on both sides, Heather. Chris lost men. Dozens were wounded. And we lost two of my immortal brethren."

Silence enveloped them.

"Do you fear me now?" he asked hesitantly.

"No." The inflection in her voice told him nothing.

"What are you thinking? I can't tell if you're angry or uneasy or . . ."

"Honestly, I'm not sure what I'm feeling right now. I'm a military brat. So it's hard for me to hear about soldiers being slain in such numbers."

"Those men weren't military."

"But they still probably had families."

"They didn't. Shadow River was very selective when it came to recruiting soldiers. They knew they would eventually kill every man they infected with the virus, so they couldn't afford for the soldiers to leave behind family members who might ask questions, file wrongful death lawsuits, or bring unwanted media attention to the program. And, if it helps, Lisette and the other telepaths read the minds of many of the mercenaries and said those men would've sold their own daughters, if they'd had any, for a profit. They were not honorable men. They were in it for money, not country. They would have fought for whatever government or terrorist organization offered them the highest pay, even if it meant killing their own countrymen."

A couple more minutes of tense silence ticked away as Ethan waited for her to respond.

"I know I already asked this," Heather said finally, "but I feel the need to do it again. Are there any other revelations you'd care to make while I'm sitting down?"

He fought a smile, relieved that she still seemed to feel no malice toward him. "I think that's enough for today."

"Good. This is all a little hard to take in. I mean, the whole vampires-being-real thing was big enough. Immortals, and *gifted ones*, and Shadow River thrown on top of that kinda has things teetering toward being too much for me, at least for now."

"I imagine so. I apologize for hitting you with all of this at once. I'm just concerned for your safety."

"At least I understand now why you were so pissed at Chris for offering me the job."

"You aren't going to take it, are you?" He *really* didn't want her to take it. Lisette had been right. The enemy they faced now was more dangerous than all of the enemies they had faced in the past combined simply because they had no way of knowing when or how he would strike next. Gershom was as old and powerful as Seth and Zach and, for whatever reason, was bent on triggering fucking Armageddon.

"I don't know," she admitted. "I'm feeling a little brain dead right now and can't think about it, *but,*" she added when he opened his mouth to again try to dissuade her, "your objections and concerns for my safety will play a role in my decision when I make it."

He supposed he couldn't hope for more than that.

"You look beat," she said, her lips curling up in a sympathetic smile.

He sighed. "I am."

"Me too. I think all of the adrenaline and fear and everything else has just sucked the energy right out of me. Would you like to try to get some sleep?"

His pulse leapt as images of lying beside Heather filled his mind . . . of turning toward her in bed, pulling her to him, and—

"Your eyes are glowing again," she whispered.

He swore and brought a hand to them as if he could rub the damned luminescence out of them. "I'm sorry. I had a fleeting image of lying in bed with you and . . ."

"Oh." Her tone reflected surprise and he couldn't decide what else.

"I know. But I promise I'm not a total degenerate. I'm just tired and seem to have no control over my body when I'm around you." Lowering his hand, he forced himself to meet her gaze and almost did a double take.

A wide smile brightened her features. "That is so cool."

He arched a brow. "What is?"

"I don't have to guess if you're attracted to me because it's all right there in your eyes. And I don't mean in a corny chick-flick kind of way. But in a *Bam!* in-your-face kind of way. It's like a sexual barometer or a mood ring."

He laughed. "Well, it's not so cool from my perspective, because I can't hide it. *You*, on the other hand, *can*, so I have no idea what you think of me."

Her smile softened as she studied him. "I'm attracted to you, too, Ethan. But I'm annoyingly old-fashioned and don't take sex as casually as most of my peers do. Feel free to blame my grandparents. I spent a lot of time around them when I was growing up."

"I'm a century older than you, or thereabouts, so you *can't* be more old-fashioned than *I* am." He grimaced. "Hell. I probably shouldn't have mentioned my age, should I?"

"Relax. You don't look a day over sixty."

Sixty!

She burst into laughter and patted his knee. "I'm just kidding. You know you're hot."

Ethan groaned. "You're evil."

"And you're tired. Why don't you sleep for a bit. I signed the confidentiality agreement, so you don't have to worry about me trying to sneak pictures of your fangs or calling all the news outlets while you rest."

Smiling, he shook his head. "And what will you do while I sleep?"

"Find a permanent marker and draw a mustache and bushy eyebrows on your face."

He laughed. "I *really* like you, Heather."

"I like you, too. So . . . get some sleep. The bedroom is through there."

"What *will* you do while I rest?"

"Unless I'm called in to observe an interrogation, I'll just read a book. Watch TV." She winked. "Paint my toenails."

"Damn, I hate to miss watching you paint your toenails."

She laughed.

"May I crash here on the sofa beside you?" For some reason, he just wanted to be near her. Perhaps because he knew he would have no excuse to remain with her or to even see her again once the rain began to fall tonight.

She grinned. "Yes, you may crash on my sofa."

Smiling, Ethan tugged off his boots and propped his big feet on her coffee table. Slouching down on the soft cushions, he folded his hands on his stomach and closed his eyes.

The sound of her heartbeat soothed him as her scent followed him into dreams.

Chapter Six

"Stupid weathermen," Heather muttered. Her gaze shifted from the television screen to the large immortal warrior who slumbered on her sofa.

Ethan had slept deeply all day while she had puttered around the house, trying to stay busy so she wouldn't just sit and stare at him.

He was incredibly handsome, with all of the heavy muscle of a cover model, but none of the soft pretty-boyishness. Perhaps it was the dark beard stubble that lent him a rugged air. Or maybe the strong, angular jaw.

She had caught up on all of the household chores she abhorred, had showered and changed, then had finally given up on trying to ignore Ethan a couple of hours ago and had reclaimed her seat beside him.

He hadn't changed positions all day until then. She had wondered if something might be wrong, how someone with exceptionally keen hearing could sleep through all of the racket she had made washing dishes, slamming the stubborn dryer's door, or blow-drying her hair.

But as soon as she had sat next to him, he had shifted. Drawing his legs up onto the cushions, he had curled up beside her and lowered his head to her lap, the back of his

head resting against her belly. While she had stared down at
him, unsure where to put her hands, he had snuggled closer
and draped an arm across her legs, curling one hand over
her hip.

Of course her heart had begun to pound like a sledge-
hammer. But his eyes had never opened. So she had reached
for the nearby universal remote, turned the television on,
and channel surfed while she gave in to temptation and combed
her fingers through his short locks.

His hair smelled like her lavender-scented shampoo and
was so soft.

Such contentment suffused her that she damned near fell
asleep herself.

It was nice, having him curled up against her. She cursed
her mind for leaping forward and wondering how nice it
would be to have him curled up against her in bed. Naked. All
of that fabulous strength pressing down on her.

He's immortal. You're human. She frowned. *Or a* gifted one.

That was going to take some getting used to.

She had super-advanced DNA. How bizarre was that?

"That feels nice," Ethan muttered.

Heather jumped. "I thought you were asleep."

"I was." He sighed and tightened his hold on her hip as if
he didn't want to let her go. "What time is it?"

"Eight thirty."

"At night?" he asked, sounding more alert.

"Yes."

Raising his head, he squinted at the windows. "Has the
sun set?"

"Barely."

Groaning, he sat up, lowered his feet to the floor, and
slumped against the cushions beside her. "Sorry about that. I
didn't mean to sleep so long."

She fought a smile as she eyed him curiously. Several
strands of hair stood up on one side of his head. "I'm a little

surprised you slept so deeply," she commented. "I would've thought a vampire—or rather an immortal—would wake at the slightest sound."

Grimacing, he combed his fingers through his hair and tamed the rebellious strands. "Normally, I do. But when I suffer severe enough wounds, I tend to slip into a healing sleep and rest much more deeply, especially when . . ."

"When what?"

He offered her an apologetic shrug. "When I need blood."

She swallowed. "You need blood?"

"Yes. My wounds may have healed, but I won't be at full strength until I get an infusion."

She considered his words. *Infusion* sounded almost clinical. "So you don't . . . bite people or *drink* blood?"

"I only bite people when I'm desperate and don't have a ready supply of blood. Immortals have our own blood banks to which members of the human network routinely contribute. And no, I don't drink the blood. My fangs siphon the blood directly into my veins."

She studied him. "Are you desperate?" Because she was the only blood supply present.

"No," he assured her with a smile. "Even if I were, I wouldn't bite you."

"Well," she huffed in feigned offense. "I guess my blood isn't good enough for you."

He chuckled. "I'm sure your blood would perk me right up." His eyes said *as would other things*. "But I won't risk exposing you to the virus."

"Is it that pervasive?" she asked. "Would one bite turn me into an immortal?"

"Only if I drained you nearly to the point of death, then returned your blood to you infected with the virus. Otherwise, I would have to bite you several times before the virus would gain a strong enough hold on your immune system to conquer it and transform you."

"Oh." She didn't know what else to say to that.

He motioned to the windows. "Did it rain while I slept?"

"No." She nodded to the television. "But according to the big blob of red on the radar, it will within the next half hour."

As though to punctuate her words, thunder rumbled outside.

Ethan didn't seem particularly thrilled by her announcement.

"What's wrong? I thought you said rain would wash away the scent of our battle with the vampires and prevent any more from tracking us here."

He offered her a sheepish smile. "It will. I guess I was just hoping I'd have an excuse to stay with you a little longer."

Her pulse did a funny little fluttery thing. "You can't babysit me forever, Ethan."

"I'm not babysitting you. I'm watching over you." His lips quirked up. "When I'm not sleeping, that is. Should I check my reflection in the mirror to see if you've drawn me a dapper mustache and bushy eyebrows?"

She grinned. "I couldn't find a permanent marker."

As he laughed, his cell phone rang.

Ethan retrieved his phone and took the call. "Yeah?"

"It's Ed. Just checking to make sure you're still among the living."

"I am."

"And are you still with the woman?"

Ethan sighed at Ed's hopeful tone. "Yes."

"Good for you," he praised with annoying enthusiasm, then went all business. "Seth has called a meeting. He wants everyone at David's place in an hour."

"I'll be there."

"You want me to bring you anything?"

"A change of clothes would be nice." David kept a ready supply of clothing at his home for Immortal Guardians and their Seconds to plunder, but why raid it if it wasn't necessary?

"Got it. See you there."

Ethan tucked his phone away in a back pocket.

Lightning flashed beyond the curtains, followed by the grumble of thunder as the first drops of rain struck the ground outside with a tentative pitter-patter.

There went his excuse to linger.

"Everything okay?" Heather asked.

He nodded. "May I use your bathroom?"

"Of course."

Rising, he crossed to his duffel bag and dug around in it until he found the toothbrush and minty toothpaste he always carried with him. Battling vampires could get ugly. He had, on more than one occasion, had to use his teeth to rend flesh or give himself a quick infusion when wounded severely. And unlike some of the other immortals, he had never developed a fondness for the taste of blood.

Not that he would tell Heather any of that.

She arched a brow and smiled. "What *don't* you carry in that bag?"

"An umbrella," he retorted with a grin.

She laughed. "Bad luck there."

Ethan availed himself of her bathroom. When he returned to the living room, he found Heather standing at the window with the curtains open, staring out into the darkness.

Lightning flashed, brightening her features momentarily.

The rain pummeled the ground in earnest now.

"It's really coming down out there," Ethan commented, tucking the toothbrush and toothpaste away and zipping his duffel bag closed.

"Yes."

He crossed to his coat and withdrew her 9mm from an inside pocket. "Here. I'm sorry I had to take it from you."

Accepting the weapon, she stared up at him. "I'm sorry I probably would've shot you with it if you hadn't."

Damn, he hated to leave her.

Spying a pen and a pile of mail on the coffee table, Ethan picked up an envelope, turned it over, and wrote on the back of it. He handed it to her. "My number. If you need *anything*"—*or just want to talk*, he added mentally—"please don't hesitate to call me."

She took it and stared down at it.

Ethan forced himself to don his coat and retrieved his duffel bag. His boots thudding across the wooden floor sounded loud in the silence.

Heather followed him to the door.

"I'll check the area to ensure no vampires made it this far before the rain began to fall," he told her.

She nodded.

Opening the door, he stepped out into darkness and dropped his duffel on the front porch. "I'll be right back."

A quick search of the surrounding forest and meadowland confirmed no vampires had come looking for their deceased comrades. Already the scent of blood in the clearing had been washed away by the downpour, as had Ethan's and Heather's scents.

Ethan returned to the porch, his hair and coat dripping.

Heather waited for him in the doorway, the 9mm clutched in one hand.

"All clear," he told her, wanting so badly to kiss her again.

She nodded. "It still feels like I've known you for a year," she murmured.

"Oddly, it feels the same for me." Stepping closer, he cupped her face in cool, rain-slick hands. He heard her heartbeat pick up its pace even as his own did the same.

Lowering his lips to hers, Ethan delivered a slow, gentle kiss, memorizing her taste, the feel of her soft cheeks beneath his palms. He raised his head, saw the amber glow of his eyes reflected in hers. "Be safe, Heather."

She nodded. "You, too."

He lingered a moment longer. Then, stepping back, he picked up his duffel bag, strode to his car, and drove out of Heather's life.

David was the second eldest and second most powerful Immortal Guardian on the planet. Or at least he had been until Zach had grudgingly joined their ranks. Nevertheless, David remained Seth's second in command, having helped him guide and corral the Immortal Guardian group for thousands of years.

David also treated all immortals, their Seconds, and members of the human network like family. He opened his homes to them all. Did everything he could to provide a family-like atmosphere and dispel the loneliness that crept up on them from time to time. And provided the warmth and stability so many of them needed to keep plodding along in this existence.

For some time now, David had made North Carolina his primary home. A fortunate thing for Ethan, because David's home here—in recent years—had abounded with activity. All meetings were held there. Most of the immortals in the area spent their downtime there. And Ami, the young mortal from another planet whom Seth and David both loved like a daughter, lived there with her husband Marcus and their beautiful, miraculous baby girl.

Even before Ami had become the first mortal to give birth to an immortal's baby, she had won the hearts of all the

Immortal Guardians. She had been tortured by one of their mercenary enemies for months and had emerged from it changed. She feared all strangers now. Was almost painfully shy. Yet she was one of the fiercest fighters any of them had ever seen.

When Ami had again been targeted by mercenaries, all immortals in the area had felt the need to watch over her and protect her, so David's large house had become a home away from home for most of them, many even sleeping there during the day now to provide added security.

As they apparently had today.

Several cars already lined the long, curved drive when Ethan arrived. For once, when he headed up the walk and heard the bustle of activity inside, he didn't smile or feel relieved that the loneliness that afflicted him would soon be dispelled, at least for a time.

Heather weighed heavily on his mind. He hadn't liked saying good-bye to her. Had wanted to find some excuse—*any* excuse—to delay his departure. It puzzled him.

He had saved other mortal women in the past. Granted, they had all been drugged by vampires' bites. But it hadn't bothered him in the least that they wouldn't remember him or that he would never see them again.

He knew, without a doubt, that Heather would not be so quick to leave his thoughts.

No, Heather would linger a long time.

Chatter and laughter washed over him as he opened the front door and entered.

It looked as though he was one of the last to arrive. The dozen or so other immortals in the area and their Seconds all filled the huge living room, sprawled in the many chairs and love seats and sofas the room boasted.

Several called a greeting to him.

Ethan waved and closed the door behind him. As he shrugged off his coat and hung it beside the many others that adorned the hooks beside the door, he saw all eyes return to a tiny figure in the center of the room.

Adira, Marcus and Ami's baby girl, tottered from warrior to warrior, her little hands curling over black-clad knees to help maintain her balance as she grinned up at them. Every warrior smiled with indulgent affection and patted her little back or drew a large hand over her bright orange curls while offering words of encouragement.

How they all adored her.

One of the cats that had found a home with David slunk over to rub up against Ethan's legs. Adira's pretty green eyes latched onto it and lit up as she began to make her way forward.

She had almost made it to them when she lost her balance and sat back onto her bottom.

Ethan scooped her up and smiled at her, his somber thoughts fleeing. "Hello, princess."

She grinned up at him, revealing four teeth. Her little chin slick with drool, she curled her fingers into his shirt.

Ethan had been utterly terrified the first time Marcus had let him hold her. He hadn't been around children since he had been a child himself. Hell, almost a year later, she still felt far too fragile to Ethan. Even with all of her adorable rolls of fat. The child was built like the Michelin Man. Either that or an NFL linebacker.

The door opened behind Ethan.

Adira's face lit up. "Wo! Wo!" Kicking her little legs in excitement, she stretched her arms out to the latest arrival.

Ethan didn't even have to look to know who it was. Turning, he shook his head as the most antisocial immortal on the planet smiled down at Adira.

"Hello, poppet," Roland said, his deep voice warm with affection. As far as Ethan knew, Roland was the only immortal in the room who had fathered children—a son and a daughter—before his transformation. Unlike Ethan and the others, Roland had been comfortable caring for the babe from the get-go and clearly adored his best friend's child.

Beside Roland, his petite wife Sarah grinned up at Ethan, then waved at the baby. Sarah, too, had found a home in the hearts of all immortals. She had been the first *gifted one* in history to *ask* to be transformed so she could spend eternity with Roland.

"Wo! Wo!" Adira repeated.

"Hi, cutie," Sarah said with a smile.

"Hi, yourself," Ethan retorted and winked.

Sarah laughed.

"Wo! Wo! Wo!" Adira damned near hurled her little body out of Ethan's arms in an attempt to get to Roland.

"Let Uncle Roland doff his coat first, sweetling." Roland removed his coat in a blur of motion, helped his wife remove hers, then hung them up and held out his arms. "There's my girl."

Ethan obligingly transferred the squirming toddler to her favorite *uncle's* arms.

Sarah shook her head and smiled up at Ethan. "She adores this man."

Ethan remarked in a loud whisper, "I don't see the appeal."

"I heard that," Roland grumbled.

Sarah and Ethan shared a laugh.

As the three of them headed into the living room, Roland held Adira high above his head, then bent his arms so she'd dangle upside down behind his back, then straightened his arms and lowered her in front of him, then lifted her high and dangled her down his back again, all the while making what Ethan guessed were supposed to be airplane sounds.

Judging by the expressions of the others in the room, all felt as Ethan did: It was damned odd to see the dour immortal's face wreathed in such a wide smile, to see him so playful and affectionate.

Adira shrieked and giggled and drooled down Roland's

neck. And chest. On his shoulder. Apparently toddlers did that a lot while they were teething.

Roland didn't seem to care. Sarah and Adira had fostered *so* many changes in him. Not that Roland wasn't still one of the most ruthless warriors among them. As Krysta had once confided, Roland looked like he could kill a man, prop his feet on the body, and eat a sandwich. He just had a serious soft spot for these two ladies.

As Roland and Sarah sat on the sofa across from Marcus and Ami, Ed sidled up to Ethan.

"So?" his Second asked, raising his eyebrows.

"So?" Ethan repeated. No way in hell was he going to discuss Heather in a room full of preternaturally sensitive ears.

Ed had been with Ethan long enough to guess his train of thought and didn't push for details. "So I brought you a change of clothes. You look like you could use some blood."

"I could, actually," Ethan admitted and followed Ed into the spacious kitchen.

Sheldon, Richart's young Second, passed them on his way out, a gargantuan sandwich on the plate he carried. "Hey, man. How's it goin'?"

"Same old same old," Ethan lied.

"I hear ya."

Ed retrieved a couple of bags of blood from one of two refrigerators the kitchen boasted. (Large warriors tended to consume large quantities of food.)

Ethan sank his teeth into the first bag and let his fangs siphon the blood into his greedy veins. Strength flowed into him alongside it. He swiftly drained a second bag. Much better.

He heard the front door open and close, heralding more arrivals.

"Okay, guys," Darnell said in the living room, "let's do this."

Ethan and Ed headed into the dining room and sat at the long table that dominated it.

Marcus and Ami sat beside each other on the side opposite Ethan, near one end of the table. Sarah and Roland, who still carried Adira, took the chairs beside them.

Lisette appeared at Ethan's elbow and settled herself in the chair beside him. Zach took the chair on her other side. Lisette's brother Richart seated his wife, Jenna, next to Sarah, then claimed the seat beside her. Richart's Second Sheldon and Lisette's Second Tracy sat across from Ethan, beside Richart.

Ethan studied those two. Rumors abounded that Tracy and Sheldon might be sleeping together. What an odd pairing. Sheldon, the "kid brother" everyone razzed, the youngest Second in their midst. Tracy, a good nine years older and—from what Ethan had observed over the years—usually attracted to rugged bad boys. (Hell, he had even seen her flirt with Ed a time or two.) What about Sheldon would attract her?

Ethan's stomach growled as he transferred his attention to Sheldon's sandwich.

"You want half?" Sheldon asked, following Ethan's gaze.

Nodding, Ethan accepted the tasty offering with a smile. "Thanks. I forgot to eat earlier." Maybe Sheldon tempted her with his sandwiches, he thought after his first bite. Damn, it was good.

While Ethan swiftly devoured the sandwich, Richart's twin Étienne, his wife Krysta, and their Second Cam, along with the German immortal Alleck (Ethan didn't really know him) and the network doctor Linda, took all but one of the remaining chairs on the opposite side of the table. Bastien seated Melanie and himself beside Zach. Their Second Tanner took one of the last two chairs on that end.

Ethan thought the other immortals *might* have begun to

thaw toward Bastien. Ethan's eyes slid toward Roland and caught the glower that one sent the immortal black sheep.

Well, *some* of them had softened toward him. Ethan didn't think Roland would ever forgive Bastien for kidnapping Sarah and giving her a concussion. And Sarah wasn't exactly thrilled about Bastien's having tried to kill Roland more than once. So . . . yeah. Some tension lingered there.

The remaining chairs on Ethan's side were claimed by Krysta's brother Sean and his Second Nichole, the British immortal Edward and his Second Desmond, and Aidan and his Second Brodie.

Ethan thought Aidan downright peculiar. Seth had transferred the immortal to North Carolina last year just before the Immortal Guardians' final showdown with Shadow River. Born around seven or eight hundred BC, the Celt seemed bizarrely entertained by . . . well . . . everything that went on around him. Ethan would swear the man had smiled through every battle in which they'd fought together. Hell, he was smiling now, faintly.

Although every once in a while, Ethan caught a glimpse of weariness in the elder immortal's eyes. Not physical weariness. More of a world weariness. Perhaps the odd pleasure he exhibited was simply relief at having new challenges to dispel the boredom that doing the same damned thing every night for millennia could generate. Ethan had only been immortal and fought vampires nightly for a hundred years. He couldn't imagine doing it for nearly three thousand. Alone. No wife. No girlfriend.

Ethan's thoughts returned to Heather. Damn, he'd hated to leave her tonight. The way they'd met might have been fucked up, but he had really enjoyed her company. He couldn't remember the last time he'd laughed so easily or so often.

Darnell, David's Second, strolled into the dining room and seated himself in the last remaining chair near the head of the table. David followed. Even had David not stood six foot seven inches tall and had shoulders as broad as Ethan's, the elder immortal would have commanded attention. Thousands of years old, he fairly oozed power. With skin as dark as midnight, the face of a pharaoh (as Ethan had once heard Sarah describe him), and a mass of pencil-thin dreadlocks that fell to his hips, he had been on the planet long enough to have witnessed biblical events.

David possessed multiple gifts, all of which Ethan would *love* to possess. David could heal with his hands, shape-shift, read minds, move things telekinetically . . . *and* he could withstand several hours of exposure to daylight. David was not someone *anyone* would want to cross. He was unbeatable in battle. And fiercely loyal to his immortal family and the humans who aided them.

David lowered his powerful frame into the chair at the head of the table and greeted them all with smiles. Adira instantly slid off Roland's lap and began to toddle her way down the table toward him. Immortals smiled over their shoulders as she grasped the backs of their chairs to help her maintain her balance. When she reached David, Adira thrust her arms up toward him.

Smiling, David gathered her against his chest. "Hello, sweetheart. How's our girl tonight?"

The front door opened. Chris Reordon entered, his crappy leather briefcase clutched in one hand, and swung the door shut behind him. "Evening, everyone," he said as he joined them and took one of the only two seats left, which would put him at Seth's elbow when Seth arrived.

Ethan glanced around the table and felt sorrow lodge in his throat. Stanislav and Yuri should be at this table, their Seconds—Alexei and Dmitry—with them. The Russian immortals' deaths, at the hands of mercenaries, still struck Ethan like a kick in the gut at moments like this when they all gathered together.

Ed had told Ethan that Dmitry and Alexei were both

serving as guards down at the network for now, neither yet ready to serve as another immortal's Second.

David glanced at Zach. "Is Seth still in Mozambique?"

Zach nodded. "Last I heard."

While Adira stuffed one of David's dreadlocks into her mouth, David turned his head to one side and closed his eyes. "Seth." A moment passed. "Yes." He opened his eyes. "He shall be here shortly. He's at the network."

"That is so cool," Sheldon said, voicing Ethan's own thoughts.

David smiled.

Once again, Ethan bemoaned the fact that he had been born with such a boring gift. But his bloodline had been diluted so much over the millennia by ordinary human DNA that he was fortunate he had any gift at all.

"Where's Cliff?" Ami asked. "Won't he be joining us?"

Several others nodded. Cliff was the only vampire ever to be privy to their meetings. He really *had* become one of them in recent years.

Chris cleared his throat. "I thought it best that he not be present, considering what we're going to discuss."

Seth, the leader of the Immortal Guardians, abruptly appeared beside the chair at the foot of the table. Six foot eight, with long, black hair that reached his waist, he was the wisest and most powerful among them. Seth possessed all of the gifts the others held combined *plus* some they didn't.

"I apologize for the delay," Seth said, seating himself. He smiled at Adira, who grinned back from her perch on David's lap. "Hello, sweetheart."

Adira babbled something Ethan couldn't translate.

Seth nodded to the others. "Shall we begin?"

Chris opened his briefcase and drew out a laptop computer. "Some of you are already aware that there was an incident at the network this morning."

A few nods.

Krysta glanced around. "We didn't hear about it. What happened?"

"Shortly after dawn, Cliff suffered a psychotic break," Chris announced.

Gasps and *Oh no's* circulated the table as expressions filled with dread.

"He attacked Dr. Whetsman and did his damnedest to kill him. We had to take Cliff down with a buttload of bullets and tranquilizer darts."

"Is he okay?" Tanner asked, his brow furrowed. He had served as Bastien's Second—in a manner of speaking—back when Bastien had raised his vampire army, so Tanner and Cliff had been friends for years.

Melanie addressed the table. "He still hasn't awoken. It took double the usual dose of the tranquilizer to drop him. And we don't know what his mental state will be when he finally *does* wake up."

Chris opened the laptop. "We had no idea what triggered the break at first. We assumed Whetsman was being his usual self and had just said something assholish. Then Zach read Whetsman's thoughts and discovered that Whetsman had shot Linda."

All eyes went to Linda.

"I'm okay," she assured them. "Zach healed me." She sent Zach a smile. "Thank you."

Zach nodded.

Chris set a movie into motion on the laptop's screen. "This footage was taken from various surveillance cameras on the premises. Here is where Linda confronts Whetsman. He forces her with a concealed weapon to accompany him to his vehicle, then leans in and shoots her, out of sight of the cameras."

"What the hell?" Sheldon blurted. "Why did Whetsman shoot you?"

"Because I caught him smuggling vials of the sedative out of network headquarters," Linda answered.

Silence reigned.

The video continued.

"Whetsman went back inside to get the vials he had to leave behind when Linda tried to thwart him," Chris narrated. "He ran into Cliff—"

"Did Cliff hear Whetsman shoot her?" Sheldon asked.

Chris paused the video. "No. Cliff . . . hasn't been sleeping well lately."

Seth leaned forward. "He only sleeps in short snatches. His dreams are often so violent they wake him up, and . . . he hears voices now."

"Shit," Tanner murmured.

Chris nodded. "When it's bad, he wanders the halls, looking for a distraction. It appears he had just awoken from one of his nightmares and was walking it off when he ran into Whetsman." Chris set the video into motion once more. "We think Cliff may have smelled Linda's blood or fear on Whetsman and . . ."

Cliff's eyes flashed amber as he suddenly tore into Whetsman, shaking him like an animal would a chew toy. Chaos erupted onscreen as the guards fired their weapons, hitting the young vampire with enough bullets to make him drop the doctor. Which only seemed to piss Cliff off more. When the doctor ran, Cliff plowed through the guards, followed him upstairs, and caught him just before he reached the front door.

Damn. He messed Whetsman up before blood loss and the tranquilizer finally took him down.

Seth leaned back in his chair. "It appears Cliff has solved a mystery for us. We've wondered for some time now how Shadow River got their hands on the sedative they used against us. How they knew they needed to up the dosage in order to totally and instantly incapacitate one of us on the battlefield. Well, according to what Zach and I saw in his thoughts, Whetsman gave it to them."

"Why, for fuck's sake?" Bastien demanded.

"For money, no doubt," Roland pronounced with a scowl.

"Actually," Seth corrected, "he did it at Gershom's bidding."

The quiet that enshrouded them then grew so heavy that even little Adira seemed to feel it. Her face sobering, she leaned into David's chest and stuck two fingers in her mouth.

When no one else spoke, Ethan said, "What?"

"Whetsman's mind is a mess," Seth told them. "His brain is riddled with scar tissue where large portions of his memory have been erased."

"Erased?" Ethan asked for clarification's sake. "Or buried?"

Seth and David had told them that they preferred to *bury* memories when necessary because erasing them completely could cause brain damage.

"Erased," Seth confirmed. "As you know, we identified Gershom as the Other who is hell-bent on sparking Armageddon. Matching me and Zach in age, Gershom is capable of mind control, of planting instructions in one's subconscious, impulses one would be helpless to deny. And he has apparently been doing such with Whetsman for over a year now, essentially making Whetsman his puppet."

"Shhhhhit," Sheldon whispered.

Melanie nodded. "I didn't notice anything different in his behavior. Nothing at all."

"I didn't either," Linda said. "If I hadn't actually *seen* him with the vials of sedative, I never would've guessed anything was up."

Seth sighed. "That's how mind control works when implemented by an elder."

Lisette looked from Seth to Zach. "If Gershom wanted the sedative, why didn't he just pop in and take it himself? He certainly has the power to do it. Why involve Whetsman?"

"We don't know," Seth admitted.

"Plausible deniability?" Zach suggested. "He's already attempted to lay the blame for his actions at my feet once. Perhaps he thinks if he avoids being captured on surveillance video that he can still make that claim."

Aidan cleared his throat. "If he were to erase the guards' memories of his presence in the network, none would remember seeing him so none would have any reason to look at the video footage again. No one would even know they had caught him on tape."

Chris shook his head. "Erasing the guards' memories wouldn't have kept us from seeing him in the surveillance footage. *Certain events*," he said with a distinct edge in his voice as he sent Aidan a cutting look, "drove me to enhance network security. So video surveillance footage isn't just monitored twenty-four seven by the guards on duty at network headquarters. It is also streamed live to guards on duty at two undisclosed locations, many miles away. Unless Gershom can be in three places at once to wipe the other guards' memories at the same time, those guards will alert us to the Other's presence in our midst *if* the special alarms I had installed to detect preternatural motion don't warn us first."

Damn. Chris really *did* think of everything, didn't he?

Roland's scowl deepened. "If he uses the mortals at the network to do his bidding for him, then any one of the network employees could potentially betray us."

Ethan waited for Chris to explode with anger as he usually did when the dedication of his employees was questioned. But he didn't.

Chris sighed. "I can only protect you from what I can see. I can't see someone fucking with my employees' brains and turning them into puppets. I don't know *how* to combat that."

David cuddled Adira closer, rocking a bit from side to side.

"Seth, Zach, Aidan, and I will have to take turns scanning network employees' minds for any anomalies."

"Not Aidan," Chris declared. "Lisette and Étienne can help you instead."

David shook his head. "Younger telepaths wouldn't know what to look for."

"Then bring in another elder," Chris snapped, "because I don't trust Aidan."

Ethan examined all involved. Why didn't Chris trust Aidan? Was it because Aidan was still new to the team in North Carolina? Or had something happened? Seth and David shared a long look. Ethan was pretty sure they were consulting each other telepathically. He'd been around Lisette and her brothers enough to recognize the signs.

Seth turned to Chris. "For now, we'll accede to your wishes. David, Zach, and I will scan the minds of your employees."

"And Seconds," Roland added.

All of the Seconds at the table frowned.

"We don't know what Gershom's plan is," Roland contin- ued, "so we don't know how he might try to fuck with us next."

"I agree," Zach said.

Seth nodded. "So be it. I'm sorry, Seconds, but after what happened with Whetsman, we can't take any chances."

"Okay," Sheldon said, face somber, then tapped his temple with one finger. "But I gotta warn you, you're gonna see a *lot* of porn up there."

Tracy laughed and jabbed her elbow into his side. "Freak."

Grinning, Sheldon clutched his abused ribs. "Seriously, though, I'd rather you guys read my thoughts however often you need to than end up being some asshole's puppet. It would kill me to find out I had betrayed you while under someone else's control. So . . . scan away."

The other Seconds reluctantly nodded.

Zach glanced at Seth and David. "I don't know about you,

but I'd rather not be the one who scans Sheldon's mind. Who knows *what* you'll find up there."

Ethan and the others laughed.

"There's one question," Roland commented as the chuckles died, "that we've failed to ask tonight."

"What's that?" Marcus asked.

Roland's gaze circulated the table. "We defeated Shadow River a year ago. Why is Whetsman still stealing the sedative?"

None could answer that one.

Chapter Seven

Heather stared at the television but, if asked, wouldn't have been able to say what show she watched. Or *didn't* watch, as the case may be.

Two weeks had passed since she had helped Ethan defeat those vampires in the clearing. Two weeks since she had found herself thoroughly enchanted by the powerful immortal who, like her, had always been different.

Ethan hadn't called once. Hadn't returned to check on her. He had, it seemed, walked out of her life without a single glance back.

How crazy was it that she felt so . . . heartbroken?

No. That was a bit much. But disappointed didn't quite cover it.

Heather had gone on with her life as usual. She'd been called in to observe a few interrogations by local law enforcement. She'd also given a lecture at the University of North Carolina in Greensboro. Those were always fun. Her student and faculty audience always began by viewing her with a healthy dose of skepticism, if not outright mockery, and left with wide eyes and faces that were either flushed with embarrassment when she demonstrated her so-called FACS knowledge by revealing their lies or with faces wreathed in impressed smiles.

Through it all, she had been unable to stop thinking about Ethan. About his handsome face. His teasing grin. About the laughter they had shared and the kisses that had heated her blood. About . . .

Her gaze slid to the clock on the wall.

About the dreams.

Not the dreams that had plagued her for a year, but the *new* dreams that had been haunting her ever since she had watched Ethan get in his snazzy car and drive away.

10:47 p.m.

Her stomach tightened into a knot.

Reaching for the remote, she muted the television.

No vampires had come looking for her. Ethan must have been right about the rain washing away the scents of blood and battle. Life had been depressingly mundane.

When she was awake.

Gravel crunched in the driveway.

Leaning forward, Heather lowered her feet to the floor, sat up straighter, and curled her fingers around the grip of the 9mm on the coffee table.

A car door opened. Shut.

Again she consulted the clock.

10:49.

Damn it. Please be wrong, she silently implored.

Ethan stared at the front of Heather's comfy little home. Though warm light shone behind the curtains, he heard no movement inside, no television droning, no flip of a page that would indicate Heather read a book or a magazine.

Was she asleep? Curled up in bed with the covers tucked

beneath her chin, her slender body encased in a barely there nightgown?

He checked his watch.

10:49 p.m. Early for him. But mortals tended to keep different hours. He didn't know how often or how early Heather got called in to advise or observe interrogations.

Was this too late to call?

He wiped his hands on his pants. *I can't believe my palms are sweating. What the hell am I doing?*

Calling himself six kinds of a fool, he collected the items he'd set on the roof of the car and strode up the wooden stairs. Bending, he set the goods to one side, out of her line of sight. Then, taking a deep, bracing breath, he knocked on the door.

Sneaker-clad feet carried Heather to the door.

Good. He hadn't woken her.

The light behind the peephole darkened. The rattling of bolts being turned and a chain being removed preceded the opening of the front door.

Heather peered up at him. "Ethan. Hi."

"Hi." He smiled. She was as beautiful as he remembered. It had been hell, trying to stay away. He had only made it two weeks before he had given in and come to see her. He knew he shouldn't lure Heather into his world, especially with Chris Reordon waiting in the wings to recruit her, but . . . he had been unable to stop thinking about her.

"What are you doing here?" she asked and looked past him. Not the friendly, flirty response he had hoped for.

His gaze drifted beyond her. Did she have a guest? A *male* guest?

His hackles rose. "Are you alone?"

"Yes."

But she neither opened the door wider nor welcomed him inside.

Had he read things wrong with her?

"I was just hunting nearby," he began.

Alarm swept across her features. "Hunting vampires? You saw more vampires hanging around?"

"No," he hastened to assure her. "No. You're safe, Heather."

She didn't relax. Nor did she stop visually searching the yard behind him.

"I meant I was hunting in the *area* and . . . was passing by on my way home and just thought I'd . . ." He rubbed the back of his neck and sighed. "Ah, hell. I suck at this."

"Suck at what?"

"I wasn't hunting nearby," he admitted. "I was hunting forty miles away. But I can't stop thinking about you and wanted to see you again." Bending, he retrieved what he hoped she would see as a romantic gesture. When he straightened, he held a newspaper in one hand and a stainless steel coffeepot in the other. He offered her a sheepish smile. "It seemed like a good idea at the time."

Heather bit her lip. And he *did* think he saw a little *Aww, how sweet* enter her pretty brown eyes.

Stepping closer, he leaned against the door frame opposite her. "I'm afraid I don't really know how to do this."

He heard her heartbeat pick up. "Do what?"

"Date. I haven't tried to court a woman in about a century. I don't know how to get things going and can't ask Ed or he'll never let me live it down." Damned if he didn't feel like a teenager with his first crush.

Her throat moved in a swallow. "You want to date me?"

"If dating you means spending lots of time with you, getting to know you, and exploring every inch of your delectable body as soon as you're ready to take things further, then yes. I *really* want to date you." He held up his goodies. "I remembered your neighbor with the newspaper analogy and . . ." He released a rueful chuckle. "As I said, I don't know what I'm doing. I don't even like coffee. I just liked the idea of it and wanted to see you again."

"Oh, Ethan. It's perfect."

His heart leapt.

"But I really wish you hadn't come." Stepping back, Heather opened the door.

Disappointment struck. "Why?" He had been so sure she'd felt the same spark.

She brought the hand he hadn't realized she had been hiding behind her back around and raised a Walther PPQ 9mm. "Because I dreamed you would."

As Ethan gaped down at her, she pulled the trigger.

The coffeepot Ethan held clattered to the floor as he jerked his head to one side and ducked the bullet Heather fired.

Just as she had dreamed every night for a week, vampires poured from the foliage that bordered her front yard.

Heather squeezed the trigger again and again, striking vampires in the chest to slow them down, then hitting them in the major arteries.

Ethan swore and drew two sais. "Get inside!" he shouted as he turned and tore into the vampires who made it to the front porch.

"It won't do any good!" She ejected her empty magazine, drew another from the substantial pile she had stacked on the table just inside the door, slammed it home, and advanced the first bullet into the chamber.

"The hell it won't!"

Warm blood slapped Heather in the face as Ethan's blade slid across the throat of a vampire determined to get past him. Gasping, she wiped her eyes and mouth with her sleeve and fired her Walther. Again and again and again until she'd emptied the magazine.

One of Ethan's large hands, still curled around the grip of a sai, touched her chest and gave her a shove.

As Heather stumbled backward, he caught the door with

two fingers and swung it closed, shutting himself outside with over a dozen vampires. "Call Chris! His number is on the contract you signed!"

Heather tripped and landed on her ass with a curse. Scrambling to her feet, she lunged for the table and grabbed another magazine. A vampire crashed through one of the front windows as she slammed the full mag home and racked the slide.

Glowing blue eyes turned her way as the vampire picked himself up off her floor and flashed deadly fangs.

"Oh shit." Heather fired her 9mm before the vamp had the foresight to leap forward.

Crimson liquid sprayed from his jugular, splattering the walls and floor and furniture as he brought his hands up to his throat and staggered around the room.

A second vampire catapulted himself through the window. Then a third.

Outside, Ethan swore. "Heather!"

"I'm okay!" she shouted. "Just stay out there!"

Please, stay out there, she silently entreated as she emptied her magazine into the vampires, ejected it, and slammed another full mag home.

Adrenaline—fueled by pure panic—flooded Ethan's veins, lending him even greater strength and speed. He didn't fear for his own safety. He feared for Heather's, knowing what would undoubtedly happen to her if he didn't live.

How many fucking vampires *were* there? Two dozen? Three?

Where were they all coming from? And why the fuck were they there?

He had lost count of the number he had struck down, but the bodies shriveling up at his feet began to pile up enough to trip the vampires clamoring toward him. Were his back not up against the house, Ethan would not have survived an attack by so many. The fact that the vampires could only come at him from three directions instead of four helped, but Ethan was a young immortal. Not as powerful as the elders. The odds of him defeating this many vampires were slim to none.

A fourth vampire dove through the front window.

Ethan swore and hurled a sai at a fifth who sought to follow, nailing him in the heart. Palming one of the many daggers inside his coat, Ethan continued to fight and wished like hell he were telepathic and could call out to Seth or Zach or *any* immortal nearby to come to his aid.

Gunshots resumed inside. Two bullets burst from the wood to Ethan's left and embedded themselves in one of the vampires he fought. Ethan hoped like hell Heather wouldn't accidentally shoot him while she fended off the vamp inside.

The sound of glass shattering warned Ethan that vampires had found another way in.

Why were they so intent on getting to Heather? What the hell?

Kicking open the door behind him, Ethan backed inside. "Heather?"

"I told you to stay outside!" she shouted, steadily firing her weapon.

A vampire rushing in from the back of the house dropped.

Ethan kept backing up until he was within a few feet of Heather. Close enough, he hoped, to help her fend off the steady stream of vampires intent on reaching her.

Another window shattered, behind them this time.

Heather grunted.

Heart stopping, Ethan sliced at his two foremost opponents and spun around.

A vampire had come up behind Heather and locked his arms around her. As Ethan turned, the vampire lowered his head and buried his fangs in her neck.

Heather cried out. Pain and tears filled the brown eyes that met and held his.

A vampire's bite didn't generate the erotic pleasure found in so many movies and books. Instead, it would have felt like someone had just stabbed Heather with two large needles.

As Ethan took a step toward her, she jerked the hand holding her weapon up, pressed the barrel to the vampire's forehead, and fired.

"No!" Ethan roared, afraid the vamp would tear her throat out.

The vampire's head jerked. Abandoning his hold on her, he stumbled back a step and raised a hand to the hole in his fore-head.

Heather turned to face him and shot the vampire again. And again. Until he dropped.

Agony streaked through Ethan's right side as a vampire's blade pierced it. Another blade sliced across his left ham-string. Growling in pain, he staggered forward and turned to again swing his blades at the bastards.

A fucking machete cut across his stomach.

Ethan's speed slowed. His strength began to wane as blood poured from his wounds.

He needed to end this. *Now.* Or he wouldn't be able to. Not with the wounds he was racking up and the blood he was losing.

Ethan did his damnedest to push the vampires back, away from Heather, who somehow managed to remain lucid enough to aid him, firing her weapon whenever he didn't block her aim.

Beneath the steady barrage of her bullets and Ethan's blades, the vampires' numbers began to dwindle. Soon Ethan found himself fighting the last three vampires.

His breath came in short gasps, each feeling like a blade

burying itself in his chest. He swung his sai, struck a femoral artery. Threw a dagger, pierced a brachial artery.

One vampire down. Two more to go.

Barely able to remain upright, Ethan heard Heather's 9mm fall silent after a series of clicks. Was she out of magazines?

Her gun sailed over his shoulder and struck a vampire in the forehead.

Ethan would take that as a yes.

One of the vampires who faced Ethan nearly matched him in height. The other was several inches shorter. Both, thanks to the many injuries Ethan now sported, surpassed him in speed and strength.

As Ethan fended off the attack of the taller vampire, the other one left his peripheral vision. The taller vamp's blade cut across Ethan's chest half a second before Ethan cut the vampire's throat.

A weight struck Ethan's back. Stumbling forward, he turned . . . and felt his heart stop.

Heather stared up at him with eyes full of pain, the tip of a long blade sticking out of her stomach.

The second vampire had circled around to come up behind Ethan and Heather . . .

She must have thrown herself between them to keep the vampire from stabbing him.

"What have you done?" he whispered, horror stealing what breath remained in his body.

The vampire behind her directed a smile full of malice at Ethan over her shoulder, then yanked the blade out of her.

Heather screamed.

Ethan dropped his dagger and wrapped an arm around her as her knees buckled and she crumpled toward the floor. Fear and fury flowed through him, battling for dominance even as they lent him strength. Roaring his rage, Ethan swung at the vamp with his sai, limping forward, Heather still clutched to him, forcing the vampire back.

That malicious smile fled as the vampire stumbled over one of his fallen companions.

Ethan struck a killing blow, then struck another and another until the vampire fell to the floor and breathed his last breath.

Panting, Ethan wrapped the arm wielding the sai around Heather and held her close. Tried to listen for more vampires over his own labored breathing.

No sounds came to him from outside the house. Even the insects and nocturnal animals had been silenced by the violence.

Afraid to trust his senses—they sure as hell hadn't warned him that a couple dozen vampires hid in the damned bushes earlier—Ethan backed into a far corner of the living room, away from the windows, knelt, and lowered Heather to the floor.

"Heather?" A crimson stain spread rapidly across the front of her T-shirt as more blood pooled on the wood floor beneath her.

Ethan tore the material open and examined the ragged hole in her abdomen. Had the vamp severed her abdominal aorta? Ripping the rest of her shirt off, he wadded half of the soft cotton into a ball and pressed it to the wound, then wadded the other half up and tucked it beneath her back.

She moaned. Her eyelids fluttered, then opened. Dazed brown eyes rolled around, then struggled to focus on his face.

Ethan set his sai on the floor beside him and drew his cell phone from his back pocket with a hand that shook. "Shh. Just lie still. Everything's going to be okay."

"Hurts," she whispered.

"I know it does, honey." He dialed Seth's number, brought the phone to his ear. "Why did you do it?" he asked her while it rang. "Why did you throw yourself between us like that? I'm immortal. Stabbing won't kill me."

"C-couldn't let him . . ." she wheezed as blood stained her lips cherry red.

"Heather?" he called as she seemed to fade. "Heather, I need you to stay with me, honey. Can you do that? Just stay with me a little longer and I promise I'll bring you coffee and a newspaper every night until you grow to hate the damned drink."

"Yes?" Seth answered.

"Seth," Ethan nearly shouted with relief. "I need you. Now."

Seth appeared a few feet away. As soon as he saw Ethan and Heather, he rushed forward and knelt beside them, pocketing his phone.

"She's lost a lot of blood," Ethan told him as Seth nudged Ethan's hand aside and peeled back the wadded-up T-shirt. "She was bitten by a vamp, then was run through with a blade."

More blood welled and spread out to pool in her belly button.

Seth splayed a large hand on her pale, slick stomach. His hand began to glow.

Heather hissed in a breath and stiffened. Her legs moved restlessly on the floor as though she wished to scoot away from Seth.

Ethan took one of her hands in his and leaned down until his face hovered just above hers. "It's okay," he murmured. "Just look at me, Heather. Focus on me and it'll be over in a minute. I promise."

Her eyes opened and clung to his. Her fingers tightened to the point of pain.

Ethan could feel the heat radiating from Seth's hand as he worked.

Then Heather's grip loosened. Her shoulders relaxed. The tension in her face eased. But she didn't look away. Not until her eyelids grew heavy and closed, her head rolling to one side.

Seth sat back. "I healed her wounds, but she isn't out of the woods yet. She needs blood. A lot of it. We need to take her to the network."

Ethan didn't hesitate to gather her into his arms. When he rose, the pain of his own wounds rushed back, sweeping over him like a tidal wave. He staggered and would have lost his balance if Seth hadn't grabbed his arm to steady him.

"Give her to me," Seth ordered, concern darkening his features.

"No," Ethan growled through the pain.

Seth opted not to argue.

Heather's living room darkened, then vanished, replaced by the bright lights of the network's infirmary.

The network's *empty* infirmary. Where the hell *was* everyone?

Ethan opened his mouth and drew in a breath to bellow for help, but ended up grunting when his ribs and lungs protested.

"Melanie," Seth spoke in a normal voice. "We have an emergency in the infirmary."

Melanie rushed through the doorway. "What's up?"

"Miss Lane needs a blood transfusion. Chris probably has her blood type on file."

"Put her there." Melanie pointed to a hospital bed, then rushed away in a preternatural blur of motion.

Dimly, Ethan was aware of her speaking in the background, probably consulting Chris, as Ethan limped over to the bed and carefully deposited Heather atop the covers.

A breeze ruffled his hair as Melanie zipped up beside him and set up an IV in record time. Blood slithered its way down a tube and into Heather's arm.

Seth curled a hand around Ethan's biceps and gently drew him back. "I can't heal you while you're touching her."

Ethan released Heather's hand with great reluctance.

Seth flattened his other palm on Ethan's chest.

Heat flowed into Ethan and spread to his head, fingers, and toes. He gritted his teeth as broken bones shifted back into position and fused together. Wounds closed. Punctures sealed themselves. And, at last, the pain abandoned him.

He sighed with relief.

Seth patted his back, then withdrew his touch. "What happened?"

Ethan reached over and reclaimed Heather's hand. "Heather threw herself between me and a vampire to keep him from stabbing me."

Melanie glanced at them. "Is it okay if I hear this? I need to remain here for a bit. I'm not liking her vitals, and I want to make sure—"

"Of course," Seth assured her.

Ethan again felt panic rise. "I thought she was going to be okay."

"She will be," Seth promised, all calm assurance. "Once her blood volume returns to normal, she'll be fine. Now tell me what those vampires were doing at her home. And in such large numbers."

"I don't know," Ethan said, baffled. "The rain completely eradicated the scent of our skirmish a couple of weeks ago. I checked twice to be sure. So they couldn't have come looking for the others or seeking retribution and followed the scent to her door. Yet . . . Heather lives far enough from town that I just can't believe it was a coincidence. Two vampire attacks in a half-mile radius out in the sticks?"

Seth crossed his arms over his chest. "What were *you* doing there?"

"I was . . ." Ethan fought the urge to shuffle his feet. "I was . . . Ah, hell. I was trying to date her."

He saw Melanie glance at Seth from the corner of her eye.

130

Dianne Duvall

"Could they have followed you there?" Seth asked, no condemnation in his tone.

"Not at the speeds I was driving." Unease trickled through Ethan. "It was odd, though. Nothing tipped me off that they were there. I didn't see a single blade of grass flattened by a shoe that would've indicated that one or more of them had crossed her front yard. Didn't see a broken branch or dislodged leaves that would've told me someone hid in the bushes. And you know—with my gift—I wouldn't have missed visual clues like that. I didn't hear their heartbeats. If they didn't arrive until after I did, I didn't hear them approach. Didn't hear footsteps. Didn't smell them either."

"Were you upwind?"

Ethan thought about it. "Yes. But that would only explain why I didn't *smell* them, not why I didn't *hear* them."

"No." Seth's brow furrowed. "Even had they avoided crossing Heather's lawn and been there, lying in wait, you should have heard their heartbeats, the slightest shuffling of their feet or clothing when they changed positions."

Ethan agreed one hundred percent.

"How distracted were you?" Seth asked.

"I wasn't *that* distracted," Ethan protested. Sure, his mind had been on Heather. But that wouldn't have shut down all of his senses.

"Were the vampires after you or her?"

"I think they may have been after her. Had they wanted me, they would've remained outside and simply overwhelmed me with their numbers."

Melanie glanced at Ethan. "Not if they thought they could use her against you."

Seth nodded. "Did they seem to want to *kill* you or *capture* you? Bastien mentioned that some vampires think they'll live longer and be stronger and faster if they exist solely on the blood of an immortal."

"I'm pretty sure they wanted me dead. They scored enough hits that I would've bled out if I had been a vampire. And toward the end there, I don't think I was far from having my head removed."

Heather sighed suddenly. "Threw my gun," she mumbled.

Ethan moved closer to her, stroking the hand he held. "Heather?"

It took her several tries to open her eyes. Then she seemed to have trouble focusing. "Can't believe . . . threw my gun." Her words slurred as though she were drunk. "Can't believe I . . ."

"You can't believe you threw your gun?" Ethan supplied for her.

She gave her head a groggy shake. "Can't believe I . . . threw like a girl."

Seth and Melanie both laughed, then caught themselves and corralled their mirth.

Melanie smiled up at Ethan. "Was she by any chance bitten by a vampire?"

"Yes."

"I thought so. She'll probably be a little loopy for a while, then."

If the chemical the vampire's bite had exposed Heather to only left her a little loopy, then she had fared better than most mortals did when bitten.

Yet again, Ethan wondered how Heather had maintained enough control to continue firing her weapon with any accuracy after that vampire had sunk his teeth into her.

Heather couldn't seem to get her mind to focus. Her eyes either, for that matter. When she opened them, the room around her tilted and rolled as if she had just come off a three-day bender.

Voices spoke around her. One female, two male.

And a hand clung to hers. Large. Warm. With long fingers woven in between her own.

"Ethan," she murmured. Relief filled her when his huge, muscled form leaned over her and his handsome face swam into view.

"Hey," he said with a soft smile and stroked her hair back from her face.

Heather could have purred like a cat, it felt so good. "Handsome."

His smile broadened.

Her own smile faltered as her vision cleared and she got a good look at him. The hair above one ear was matted with blood. His face, neck, and clothing were splattered with it.

"You were wounded," she breathed and clumsily tried to sit up.

"Whoa." Ethan urged her back down. "It's okay. I'm okay. Just lie back and rest."

A pretty brunette in a white lab coat appeared beside him and reached for Heather's arm, checking a tube that was taped to it.

"Am I in a hospital?" Heather asked. Her tongue felt weird. Thick. She kept slurring her words. And her thoughts jumped around in her head like children in a bouncy house.

"You're at network headquarters," Ethan told her.

The brunette smiled down at Heather. "Hi, Heather. I'm Dr. Melanie Lipton. You're going to be fine. I'm just giving you a transfusion to replace the blood you lost."

Heather nodded. The room did that tilt-and-roll thing again. "A vampire stabbed Ethan in the back. Would you please check it?" She grabbed Ethan's shirt with her free hand, intending to turn him around so she could see his back, but two hundred plus pounds of muscle that didn't want to be budged simply couldn't be budged.

Ethan's lips tightened. "He didn't stab *me* in the back. He stabbed *you* in the back, because you threw yourself between us."

Really? The foggy remnant of a memory teased her. Pain. Seeing the point of a blade emerge from her stomach just before she stumbled into Ethan's back. "Oh. Right. Good."

His eyes flashed bright amber. "Good?" he repeated, fury darkening his features. "The hell it was! You sacrificed yourself to save me! What were you thinking? I'm immortal. *You're* mortal. *Incredibly, incredibly* mortal. You would've *died* if Seth hadn't gotten to you in time! You could've—"

"I wasn't thinking," she admitted, cutting off his rant. Her pounding head couldn't take the yelling. "And it never ended that way in the dreams. The vampire always—"

"Wait," Ethan interrupted. "You dreamed this would happen? You dreamed vampires would attack again?"

"Yes."

He stared at her. "When?"

Heather wondered why he looked so pissed. "When what?" She could've sworn he paused to count to ten.

"When did you dream it?" he gritted.

"Every night for the past couple of weeks." Fatigue seeped into her like a sedative.

"And you didn't think to call me?"

Heather closed her eyes.

"Heather?" Pause. "Heather?"

She pried her eyelids open and stared up at the handsome face hovering above her. "Ethan." She smiled. "You brought me coffee."

He looked to the brunette.

The brunette pursed her lips. "Did I mention she may be loopy for a while?"

Ethan sighed. "Yes, but I actually *did* bring her coffee."

"I thought you hated coffee," a deep voice rumbled beyond Heather's view.

"He does," Heather murmured. "But he wanted to come around the hedges."

Silence.

The doctor cleared her throat. "If that's a sexual metaphor, please don't explain it to me."

Masculine laughter.

"So tired," Heather complained. She couldn't keep her eyes open. "Could use that . . . coffee . . . bout now."

"Sleep," Ethan murmured. His lips brushed her cheek. "We'll talk later."

"Don't leave," she whispered.

"I won't. I promise."

Comforted, Heather let slumber claim her.

Chapter Eight

Seth watched Ethan stroke Heather's hair. The younger immortal was clearly smitten. "What did she mean about the dreams?"

Ethan straightened, but didn't relinquish his hold on the mortal woman's hand. "Did Chris fill you in on how Heather and I met?"

"We were all concerned about Cliff at the time, so Chris just gave me the basics. He said she came to your aid while you were fighting vampires in a nearby clearing."

Ethan nodded. "Heather dreamed the vampires and I would end up fighting there and that she would be dragged into it. Dreamed it exactly as it happened, almost every night for a year before it finally *did* happen. Apparently she dreamed of tonight's battle as well."

Alarms sounded. "Heather isn't precognitive," Seth said.

"Did Chris tell you that?"

"No."

Ethan stared at him for a long moment, then blinked. "Oh. Right. I forget sometimes that you know everything."

"Smart-ass," Seth muttered.

"Not really. I'm just a little slow to process things at the moment. It's been a long night and I'm not at my best."

Melanie frowned. "Oh, Ethan. I'm sorry. I haven't even offered you blood. Let me get you some." She darted away before he could thank her.

"Heather told you she dreamed it *exactly* the way it happened?" Seth asked.

"Yes. There were no deviations at all. She said that's never happened before. Except, now it's happened again."

Seth studied the unconscious *gifted one*. It didn't make sense. Telepaths didn't have prophetic dreams. Sometimes they were sucked into the dreams of those slumbering in their general vicinity. But Heather had no nearby neighbors and certainly had no neighbors with precognitive abilities.

Seth delved into her mind, seeking an explanation.

The one he found jarred him.

"What?" Ethan asked, his bloodstained face creasing with worry. "Is something wrong?"

Fortunately, Melanie returned just then with a couple of bags of blood she offered Ethan. "Here. If you need more, let me know. And if you'd like to clean up, Bastien always keeps a change of clothes here. He won't mind if you borrow them."

Ethan took the blood bags and arched a brow. "He won't?"

She winked. "Not if I tell him not to."

Relieved by the diversion, Seth caught Melanie's eye. "Where *is* Bastien?"

"Out hunting with Cliff," she said, her expression sobering. "Thank you again for allowing it."

He nodded. Seth agreed with Bastien that the violence of the hunt gave Cliff an outlet he needed and hadn't wanted to take that away from him just yet.

Ethan set the first bag, now empty, on the bed and lifted the second. "How's Cliff doing?" He sank his fangs into the bag.

Melanie sighed. "He's walking on eggshells, as if he thinks any slip in control at all will make him lose it again. He's handling it, though. I think the fact that no one blames him for kicking Whetsman's ass helps. But after what happened, some of the guards—the ones he inadvertently hurt trying to get to Whetsman—are more leery of him. And he knows it."

"What about Bastien?" Seth asked. "How's he taking it?"

Her shoulders slumped a little. "He wakes up every evening fearing this will be the night that Cliff will ask him to end it."

Seth backed away a step. "I think I'll join them on their hunt, then. See how they're doing. Ethan, I want you to remain here with Heather. Stay close. Don't let her out of your sight. And see what she can tell you about the latest dreams when she awakens."

"Okay."

Melanie held up a finger. "You might want to call ahead. For Cliff's sake."

Seth nodded. Retrieving his phone, he dialed Bastien's number.

"What?"

"It's Seth. I'm on my way, I just have a quick stop to make first."

"Okay. Thanks for the heads-up."

Seth teleported to the reception room outside Chris Reordon's private office. His eyebrows flew up as his gaze fell upon the shapely bottom of a woman who was bent over behind the desk, looking for something in the lowest drawer of a file cabinet.

The length of her gray skirt was conservative by today's standards, stopping just three inches or so above the knee. But it had ridden up a bit and clung to her like a second skin, outlining beautiful legs that seemed to go on forever despite her diminutive height. The pale blouse above it was a little looser, but still followed the lines of her slender body closely as she moved. The shoes on her feet were . . .

He smiled.

Brightly colored sneakers. This must be the extremely

efficient, ever-elusive assistant Chris raved about so much. His "right-hand man" without whom he couldn't function. Anyone who did whatever had to be done to enable Chris to accomplish the monumental tasks for which he had become known wouldn't be caught dead wearing high-heeled shoes. Such would've hampered her movement too much and—

The woman straightened suddenly, spun around, and fired a weapon at Seth.

A brief prick of pain struck.

Seth glanced down at the dart sticking out of his chest, then met the woman's widening eyes and arched a brow.

Her full lips parted. "Oh." She dropped her gaze to his feet and followed the long, long path up to his head. "Oh crap. I . . . I think I may have just screwed up royally."

Seth grinned. "You must be Kate." Striding forward, he held out his hand. "I'm Seth."

She rounded the desk, dismay filling her hazel eyes, and clasped his hand. "I am so sorry, sir. Things have been a little crazy around here lately and . . ." She glanced around. "Can you read my mind?"

"Yes." Right now it was full of swear words as she castigated herself for trying to tranquilize her boss's boss.

After Aidan breached network headquarters last year, she thought to him, *and broke into Mr. Reordon's office, I started keeping a tranquilizer gun on hand. Since you guys are so fast—the vampires, too—I thought it would be best to shoot first and ask questions later if I sensed someone had snuck up behind me without making a sound.*

Wise reasoning, he praised her telepathically, releasing her hand.

Thank you. I've been jumpier than usual since the incident with Cliff. And finding out the Other might be nearby, doing that creepy mind-control thing . . .

She knew about Gershom?

Seth forced himself not to frown. *How much do you know about the Other?*

She bit her lip. *Everything Mr. Reordon knows,* she admitted. *I can't help him nearly as much if I'm not privy to all the details. But the information stops with me.*

A quick scan of her mind showed him she was completely trustworthy. And totally attracted to her boss.

Seth smiled and plucked the dart from his chest.

"Again, I'm so sorry about that," she said aloud.

"Don't worry about it. I'm fine. And don't think twice about doing the same in the future."

She nodded.

"Is Chris around?"

"No, I sent him home."

Seth would've loved to have seen that. Chris Reordon didn't take orders from *anyone*. Hell, sometimes he even balked at taking orders from Seth.

"He's been getting by on naps here at the office ever since the Whetsman incident," Kate continued, "and that just isn't enough. He needs rest. Is there something I can help you with until he gets back?"

Seth almost laughed. *Oh* yeah. If Chris ever got his head out of his ass, took a break from his workaholic schedule, and realized what a prize his assistant was, the two would make a perfect match. Kate didn't ask Seth if he'd like to teleport to Chris's home and talk to him there. She asked if *she* could help Seth instead, basically warning him not to bother Chris because the man needed sleep.

"Thank you," Seth said, "but no. I'll wait to speak with Chris later. Would you please have him call me when he returns?"

She smiled. And Seth realized she had actually been gearing herself up for battle in case he had asked her to wake Chris or suggested he intended to teleport over there and wake him up himself. "Of course, sir." She held out her hand. "And may I say what a pleasure it is to have finally met you?

I've heard so much about you and am so grateful for the work you and your Immortal Guardians do."

Seth took her hand and, instead of shaking it, brought it to his lips to press a kiss to her knuckles. "The pleasure was all mine." In her mind, he said, *Thank you for taking such good care of our boy. Chris is like family to us.*

Her smile stretched into an appealing grin.

Winking, Seth released her hand and teleported to Bastien and Cliff.

The two were seated atop a building on NCCU's campus. Seth could detect no scent of blood on them, so they must not have slain any vampires yet.

"How's the hunt?" he asked as they rose and faced him.

"Slow night," Bastien said, careful to let no concern for his friend enter his voice.

But Seth could see it in the British immortal's eyes.

Cliff nodded without speaking. The young vampire had been quieter and more subdued since the incident.

"Is something up?" Bastien asked.

"We have a situation," Seth told them. "I could use your help with it. Can you postpone tonight's hunt for an hour or so?"

Both nodded, gazes sharpening.

Seth closed his eyes and did a quick mental search for Aidan. Once he found him, Seth touched Bastien's and Cliff's shoulders and teleported them to the Celt's side.

Aidan smiled at them, a tire iron held in one hand. "I thought I felt a disturbance in the force."

Cliff laughed.

Bastien smiled.

Seth shook his head. "What have you been doing?"

Aidan held up the tire iron. "Helping a lovely woman change a flat tire."

Bastien arched a brow. "A lovely *gifted one*?"

"As it happens, yes."

Seth sighed. "Did you flatten her tire, Aidan?"

"Yes, I did," the nearly three-thousand-year-old immortal admitted without remorse. Seth had transferred Aidan to North Carolina a year ago when loneliness had driven the immortal to break into network headquarters, violate security protocols, and steal a list of names of female *gifted ones* in the area. Aidan had hoped that he might be lucky enough to arrange a chance encounter with a woman who could love him and would be willing to transform for him as Sarah had for Roland. A woman who would want to spend the rest of eternity with him.

"Give Chris her name," Seth ordered, "so he can reimburse her for the cost of a new tire."

"I already reimbursed her. Tucked some cash in her purse. She just doesn't know it yet."

Cliff raised his brows. "So? Any sparks flare?"

Cliff, Bastien, and Melanie were among the few who knew why Aidan now resided in North Carolina.

"Sadly, no," Aidan told them. "She's distressingly attached to the mortal man she loves. So, what can I do for you gentlemen?"

"I could use your assistance with something," Seth said.

"If I can help you, I will."

Seth teleported them all to Heather's home.

Noses crinkled at the strong stench of death and decay as gazes raked the empty piles of clothing scattered about the living room floor. Blood streaked the walls and ceiling. Crimson stains marred the furniture.

Seth closed his eyes and summoned Zach.

Zach appeared at his elbow.

"We have a problem," Seth told them.

Zach studied the room. His boots thudded on the wood floor as he crossed to a broken front window and bent to peer outside. "Any of those piles of clothing out there Ethan?"

"No," Seth answered. "He and Heather survived the attack and are at network headquarters."

Bastien frowned. "Isn't Heather the mortal woman who fought vampires with Ethan a couple of weeks ago?"

"Yes." Seth gave them a quick rundown of the two battles as he had seen them in Heather's thoughts.

"That *is* a problem," Zach pronounced.

"Why?" Cliff asked.

"Seth said Heather is telepathic," Zach explained. "Telepaths don't have precognitive dreams."

Aidan's eyes lit with interest. "She's a *gifted one*?"

"Yes," Seth said, "and she's smitten with Ethan."

"Lucky bastard," Aidan muttered.

Cliff looked at Zach and Seth. "Couldn't precognition be a latent ability that has only recently begun to manifest itself?"

Yet again, Seth wished Cliff were immortal. He hated to lose such a bright, honorable man to insanity. "No. *Gifted ones* generally become aware of their abilities at a very early age. They don't suddenly acquire them as adults."

Bastien scowled. "Then why did she have the dreams?"

Seth drew in a deep breath. "Because Gershom planted them in her subconscious mind."

Zach swore. "You saw him in her memories?"

"No. I only saw the dreams he planted. I suspect he also orchestrated both vampire attacks. Like Ethan, I just don't see them being a coincidence. Not out here in the sticks."

"To what purpose?" Bastien asked.

"I don't know."

Heavy silence enshrouded them.

"Can you show us the battles?" Zach requested.

Nodding, Seth held out his hand, palm down. "Touch my hand."

Zach, Bastien, and Aidan stepped forward and covered Seth's hand with theirs.

Cliff hesitated.

"You, too, Cliff," Seth invited.

Wiping his hand on his black cargo pants, Cliff added his to the pile.

Seth closed his eyes and replayed the images of battle he had found in Heather's memories. He would've preferred to do it from Ethan's perspective, since Ethan would recall even the most minute detail, but couldn't read Ethan's mind without causing him considerable pain. Ethan's brain was just wired differently than other people's. Seth had never been able to determine why.

Seth opened his eyes.

The others lowered their hands and stepped back.

"The first encounter seemed accidental," Zach murmured.

"And yet," Seth countered, "Gershom knew it would happen and showed Heather over and over again in advance to lure her into it."

Bastien scowled. "Did he guide Ethan to the battle? Fuck with his thoughts and use him like a puppet the way he did Whetsman?"

Seth shook his head. "I doubt it. Ethan's mind is incredibly hard to penetrate. Zach and I are the only immortals who can do it and we can't do it without giving him a nosebleed."

Zach nodded. "And that's just to *read* his thoughts. Exerting enough power and enough of a push to force impulses in there may very well kill him. So I'm not certain it's *possible* to manipulate Ethan."

Another tense, thoughtful pause ensued.

"The vampires in tonight's battle seemed intent on getting to Heather," Aidan said. "Why? Could she have some meaning to Gershom?"

Seth had wondered the same thing. "If so, it isn't fondness. Had Ethan waited even a moment longer to call me, she would have died tonight. Gershom did nothing to aid her during the battle or to prevent her from being run through. Nor did he heal her afterward."

The four warriors looked as puzzled as Seth felt.

"I'm not seeing a motive," Bastien murmured, "a connection."

Zach shook his head. "Nor am I."

"Nor I," Aidan added.

"Could these attacks be related to Whetsman trying to steal more of the sedative?" Cliff asked. "Could the vampires be part of another mercenary army?"

"They didn't fight like mercenaries," Seth said. "But I suppose anything is possible."

"What do you want us to do?" Bastien asked.

"I want you, Aidan, and Cliff to return to network headquarters. Spend the rest of the night there, as well as the day, while Heather recuperates. Ethan will wish to remain with her, I'm sure. Stay vigilant and keep your senses open to anything that would indicate Gershom has come looking for them, and contact me if you have even the slightest suspicion that he has. If he strikes before you can call me . . . Aidan, teleport Heather to safety. Teleport multiple times to multiple countries around the globe to throw Gershom off track. Bastien, you, Ethan, and Cliff try to keep Gershom busy to buy Aidan some time until I can join you."

"Does Ethan know any of this?" Bastien asked.

"No. I'll speak with Ethan and Heather once she's back on her feet."

Zach spoke. "He won't want to leave her side if something foul goes down."

"Aidan won't give him time to object. Will you, Aidan?"

Aidan smiled. "Nope."

"Again," Seth stressed, "stay vigilant. And let the other vampires out to play if things get nasty."

The three nodded.

"Zach, I want you to sniff around here—inside and outside Heather's home—and see if you can catch a whiff of

Gershom. He had to have been close to have planted those dreams, then would've had to return several times to ensure they continued to plague her every night for a year. If he orchestrated tonight's attack, as we suspect he did, he may have been sitting on the damned roof the whole time it went down. It would certainly explain why Ethan wasn't able to detect their presence before they attacked."

Zach nodded. "What will you do with the woman once she's well?"

Another problem. "She can't return here. If Gershom came for her, Ethan would be no match for him."

"Nor would he sense Gershom's presence," Zach added. If possible, his look turned grimmer. "But Ami might if Heather stayed at David's."

Bastien swore. "Hell, no! And put Ami and the baby in Gershom's line of sight?"

Seth held up a hand. "I agree. It's too dangerous." He looked to Zach. "So I'd like Ethan and Heather to stay with you and Lisette until we get to the bottom of this."

Now Zach swore foully.

"You don't like it," Seth said, "but you see the wisdom of it."

"Yes," he growled.

"You may be able to sense Gershom's presence. And if you can't and he comes for Heather or Ethan for whatever purpose he has in mind, you can probably defeat him . . . or at least hold him off until I can join the fight. Then we can end this."

Zach loosed another growl of defeat.

"So," Cliff said, "you're going to use Ethan and Heather as bait?"

Seth didn't like it either, but . . . "One or the other of them means something to Gershom. Otherwise he wouldn't have brought the two together and orchestrated the vampire attacks. I don't know which one or what his purpose is, but it's the only thing we have to go on right now, and both of

them need to be protected. I would protect them myself, but
am called away too often to aid immortals and their Seconds."

"Are you going to tell Ethan and Heather *all* of it?"
Bastien asked.

"Yes," Seth decided.

He was not looking forward to Ethan's response.

Heather sighed as sleep receded.

She almost hated to relinquish her hold on it. It had been
a long time since she had slept so peacefully, free of violent
dreams battling vampires. A year, in fact.

That was a long time to go without a good, restful sleep.

As she let consciousness creep in, her senses went to work,
cataloging all of the things she would know if she would just
pry her heavy eyelids open.

She lay in a bed. In an empty room?

No. Somewhere a piece of paper rasped as though a page
had turned. And a conglomeration of thoughts and voices
from the minds of males overlapped one another and pummeled her until she consciously blocked them out.

Quiet descended. Much better.

Her nose was cold. But an appealing scent teased it. Masculine. Familiar. *Very* nice.

The rest of her, however, was toasty warm thanks to the
large male body curled up beside her.

Her eyes flew open. Heather turned her head on the pillow.
Her breath caught.

Ethan.

Damn, the man was beautiful.

He must have showered. Her last, vague image of him had
been a bloody one. Now the jet-black hair that teased her nose
gleamed in the overhead lighting and smelled like fresh rain.
His handsome face had been scrubbed clean, the dark stubble
from yesterday darker and more pronounced, lending him a

yummy rugged appearance. Those iridescent eyes of his were closed in slumber. His soft lips, parted ever so slightly, touched her hospital gown–clad shoulder.

He lay on his side, her right hand clutched to his chest with his left. The hard muscles of that bare chest provided much of the heat that warmed her. His right arm rested upon her belly, his fingers curled over her side. The heavy weight caused her no pain, so her stab wound must have been healed.

His left leg stretched along the length of hers. His right weighed down her thighs. Between them, through the material of whatever pants he wore, she could feel the long, hard length of him against her hip.

He was aroused.

Her eyes flitted back up to his face. But he was asleep.

And she *so* wanted to wake him . . . until she reminded herself that they weren't alone.

Her gaze slid to the other side of the bed.

A young African American man reclined in a chair next to the bed, Bose earbuds in the ears nearly hidden beneath thick dreadlocks. His angular jaw was clean shaven, his chocolate skin as flawless as a cover model's.

Heather wondered idly if *everyone* in the Immortal Guardians' world was handsome.

When he noticed her staring, the man removed his earbuds and offered her a smile that didn't reach his eyes. "You're awake."

She nodded.

He held up the earbuds. "Sorry about that. I listen to audiobooks and music to block out the voices." He began to wrap the earbuds' cord around an iPod.

"Block out what voices?" she asked, quietly enough—she hoped—not to wake Ethan. "The voices of the employees?" She seemed to recall Ethan telling her that they were at network headquarters. This must be another immortal if he could hear all the voices in the building.

"No." He set the iPod on a rolling tray beside the bed. "The voices in my head."

"Oh. You're a telepath?" There seemed to be a lot of those in the Immortal Guardians' world.

"I wish," he said, his tone almost wistful. "No, I'm a vampire."

And, according to Ethan, the virus drove vampires insane. *Oh shit.* She tensed.

"Relax," a voice with a . . . Scottish? . . . accent murmured. "Cliff is on our side."

Cliff. She knew that name. The other immortals had mentioned him. Something about a psychotic break. They had all seemed quite concerned about him.

Heather tilted her head enough to peer around Cliff and saw a large male who could easily pass for Ethan's brother sitting at a table across the room, reading a book. His eyes never lifted from its pages. "Are you a vampire, too?"

"Aidan is immortal," Cliff supplied. "A very old immortal who can kick my ass without lifting a hand, so you don't need to worry about me losing it and attacking you or anything."

"Okay." This was so weird.

Aidan's lips quirked up.

Heather returned her attention to Cliff. Relaxing her guard, she peeked into his mind . . . then fought the urge to recoil. Those were some ugly, ugly thoughts. But he was doing his damnedest to eradicate the ones he could and ignore the rest.

She nodded to the earbuds. "I do that, too, sometimes. I'm telepathic. And when I'm tired or stressed, I can't always block other people's thoughts. Were you listening to a book or music?"

"A book."

"Which one?"

"Walter Mosely's latest. David gave it to me."

"I haven't met David."

Cliff hooked a thumb over his shoulder at Aidan. "He's even older than this one. And this guy's ancient."

"Watch it, youngster."

When Cliff smiled again, Heather understood why it didn't reach his world-weary eyes. The struggle he waged inside must be exhausting. He tilted his head to one side. "Are you afraid of me?"

Heather looked past him to Aidan. "Can you really kick his ass?"

Aidan slid Cliff a sly look. "Hang on to your chair, vampire."

Cliff lowered his hands to the arms of his chair just as it leapt into the air a good four feet and spun in a circle.

Heather's mouth dropped open.

Cliff laughed and flashed her a genuine smile, his brown eyes finally lightening. "What'd I tell ya?" His chair returned to the floor.

That was so cool! If Ethan weren't sleeping beside her, Heather suspected she would've jumped up and down like a child, raised her hand, and shouted, *Me next! Me next!*

Aidan laughed. "I can see why Ethan likes you."

Heather glanced at Ethan, who hadn't moved. "How long has he been sleeping?"

"Several hours," Cliff said. "Immortals and vampires tend to sleep deeply after we've been severely wounded."

Heather took stock of her own body and felt no pain. A quick check revealed no tubes feeding her painkillers. "Are my wounds gone?"

"Yes. Seth, the leader of the Immortal Guardians, healed you with his hands, then Melanie gave you a transfusion—human blood—to replace the blood you lost." Cliff eyed her speculatively. "Is it true that you shot a vampire in the head when he sank his fangs into your neck and tried to drain you?"

"Yyyyes," she answered cautiously. Would Cliff be angry that she had killed a fellow vampire?

"That is awesome," the young vampire praised.

"It is," Aidan agreed. "I'm surprised you even remember that, having been bitten."

"It's a little hazy," Heather confessed. "And I'm not sure if I'm remembering the battle last night or the dreams that came before it."

"You should have told me about the dreams," Ethan mumbled. Tightening his arm around her waist, he snuggled closer.

For some reason, Heather felt heat creep into her cheeks. It hadn't bothered her to have Ethan curled up beside her while he'd slept. But now that he was awake, it seemed too intimate with the others watching.

She turned her head on the pillow and met Ethan's piercing brown eyes. "I wanted to tell you. But in the dreams, the vampires didn't appear until *you* did. I knew if I called you, you would race over to check on me. And I assumed, when you did, the dreams would come true. I thought maybe if I kept my distance, I could keep it from happening. I didn't expect you to—"

"Come around the hedges?" He pressed a kiss to her shoulder.

Her heart skipped a beat. "Yes."

Cliff's forehead crinkled. "Is that a metaphor?"

Ethan laughed and turned his attention to the vampire. "Not for what *you're* thinking. What are you doing here, anyway? I sense it's still daylight."

Cliff shrugged and pointed to his head. "Couldn't sleep. Too much noise up there."

Ethan pushed himself up onto one elbow. "That sucks." "Yeah."

Ethan looked to Aidan. "And what are *you* doing here?"

"Babysitting you."

"Well, I'm awake now, so you can go get some rest."

"No, I can't. The two of you aren't to be left alone."

Ethan frowned. "Why?"

"Ask Seth when he returns," Aidan countered. "And don't even try to read my thoughts, little telepath. My mental walls are far too strong for you to breach."

Heather bit her lip. How had he known? She hadn't intended to read *all* of his thoughts. She had just wanted to take a peek and find out why she and Ethan couldn't be alone.

"It isn't that you can't be alone," Aidan offered. "It's that you can't be left unguarded."

"Are you reading my thoughts?" she demanded.

He quirked an eyebrow at her. "Weren't you going to read mine?"

Yes, damn it.

He laughed and looked at Ethan. "Why couldn't *I* be so lucky?"

Ethan sat up and ran a hand through his short, tousled hair. "Why do we need to be guarded? Does Seth think the vampires will come for us here?"

Heather watched the play of muscles in Ethan's bare back and tried not to let it distract her. But he looked *really* good. Pure temptation. He was so close. So warm. And probably still hard for her beneath the blankets and the sweatpants she could now see he wore.

"Marshal your thoughts, woman," Aidan pleaded with a comical grimace. "You're broadcasting, and this is getting a little uncomfortable."

Heather's face went up in flames as Ethan glanced down at her with interest and Cliff casually raised a hand to his mouth to hide a smile.

"What exactly are you thinking?" Ethan asked, his voice still low and husky from sleep, which only made things worse. Because she could imagine him saying other things to her in that low and husky voice while he—

"Heather!" Aidan barked.

She jumped and covered her face. "I know! I'm sorry.

It's . . . the vampire's bite. You said it contained a chemical that drugged me, right?"

"That's been out of your system for hours," Ethan said with a grin.

"Well . . ." She threw her hands up in exasperation. "I don't know what to say. You've been in my head for a year now and then you kissed me and were all irresistible charm when we finally met—"

"Dude, you kissed her?" Cliff chimed in. "Awesome!"

Heather rambled on as though he hadn't spoken. "Then you showed up tonight with your coffeepot and newspaper and boyish smile—"

"I thought women liked flowers and chocolates?" Aidan remarked.

"And now I wake up with you all over me and looking like"—she motioned to his gorgeously muscled chest and flat washboard abs—"*that*. So . . . of course I'm going to have some . . . inappropriate thoughts."

"That is so cool," Cliff said.

Ethan's eyes lit with an amber glow. "Aidan?"

"Yeah?"

"You don't have to be in the same room with us to guard us, do you?"

Heather's breath caught. Her pulse picked up at the heat in Ethan's gaze.

"Sadly, I do," Aidan countered. "But even if I didn't, if the two of you made love in here, I and every vampire on the floor would hear you."

"Well, screw that!" Heather blurted. She was *not* an exhibitionist, visually or verbally.

Cliff laughed as Aidan continued.

"And if you sought the privacy of the soundproofed room Chris recently added, I wouldn't hear it if you were attacked."

The glow in Ethan's eyes faded as he turned his head and

studied Aidan. "Anyone who attacked us in a room down here would have to get by you and all of Chris's men first."

"Not necessarily."

Heather looked at Ethan. What did that mean?

Ethan looked as confused as she felt. "Just what the hell is going on?"

Chapter Nine

"I'm sorry, could you repeat that?" Ethan requested.

Seth had returned to the infirmary at sunset and, instead of letting Ethan and Heather leave, had given Heather a change of clothes he'd nabbed from her home, then teleported the two of them to Zach and Lisette's house.

Now Ethan and Heather sat, shoulder to shoulder and hip to hip, on a living room sofa, their linked hands resting on Ethan's thigh.

Across from them, Seth manned a wingback chair. Zach propped up the fireplace mantel, his arm curling around Lisette's shoulders as she leaned into him. Their Second, Tracy, occupied a love seat nearby, her brow furrowed.

"The prophetic dreams Heather has been having," Seth obligingly repeated, "were planted in her subconscious by Gershom."

Shit. That was what Ethan had thought Seth had said.

This was bad. This was *so* bad.

Ethan tightened his hold on Heather's hand. "Why?" Why would the Other single out Heather and fuck with her mind?

"We don't know," Seth admitted. "That's what we're trying to determine."

A leaden hush descended.

"Who is Gershom?" Heather asked, the question timid, as though she too recognized the gravity of the situation.

Ethan looked to Seth. How to explain it?

"I have led the Immortal Guardians for thousands of years," Seth told Heather.

Her eyes widened. "You're that old?"

"Yes. Zach is, too. Aside from David, my second in command, no one else can even come close to us in terms of age and power . . . except for the Others."

"The Others?" she parroted.

"That's what they call themselves, yes."

"There are over a dozen of us. Of *them*," Zach corrected himself. "Seth and I are . . . willing exiles, if you will. Defectors."

Heather's brow creased. "I'm sorry. I'm not following you. You keep saying others. Other what?"

Seth leaned forward and braced his elbows on his knees. "Others are the eldest immortals on the planet. As such, we possess incredible power. Power that can alter the world if we wield it. But we decided long ago that we would not, under any circumstances, interfere with the natural course of mankind. We believed—and had good reason to do so—that any interaction with humans would alter that course and inevitably bring about Armageddon."

Heather stared at him. "Armageddon. As in the end of the world."

"Yes," Seth confirmed. "We really did have good reason to believe it, but I can't go into that with you."

Heather cast Ethan a questioning look.

"David once compared it to time travel," Ethan attempted to explain. "Have you ever seen time-travel movies in which those who traveled back in time were warned to alter nothing, that even stepping on a bug or killing a butterfly could change the course of history?"

"Yes."

"That's what the Others believe. That any interaction at all with humans will irrevocably set into motion changes that will bring about an apocalypse and destroy us all."

Her gaze slid to Seth. "I don't understand. You're here, right now, interacting with *me*. And you protect humans from vampires every night. Doesn't that contradict what you just told me?"

"As Zach said, he and I defected from the Others. I fell in love with a human woman many millennia ago and was willing to risk everything to be with her. Once I became part of the mortal world and began living amongst humans, I couldn't let vampires prey upon them unchallenged. Since vampires and immortals share similar characteristics in terms of speed, strength, and regenerative capabilities, I believed immortals protecting humans from vampires would *balance* the playing field rather than tilt it. And such gave immortals a purpose."

Heather's gaze slid to Zach.

Zach's lips tilted up a bit. "I thought Seth was full of shit and sided with the Others until recently." He glanced down at Lisette. "Until I understood what it meant to be willing to risk all for the woman you love."

Smiling up at him, Lisette rose onto her toes and pressed a kiss to Zach's chin.

"The Others," Seth told Heather, "believe we're in the wrong and still maintain that any interaction with humans will bring about Armageddon . . . and their own demise. They would like nothing more than to kill me—and Zach—to end our interference in the matters of mankind. But last year, one amongst them . . ."

"Lost his fucking mind," Zach snarled.

Seth glanced at Zach, then nodded at Heather. "Yes. Gershom apparently *has* lost his mind and actually *wants* to bring about Armageddon. At least, that is what we believe, since we can find no other explanation for his actions."

Heather looked up at Ethan. "Seriously? He wants the world to end?"

Ethan sighed. "Yes. He already tried to get things rolling once by giving Shadow River the virus so they could raise their mercenary vampire army."

Her throat moved in a swallow. "That would do it." Then the color fled her face as she studied them all. "And now you say this Other, this Gershom, is screwing with my head, planting dreams in my subconscious?"

"Yes," Seth acknowledged.

"Why?" she asked as her hand began to tremble in Ethan's grasp. "Why me?"

"We don't know," Seth answered.

Zach cleared his throat. "It could be your connection to your father. I understand he's a high-ranking officer in the army."

"He is. But if this Gershom wants to use my father, why not plant the dreams in my father's mind? Why go through me? What did he think I would do? And if I'm so important to him, why did he mislead me in the last set of dreams? Why did he let that vampire stab me?"

Ethan frowned. "What do you mean? Mislead you how?"

"In the dreams of the battle we fought last night," she told him, "you always died."

Shocked silence took the room.

"What?" Ethan breathed.

"*That's* why I didn't call you and tell you about them," she said, her face full of sorrow. "I was afraid it would make them come true. In the dreams, I was always leaning down to grab one of the fallen vampires' weapons when that last vampire came up behind you and stabbed you in the back. In the dreams, you fell to your knees and . . ." Her voice faltered.

"He took your head," Seth said grimly. "In the dreams, the vampire decapitated you."

"Yes," Heather whispered.

Ethan stared at her. "That's why you threw yourself at my back? Because you knew if he stabbed me it would weaken me enough for him to decapitate me?"

She nodded. "I couldn't let him kill you."

Releasing her hand, Ethan wrapped an arm around her shoulders and drew her close. "What does it mean?" he asked Seth. Zach. Lisette.

Seth shook his head, his expression grim. "We don't know. We can't even decide who his real concern is. Is it Heather and her connections? Or is it you? Did he purposely mislead her in the dreams so she would save your life?"

"If he wanted to save my life, why did he orchestrate the vampire attacks in the first place?" Ethan demanded, frustration rising. "I mean, what the fuck, Seth? I don't know this guy from Adam. What the hell would he want with *me*? I don't even have a mind he can control. My damned head is too hard." Unease trickled through him. "Wait. That couldn't be it, could it?" He looked back and forth between the elders. "He can't control my mind, can he? Could he want to manipulate me the way he did Whetsman because he knows you never read my thoughts and wouldn't guess it?"

Seth visually consulted Zach for a long minute.

Ethan didn't like the look in his eyes, when Seth again met his gaze.

"It's possible. We hadn't considered it from that angle."

Ethan swore.

"But," Seth qualified, "considering the pain it would cause you, I find it hard to believe he would be able to get you to sleep through his intrusion."

"But you'd know it if you saw it, right?" Ethan pressed. "You'd see some evidence that he's tampered with my mind if you took a look?" He did *not* want to end up like Whetsman. Ethan did *not* want to be some prick's puppet and end up betraying his friends.

And he didn't want to hurt Heather.

"Yes," Seth responded, no less grim.

"Then do it," Ethan said.

Seth swore. "That isn't necessary. We aren't there yet. We can just monitor things and see what happens—"

"Do it, Seth," Ethan gritted, understanding his leader's reluctance.

The elder dragged a hand down his face and again looked at Zach.

Hell, even Zach looked grim.

Lisette's face filled with dread. "Ethan, you don't have to do this."

Again Ethan thought of Whetsman, who had worked with Gershom for who knew how long and had aided Shadow River, something that had inevitably resulted in a loss of lives, both mortal and immortal.

Yes, he did.

Straightening, Heather frowned up at him. "Why don't they want Seth to read your mind?"

He tried to shrug it off. "Because it will hurt like hell, but I can take it."

"It can also cause brain damage," Seth told her. "Brain damage I won't be able to repair. Ethan's mind is wired differently. Negotiating it is extremely difficult."

Alarm filled her features. "Then don't do it!" She turned back to Ethan. "Ethan, don't. You don't have to. Seth said he can wait and—"

"And what? See if I hurt my friends? See if I hurt *you*?" Ethan shook his head. "Fuck that. I'm not going to let this asshole turn me into a weapon he can use against you all. The last time he did that, we lost two immortals and seven members of the network. Seth, just do it and get it over with."

"Zach," Seth said.

Straightening away from the mantel, Zach crossed the room and circled the sofa to stand behind Ethan. He rested his hands on Ethan's shoulders. "I'll try to alleviate some of the pain."

Ethan nodded and tried to ease away from Heather.

Heather clung to him like a vine.

"You'll have to release him," Seth informed her.

She hesitated, face stricken, then took Ethan's face in her hands and leaned up to kiss him. A long, hungry kiss full of desperation that he eagerly returned.

No one voiced an objection as the kiss lingered.

When Heather finally broke the contact, she pressed her forehead to his. "You owe me coffee."

He nodded, unable to speak.

Her brown eyes full of fear, she eased away from him and curled up on the opposite end of the sofa, arms wrapped around herself as though she fought the urge to reach for him again.

Ethan looked to Seth. "Do it."

Across the room, Lisette mouthed, *I love you*.

Ethan forced a smile.

Seth eased out of his chair and down onto his knees. Shoving the coffee table aside, he moved forward until he knelt in front of Ethan and took Ethan's jaw in one large hand. "Are you sure?" he asked one last time.

"I'm sure."

Agonizing pain struck, as though someone had fired a damned Taser at Ethan and the barbs had embedded themselves in his head. Jolt after jolt of fiery pain pummeled him as that imaginary finger held down the button and sent what felt like a powerful electrical current burning its way through his brain. Ethan's teeth clamped together as every muscle in his body jerked and tightened. Beneath the torturous assault, he could feel warm tendrils of . . . *something* seeping through him. Zach, trying to alleviate the pain. But it was about as effective as a mother pressing a kiss to a child's arm after it had been broken.

Warm liquid tickled Ethan's upper lip. Then his chin. His jaw beneath his ears.

Ethan tried to hold his shit together for Heather's sake, but soon bellowed from the pain until darkness opened its gaping maw and swallowed him whole.

In a windowless room, men with dour faces sat around a large, beautifully polished oak table. Some wore military uniforms decorated with multiple medals and insignia. Others wore business suits that identified them as either leaders of the intelligence community or political advisors.

On one wall, large monitors flashed with color, images, and text.

Outside the door, heavily armed guards ensured none breached the inner sanctum.

Thick files full of information on the destroyed army base and one Private First Class Nick Altomari rested on the table before each man.

"Could he be in collusion with the perpetrators of the attack?"

General Lane addressed the man videoconferenced in via the laptop at the head of the table. "It's a possibility, sir."

"Not according to our psychiatrists," a second man objected.

"Well, what do *they* say?" the first man asked.

"That whatever he saw traumatized him so much that it drove him insane. That his mind couldn't take it and has fabricated this . . . I don't know . . . fantasy-world explanation to help him deal with what happened that night."

"Or to deal with the guilt," yet another offered. "For all we know he could have orchestrated the whole damned thing."

"I say we have our interrogators lean on him harder until he cuts the shit," a gravelly voice farther down the table barked.

General Lane shook his head. "There's an alternative to that."

"What?" the man with the gravelly voice snorted. "Your daughter?"

General Lane ignored him and looked to the head of the table. "Mr. Chairman, my daughter has helped us countless times in the past with interrogations. She is the best in her field."

"What exactly *is* her field?" the chairman asked.

"She's a FACS specialist. She reads facial expressions and can tell by even the most minute changes whether or not someone is telling the truth."

Grumbles and snide comments erupted.

"She's been more effective at telling truth from bullshit," General Lane said over the noise, "than a lie detector at every turn."

"Hell, I can beat a lie detector," the gravelly voice declared.

"But you can't beat her. She'd know it in an instant if you tried." General Lane returned his attention to the chairman. "My daughter is the reason we knew the Brooklyn cell intended to blow up Grand Central Station. She's the reason we stopped them."

Some of the mutters ceased, but a few assholes continued to voice their disbelief.

"Has she ever been wrong?" General Lane challenged them.

Silence.

"We can't risk knowledge of this leaking to the public," the chairman intoned.

"It won't," General Lane vowed. "She signed a confidentiality agreement when we first started calling her in. She won't violate it. She's completely trustworthy. That's why the DHS, NSA, FBI, and CIA all use her. They know she won't talk and she's always accurate."

More silence.

"You aren't actually considering this?" the gravelly voiced bastard asked.

"Bring her in," the chairman ordered. "At the very least, she should be able to tell us enough for us to decide whether or not we need to loosen the reins on our interrogators."

Heather watched in horror as Seth . . . did whatever the hell he was doing to Ethan's mind.

Ethan clenched his teeth together until she feared they would crack. His face reddened. The cords in his neck stood out as blood streamed from his nose and ears in steady rivulets. His hands gripped the sofa cushions so tightly the fabric tore.

Then he bellowed in agony.

"Stop!" Heather begged, rising onto her knees. "Please!"

Hands grasped her shoulders. Small, but powerful enough to restrain her.

Heather looked over her shoulder.

Lisette stood there, as grim-faced as the others, her eyes glistening with tears.

"They're killing him," Heather choked out.

Lisette's throat moved in a swallow as she shook her head. But she didn't deny it.

Heather looked back at Ethan.

Seth's hand on Ethan's face began to glow with a golden light.

Convulsions abruptly shook Ethan's big body, cutting off his roar. His mouth clamped shut. Blood seeped from between his lips.

Had he bitten his tongue? Or was he . . . ?

Ethan's eyes closed. A long breath left him as his body went limp.

Seth's hand lost its glow.

When Seth released his hold, Ethan's head lolled forward

to hang low. Had Zach not held Ethan's shoulders, Ethan would have folded over and fallen off the sofa.

A sob caught in Heather's throat.

Was he dead?

She waited, watching in horror for the first signs that would indicate he was shriveling up like vampires did when they died.

Seth sank back on his heels. "He needs blood."

Relief, almost painful in its intensity, overwhelmed Heather.

Seth looked up at Zach. "Get David. His will nourish Ethan the most."

Nodding, Zach stepped back from the sofa and vanished.

Heather lunged forward as Ethan began to slump over and guided him down until his head rested in her lap. The backs of her eyes stung with salty tears that spilled over her lashes as she combed her fingers through his hair.

"Is he okay?" Lisette asked in a choked voice.

Seth sighed. "We won't know for sure until he awakens."

"Did you at least find the answers you sought?" Heather asked, not quite able to suppress the fury she felt over Seth's having caused Ethan so much pain.

"I believe so, but—again—won't know for certain until he awakens."

Zach reappeared with a tall, strikingly handsome man with skin as dark as midnight and pencil-thin dreadlocks that fell to his hips. This was David, the immortal Cliff had mentioned?

He must be. Cliff had said David was even older and more powerful than Aidan. And this man exuded power.

"Zach said Ethan needs my blood," David said, his voice deep. When his gaze found Ethan, David swore. Striding forward, he knelt beside Seth in front of the sofa and started rolling up one sleeve.

Heather waited for someone to offer him an explanation. No one did.

David gently opened Ethan's mouth and nudged his upper lip back.

No fangs.

When he touched his fingers to Ethan's jaw, Ethan's fangs descended.

David pressed his arm to Ethan's mouth, shifting it slightly until it was positioned just so, then applied enough pressure to make the fangs sink deep.

Heather continued to stroke Ethan's hair.

Minutes passed, during which she concluded that Seth and David were communicating telepathically. She would have tried to listen in, but her own thoughts were too chaotic for her to focus.

David glanced at her. "You must be Heather."

She nodded.

"I'm David." He offered her his free hand.

Heather shook it, her small hand swallowed by his.

When she would've withdrawn it, David tightened his hold on her fingers and gave them a squeeze. "Thank you for saving our boy's life last night."

She nodded, but said nothing as bitterness flooded her. Yes, she had saved Ethan's life. But for what? So Seth could nearly take it or give him brain damage?

David gave her hand another squeeze, then let it go. "Our world can be a dangerous one," he confided, his voice kind. "Sometimes it compels us to make difficult decisions, not unlike the one you made last night when you threw yourself between Ethan and the vampire's blade. I know you're angry. But please keep in mind that *Ethan* made this decision. Not Seth. Seth didn't even suggest it. He takes no pleasure in harming those he loves."

Swallowing hard, she nodded. Had he and Seth and Lisette all heard her thoughts? Her silent accusations?

She forced herself to look at Seth, saw the self-condemnation in his dark eyes, and blinked back tears. "I'm sorry. I'm just . . . afraid for him."

"As am I," he admitted, then nodded to David. "That should be enough."

As David withdrew his arm, Ethan's fangs receded.

Heather had hoped that whatever blood did for immortals and vampires would make Ethan rouse swiftly. But it didn't.

Lisette cleared her throat. "Why don't we make him more comfortable? He can rest in one of the bedrooms downstairs."

While they waited to see how much damage had been wrought.

Ethan bit back a groan as darkness fell away and light brightened the backs of his closed lids. His head hurt like a bitch. What the hell?

He started to raise his right hand to grip his forehead and try to force back the ache, but couldn't. A weight rested upon it.

Cracking open heavy lids, he squinted down.

Heather. They lay in bed together, Ethan beneath the covers and Heather above them. Almost as they had in the infirmary. Only this wasn't the infirmary.

He squinted at the room around them. Lit by the glow of a solitary candle, it seemed vaguely familiar. Was this . . . Richart's room at Lisette's house? Or Étienne's room?

Why did the candle seem so damned bright? Looking at it increased the pounding in his head, so he returned his attention to Heather.

"She hasn't left your side," a voice ventured softly.

Ethan glanced over and found Lisette standing in the open doorway, garbed in hunting clothes. "What happened?"

Her pale, slender throat moved in a swallow. "Do you know me?"

"Know you how?" he asked, confusion mingling with the pain in his head.

"Do you recognize me?" she asked, taking a step into the room.

"Of course, Lisette. What the hell is going on? What happened?"

"Do you know your name?" she pressed. "Do you know *her* name?"

"Yes. I'm Ethan and she's Heather. Why are you behaving so oddly? And why do you look like you're about to cry? Did something happen to Zach?"

A tear spilled over her lashes. Swiping a hand across her cheek, she shook her head.

Alarm shook him. "Lisette . . ."

She held up a hand, then pulled a cell phone from her back pocket and dialed.

"Yes?" he heard Seth answer.

"He's awake."

Seth appeared beside Lisette. Zach crowded into the doorway behind her.

Seth approached the bed. "How do you feel?"

"Alarmed. What the hell happened?"

"You don't remember?"

Heather roused as his voice rose. When she lifted her head and saw Ethan staring back at her, she stilled. "Ethan?"

"Yeah?"

Lunging upward, she threw her arms around his neck and hugged him tight. "I was so afraid," she whispered, her lips brushing his ear. "I thought he'd killed you."

And it all came rushing back.

"Oh shit." Ethan looked to Seth. "You read my mind." And he wasn't sure he wanted to know what the elder had found up there.

"You remember?" Seth asked. "You remember everything leading up to my reading your mind?"

"Yes. Heather nearly died when we fought vampires at her home. You healed her and took us to the infirmary. We both slept. Then you brought us here and . . ." He looked from Seth to Zach and back. "What did you find?"

"You remember all of it?" Seth pressed.

"Yes. Zach held me still and tried to ease the pain. You touched my face. Then it felt like someone fucking Tasered my head." He glanced around. "I'm not sure how I got down here, though. I must have blacked out."

Relief swept Seth's features. "You did. And everything is good. I found nothing in your mind that would indicate that Gershom has been manipulating you. No scar tissue that would indicate memories had been erased, although—since you're immortal—erasing memories may not cause scarring. But there were no instructions or directions or impulses or even dreams planted in your subconscious."

Ethan sighed, the tension leaving his limbs. "That's good."

"Even better," Seth said, smiling, "I tried to plant a command of my own in your subconscious to prevent you from remembering the pain I had caused you or that I had dabbled in your mind, and it clearly didn't take. I assume your gift would not allow it. So I firmly believe it would be impossible for Gershom to use you in such a fashion, to plant any commands without your remembering him doing it as you did this. You are impervious to mind control."

The relief that statement spawned was heady, leaving Ethan a little light-headed. Or maybe he was still recovering from Seth plowing through his brain.

Heather sat up beside him and helped him ease up to lean against the headboard. "So, that's a good thing, right?"

"A very good thing," Seth assured her. "Ethan can rest easy now that Gershom can't use his hard head against us."

Ethan laughed, then groaned and clutched his head as pain shot through it.

Seth moved closer, leaned down, and touched his fingers to Ethan's forehead.

Instant relief.

"Thank you."

Seth withdrew his touch. "I'm sorry, Ethan."

Ethan shook his head. "You were just doing what I asked you to do."

Lisette cleared her throat. "If Ethan can't be used as a weapon against us, what interest could Gershom have in him?"

Zach curled an arm around her shoulders. "I think we can safely conclude now that Ethan isn't the one who interests him. I think Heather is his target."

Ethan took Heather's hand.

His target for what?

Seth left. Zach and Lisette headed . . . Heather wasn't sure where. Upstairs, she thought, since she couldn't hear anything down here. No movement. No muted conversation.

Sliding off the bed, she crossed to the door and closed it.

"Are you okay?" Ethan asked with touching concern as she returned and climbed back onto the huge bed.

She nodded. "Are you?"

He smiled. "I'm good."

Heather knelt beside him and sat back on her heels. "What about your head? Does it still hurt?"

"No. David's blood helped me heal and Seth took away the pain."

"Good."

Silence fell. Then they both spoke at the same time.

"Ethan—"

"Heather—"

They laughed.

"Go ahead," Ethan said. "You first."

She nodded, a little nervous all of a sudden. "I like you, Ethan."

His smiled softened. "I like you, too."

"I mean I *really* like you. Every time I'm around you, I feel a connection to you that I've never felt before. I know the dreams make me feel as if we've known each other longer than we have, but it's more than that. You make me laugh. And I always want to spend more time with you than we have together. I can't wait to see you again when we're apart . . ." Her heart began to pound. "I know I told you I was ridiculously old-fashioned when it comes to sex. And I am. Normally I would spend a lot more time getting to know you before I jumped into bed with you, but . . ."

His eyes turned watchful. "But?"

Heather shook her head. "I don't know how much time we have. I almost died two nights ago. You almost died last night. This Other is screwing with my head for who knows what reason and . . ." Leaning forward, she clasped his face between her hands and lowered her lips to his.

His mouth parted, eager to join with hers. Her pulse leapt when his tongue began to tease and tempt hers. Sliding his arms around her, Ethan pulled her off balance so she toppled over onto his hard, muscled chest.

Heather ended the long, desperate kiss, already breathless. Raising her head a few inches, she stared down into Ethan's glowing amber eyes. "I want to make love with you, Ethan. I don't know what tonight will bring or tomorrow night and I don't care at the moment. I just want to feel your body against mine and lose myself in you for the day."

He brushed the fingers of one hand across her cheek and tucked a lock of hair behind her ear. "Are you just doing this because you think your days are numbered and you don't want to die without having sex one last time?"

"I'm doing this," she corrected, "because I think Zach is right. I think I'm Gershom's target. I don't know why he keeps screwing with my head, but it's probably going to get me killed. So, yes, I believe my days *are* numbered. And I don't want to die without making love with *you*." She stroked his handsome face. "I think, if we were given time, we could have something together, Ethan. Something that doesn't even come along once in a lifetime for some people. Just talking and shooting the breeze with you has been more fun for me than sex with my ex-boyfriends ever was."

"Your ex-boyfriends must have really sucked in bed."

As she laughed, a line from one of her favorite movies came to her. "Have you ever seen that movie *Romancing the Stone*?"

He nodded. "That's the one about Joan Wilder, the romance author, right?"

"Yes. Joan says something to Jack—while they're trying to find the treasure—that summarizes perfectly how I feel about you."

"What does she say?"

Heather brushed her lips against his. "You're the best time I've ever had, Ethan."

His eyes flashed brighter seconds before his hand locked on the back of her head and brought her lips down to his for a crushing, pulse-spiking kiss.

Chapter Ten

Heat coursed through Ethan, replacing the cold left behind in the wake of his headache. His body hardened. His heart raced, slamming against his ribs so hard he wouldn't be surprised if Heather could feel it. Rolling her beneath him, he devoured her, his tongue diving between her lips to stroke and tease and tempt. Damn, she tasted good.

He clutched her tighter, slid a thigh between hers as he drew a hand over her hair, her slender, vulnerable neck, and down to clasp a full breast. So perfect.

She moaned as he kneaded the soft flesh and drew a thumb across the hardened peak that pressed against the fabrics of her shirt and bra.

He heard Lisette murmur something about earbuds upstairs seconds before music rose on the morning. Music he knew she played loud enough to drown out Ethan and Heather's lovemaking. Lisette had never soundproofed her bedrooms. She had never felt the need to. So assaulting her sensitive ears with loud music was the only way she could afford them privacy.

Zach, on the other hand, lacked that luxury. He had to remain on guard at all times. If he followed Lisette's example, he wouldn't hear it if Gershom teleported down to this bedroom and attacked or did whatever the hell else he had in mind.

It really chapped Ethan's ass that Zach would hear them. Would hear every moan and groan and sigh of ecstasy. But Heather was right. Both of them had nearly died in the past forty-eight hours. They had no idea how much time they would have together, and didn't have the luxury of waiting until they had complete privacy.

Ethan just hoped Zach would never give Heather any indication that he had heard them.

Heather buried her fingers in Ethan's hair, slid a leg up over his hip.

"Let's get these clothes off," he murmured, frustrated by the material that separated them.

"Okay." Sitting up, she reached for his shirt and tugged it up out of his pants.

Ethan sat up and raised his arms to help her pull it over his head.

She tossed the shirt aside, then drank him in with a heated gaze. "Holy crap, you're gorgeous," she whispered, her eyes burning with need.

Need and something else. Unease?

"What's wrong?" Ethan asked, touching her face. "Have you changed your mind?"

Heather studied every inch of Ethan's body. His broad shoulders. The heavy muscles of his chest and arms and abs. So perfect. And *she* was anything but.

She met his glowing gaze, "No. It's just . . ."

He raised his eyebrows and sent her an encouraging smile. "What?"

Heather loosed a miserable sigh and mentally cursed every man she had ever dated. "You're perfect," she declared, and cringed when it emerged almost as an accusation.

He grinned. "And you're not?"

"No, I'm not," she said. "Trust me when I say I'm aware of every single one of my flaws because my damned telepathy allowed me to hear past boyfriends mentally catalog them."

All levity fled his handsome, perfect features. "I don't understand. What flaws? I don't see any."

"You will when I'm naked," she muttered, cursing the insecurity instilled in her by the men of her past.

He considered her thoughtfully. "How attached are you to those clothes?"

Heather blinked. "Not very. Why?"

He blurred.

Heather felt a tug and looked down. Her mouth fell open. "Holy crap!" She was completely naked.

Ethan laughed. "One of the perks of being immortal."

She reached for the covers.

Ethan captured her hand and brought it to his lips, stopping her. "Don't. Let me see you."

She swallowed. "What about you? You're still semi-clothed."

Rolling off the bed, he stood beside it, blurred, then stilled, as bare as she was.

Wow. Ethan could easily grace the pages of one of those hunky guy calendars. His body was perfectly sculpted, thick with muscle, and very aroused.

She swallowed.

"Now," he said, his voice lowering to a purr as he knelt on the bed beside her, "let me see if I can find all of these flaws the imbeciles you dated in the past thought they saw. Lie back."

Heather did as ordered, her heart pounding in her chest.

Ethan clasped one of her hands and brought it to his lips to kiss her palm. A little jolt of desire shot through her when he nipped it with his teeth, then soothed it with his tongue. Releasing her hand, he slid his fingers up her arm. Every inch of flesh he touched tingled, making her burn with renewed passion. Over her shoulder. Across her collarbone. And down.

Her breath caught when he closed his large hand over her breast.

"Beautiful," he proclaimed in a hoarse whisper, then tweaked the sensitive tip with fingers and thumb.

Heat pooled low in her belly. She shifted her legs restlessly as the ache within her grew.

Lowering his head, Ethan claimed her other breast with his lips, stroking and sucking and laving until she forgot all of her insecurities.

Heather buried her fingers in his hair, wanting more.

But he wasn't finished exploring. Abandoning her breasts, Ethan kissed a path down her stomach, dipped his tongue into her navel, then continued lower.

Heather gripped the covers when he urged her legs apart, settled himself between them, then dipped his head. A low moan escaped her at the first brush of his tongue against her clit. Fiery sensation sliced through her as he closed his lips around the sensitive bud, that talented tongue of his flicking and stroking. Driving the need higher. Making her arch up against him, call his name, and urge him on.

He slipped a long finger inside her.

She bit her lip. *So good.*

A second finger joined the first.

She panted as he stroked her . . . with his fingers . . . his mouth . . . that wicked, wicked tongue. Feeding the need. Taking her higher and higher until she threw back her head and cried out as she came. Hard. The ripples of pleasure going on and on, prolonged by Ethan's talented mouth and fingers.

At last, Heather collapsed against the sheets.

Ethan kissed his way back up her body and rose above her as she fought to catch her breath. "Absolutely perfect," he growled. His eyes glowed brighter than she had ever seen them, and fangs peeked out from between his lips.

Heather believed him.

Clasping his face in her hands, she drew him down to her, kissed those soft lips, and said one word. "More."

Ethan's pulse pounded in his ears. With Heather's taste still on his tongue, her beautiful body beneath him, and her hands on his face, he trembled with the need to fulfill her request.

More, she'd said. Ethan wanted more himself.

She caressed a path down his neck to his chest. When she found his nipples with her fingers and delivered sharp pinches, he groaned. Shit, he needed to be inside her.

As though she had heard his thoughts, she slid a hand down his stomach, pausing to play with the muscles there, then lower still and curled her fingers around his hard, aching cock. "I want you inside me. Now."

She didn't have to say it twice.

As soon as she guided the sensitive crown to her entrance, Ethan plunged inside.

So warm and tight and wet, squeezing him with such delicious pressure.

She sucked in a breath.

Ethan raised his head, afraid he'd hurt her. "Heather?"

Her eyes met his, full of smoky desire. "So good," she moaned. Sliding her arms around his back, she gripped his ass with both hands and urged him on.

He found a smile and withdrew almost to the tip. "Want more?"

"Hell yes."

Ethan plunged inside, drew back, and plunged inside again. Driving into her tight, warm body. Finding just the right angle to give her the most pleasure until she cried out with every thrust, her fingernails digging into his ass. Ethan's own pleasure mounted as she threw her head back, her hips rising to meet him again and again with surprising force until she stiffened and cried out with another orgasm. Her body clamped down around him, pulsing and squeezing and sending him over the edge.

Ethan stiffened above her and shouted with his own release as pleasure seared him, suffusing every muscle and setting his blood afire.

Breathing hard, he rolled them to their sides and held her close, their bodies still joined.

Her warm sheath continued to tighten and relax around his cock as little aftershocks struck her.

He leaned back just enough to see her face.

Her pretty features damp and flushed with satisfaction, she gave him a tender smile that seemed to burrow its way straight to his heart, affecting him even more deeply than the momentous lovemaking they had just shared.

Ethan pressed a light kiss to her lips, then urged her to snuggle against him.

His breath calming, he refused to think about the future and the dangers it might bring. Instead, he allowed himself to absorb the peace she brought him and let it lure him into sleep.

Zach woke when Lisette rolled away and slipped from the bed. He had been resting lightly all day, waking at the faintest sound or slightest movement. Through cracked lids, he watched her don a robe, belt it, then leave the room and head down the hallway.

He sighed, knowing she worried for Ethan and the woman. This was the third time she had checked on them.

Though he wouldn't admit it, Zach was worried, too. He

just couldn't decipher the meaning of it all. The last time Gershom had tampered with human affairs, his game plan—when viewed in retrospect—had been clear. This thing with Ethan and Heather . . .

What the hell did it mean? *Was* this another scheme meant to kick-start an apocalypse? Or could Gershom simply be fucking with Seth?

Had Ethan died in that vampire skirmish, it would have been a major blow to the Immortal Guardians' leader, who had just lost two immortals the previous year. And last time, Gershom had seemed to delight in propagating confusion and pitting Seth against his immortals.

When Lisette didn't return, Zach drew on a pair of sweat-pants and went looking for her.

He found her in the open doorway to Ethan and Heather's room. One small shoulder braced against the door frame, she stared at the slumbering couple entwined beneath the covers.

Zach leaned against the door frame opposite her. "Does it bother you?" he asked, preternaturally soft so as not to wake Ethan. His stomach tightened when he failed to glean anything from her expression.

He had tried—*really* tried—to get past the fact that Lisette and Ethan had been lovers for damned near a century, but he just hated the thought of any man other than himself touching her. The fact that he *knew* Ethan and, thus, could picture the two together only made it harder.

Lisette gave her head a slow shake. "It'll only bother me if she hurts him."

Zach glanced at Heather. "I don't think that's going to happen. They haven't known each other long, but she already cares for him and craves his company the way I do yours."

"I think he feels the same way about her," she responded, her face impassive.

"Do you miss him?" Zach cursed himself as soon as the words left his lips.

Lisette titled her head back and looked up at him. Although she stood at about five foot six, she was still more than a foot shorter than Zach. "Yes."

His stomach sank so fast and hard he was surprised it didn't crush his feet.

"I miss laughing and talking with him," she continued. "I miss hanging out and watching games with him, arguing over a ref's call or whether or not a player flopped."

"You do all of that with me now."

"I know. And I thoroughly enjoy it. I love you, Zach. I always will. The fact that I miss some of the things I used to do with Ethan doesn't mean I love you any less or that I don't enjoy doing them with you. It just means . . ." She shrugged. "Ethan was my best friend for a long time. Didn't you miss Seth after he defected?"

Zach snorted. "I was too pissed."

Smiling, she rolled her eyes. "*After* you stopped being pissed, did you miss him? Did you miss hanging out with him? I know you had the Others. But you and Seth were friends."

Zach sighed. "Yes. I missed him."

Reaching out, Lisette drew a hand up and down his arm in a reassuring stroke. "I can guess what you're thinking. It kills you to know Ethan and I slept together. But sex with Ethan was never the way it is with you."

Zach sent her a self-deprecating smile. "I'm sure it wasn't. Ethan didn't come to you a virgin."

She grinned. Taking a step forward, Lisette leaned into Zach's form and slid her arms around his waist. "You sure as hell didn't make love like a virgin. Your skill and the speed with which you can make my body burn still astounds me."

Zach locked his arms around her. "Flatterer."

She shook her head. "Sex with Ethan was a release, Zach. Nothing more. A sandwich to sate a hunger. A balm for the loneliness that plagued us both." Rising onto her toes, she kissed his chin. "When you and I make love, you hold my heart in your hands."

His own heart began to pound.

"It isn't just our bodies that become one. I feel complete when I'm with you. Whole. Happy. And find pleasure that I didn't even know was possible. *No one* else has ever made me feel that way. No one but you. I adore you, *mon coeur*."

Dipping his head, Zach buried his face in the crook of her neck. "I love you, Lisette. I don't ever want to lose you."

"You won't," she promised.

"I don't want my jealousy to come between us."

"It won't." She patted his back. "Should it ever start to grate on my nerves, I'll just kick your ass."

Laughing, Zach raised his head. "You're welcome to try anytime."

Lisette took one look at his glowing eyes, felt his body harden against hers, and laughed. "I still think you're strange."

"Because your kicking ass turns me on?"

"Yes." Stepping back, she took his hand. "Now stop worrying about Ethan. For the last time, he and I were never in love."

"I doubt he would agree with you. There was love on his part."

She shook her head. "It was infatuation." When he opened his mouth to protest, she held up her free hand. "If you and I spent a century together, then you lost me, would you be ready to make love with another woman a year later?"

"Hell no. I wouldn't *ever* want to make love with another woman."

"Then there's your answer. Now come to bed and whisper to me all of the naughty thoughts that are making your eyes glow and your body strain toward mine."

Smiling, eager to feel her bare body against his, Zach followed her back to their bedroom.

Ethan opened his eyes after the couple left.

"Hey, Zach?" he heard Lisette whisper as their footsteps faded down the hallway.

"Yeah?"

"I'm dying to know . . . How was the sex between Ethan and Heather?"

Ethan nearly groaned.

Zach huffed a laugh. "Based on what I heard? Very satisfying."

"Good," she said, a smile in her voice. "Now, back to those naughty thoughts of yours."

Ethan smiled.

Hugging Heather closer, he pressed a kiss to the top of her head and let sleep reclaim him.

The buzzing of a cell phone on vibrate roused Heather as the plastic gadget quivered on the bedside table.

"Holy crap, that's annoying," Ethan grumbled.

Heather laughed, wondering how many times it had vibrated before it had woken her.

"I have no idea where my cell phone is," he continued, sprawled on his back, his voice rough from sleep, "so I assume that's yours. Otherwise I would have long since hurled it against the wall."

Curled up beside him, one leg draped across his hips and an enticing erection, Heather rose onto one elbow. "Hi there, Grumpy," she said with a smile as she brushed her tangled hair out of her face.

He grinned up at her, all signs of crankiness evaporating. "Hi, yourself." The man was just too good-looking. Even with his eyes heavy from sleep, his hair mussed, and stubble that was well on its way to becoming a mustache and beard, he made her body tingle.

The phone stopped buzzing.

Heather folded her hands on Ethan's chest and rested her chin on them. "Today was . . . incredible." They had spent hours making love, getting to know each other's bodies, learning every curve, every millimeter of flesh that elicited moans when stroked.

"Yes, it was," he agreed softly. "No regrets?"

"None." She slid her body over onto his, covering him like a blanket, and eased up just enough to lower her lips to his.

The phone vibrated again, buzzing against the wooden table.

Ethan growled.

Laughing, Heather sat up and straddled his hips as she reached for her cell. "How many times has it rung?"

"Three times in the past hour," he complained, his hands going to her hips and adjusting her position so that his hard cock teased her center.

Heather moaned. "Hold that thought." Her eyes on Ethan's gorgeous self, she answered the call. "Heather Lane."

"Hi, sweetie," her father said. "Where've you been? I've been trying to reach you for over an hour."

"Dad!" Feeling absurdly as if he had just walked into the room and caught the two of them making love, she slid off Ethan's body and drew the sheet up to cover her breasts. "Hi. What's up?"

Ethan grinned, his glowing amber eyes sparkling with amusement.

"Are you working?"

"No. Not at the moment." When Ethan reached over and tried to tug the sheet down, Heather slapped his hand.

He leaned back, laughing without making a sound, and tucked his hands behind his head, elbows splayed.

Wow, he was built. In that position, his biceps looked bigger than her head.

"Good," her father said. "We have a situation here and could use your help."

Damn. She so didn't want to leave this bed. Or Ethan's company.

Noting the frown that replaced Ethan's smile, she wasn't even sure she *could*. He must be listening to both ends of the conversation.

"How soon do you need me?" she asked.

"Now. I'll send a car to pick you up in twenty minutes."

Ethan shook his head.

"Now's not a good time, Dad," Heather stalled, trying to think of an adequate reason.

The door burst open.

Zach stepped into the room.

Ethan's scowl deepened as he reached down and dragged the blankets up to his waist.

"I thought you said you weren't working," her father said in her ear.

"Say you'll do it," Zach whispered, his deep voice barely audible.

Ethan bolted upright.

For a second, Heather thought he was going to jump out of bed and kick Zach's ass.

Ignoring him, Zach pointed an authoritative finger at her. "Tell him you'll do it."

Not knowing what else to do, Heather complied. "You know what? It's fine, Dad. I can come in. I just need a little time to finish up what I'm doing here. Can you give me an hour?"

"That's fine. You're at home?"

Heather looked at Zach, who nodded. "Yes."

"The car will pick you up there in an hour."

Heather ended the call.

"Are you out of your fucking mind?" Ethan ground out, glaring daggers at Zach.

Lisette peeked around the door frame, then entered and stood beside Zach. Both were garbed in black pants and black shirts similar to the ones Heather had seen Ethan wear.

"Why the hell did you tell her to do it?" Ethan demanded.

"If Gershom is interested in her because of her connections," Zach said, "then *removing* those connections could—"

"What?" Ethan interrupted. "Make her safer? Take her off his radar?"

"Possibly. Or it could get her killed. The Other we're dealing with is mentally unstable. We don't know *how* he will react if we take away his toy. And as long as *he* thinks he can use her, *we* can use her to locate and destroy him."

All of the happiness that had filled Heather upon waking in Ethan's arms vanished.

"So you want to use her as bait," Ethan spat, his amber eyes brightening with fury. Throwing back the covers, he rose and faced the powerful elder.

Heather scrambled to ensure the sheet still covered her. *Crap.* This wasn't good.

Lisette tossed Ethan a pair of sweatpants she found Heather-didn't-know-where.

Ethan swore and pulled them on.

"Yes, Ethan," Zach responded, his face darkening as he took a step forward. "We want to use Heather as bait. We want her *and* you to help us *prevent Armageddon*."

"Zach," Lisette cautioned, touching his arm as Zach's eyes acquired a golden glow.

Ethan's eyes glowed even brighter. "We can find another way—"

"*What* way?" Zach snarled. "We can't find the fucker, Ethan. We've been looking for him for a year now and have nothing to show for it. This is the first real opportunity we've had to lure him into our clutches since we found out he was behind Shadow River. Something about Heather has caught his attention. There's something or someone in her life that he thinks he can use to his advantage, and we aren't going to find out what or who if we keep her hidden in Lisette's basement."

"It's *our* basement now, darling," Lisette murmured.

Ethan motioned to the doorway, every movement stiff with anger. "It's the middle of the fucking afternoon! I can't protect her out there!"

"But *I* can," Zach said. His tone softened. "I can, Ethan, and I will. I vow it to you. Heather will not leave this house without me. I will go wherever they take her. And I will keep her safe."

Ethan's anger seemed to cool a bit at that.

Heather hesitantly raised an index finger. "Actually, about that . . ." As all eyes focused on her, she *really* wished she weren't naked and wrapped in a sheet. "My dad only sends a car when the case I'll be helping them with is highly classified." She studied them. "It doesn't happen often. But . . . when it does I usually don't even know where I'm taken. The windows in the back of the car are blacked out. A partition like the one in limos keeps me from seeing the route we take. The car parks in a basement parking garage that looks like *all* basement parking garages do. Then I'm escorted into a nondescript elevator that takes me to this or that floor in a building I can't identify."

All stared at her.

"What?" she asked as the silence stretched.

"What the hell do you do for your father?" Ethan asked.

She shrugged. "Exactly what I told you. I read the minds of men they're interrogating and let them know if the guys being questioned are bullshitting them. If I see anything important in their minds that can't be passed off as something I gleaned from reading their expressions, I tell my dad later when we're alone."

Lisette frowned. "Have these suspects been legally detained?"

"Of course," Heather assured her. "Some are innocent, and I help clear them. Others pose a serious threat to national security."

"Are members of the military present in this building?" Zach asked.

"Yes. The guards are definitely military, as are most of the other men and women I encounter there. Anyway, my point is, you won't be able to accompany me inside. There's no way you'd get past security. You also won't be allowed to accompany me in the car. And I doubt the soldiers in the front seat would react well to your following us on the drive there."

Ethan sighed. "They won't know he's following you. Zach can shape-shift."

Heather's mind went blank with surprise. She looked from Ethan to Zach. "What?"

"I can shape-shift," Zach told her as casually as he might admit he could play the piano. "I'll shift into the form of a bird and follow the car to whatever installation you're taken to."

Heather just stared at him. "Seriously?" It sounded so . . . B-movie.

Zach released a beleaguered sigh. In the next instant, his form melted into that of a huge lion as empty clothing fell to the floor.

"Holy shit!" Heather scrambled backward off the bed, keeping a death grip on the sheet.

Ethan threw up a hand. "It's okay, Heather. It's okay."

Lisette buried the fingers of one hand in the lion's thick, dark mane.

His paws planted on the clothing Zach had been wearing,

the lion turned his big-ass head and rubbed it against Lisette's chest.

Heather pointed a shaking finger at the beast. "He just . . . I mean, he just . . . He was . . ."

The lion shifted back into Zach.

Heather got a brief glimpse of the elder's naked body before the clothes at his feet covered him as though he had never removed them. Her eyes bugged. "Y-you . . . you . . . you . . . and then . . . *huge* lion . . ."

Zach raised his eyebrows, lips twitching.

"Seriously?" she blurted in a near shout. "You can *do* that?"

The immortals all laughed.

Heather looked at Ethan, who shrugged.

"I told you there were a lot more exciting gifts out there than mine."

Heather returned her attention to the elder. "You weren't kidding."

Zach arched a brow at Ethan. "So we're a go?"

"Not until I talk to Seth."

Zach grumbled something Heather couldn't hear.

Ethan must have, though, because he arched a brow and gave Zach the finger.

Leaning back against the wall, Zach closed his eyes and tilted his face toward the ceiling. "Seth?" A pause. "No, Ethan just has a question for you."

The Immortal Guardians' leader appeared out of nowhere, a baby held against his chest. "What's up?"

Heather blinked. Seth was a daddy?

The large male swayed from side to side, adding a slight bounce while he patted the baby's back with one large hand. Seth's eyes met Heather's. "She isn't mine. I'm just watching her so her parents can get some rest."

Heather titled her head to one side so she could get a better look at the little one. She was a beauty. With solemn green eyes and flaming orange curls. Pale skin. Cute little rolls of fat.

Lisette reached up to brush a hand over the baby's hair. "She's not sleeping well today?" Smiling, she whispered a greeting to the baby.

The baby reached out and grabbed Lisette's finger for a moment, then tucked her hand back against Seth's chest once more.

Seth shook his head. "She's having nightmares again."

Babies had nightmares?

Heather hadn't been around little ones since she was a teenager, but didn't remember any of the babies she had babysat having nightmares. "How old is she?"

"Almost a year," Seth answered. He glanced at Zach, then Ethan. "So, what's going on?"

Ethan filled him in.

Seth nodded. "I agree with Zach."

Ethan swore.

"I don't like it either," Seth said, "but Zach will protect Heather and keep her safe."

Lisette crossed her arms over her chest. "You're all forgetting something."

The men looked at her in question.

"None of you have asked Heather what *she* wants to do. *Her* life is the one that will be in jeopardy. And *she* is the one who will have to lie to her father and pretend nothing is amiss."

All eyes focused on Heather.

Her heart fluttered with sudden nerves.

Ethan circled the bed to stand in front of her. "I'm sorry, Heather. Lisette's right. This should be *your* decision, not ours. I didn't mean to try to make it for you. I'm just worried."

"I know. Honestly, I don't see that I have much choice. If this Gershom asshole wants me for my connections, then I should keep working as usual to give you guys time to find him. If you're all wrong and nothing else happens . . ." She shrugged. "I'll have to go back to my regular life, or at least the day job part of it, eventually anyway."

"It's settled, then," Seth pronounced. "Thank you, Heather, for working with us. Zach will protect you as promised."

"I still don't think he'll be able to accompany me inside the building," she warned.

"He won't have to," Seth said. "He'll be able to hear everything that happens from outside. And if something goes wrong, their security—no matter how tight—won't be able to keep him from reaching you."

"Oh. Okay." That was a little scary. One man being able to defeat a building full of soldiers armed with automatic and other deadly weapons?

Seth hadn't been exaggerating when he had said he, Zach, and the Others wielded enough power to alter the world.

Hell, if they chose to do so, they could *conquer* it.

Chapter Eleven

As Heather followed her escort into the parking garage's elevator, she wondered if Zach was somewhere overhead, circling the building in whatever bird form he had chosen.

The soldiers who had picked her up in the car remained silent as the elevator carried them upward. When the doors slid open once more, a man in a business suit waited for them.

"Heather Lane?" he asked.

"Yes."

"Follow me, please."

Onward they strode, the suit in front, the soldiers in back, down a series of nondescript hallways. A white ceiling. White walls. A white floor marred by occasional dents and dings and smudges.

Boots clomped behind her in a rhythm that made her wonder if soldiers always inadvertently synced up their steps when they walked side by side.

Heather's sneakers, on the other hand, made no sound. When Zach had teleported her home, she had taken a quick shower and changed into jeans, a T-shirt, and a blazer. She would have been happy to leave off the blazer, but had encountered enough good old boys among the higher-ups in the military and law enforcement agencies to know that they tended to be less assholish toward her when she added that little bit of professional accoutrement.

At last, the suit stopped before the first of two doors in a short corridor. Both doors bore keycode entries. Armed soldiers manned each.

The man typed in several numbers, angling his body to hide his hand as if he thought Heather might try to see the code and what . . . spring the prisoner?

News flash, she thought, *I don't need to watch you type it in. I can pluck every keycode and password you know from your thoughts.*

When a click sounded, he pushed the door open and held it for her.

Heather's father and another man in a suit waited within. Beside them, a soldier sat at a table loaded down with electronic equipment used to record audio and video and to monitor the vitals of the suspect being questioned.

Heather stepped inside.

Her father nodded to the suit, who stepped back into the hallway and closed the door.

General Lane opened his arms and drew her into a hug. "Hi, baby. Thanks for coming in on such short notice."

"Sure." She gave him a squeeze and stepped back. "Mac," she greeted the man who stood beside him.

Mac nodded. "Good to see you again, Heather."

Mac was a bit of a mystery. She could never decide who he was or what role he played in the greater scheme of things. Was he military? Ex-military? General counsel? Military Intelligence? From another branch of the government? FBI or CIA? Maybe NSA?

She had tried to peek into his thoughts once and caught him picturing her naked. He was more than a little attracted to her and always seemed to focus on that when in her presence, so she had given up and stopped looking for anything else.

He seemed like a straight-up guy, though. She liked him

far more than she did some of the other men who had been present while she worked. Most viewed her abilities with skepticism and a run-along-and-play-little-girl-while-the-*men*-take-care-of-business attitude. They wouldn't have even let her in the building if her father hadn't been the one to summon her.

Neither General Lane nor Mac bothered to introduce her to the soldier who sat at the table, deciphering the data the equipment sent.

"So," she said, "how can I help you?"

Mac spoke before her father could. "I've been told to remind you that everything you see and hear today is classified."

"Of course."

General Lane nodded to the large window that she knew was instead a two-way mirror. "We have a situation."

Beyond the glass lay yet another stark white room. Small. Boasting only a table and two chairs: one on the opposite side of the table, facing the mirror, and one with its back to the mirror.

A soldier sat in the chair facing them. Perhaps in his mid-twenties, the guy looked strung out, with hollow cheeks, and dark circles beneath his eyes. One of his knees bobbed up and down under the table in a rapid rhythm. And he couldn't seem to sit still. Leaning forward one moment. Leaning back the next. Then leaning forward again. Shifting as though the monitors attached to his chest chafed. Dragging a hand over his closely cropped hair. Then drumming an anxious beat on the table with his fingers.

If she had seen him on the street, Heather would've thought the man a drug addict in need of a fix. "What can you tell me?" she asked.

Her father moved to stand beside her, his arm brushing her shoulder. "A small military base was attacked and destroyed two weeks ago. One of ours."

Shock rippled through her, accompanied by a twinge of unease. "What?" She had seen nothing about it on the news.

"It was a classified installation," he said.

Which explained the no-news thing. "Here in the States?"

"No. But the location is need-to-know only."

"Okay."

"Every soldier who manned the base was killed." Her father pointed to the strung-out man in the next room. "Every soldier except for him. He's the sole survivor."

"Who did it?" Heather asked, stunned.

"That's what we're trying to find out. The surveillance equipment on site was either destroyed or tampered with, because the images of the onslaught are all too blurry or distorted for us to identify the attackers."

"No one has claimed responsibility?" It had to have been terrorists, right? Terrorists were *always* eager to claim or tag their work online.

"No one," Mac answered. "No tapes have been released. We've heard no chatter relating to it, or anything close to it, at all."

Heather nodded to the suspect. "How did *he* survive when on one else did?"

"That's what we want to know. That and whether or not he might have been involved in planning the attack. It seems unlikely that he would've been the only survivor if he wasn't."

"Was he injured? Or did he walk away unharmed?" If he walked away unharmed, she could see why they were suspicious.

"He suffered some deep cuts on his arms and torso," her father said, "and almost bled out before we found him."

Any bandages the soldier sported lay hidden beneath his uniform. "Has he given you anything at all?"

Her father and Mac shared a glance.

"Only babbling nonsense," Mac murmured.

Her father sighed. "According to the psych eval that was

ordered after listening to his account, whatever happened during the attack caused him to have a mental breakdown."

"But there are those who disagree and think he's bull-shitting us," Mac inserted. "Faking it to cover his own ass."

She arched her brows. "*You* think he's bullshitting?"

"Yes."

She studied her father. "And you?"

"I want you to tell us if he's bullshitting. A lot is at stake either way."

She examined the soldier once more and noticed a gold chain around his neck. "He's religious?" she asked, her eyes on the cross that peeked from beneath his rumpled shirt collar.

"Not until now."

Mac snorted. "Apparently his mental breakdown made him find God."

"Will you be interrogating him while I observe?" she asked Mac.

General Lane shook his head. "I want *you* to sit down and talk with him, see if you can get him to tell you what happened. He stopped cooperating with us when we refused to believe him."

"You want *me* to talk to him? Alone?" Usually she just observed, sometimes in the room with them, sometimes from behind the mirror. "Is it safe?" The last thing she needed was for the soldier to attack her and have Zach come charging through the facility to rescue her.

"I wouldn't ask you to do it if it weren't," her father assured her.

"Okay then." Heather stepped out into the hallway.

The dour suit waited for her in front of the next door. As soon as he saw her, he turned his back, typed in a code, and opened it for her.

Heather stepped past him into the interrogation room.

The soldier looked up. One hand went to the cross on his chain.

The door closed behind her.

"Hi," Heather greeted him and, bolstering her nerves, offered her hand. "I'm Heather."

He hesitated a moment before taking it and giving it a shake. A wince rippled across his features as he lowered his arm again. "Nick."

"I'd say it's nice to meet you, Nick, but under the circumstances . . ." Circling the table, she seated herself in the chair opposite his.

"Are you a lawyer?"

"No."

"You here to shrink me?"

"No. I'm just here to talk."

"Sounds like a shrink to me."

She forced a smile and, wanting to ensure he really wasn't a danger to her, began to comb through his thoughts.

Wow. They were all over the place. Totally chaotic and teeming with fear. Fear that the others were right, that he had lost his mind and killed his friends.

"You're prettier than the other shrink," he spoke into the awkward silence.

"I'm not a shrink."

"Then what are you?"

"I'm just a consultant the military occasionally calls in to chat with . . ."

"Victims?" he asked, his expression giving nothing away. "Suspects?"

"Either or," she replied.

He quieted. "You remind me a little of Cindy."

As soon as the words left his mouth, the image of a young, pregnant woman flashed in his mind. A snapshot moment in which she smiled for the camera and exposed her big belly.

The maelstrom of his thoughts quieted. Then Heather saw

darkness and a man's head hitting the ground beside a fallen body.

She forced her lips to hold what she hoped was a kind smile. "Who is Cindy?"

The soldier looked down at the table. "Does she even know Wes is dead?" he asked. His red-rimmed eyes shimmered with tears when he raised them. "They won't tell me. Does she know? Is she okay? Is the baby okay?"

"I don't know," Heather admitted. "I can try to find out, if you want me to."

He nodded. "Thank you. I'd appreciate that." He blinked back the tears.

"Can you tell me what happened, Nick?"

His lips turned down as his face tightened with a grimace of frustration. "I've already told them a million times. They don't believe me. *You* won't believe me."

"You won't know that until you give me a try."

He studied her a long minute, his eyes desperate and hopeless and heartbreaking.

Heather steeled herself against the sympathy that rose within her and kept trying to sift through his tumultuous thoughts.

"It was dark," he began. "Late. Wes and I were manning the southwest guard tower. Nothing but jungle outside the gates. Just enough moonlight to let you see the tops of the trees."

She saw the scene come to life in his mind as he spoke. "Go on."

"You ever seen that TV show *Lost*?"

"Yes. The first couple of seasons anyway."

"Remember, in the first season, when the trees would start to jerk and sway as a monster or some shit stomped through the jungle? As if whatever was moving around out there was so big that just bumping up against the trees nearly toppled them?"

"Yes."

"Well, that's what happened. We saw the trees in the distance start to jerk and sway as if something plowed through the jungle toward us. I didn't know what it was. It wasn't vehicles. There weren't any engine sounds, and the only way a truck would shake a tree like that was if it slammed into it." He paused. "We didn't hear any crashes."

Snarls and growls and guttural noises rose on the night in his memory.

Heather's heart began to pound.

"It kept getting closer, so I told 'em to hit the lights. A warning was called over the speakers. Whoever or *whatever* was coming ignored it, so we lit 'em up. Fired everything we had into the trees. I thought for sure that would stop 'em."

He braced his elbows on the table, which began to vibrate.

Heather knew that, were she to look beneath it, she would see his knee bobbing up and down even more violently than it had before as his agitation increased.

Hell, she had to fight to keep her own knee from bobbing. The images in his mind were straight out of a horror movie.

"They threw something at the lights," he went on.

"They?"

"The things coming for us. Shattered *all* of them so everything went pitch black. Then the explosions started—flashes of light—as they tripped the land mines outside the walls." He dug the fingers and thumb of his free hand into his eyes as if he wished he could rub away the memory. "Guys started screaming. It was so fucking dark. I couldn't see shit and grabbed one of the night-vision monocles." He ceased abusing his eyes and smoothed a hand back over his head. "Budget was tight. We didn't have enough of the night-vision monocles to go around, so we just kept a couple in each guard tower to be used as necessary and usually never touched the damned things. Didn't need to, because we always had the lights."

Heather leaned forward. "What happened, Nick?"

"Guys were screaming. All over. In the other towers. On the ground. I grabbed the monocle and . . . something hit Wes. Took him down. When I turned around . . ." He swallowed hard. "His fucking head was on the floor beside him."

Had Heather not seen that and worse, up close and personal, lately, she would've been sickened by the images she found in his mind then. "Who attacked the base, Nick?" she pressed. "Who was it?"

In his mind, she saw Nick attach the monocle to his scope, raise his weapon, and peer through it.

Oh shit.

"Vampires," Nick said. "Vampires attacked the base."

And killed everyone in it except for Nick, whom they apparently left for dead.

A slew of curses filled her mind, spewed by Zach from wherever he was outside the building. Apparently, he really *could* hear everything that went on in here.

Heather jumped when knuckles rapped on the two-way mirror, her father summoning her back. Panic swamped her. *What do I do?* she asked Zach mentally. She couldn't tell them it was all true, that Nick wasn't lying when he said vampires had attacked the military base. The immortals didn't want humans—particularly those in the military or mercenary profession—to know vampires existed . . . with *very* good reason.

More mental curses.

Another rap on the mirror.

Zach?

Don't tell them it's the truth, he advised. *Tell them Nick is difficult to read because of his current state of agitation,*

*but that he seems to believe the things he says are true. I'll
monitor their thoughts and . . . hell. Hopefully they'll take that
as confirmation that he's nuts and look elsewhere for the
culprits.*

And if they don't?

*They aren't going to believe vampires took out a military
base.*

Heather supposed it *would* sound crazy to anyone else.
Hell, even after dreaming about vampires every night for a
year, she hadn't believed they actually existed until she had
come face-to-face with them.

She rose.

Nick's hand shot out and gripped her wrist. "I'm not crazy.
They were there. They were real." His eyes begged her to confirm it, as though even *he* had begun to question his sanity.

Heather tugged her arm from his grasp. "I'll see what I can
find out about Cindy."

Slumping back in his chair, he returned his gaze to the
table.

Heather knocked on the door. The suit opened it, then led
her back to the room with her father and Mac.

"Well?" Mac demanded as soon as the door closed behind
her.

Heather looked through the mirror. "I had a hard time
reading him. He's very agitated."

"No shit," Mac snorted.

Heather shrugged and shook her head. "He seems to believe everything he's saying."

Mac swore. "That's it? That's all you've got for us?"

"Give us the room, gentlemen," General Lane ordered.

The soldier seated at the table instantly stood and headed
for the door. Mac followed.

Once both had gone, Heather forced herself to face her
father.

She really didn't want to lie to him.

But you have to, Zach reminded her.

I know.

General Lane reached over and flipped switches on several instruments. The red light on the camera mounted to the ceiling in one corner went dark. "It's just the two of us now," he said, straightening. "Tell me what you heard." He must be desperate if he would ask her here instead of waiting until later.

Heather crossed her arms beneath her breasts and shrugged. "As I said, he's very agitated. His thoughts are all over the place. He's worried about this Cindy, whoever she is."

"She's his best friend's wife. Her husband was decapitated in the guardhouse Nick manned."

"Does she know?"

"No. We haven't decided what to tell the families yet." He sighed. "You didn't see anything that could help us? No uniforms you could identify or anything that would label those carrying out the attack as terrorists?"

She shook her head. "Just darkness and flashes of explosions and . . ." *a man with long, sharp fangs and glowing eyes.*

"Vampires?" her father asked.

"Nick's friend, dead on the ground beside him," she said instead.

"Can you at least tell me if Nick was in on it?"

"I don't think so, Dad. If he had been part of the attack, he'd be worrying over whether or not he was going to get away with it. I didn't see anything like that in his thoughts."

Her father studied the soldier in the next room. "Is he insane?"

"I've never looked inside the mind of an insane person before. I can't make that call." She looked at Nick. "But I *have* read enough soldiers with PTSD to know that Nick is suffering from it big-time."

"PTSD doesn't make you see vampires," General Lane snapped.

"Well, I don't know what to tell you. Were there *no* other survivors?"

"None."

Heather felt like crap, letting him down this way. "I'm sorry I can't be more helpful."

He nodded. "I think this is a first. The shrink must be right. Nick must have had some kind of breakdown if even *you* can't sort through his thoughts and tell us what happened."

Hell.

"Maybe they can find some meds to help him. If they do, will you come back in for us?"

Heather nodded, knowing no medication on the planet would alter the fact that vampires had just destroyed a U.S. military base.

Chapter Twelve

Heather could feel Zach's impatience while the soldiers drove her home. Every minute seemed like an hour. And with the passing of each, her thoughts grew more chaotic.

Once home, Heather thanked the soldiers and stood in her empty living room, listening to them back the car out of her driveway.

Zach appeared in front of her, looking even more grim than usual. He rested a hand on her shoulder. The lights went out. When they came back on, a large, beautiful study or home office had replaced her living room. Floor-to-ceiling bookshelves lined every wall, boasting thousands upon thousands of books. Two desks consumed some of the floor space. One small and vaguely feminine. One large and as overtly masculine as the figure seated behind it.

David looked up from the book he perused.

"Summon Seth," Zach said. "And tell him to bring Chris. The shit has hit the fan."

Releasing Heather, Zach vanished.

David met Heather's gaze and arched a brow. "I take it things did not go well with your father?"

She bit her lip. "It isn't so much that the visit didn't go

well. It's what we learned while we were there. Zach's right. It's bad. It's . . . it's really, really bad."

Setting his book aside, David closed his eyes.

Seth appeared at his elbow, breathing hard. The black clothing and long, black coat he wore glistened with wet patches Heather assumed were blood. Crimson liquid coated the katana he clutched in one hand. Speckles of it dotted his face and neck. "What?" he asked David.

"Zach has news. Bad news, apparently. He wants you to fetch Reordon."

Seth glanced at Heather, took in her no doubt worried-as-hell look, and nodded. "Let me clean up first." He vanished.

Heather looked to David.

David shrugged. "It's always nighttime *somewhere* in the world. And where there is nighttime . . ."

"There are vampires." That sucked. Did the powerful Immortal Guardians' leader ever get a break?

Zach reappeared with Lisette and Ethan.

The tightness in Ethan's face eased when he saw Heather. Crossing to her side, he wrapped his arms around her and hugged her tight. "You okay?"

Nodding, she leaned into him. They'd had such a nice morning together. Who would've thought the day would take such an unpleasant turn?

Seth strode through the doorway behind them, *sans* katana. Clean clothing now adorned his tall frame. His long hair was wet and slicked back from his face, his skin clean.

He showered that fast? she thought with awe, releasing Ethan and shifting to stand beside him.

Winking at her, Seth drew out a phone.

"Where's Reordon?" Zach asked.

"I'm calling him now. Chris?" Seth spoke into the phone. "Seth. Are you busy? Zach has news and wants you to be privy to it . . . Okay. I shall be there momentarily." Pocketing the phone, he looked to Zach. "How big is it?"

"Gargantuan."

"Gargantuan warrants a meeting." Seth tucked his phone away, then withdrew a silver pocket watch on a chain from a front pocket. He flipped it open and regarded its face. "The sun will set in about two hours. I want everyone and their Seconds here no later than an hour after that. David, have Darnell start making the calls. I'm going to fetch Chris."

As soon as David nodded, Seth vanished.

"Darnell," David called.

A handsome African American man poked his sleek, bald head into the study. "Yeah?"

"Call a meeting," David said. "Have everyone here an hour after sunset."

"Will do." Darnell started to withdraw.

"And, Darnell?" David added.

Darnell looked at him expectantly.

David motioned to Heather. "This is Heather Lane."

Eyebrows rising, Darnell stepped into the room and regarded her with interest. "Ethan's Heather?"

"Yes," Ethan confirmed, surprising Heather with his claim. "*My* Heather."

Darnell strode forward with a smile and held out his hand. "It's nice to meet you. I'm Darnell, David's Second."

Heather liked him instantly. He had one of those open faces that told you he was a no-shit guy and a smile too charming to resist.

Smiling back, she shook his hand. "It's nice to meet you, too. If you're a Second, does that mean you're human?"

"*Gifted one,* actually. From what I hear, you're telepathic?"

"Yes."

"Then all I ask is that you avoid intruding upon my thoughts whenever possible. It took me forever to get the rest of these guys to stop examining them at will. But I like my privacy."

"I totally understand and haven't taken so much as a peek."

His smile widening, he patted their clasped hands with his

free hand before releasing her. "I appreciate that. And I have to tell you, I'm impressed as hell by what I've heard about you. Not many of us have been able to use our gifts outside of the network without others learning that we're different. The FACS thing was a stroke of genius."

She warmed under his praise. "Thank you."

Ethan slid an arm around her waist and drew her up against his side.

"And shooting the vampire—the one who bit you—in the head?" Darnell continued. "That was gutsy as hell."

Heather laughed. "Not really. I was scared to death."

"Which made it even gutsier."

Ethan's arm tightened. "Stop flirting with her, damn it."

Darnell rolled his eyes. "Dude, you're practically wrapping your body around her to stake your claim. I'm not flirting with her. I'm just being friendly." Leaning closer to Heather, he whispered, "I would totally flirt with you if you weren't into Ethan. I love strong women."

Again Heather laughed. "And I might just be tempted to flirt back."

Ethan growled.

"*If* I weren't into Ethan, that is," she added with a grin.

Darnell winked. "That's my cue." He nodded to David. "I'll go make those calls now."

"Yes," David advised with a wry smile, "I think that would be best."

Seth reappeared with Chris Reordon as Darnell left and closed the door behind him.

Chris dumped his shabby briefcase in one of the chairs that faced David's desk.

Seth crossed to stand beside David. "So, what's the news?"

Ethan kept an arm around Heather as she and Zach re-capped her visit with her father and took turns relating what they had found in Nick's mind.

"Vampires attacked an American military base?" Ethan asked, finding it difficult to believe.

"And killed everyone in it save this Nick fellow," Zach confirmed.

"How the hell is that possible?"

David frowned. "And how could we not have heard about it?"

"It sure as hell wasn't on the news," Chris said. "Nor have any of my contacts said anything about it. An American military base that the sole survivor claims was attacked and destroyed by vampires? My phone should be ringing off the hook. This base—*and* the attack—must be one hell of a secret."

Seth's brow furrowed. "You've heard nothing at all from your contacts?"

"Not a peep," Chris answered.

Heather shifted. "My father said it was all highly classified. If the base is top secret, the military can't exactly tell the public it was destroyed. Do your contacts have access to classified information?"

"*Some* classified information. Not all," Chris said. "Honestly, that's why I was trying to recruit *you.*"

Damn it. Ethan wished Chris would let that drop.

Seth wagged his head slowly back and forth. "It had to have been an *army* of vampires to defeat so many well-trained and well-armed soldiers. Yet no immortals have reported seeing any signs that vampires may be amassing again. Even with the increased numbers we have here in North Carolina, we've seen no evidence of an army forming, no signs that they may be organizing. And I would think, if one were to form anywhere, it would be here."

Ethan agreed. "Other than hunting in larger packs—and they've been doing that for years now, thanks to Bastien—the only unusual vampire activity we've seen of late is the second attack at Heather's place. The first fight, in the field, felt random to me even though we suspect it was orchestrated by Gershom. Those vampires didn't see me coming and sure as hell didn't expect to run into Heather and her 9mm. The second group of vampires seemed to have no knowledge of the first group. If they were all part of a growing army and the second group was there to avenge the first, I would think they would've at least mentioned it."

Lisette's brow furrowed. "Where *was* this military base? It couldn't have been on any island guarded by an immortal. As soon as the immortal heard the battle and saw what was transpiring, he would have summoned Seth."

Zach began to pace. "That's the hell of it. I don't know. Nick and the other men weren't told where the base they manned was stationed. Not the name of the island. Not the general location. Hell, not even in what ocean it may be found. It's all very hush-hush."

"Was it another Gitmo?" Ethan asked.

Zach shook his head. "I don't think so. I saw no prisoners or detainees in Nick's memories. But it wouldn't surprise me at all if it weren't some kind of bioweapons research facility, because Nick *did* see a lot of doctors there."

"Well, shit," Ethan said. "That's even worse. A vampire army in possession of potentially lethal bioweapons? Fuck!"

"Nick may not know the location of the base," Seth said, "but General Lane *must*."

"I'm sure he does," Zach said, his every word and gesture radiating frustration, "but I couldn't find the information with a standard, harmless search. He has unusually strong mental barriers for a human. Had I delved any deeper, it would have hurt him."

Ethan's stomach sank.

All eyes went to Heather.

Heather straightened away from Ethan and took his hand

in a death grip. "He does." She licked her lips nervously. "Have strong mental barriers, that is. My mother was a telepath, too, and . . . over the years he learned to guard his thoughts and erect mental barriers neither one of us could penetrate easily. They aren't as strong as Ethan's, but . . . they're there. I can't get past them without him knowing, because just *trying* to gives him a headache. It's why I don't read his mind anymore and never hear his thoughts when I let my *own* guard down around him." She looked up at Ethan, then at Zach, Seth, and David. "You aren't going to hurt him, are you?"

The quiet that followed stretched every nerve tight.

Heather raised pleading eyes to Ethan's. "Please, don't hurt him."

He swallowed hard, not knowing what to say, unwilling to lie to her.

Seth's voice carried regret when he spoke. "We need to know the location of that base."

She closed her eyes, face pained.

"If we can examine the scene ourselves," Seth continued, "and read the minds of anyone else we find on the island, we may be able to discover something that can lead us to this vampire army. We *have* to destroy them, Heather, before they launch another attack. And we have to know if they've gotten their hands on bioweapons."

Heather opened her eyes. "Can't you just talk to him?" she pleaded.

"We would have to erase the memory of it from his mind, if we did," Seth explained. Which, because of the strong mental barriers General Lane possessed, would cause as much damage as simply reading his mind would.

"He won't tell anyone," she promised.

"I'm afraid we can't take that chance," David said. "Ethan told you of our recent troubles with Shadow River."

"My dad isn't like that," she vowed. "He isn't greedy. He

isn't a warmonger. And he knows how to keep a secret, knows the *importance* of keeping one. He's kept *mine* for twenty-nine years, and kept my mother's even after she died. If he were like those Shadow River guys, don't you think he would've used our telepathy for his own gain? Don't you think it occurred to him once in all these years that maybe the military could benefit from our abilities?"

"The military *does* benefit from your ability," Zach pointed out.

"Not as much as they would if they knew what my ability actually was," she protested. "He told them I read facial expressions, not minds. You don't think he knows the kind of career boost he could get by bringing the government an honest-to-goodness telepath who can read the thoughts of every prisoner, every political opponent, every other nation's leader?"

Ethan glanced at Chris. "Can't your contacts get us the location of the base?"

Chris shook his head. "Too much attention is focused on it at the moment. The military would know instantly if someone hacked into classified files. But my contacts *may* be able to tell us who else would likely know the information we need. Then Seth or Zach could read *that* person's mind instead of Heather's father's."

Sounded good to Ethan.

"What about Mac?" Heather blurted.

Zach turned to her. "The other man in the room with you and the general?"

"Yes. Or maybe the soldier monitoring all the equipment?"

"Neither knows the location of the base. I checked."

"Oh." The hope in Heather's face died a swift death.

"Well, *someone* else must know," Chris said. "I'll see if my guys can't give us some names."

Seth nodded. "Do it."

Heather released a weary sigh and leaned into Ethan's side.

Wrapping his arms around her, Ethan drew her close and hoped like hell Chris's contacts would let General Lane off the hook.

Heather stared at the powerful men and women seated around David's long dining room table. All of the immortals stationed in North Carolina were present, as were their mortal Seconds. And everyone had greeted Heather with friendly smiles, as though she were one of them.

Well, everyone except Roland. But Ethan had told her not to take that one's stony expression to heart. They all considered Roland the most antisocial of their ilk.

Heather could see why. Roland was quiet and didn't participate much in the conversation flowing around him. He *did* stick close to his wife, though, and always seemed to be touching her. If he wasn't holding her hand, he wrapped an arm around her or rested a hand on her thigh or leaned down to kiss her neck. Heather thought it sweet, how much the surly immortal adored Sarah. And thought it even sweeter when his dour face broke into a wide, affectionate grin when Ami's baby held her arms out to him and called, "Wo! Wo!"

Even now, the little one sat in Roland's lap, toying with the buttons on his shirt while he whispered something in her ear.

Heather felt honored to sit at a table with such powerful immortal warriors. It seemed so surreal, like sitting down to chat with a bunch of superheroes, only these guys—and gals—didn't wear colorful tights. They wore black to conceal the blood they would spill later in the night when they hunted.

A sobering thought.

The relaxed, family-like atmosphere evaporated once Seth and Chris arrived and related the day's events. All eyes shifted to Heather, who tried not to squirm beneath the attention.

Curses flowed freely.

Ethan took Heather's hand beneath the table and, linking their fingers, rested it on his thigh. "Did your contacts come up with any names for you, Chris? Anyone who might be privy to the same information General Lane has?"

Chris drew a single sheet of paper from his briefcase. "Yes." He handed it to Seth. "They seem to think these are your best bets. The first list is of helicopter pilots they believe might have been the ones who evacuated Nick Altomari and transported in some of the army personnel who cleaned up the base and collected the dead. The second list is of army and army intelligence officers who, like Heather's father, may be in the loop. But . . . I've been thinking."

Seth took the paper and examined it. "What's on your mind?"

"It may be worth the risk to try to recruit General Lane."

"*What?*" Heather and Ethan exclaimed simultaneously.

"Are you out of your mind?" Roland demanded.

Other murmured protests floated around the table.

Chris shook his head. "Heather said he understands the importance of keeping a secret, and—after all the digging I've done during the last few hours—I'm inclined to agree. If he were a man driven by greed or a lust for power or even fame, he would have long since sold out his wife and daughter. But he's a smart man and knew what would happen to them if their abilities ever came to light." He turned his head and met Heather's gaze. "Did your father encourage you when you told him you were going to pass yourself off as a FACS specialist and see if you could earn a living helping others with your telepathy without actually revealing it?"

"No," she said. "We actually had a falling-out over it. He was afraid I would slip and say or do something that would reveal I can read minds. Things were pretty tense between us for a couple of years until I proved to him that I could keep my true ability hidden."

Chris motioned to her as he addressed the others. "Clearly the man's priorities are where they should be."

"She's his daughter," Marcus pointed out, helping Adira as she scrambled from Roland's lap over onto his own. "Of course he wants to protect her. *We*, on the other hand, are strangers who all wield even more power than the vampires who just destroyed one of his military bases. If we tell him the soldier who survived isn't insane and—to prove it—flash our fangs, how eager do you think he will be to keep our secret? What reason would he have to believe we're any different from the monsters who slaughtered the soldiers who manned that base?"

"You want a reason?" Chris asked. "I'll give you two of them. We saved his daughter's life. Twice. Ethan saved it once during the first skirmish they fought with vampires. Seth saved it the second time when she was fatally wounded. You're a father, Marcus. You were, too, Roland. Don't you think that would mean something to him?"

Roland and Marcus silently consulted each other.

Neither denied Chris's words.

David cleared his throat. "There's a third reason."

All eyes turned to him.

"I think it's safe to assume that Gershom is behind this new vampire army, since he was behind Shadow River. The fact that he was forcing Whetsman to smuggle out more of the sedative seems adequate confirmation, as far as I'm concerned. And I know of no one else who would be either bold enough or stupid enough to send an army of vampires to attack an American military installation, knowing full well the response it would provoke."

Seth nodded. "It would be one hell of a way to kick-start an apocalypse. Not only would knowledge of vampires go public, it would force one of the world's largest superpowers to retaliate."

Dread seized Heather. "If Gershom directs the blame at another country . . ."

"It would mean war," Seth finished for her.

Zach leaned forward and braced his elbows on the table. "And if the American military believes another country has raised an army of vampires who are capable of such destruction, they will do everything they can to acquire the virus themselves and begin to infect troops here to raise their own."

Seth nodded. "Once that happens, countries hostile to America will find out and want to do the same, as will America's allies. *No one* wants the other guy to have the more powerful army."

More curses all around.

Heather turned to David. "Is that the third reason?"

"Third reason for what?" Sheldon asked.

"The third reason my dad would have for believing you aren't like the vampires? Because you'll warn him what will happen if the military gains knowledge of the virus?"

David shook his head. "Your father is an intelligent man. He'll draw that conclusion on his own. No, the third reason is you. Your safety is and always has been his top priority. When we tell him . . . when *you* tell him . . . that you've become a target of the leader of this new vampire army, a leader who has no qualms about sacrificing your life to achieve his goals and who may not be through with you yet, I think your father will be swayed to our side. I think his desire to protect you will force him to work with us even if doubts linger."

A tense and somber silence ensued.

Roland broke it. "I still think it's too risky. I think Seth should just read the minds of the men on Chris's list and leave General Lane alone."

"And if Seth and David find no clues at the destroyed base?" Chris asked. "If they find nothing that can help us figure out where the hell this new vampire army is forming, *then* what? I've notified the other network heads around the globe of the attack and they'll tell the immortals in their area to keep a sharper eye out for any unusual vampire activity. But if nothing has shown up on the radar so far, I don't think we can count on the vampires giving anything away in the near future. Not unless their next attack is more public. Then all bets will be off."

"Your point?" Roland drawled.

"The military is doing everything they can to find out what country or organization fostered this attack. Right now they're combing through every source of intel they have. General Lane can feed us that information and help us narrow down our search."

Heather saw the reason in it, but hoped like hell the Immortal Guardians' leader would find something at the base so all of this would be moot.

"Heather," Seth addressed her.

Her heart trip-hammered in her chest. "Yes?"

"You've not told us what *you* think on the matter."

Nervous butterflies filled her stomach. "I didn't know I had a voice in this."

"You do," Seth informed her.

"Well . . ." She rubbed her free hand up and down her thigh as her palms began to sweat. Hopefully Ethan wouldn't mind her other palm sweating, because no way in hell was she going to let go of his hand. "The downside of telling him is you'd have to erase the memory of it afterward if he didn't cooperate, and that would hurt him. Do I have that right?"

"Yes."

"Will it kill him?"

"No, but it will be immensely painful."

"He'll recover, though, like Ethan did when you read his mind, right?"

Seth hesitated. "Ethan is immortal and has greater healing capabilities. Your father is human and may not fare so well."

Her stomach churned. "Are you saying he could end up with brain damage?"

"It's a possibility."

"Irreparable brain damage?"

"Yes."

She swallowed hard. "That's a huge downside." One for which she would never forgive herself if it were to come to pass. Nor would she forgive herself if he agreed to work for the network and came to harm as a result. Ethan had told her that Chris's last group of contacts had been tortured and killed. What if that happened to her father?

"Look," Zach spoke into the leaden silence, "everyone thinks I'm an asshole."

When no one protested, Lisette shot everyone around the table a glare.

"I don't know if this will prove it or disprove it," Zach continued. "But I don't think it's fair to ask Heather to make this decision. We're essentially asking her to weigh her father's life against the welfare of the entire world. If we talk to him and he chooses not to work with us, he'll end up brain damaged and will suffer for the rest of his life. If he *does* work with us, he could end up like Chris's last group of contacts and die a torturous death."

His words reflected her thoughts so precisely that Heather wondered if the elder had been reading her mind.

"And," he went on, "if she should ask us not to enlist her father's aid and it takes us too long to locate this new vampire army—the world is a big fucking place, people—then she will know she facilitated Armageddon."

"Dude," Sheldon said, his face somber, "that sucks."

Zach reached over and took one of Lisette's hands. "The Others believe any contact with humans will bring about the world's destruction. When I fell in love with Lisette, I made the conscious decision to risk it. I chose Lisette over the rest of the world and would do so again. Yet there are some of you at this table who would condemn Heather for putting her father's welfare first."

Again, no protests.

Zach looked to Seth. "I applaud you for wanting to be fair and to let Heather have a say. But I think *you* should be the one who ultimately decides. We all trust your judgment, and it may very well spare Heather a lifetime of guilt."

Heather held her breath and fought the urge to cry in shame, because part of her *wanted* Seth to take this decision away from her.

"So be it," Seth intoned.

She squeezed Ethan's hand tighter until her nails dug into his flesh, terrified of Seth's next words.

"Aidan, you and I will go to the men on this list," he held up the piece of paper Chris had given him, "and see if any of them know the location of the base, while Zach and David keep an eye on things here. Zach, I want you to field my calls for the next few hours so there will be no interruptions."

Zach nodded.

"Once we know the base's location, David and I will teleport there and see what we can learn from the scene."

Heather nearly sagged with relief.

Then Seth snagged her gaze. "Heather, I shall leave your father out of this as long as I can. If we are left with no other option but to attempt to recruit him, I will tell you so that you may accompany us."

To help them gain his cooperation? Or to say good-bye in case things didn't go well? She had no idea how extensive the brain damage would be, so she supposed there was a chance her father wouldn't even know her or be able to speak to her again afterward.

Family is everything to me, Seth spoke in her mind. *I will do all I can to spare you that.*

The lump that rose in her throat was too big to speak past, so she answered him telepathically. *Thank you.*

"Anything else?" Seth addressed the table at large.

David nodded. "In light of these events, I want all immortals, even the elders, to hunt in pairs. And do not leave home without several of the autoinjectors that contain the sedative's antidote in your possession. Until further notice, I want you all to take the same precautionary measures when battling vampires that you did after Lisette was nearly slain last year."

Nods all around.

"Very well," Seth said. "Safe hunting to you all."

Chapter Thirteen

The scents of death permeated the balmy air.

Seth studied the picturesque beach on which he and David stood. Sunlight sparkled on water so clear he could see the pale sand on the ocean floor. Colorful fish flitted about beneath the surface, finding goodies to eat within the coral reef that blossomed like an underwater flower garden.

No drink stands, chairs, or umbrellas marred the beach's beauty. No tourists bathed in the sun's harsh beams while they fiddled with their cell phones or tablets and did everything they could, it seemed to him, to avoid conversing with one another.

All was quiet. Serene. Yielding no sign of the violence that had taken place there two weeks earlier . . . if one discounted the wide band of foliage at the beach's edge that looked as if it had been flattened by bulldozers.

David grunted. "These were young vampires. Newly turned."

Seth agreed. "And still high on their own strength."

Senses searching, they strolled into the deep green tropical forest.

Seth had wanted Zach to accompany them, but had felt uneasy leaving David's home unguarded by someone who

could defeat Gershom, should he make an appearance.
Heather and Ethan remained in David's home and, for all
anyone knew, could be putting everyone else there at risk.
None were certain yet if Gershom would attempt to use her
again.

Aidan guarded David's home as well and would cover for
Zach when the latter answered emergency calls that normally
would have gone to Seth. Just to be safe, Seth had teleported
in Chaahk and Imhotep, Aidan's equals in power and gifts.
Those three all seemed tragically excited to face a new
challenge.

Guilt pressed down upon Seth. Doing the same old same
old night after night for thousands of years had worn on
Aidan, Chaahk, and Imhotep. Seth had always tried to dispel
the loneliness of immortals by assigning them Seconds, but
an immortal could go through a lot of Seconds in a few
thousand years. That was a lot of friends to lose.

And a long time to go without love.

As leader of the Immortal Guardians, Seth was kept too
busy to dwell on the loneliness he experienced himself.
Most days.

Hell, he might—on occasion—bitch about never having
any downtime, but going days and nights without sleep could
sometimes be a good thing. It prevented him from having to
lie in bed alone, remembering what he had once had and
missing it with a desperation that made him wish his damned
phone would ring again.

"What troubles you?" David asked as they stepped over
downed trees and continued forward, following the trail of
destruction the vamps had left behind them. David knew Seth
better than anyone did.

Seth gave a weary shrug. "Things I cannot change."

"So nothing new, then?" David joked.

Smiling, Seth motioned to the dead and drooping foliage.
"This all seems a bit much, don't you think? New vampires

like to test their strength, to posture and show off, but this? Really? The guards at the base would've seen them coming from miles away. Why give them the warning?"

"Hubris? Overconfidence? A desire to see the soldiers shake in their boots?"

"If they shook in their boots, the soldiers shook while filling the trees and vampires full of holes."

The bedraggled foliage that remained standing began to sport large holes and tears as Seth and David neared the base. Some leaves bore brownish stains that drew flies. Stains that bore the scent of the vampiric virus.

"There seem to be more bullies on the planet today than when I was a mortal," David observed.

Seth snorted. "There is more of *everything* on the planet today than way back then."

Smiling, David gave Seth's shoulder a hard shove. "These vampires were already reveling in the fear they created with their little dramatic show of strength. Even Nick, according to what Zach showed us, feared fleetingly that a monster approached."

"And he wasn't wrong. It just happened to be several monsters instead of one." Seth drew in a deep breath as he passed a particularly large splash of dried blood on a tree. "You smell that?"

David inhaled. "Rage."

"Do you think it possible that they didn't know there was a base up ahead? Could this have been a random accident?"

"Gershom would have known if he was guiding them."

"That doesn't necessarily mean he would've told the vampires."

"True."

They exited what was left of the forest and stood facing a tall, thick cement wall that enclosed the entire military base as far as Seth could see. Not much of a deterrent to vampires who could leap several stories into the air with little effort.

In front of the cement wall stood two chain-link fences spaced several yards apart, each woven with razor wire. Or what remained of the fences. The vampires had chosen to plow through them instead of jumping them. Unwise, since more than one of the vampires appeared to have severed an artery in the process. The bare sand beneath the twisted remains of the fences had darkened with the color of old blood. The sand beyond bore gaping holes and craters where vampires had tripped land mines.

Beyond *that* stood the wall, then . . . only smoke-blackened remains of the base itself.

One hell of a battle had been fought here.

"How much time have you spent on American military bases?" Seth murmured.

"I don't believe I have ever been on one."

"Nor have I. What about foreign military bases?"

"Not since World War One. I know little about them."

"Perhaps it would be wise to bring someone in who does. I'm not certain I would know if something seemed out of place here, aside from the obvious damage caused by the vampires, and I want to know why this place in particular drew the attack." Slipping his cell phone from a pocket, he motioned for David to step back into the shade of the forest with him.

David couldn't withstand as much exposure to sunlight as Seth, so it helped to give him a reprieve from it whenever possible.

Seth dialed Ethan's number.

"Yes?"

"I need to speak with Heather for a moment."

A rustling ensued as Ethan murmured, "It's Seth. He wants to speak with you."

"Why?" she asked with something akin to fear. "Is it my dad?"

"No, it isn't," Seth said, knowing Ethan would hear him

even though the younger immortal no longer held the phone to his ear.

"No, it isn't," Ethan repeated.

More rustling.

"Hello?" Heather said, her voice full of uncertainty.

"Hello, Heather. Please be at ease. This does not concern your father."

"Oh. Okay. So . . . what's up? What can I do for you?"

He smiled. "From what I understand army brats, as I've heard Americans call children of servicemen and women, move around a lot."

"I know *we* sure did," she said.

"So you've seen a lot of military bases?"

"Yes. Both here and abroad."

"Would you mind joining us, then? One of the men on Chris's list gave us the location of the base."

"Oh. Good," she said, her relief unmistakable.

"But neither David nor I have spent much time on a military base, so we could use your help determining if there might be anything unique or off about this one in particular that would've made it a target."

"I don't know how much help I'll be, but I'd be happy to join you and point out anything that seems off."

"Thank you. I'm on my way." Nodding to David, Seth mentally traced the phone signal and teleported to David's home . . . then promptly gave the couple his back and stared at the bedroom wall. "My apologies. I should have asked if I was interrupting something when I called." He heard material slide over flesh as Ethan drew on a pair of pants and Heather yanked the sheet up to cover her bare body. "I shall meet you both in the living room."

Opening the bedroom door, Seth stepped out into the hallway and closed it behind him. One of the hazards of teleportation was catching people by surprise and seeing things he really shouldn't see.

He shrugged it off. He'd dropped in on immortals in so many inappropriate moments over the millennia that he'd long since ceased feeling awkward about it and didn't think he could blush if he tried.

On his way up the stairs and out of the comfortably furnished basement, Seth retrieved his cell phone again.

"Reordon," a gruff voice answered.

"Are you at home or at the network?" Seth asked.

"Network," Chris answered. "Why? Do you need something?"

"Do you happen to have anyone there who is ex-military?"

"Here right now?"

"Yes."

"Let me think . . ." A chair squeaked, and Seth imagined Chris leaning back and staring up at the ceiling. "Yeah, I do. Adam Quinly. Ex-army. He's the one we recruited from Donald and Nelson's mercenary group. He's an Iraq War vet. Good guy."

"I'd like him to accompany us to the base and help us identify anything unusual about it that might have drawn Gershom's attention."

"When do you need him?"

"Five minutes?"

"He'll be in my office in four."

"Excellent."

Seth pocketed the phone and strode down the hallway to the expansive living room. Aidan, Chaahk, and Imhotep all sat side by side on a long sofa with their backs to him and their heads tilted downward. On the floor in front of them, Adira sat, staring up at them, her pretty face somber.

None of them seemed to know quite what to make of the other.

"So this is what babies do?" Imhotep asked, his voice full of bewilderment. "They just sit there and stare at you until you start to wonder if you have food on your face?"

Seth laughed.

When the men turned to glance over their shoulders, the movement allowed Adira to catch a glimpse of Seth.

Squealing with glee, she crawled forward and used Imhotep's knee to help her stand.

The big warrior immediately held his dark hands out to either side of her, ready to catch her if she fell. "What do I do? Am I doing this right?"

"You're doing fine," Seth said, circling the sofa.

Adira toddled toward Seth, touching each man's knee on the way.

Seth bent and scooped her into his arms, kissing her cheek, then blowing raspberries in her chubby neck rolls. Giggles filled the air as she squirmed against him, leaning back and clutching him tighter all at the same time.

How he loved this baby girl.

"I don't know about you," Chaahk said, "but I'm feeling a little rebuffed."

"Why," Seth asked with a laugh, "because I didn't blow raspberries in *your* neck?"

Aidan and Imhotep laughed.

Shaking his head, Chaahk motioned to Adira. "Why doesn't she smile at *us* like that?"

Seth shrugged. "I'm prettier."

A masculine chuckle sounded behind Seth. Turning, he found Marcus striding toward them from the kitchen. In one hand, he carried a plate with a massive sandwich stacked upon it.

Seth settled Adira on his hip. "I wondered what she was doing up here alone with these three. Having a midday snack?"

Marcus shook his head. "It's for Ami. Nursing Adira leaves her perpetually hungry."

Seth nodded. It had been the same for his wife.

"What are *you* doing here?" Marcus asked. "I thought you and David were checking out the base."

"I came to pick up Heather. She knows more about military bases than I do and, hopefully, can tell us if anything seems off. We'll also drop by Chris's office and pick up one of the vets who work for the network."

Adira tugged at the leather tie holding Seth's long hair back from his face.

"I assume you're taking Ethan, too?"

"I hadn't planned on it."

Marcus looked over Seth's shoulder toward the hallway. "Does *he* know that?"

Seth glanced around.

Heather strode toward them, wearing the black garb and weapons of a Second. She shrugged when the men stared at her. "Ethan insisted."

"Do you know how to use those?" Aidan asked, eyeing the holstered 9mms.

"Yeah," she said with a bit of a *duh* inflection. "My dad's military."

Behind her, Ethan followed, his tall body encased in one of the suits the network had designed to protect immortals from sunlight when they had to venture out during the day. It reminded Seth of a scuba-diving suit, but bore an almost automobile tirelike texture that always made the immortals grumble and complain.

Fortunately, Seth had no need of such himself. "Where are *you* going?" he asked Ethan.

When Adira gave the leather tie another hard tug, Seth felt the leather loosen and release his hair.

"With you," Ethan responded.

Marcus held his free arm out to Seth.

"No, you're not." Seth transferred Adira to her father and took the leather tie from her plump fingers. "You'll be a distraction and we'll be in the sun." Reaching back, he gathered his hair at the nape of his neck and again secured it.

"That's why I'm wearing the suit," Ethan said, and held up the mask he intended to don.

"You aren't going," Seth reiterated. "You have no reason to go beyond your concern for Heather. And David and I are perfectly capable of seeing to her safety ourselves."

Ethan opened his mouth.

Seth raised a hand. "You're staying here. I want no distractions. For her or for us."

The muscle that jumped in Ethan's jaw as he clamped his lips closed said much about what he thought of the dictate. Turning Heather toward him, he lowered his head and pressed a soft kiss to her lips. "Be safe. I'll see you when you get back."

She nodded, then delivered a kiss of her own.

"Lucky bastard," Aidan muttered, his face full of envy.

The other two elders nodded.

Seth met Heather's gaze and raised his eyebrows. "Ready?"

She nodded.

Seth touched her shoulder and took her to Chris Reordon's office.

Chris and a man garbed much like Heather waited for them.

Chris motioned to Seth. "Adam, this is Seth, leader of the Immortal Guardians. Seth, Adam Quinly."

Adam thrust out a hand. "It's an honor to meet you, sir."

Seth smiled and shook his hand. "The honor is mine. This is Heather Lane. She will be accompanying us today."

Adam offered his hand to Heather. "It's a pleasure to meet you, ma'am. I've met your father. He's a good man."

Heather smiled. "Thank you."

Adam stepped back. "Does he, uh, . . . does he know about all of this?" he asked with hesitant curiosity.

"No," Seth told him. "Has Chris informed you what we will be doing this afternoon?"

"Yes, sir."

"Have you ever teleported before?"

"No, sir."

Heather thought he seemed a bit nervous, so she smiled. "It's awesome. You're going to love it."

Relaxing, the soldier grinned.

A light breeze that carried the scent of the ocean buffeted Heather as she, Seth, and Adam appeared in a tropical jungle. David waited for them in the shade. Like Seth, he wore no protective suit, so he must be old enough to not need one. She wished Ethan didn't either.

Heather glanced around while Seth introduced the two men.

"Any movement?" Seth asked David.

"None."

When Seth and David strolled through the trees, Heather and Adam followed and soon stepped out into bright sunshine.

"I thought immortals couldn't stand exposure to sunlight," Adam whispered to her.

"Apparently, the older the immortal is," she whispered back, "the more he or she can tolerate."

"Ah. Thanks."

Her first glimpse of the base shocked her.

A single road led up to the gates. A wide swath of thick sand surrounded the base like a moat. Judging by the craters blown in it, she guessed the sand concealed buried land mines. The chain-link fences, interwoven with razor wire, that bordered the moat had been reduced to a mangled mess of modern art.

Seth bent and scooped Heather up into his arms. "Follow my footsteps precisely," he ordered the others, then strode forward into the sand.

Heather couldn't help but tense. One step in the wrong place . . .

Seth didn't slow his pace at all. Didn't appear to search for signs that a mine might lay hidden in their path. He just marched forward with a few zigs and zags until he lowered her safely to her feet inside the base's tall cement wall.

David followed with as little care.

Adam took his time, carefully bringing each foot down in the large boot prints left behind by Seth and David. Sweat—spawned by nerves rather than the heat, Heather thought—beaded on his forehead and formed damp patches on his shirt. When he reached the other side, he blew out a tense breath of relief.

The eerie quiet that suffused the war-torn base as they ventured forward gave Heather the willies. It almost felt as though the place were manned by ghosts.

Ghosts who watched their every movement and did not appreciate the intruders' presence.

"A helluva fight went down here," Adam muttered, looking around.

Heather nodded. The vampires seemed to have smashed everything they could smash, like the dumbass juvenile delinquents she occasionally heard about on the news who tore up their schools for shits and giggles. Every light. Every surveillance camera. Every window of every structure. Every vehicle. *Everything* had been broken or crushed or otherwise disabled.

All four guard towers had been toppled. Trucks had been overturned, Humvees crashed.

The bodies of the slain soldiers had been taken away, but bloodstains remained where they had fallen. Many, many bloodstains. So many it sickened her.

The foursome approached the double doors to the largest building and found them locked and chained.

Seth waved a hand. The padlocks popped open. The chains unwound themselves and slithered to the ground like snakes. Another clunk sounded, and the doors swung open.

Adam stared up at the Immortal Guardians, who stood a

good eight inches or so above his own six feet. "You immortals really *could* conquer the world, couldn't you?"

"Yes, we could," Seth confirmed.

"Easily," David added.

"Well, thank you for *not* conquering it. It's a damned shame people can't know about all of the good you do."

Seth stepped inside. "That you and the other members of the network appreciate it and work so hard to help us achieve it is all that matters."

Seeing the aftermath of the vampires' attack affected Heather far more than she had expected. The vampires who had done this had not swept through, making clean kills. They had toyed with their victims. *Tortured* their victims. The evidence of it lay all around her. Bullet holes in every surface. Blood splatter on the walls and ceilings. Large circles of it on the floor, interspersed with smears left behind by boots and hands that had slipped and slid and skidded through it while soldiers struggled and clawed for purchase, trying to get away.

These vampires had delighted in the pain and fear they had inflicted, the screams they had elicited. Screams Heather could almost hear still echoing in the hallways as she and the others searched the building.

She and Adam took turns pointing out the purpose of each room. It was all pretty standard fare until they headed downstairs to the basement and stopped before some very thick doors with a keypad beside them.

"These are biohazard symbols," Adam pointed out.

Heather's cell phone rang. Frowning, she fumbled in her pocket and drew it out, then swore when she saw the caller. "It's my dad," she announced.

Seth and David shared a look.

"Answer it," Seth told her.

Heather took the call. "Hi, Dad."

"What the hell are you doing?" General Lane hissed, his fury flowing over the line.

She frowned. "What?"

"What the hell are you doing at the base? How can you even be there? That location is classified!"

Dread and fear suffused her as she met Seth's gaze with wide eyes, then spun in a circle, searching for surveillance cameras that had *not* been destroyed. Two dangled in a tangle of wires and plastic from opposite corners of the room. Aside from those . . .

"There." Adam pointed to a tiny dark hole in one wall near the ceiling.

"Who are those men with you? How the hell did the four of you get there? Do you have any idea of the shitstorm this is going to create?"

"Dad . . ." Heather looked to Seth and David, not knowing what to tell him.

Seth held out his hand.

Heather handed over her phone.

"General Lane," he began, then frowned. "We're here to try to find out what Nick Altomari couldn't tell you: Who was responsible for this atrocity . . . I can't tell you that . . . Can't . . . No . . . No . . . I can't tell you that either. Aside from you, who else knows we're here? . . . Can you keep them quiet? . . . That would be unwise . . . I assure you, General, you do not want to do that. If you value your daughter's life, you *won't* do that."

Heather's heart sank. This was so not happening.

All of the surveillance cameras they had seen at the base had been wrecked like the two obvious ones in here. The miniscule camera Adam had spotted in the wall must have been installed by the men who had come in and cleaned up the mess.

Now her father knew. His memory would have to be erased.

Her eyes began to burn with tears.

And she would lose him.

David suddenly stepped up behind Heather, turned her slightly to face the camera, and slid a hand around to grasp her neck. Though he applied no pressure, she knew it would look to her father as though he did.

"You will keep this quiet," Seth snapped, "or we will kill your daughter while you watch us do it on your hidden camera."

She squeezed her eyes closed. How had this gone so wrong?

"If you will cease . . . We are *not* your enemy, General Lane," Seth said after a pause, the anger in his voice lessening. "I have no interest in harming your daughter, but your threats may leave me little choice."

David leaned down and whispered in her ear. "We won't hurt you, Heather."

Oh, but they would . . . if they hurt her father.

Adam shoved a desk over to the wall with the camera and climbed up on top of it.

"Should you do so," Seth warned her father, "I will reveal that your daughter is telepathic and tell them *she* led us here."

Drawing a knife from the sheath on his thigh, Adam pried the tiny camera from the Sheetrock and held it up, silently asking Seth what he should do with it.

Seth drew a finger across his throat. "It doesn't matter how I found out. The point is that I know and—if you wish me to remain silent, if you wish your daughter to live—you will cease your threats and listen to me."

Adam dropped the camera onto the table and crushed it beneath his boot.

David removed his hand from Heather's neck and gave her shoulder a gentle pat.

"Wise man," Seth praised. "First, you will destroy whatever video footage your hidden cameras have captured of our presence here on the base. You will destroy it *without* making copies or letting anyone else view it. And you will ensure that the soldier monitoring the surveillance feed there will not say a word to anyone about seeing us. You're a smart man and know that the first person they will come after is the one they can most easily identify: your daughter . . . I may as well be a ghost for all the luck they would have finding me . . . No . . . Such would be futile . . . You could try, but I would advise against it. Need I remind you I have your daughter? . . . I see we understand each other . . . You will meet me tonight, and you will come alone. I shall call you soon with a time and place. Until then, *I* will be the one monitoring *your* every move, so do not think to betray me." He ended the call.

"Well," David said, "that could've gone better."

Heather wasn't one to cry easily, but damned if she didn't burst into tears at that proclamation.

David wrapped an arm around her and drew her against his broad chest. "Don't panic," he murmured, voice kind as he patted her back. "Your father is still well."

But he might not be after tonight's meeting.

"Adam," Seth said, "do you see any other hidden cameras in this room?"

Heather heard the soldier move around the room as she closed her eyes and continued to soak David's shirt with her tears.

"No, sir. We're good."

A moment later, the air filled with a dozen or so conversing voices.

"What the hell?" Ethan snapped.

Heather raised her head and felt no relief when she discovered that Seth had teleported them back to David's living room.

Ethan leapt out of the chair he had been lounging in and hurried forward. "Heather? What happened?"

Heather latched onto him like a drowning woman would a life preserver. Locking her arms around him, she squeezed as close as she could get. Sobs shook her shoulders while an uneasy hush descended upon the room.

"Is she okay?" Darnell asked softly.

No, I'm not, she thought and tuned out Seth's response.

Any chance they had had of netting her father's cooperation had died the moment they had threatened her life.

Ethan held her close. "Shh. It's okay. Don't cry, honey," he murmured, sliding his hands up and down her back in soothing strokes.

But it wasn't okay. Nor was it going to *be* okay.

In just a few hours, she would lose her father.

Though over a dozen people filled David's home, a troubled hush had befallen it. Ethan occupied the living room with Zach, Lisette, Aidan, Imhotep, Chaahk, Darnell, Sheldon, Tracy, Ed, Marcus, Ami, and little Adira. As usual, the toddler seemed to pick up on the somber mood of the others and barely made a sound.

Heather sat in a chair, some distance from the rest of them, staring blindly through a window. Ethan had claimed the chair beside her, but—aware of how the night might end—didn't know what to say or do to help her. So he just stayed close and lent her whatever silent support he could.

When Adira sensed Heather's sadness and tried to go to her, Marcus tugged her back and drew her up onto his lap.

Ethan stared at Heather's tight lips, red-rimmed eyes, and stiff shoulders and could find no hint of the playful woman who had threatened to draw a mustache and bushy eyebrows on his face if he fell asleep. He didn't have to be telepathic to know she was preparing herself for the worst. Preparing herself to say good-bye to the father she loved. Knowing that in less than an hour she might have to watch Seth erase hours of memories that, because of the mental barriers her father had built over the years to protect his wife and daughter, could either damage his brain beyond repair or kill him outright.

Ethan reached over and took her hand, so grateful when she clung to him instead of blaming him and pulling away.

As Seth and David strode into the room, Ethan hoped like hell her father would cooperate and allow himself to be swayed to their side.

Chapter Fourteen

General Lane sat in the driver's seat of a Humvee, every nerve stretched taut.

The GPS coordinates he had been given had led him to the middle of a damned field with nothing around for miles. No farms. No crops. No isolated country homes. Nothing but grass and weeds adorning rolling hills and, in the distance, trees.

He glanced at his watch. The bastards were late. "Anything?" he murmured softly.

"Negative," a voice returned in his earpiece.

Only a sliver of a moon clung to the star-filled sky. General Lane had opted to leave the headlights on. Might as well let them know he was there. And let him see the bastards coming.

If anything had happened to Heather, if they had hurt her in any way . . .

"Shit!" a voice whispered in his ear. "Targets sighted."

"What the fuck?" another murmured, astonishment in the barely audible murmur.

Five figures materialized from the blackness beyond the headlights, striding forward as casually as though they were just out for a stroll. Four men. Tall. Three of them damned near seven feet. A fourth three or four inches above six feet. All save the tallest wore black shirts, black cargo pants, long, black coats, and . . . were those swords in sheaths on their backs?

The tallest wore black leather pants and no shirt. A bandolier sporting numerous throwing knives adorned his hips.

General Lane's heart began to beat faster when his gaze alighted upon the fifth figure.

Heather. So small compared to the others. She, too, wore black cargo pants and a black shirt. No coat. Sheathed knives and holstered guns were strapped to her hips and thighs.

He frowned. What the hell?

She held the hand of the shortest man, who nevertheless towered over her.

General Lane scoured every inch of her pale, exposed skin, looking for injuries or signs that she had been beaten or harmed.

He found none.

"Target one locked," a voice murmured in his ear. Similar words were repeated by several others.

"Wait for my order," the general whispered and slipped from the vehicle.

The group stopped just inside the light cast by the Humvee's beams.

As he approached them, General Lane noted that Heather's eyes and nose were red, as though she had been crying.

Fury rose within him.

"I believe I told you to come alone," one of the men said, his voice that of the man General Lane had spoken to on the phone.

From a few yards away, the general gauged the man at standing six foot eight and could see now that he had long, black hair that fell to his waist. The way he carried himself and the fact that he had spoken first led the general to believe that this was the leader of the group.

The man to the right of him was only an inch shorter, with skin as black as midnight and dreadlocks down to his hips. The man to the left of the leader was maybe six foot four and built like a professional football player. Broader shoulders. Lots of muscle. Short, dark hair. And he kept a tight hold on Heather's hand, urging her closer as his eyes searched the night.

The man to the left of *him*, the one without a shirt, looked like a natural-born killer. Just a hair short of seven feet tall, he possessed a distinct air of ruthlessness, as if he could snap Heather's neck without a second thought and toss her body to the wolves.

Meeting the general's gaze, he arched a brow.

"I did come alone," the general lied.

The ruthless one snorted.

"Dad," Heather pleaded, "they'll know if you're lying. Just tell them the truth and cooperate. Please. You don't know what's at stake here."

Yes, he did. Her life was at stake. Which was why he hadn't come alone. He had wanted as much backup as he could afford to bring. "Are you okay?" he asked, surprised when none of the men told him to shut the hell up so they could make their demands. "Did they hurt you?"

She shook her head. "I'm fine."

The leader drew in a deep breath, searched the night, then looked to his black comrade. A moment passed. The black man nodded.

The leader turned back to the general. "Have your snipers lower their weapons."

"What snipers?" he asked, poker-faced.

"The ones in the trees and atop the hills."

Heather's look turned panicky. "Dad, you brought snipers with you? You were supposed to come alone!"

"And leave you unprotected if they kill me?"

"*They're* the ones protecting me, Dad! Tell your men to stand down."

He frowned. "What?" *They* were protecting her? What the hell did *that* mean?

"Just do it," she said, "and listen to what these men have to say."

In his ear, a voice murmured, "I have a clean shot. On your mark, I'll take out the man holding your daughter."

The man who held Heather's hand frowned and looked to the west. Shifting Heather to his other side, he nudged her toward the ruthless one, who sort of reminded General Lane of a buffer, more rugged Jim Morrison. "Zach, get her out of here."

Heather dug in her heels. "No way. I'm staying."

"The hell you are," the man said, still trying to push her toward the other. "I don't want you getting caught in the crossfire. There are six rifles aimed at us right now and one is drawing a bead on my head."

Unease and confusion struck the general.

How had he known there were six shooters? How had they known there were shooters at all? Had they been here all this time, waiting and watching?

Even if they had, *he* hadn't heard or seen the soldiers arrive and get in place, so how had they?

"All the more reason for me to stay," she insisted. Squirming out of her captor's hold, she planted herself in front of him like a shield. A short, slender shield half his weight.

"Heather," the man said with exasperation as he settled his hands on her hips, "you're a foot shorter than me. If you stay and he shoots, you won't block the shot, you'll just get showered with my brains."

The dismay that swept her features filled the general with dread.

"Then pick me up," she ordered, spinning to face the man.

He looked at her as if she'd just sprouted horns. "Are you insane?"

"No. Use me as a shield."

"I am *not* going to let you sacrifice yourself for me again. You already did that once, damn it, and I nearly lost you. So get that crap out of your head right now!"

The general's thoughts spiraled with confusion. What the hell was happening?

He looked at the leader.

The leader shrugged. "They're sort of smitten with each other. Young love and all that."

He spoke with an accent General Lane couldn't quite place.

"Fine," Heather said, the word full of defiance. Swiveling around once more, she drew a 9mm and aimed it at . . .

Shit! General Lane stared down the barrel of his daughter's gun.

"Fire a single shot," she shouted into the night, "and I'll shoot General Lane!"

The ruthless one smiled. "I like this woman, Ethan."

The leader nodded, his face relaxing. "General, how well do you trust the men you've brought with you?"

"Heather, honey," General Lane blurted, "what the hell are you doing?" Was this Stockholm syndrome? Had she fallen for her captors? They'd only had her for a day, hadn't they? What the hell had they done to her to force her to switch her loyalty so swiftly?

"General?" the leader prompted.

"I trust them with my life," he muttered absently, still trying to come to grips with the fact that his daughter had just threatened to shoot him.

"Do you trust them enough to tell them where you saw us earlier today and what transpired there two weeks ago?" the leader pressed.

"They don't have clearance."

"That's not what I asked."

"Yes," the general snapped. "I would trust them with the information, *if* necessary."

The leader studied him a moment. "Have your men lower their weapons and remove their earpieces."

"Hand over Heather first."

"Dad," Heather said, "I'm armed. You see this weapon. I would've already shot these guys if I thought they intended to hurt me."

The man with his hands on her hips grinned. "Damn, you're appealing. I *love* strong women."

Heather rolled her eyes. "Now is not the time, Ethan."

General Lane stared. "Heather—"

"I'm bored," the ruthless one interrupted.

"Zach," the leader spoke, a warning in his voice.

"This is taking too long. Why don't I just . . . move things along a little faster for you?"

The leader grumbled something under his breath. "All right. But do *not* hurt anyone."

The ruthless one—Zach—loosed a disgruntled sigh. "Fine." Then he vanished.

General Lane gasped and felt his eyes pop wide.

He just . . . *vanished*. Into thin air. There one second. Gone the next.

Odd sounds came over the general's earpiece.

Zach reappeared, his arms full of rifles. Tossing them on the ground, he brushed his hands together. "Done. Now call your men in."

"What the fuck just happened?" one of the soldiers blurted in General Lane's ear.

Another swore. "The target is now in possession of my primary weapon."

The others confirmed the same.

General Lane's mouth fell open. "How did you do that?"

The leader answered for him. "Bring your men in and we'll talk."

Heather lowered her weapon. "Trust me, Dad. You're going to want to hear what they have to say. You *need* to hear what they have to say."

Bewildered, afraid for her, the general called in his men.

The swishing of leaves and crunching of grass and weeds filled the night as six men—men so loyal to General Lane that they would do anything he requested, no questions asked—marched out of the forest and down the hills. As he watched them enter the ambient light of the Humvee's beams and come to stand on either side of him, the general wondered anew how Heather's captors had known they were there. All of the soldiers had blackened their faces, worn black fatigues, and covered their upper bodies with ghillie suits that mimicked the foliage around them so they would blend in with the night.

And they *had* blended in. These men were professionals. General Lane hadn't been able to spot them even with a nightscope.

The soldiers doffed their ghillie suits, then studied Heather's captors.

"Heather," General Lane ordered, "come stand by me."

The man behind her shook his head. "She'll stay with us for now."

The leader nodded to the soldiers. "If you don't wish these men to know what you've been investigating—what we were investigating ourselves today—then tell them to get inside your vehicle and drive away. We will see that you return home or reach a destination of your choice safely once we're done here."

Tim, one of the soldiers, glanced at General Lane from the corner of his eye. "With all due respect, sir, we aren't leaving you alone with these men."

Wayne nodded. "If you want our silence, sir, you'll have it, but we aren't goin' anywhere."

The general nodded. If they ended up having to fight their way out of this, one or more of these men might be able to get Heather to safety.

"Very well," the leader said.

"Who are you?" General Lane demanded.

"You may call me Seth," he answered and addressed the group as a whole. "Approximately two and a half weeks ago, an American military base was attacked and destroyed. Everyone within it was slain save one man."

Shock splashing across their features, the soldiers all looked to the general.

"It's true," he confirmed.

"What base?" Tim asked.

"That's classified."

"Who did it?" Wayne asked.

"We don't know. The surveillance footage was damaged and the sole survivor has suffered some kind of mental break-down."

Seth glanced at Heather.

Heather swallowed. "Here's the thing, Dad." Shifting her weight from one foot to the other, she holstered her weapon. "I wanted to tell you this before, after I spoke with Nick." She glanced at the soldiers. "Nick is the survivor." Then she met his gaze once more. "But I couldn't."

"Tell me what?" the general prodded.

"Nick didn't have a mental breakdown."

General Lane frowned. "Of course he did. He thinks vampires attacked the base."

Words of disbelief burst from the lips of the soldiers.

"He thinks vampires attacked the base," Heather con-firmed, "because vampires *did* attack the base."

Oh shit. As her words sank in, the general wanted to cry and hit something all at the same time. *What the hell did they do to my baby?* he wondered, heartbroken that her mind had obviously—

"Don't look like that!" she pleaded. "I'm not crazy, Dad. Vampires are real. They actually exist. Look, I'll prove it." She turned to face the one she called Ethan. "Smile."

His eyebrows rose. "What?"

"Smile." She poked him in the side.

He jerked and grinned, flashing straight, white teeth, when she hit a ticklish spot. "Stop that."

"Now kiss me," she ordered.

The general took a step toward her. "Heather . . ."

"Just give me a minute, Dad." Rising onto her toes, she reached up, curled a hand around Ethan's neck, and drew his head down.

Their lips met. Locked. Moved and parted as the kiss deepened.

Ethan slid an arm around her waist and urged her closer, kissing her in earnest until he appeared to forget the rest of them were there.

The leader and the quiet one with dreadlocks shared an exasperated look.

Heather broke the contact and dropped her heels to the ground. Turning to her father, she motioned to Ethan's face. "There. You see?"

General Lane's eyes fastened on Ethan and clung so long they began to burn with the need to blink.

Ethan's eyes now glowed vibrant amber. *Glowed*, as though candlelight flickered behind his irises. And the teeth that had been so straight and perfect before now included long, sharp fangs.

"What . . . the fuck?" Tim muttered.

"Those can't be real," Wayne whispered.

"The fangs or the eyes?" Rick asked.

"The fangs."

General Lane let their voices flow around him as he continued to stare.

"I've seen fake fangs that could retract before, but . . . those eyes," Tim said.

"Contacts don't do that, man," Jess informed them. "My brother-in-law is an ophthalmologist and breaks out the novelty shit every Halloween. They don't have anything *close* to that."

"Heather," the general said through stiff lips, "step away from him."

Seth arched a brow. "I see we have your attention now. Thank you, Heather, for the demonstration. Although you could have just asked Ethan to flash his fangs."

"Yes," Ethan added with unconcealed glee, "thank you, Heather."

Smiling for the first time, she drove an elbow back into his abs.

Ethan grunted and grinned.

Those fangs.

Burke, a soldier to General Lane's left, drew his sidearm and fired.

Blood spurted from Ethan's chest . . . *so* close to his heart.

Heather cried out and spun around to gape at the blood-stain on his shirt.

Ethan's eyes flashed brighter as his face twisted with rage. His form blurred as he shot forward past Heather, so swiftly he reminded the general of the Flash. Burke's gun flew into the night before he could get off another shot.

"Ethan!" Seth shouted.

When Ethan stilled, one of his hands was curled around Burke's throat, holding him up in the air. He growled, the low, deep rumble of a lion, while the soldier kicked his feet and clawed at the hand that slowly choked the life out of him.

The other soldiers all scrambled back and drew their sidearms.

Seth made a motion with one hand.

The guns leapt from the soldiers' hands and flew into the night.

"Ethan," Seth repeated, "let him go."

"He could've killed her," Ethan snarled.

"But he didn't," Seth said, his voice soothing.

Heather took a step forward, her eyes on the spreading stain on the man's shirt. "Ethan, are you okay?"

"Stay back," he said, without taking his eyes from the man he throttled.

The one with the dreadlocks sighed. "Put him down, Ethan. This is counterproductive."

Ethan yanked Burke closer until mere inches separated their faces. "If you *ever* endanger her life again by pulling some stupid shit like that, I will rip your fucking arms off and beat you to death with them." He gave him a little shake. "And you know I'm strong enough to do it."

Burke's face mottled as his eyes twitched.

Ethan opened his fingers.

Burke dropped to the ground, landing flat on his back.

Heather darted forward, grabbed Ethan's hand, and tugged him backward.

As Ethan backed away, he pointed to the downed soldier and locked his glowing amber eyes on the general. "You need to kick . . . his fucking . . . ass. He could've shot your daughter!"

Yes, he could've.

"If that bullet had hit an inch lower and an inch or two to the left," Ethan continued to rage, "or if she had moved, it could've struck her in the head!"

The general felt his hands begin to shake at the knowledge.

It had been a close call. He intended to have a long, not-so-nice chat with Burke as soon as he figured out what the hell was going on.

Who *was* this man willing to kill another for endangering
Heather's life?

Who was this . . . *vampire*?

Once she maneuvered Ethan back in line with the others,
Heather untucked Ethan's T-shirt with shaking hands and
drew it up almost to his chin.

This was *so* not going well.

The bullet had come damned close to piercing Ethan's
heart. Blood smeared his chest and washboard abs, but had
already ceased to flow.

Heather turned him so she could get a look at his back.
The exit hole was larger. Uglier. But began to shrink beneath
her worried gaze. Ethan was at full strength. She had watched
him sink his fangs into a bag of blood back at David's place
and siphon it directly into his veins. Ethan had actually asked
her to watch, wanting her to know everything about his existence. The good, the bad, and the ugly, as he'd put it.

Heather turned him to face her again. She rested a hand
beside the ugly wound and looked up at Ethan as it closed and
began to form a scar that she knew would disappear once he
had more blood or slept a healing sleep.

She hated that he had gotten hurt. Because of her.

Ethan lowered his chin and met her gaze. She hoped he
could see how sorry she was for the pain and trouble she'd
caused him. Hoped he'd see how much she hated seeing him
come to harm. Hoped he'd see . . . *everything*.

The fury at last drained from his handsome features. His
muscles relaxed. Smiling, he covered her hand with one of
his. "I'm okay."

She nodded. But she still blamed herself. They were doing
this—risking harm and revealing their existence to someone
they never otherwise would have—for *her*. To try to avoid
causing her grief by having to hurt her father.

Who should probably see this, come to think of it.

Heather held up Ethan's shirt and stepped to one side.

Gasps sounded.

Burke had been helped to his feet and now gaped at Ethan alongside the rest.

"That's not possible," Wayne whispered.

Heather recognized every man, had even chatted with a few at barbecues her father had hosted so she could read their minds and assure him he had these men's absolute loyalty.

Drawing Ethan's shirt down, she met her father's gaze, silently pleading for him to believe them and, more importantly, to *join* them. "Vampires exist, Dad. Nick isn't insane."

Her father looked stunned. Confused. Terrified for her.

He shifted his gaze to Seth. "Did you attack the base?"

"No," Seth told him. "We wish to find the vampires who *did* and destroy them before they can wreak more havoc."

"Are you *all* vampires?" the general asked.

Only Ethan had flashed fangs so far.

"If you're all vampires," her father went on, "then why are you hunting the others?"

Seth exchanged another look with David, then spoke. "We aren't vampires. We're . . . something else. Something more."

"What does that mean?" the general asked.

"Zach," Seth said.

Zach vanished and reappeared a millisecond later in front of the tight knot of soldiers.

More gasps all around.

"Tim, is it?" Zach gripped the soldier's shoulder. He must have read Tim's mind to know his name, because Heather didn't remember having heard it spoken since their arrival.

The two disappeared.

Curses filled the night.

A moment later, Zach reappeared, his hand still clutching Tim's shoulder.

Tim wrapped his arms around himself and shivered. Something white dusted his hair and shoulders and eyelashes.

Was that snow?

Even as Heather watched, the fat snowflakes melted and dampened Tim's clothing.

"Tim?" her father said, brow furrowing.

Tim shook his head. "I don't know where the hell we just were, but there was a fucking blizzard going on!"

As Zach strolled back to join the others, Seth said, "David?"

David's body seemed to melt into the form of a huge black panther.

More curses exploded from lips as soldiers scrambled backward. Eyes widened as the majestic beast padded toward them and stopped just in front of Heather's father.

Face pale with astonishment, her father held his ground.

The panther roared.

The hair on the back of Heather's neck stood on end as the rumble vibrated, like thunder, through her body.

In the blink of an eye, the panther morphed back into David, clothes and all. He looked down at her father, who Heather began to fear might have a heart attack. "As Seth said, we're something more. Vampires do not bear these and the other gifts we possess. We were born with them, much like your daughter was."

"Y-your daughter can shape-shift?" Wayne stuttered.

David answered for him. "No. She's telepathic. As am I and several others of our kind." He looked at Tim. "Yes, I can read your mind . . . Yes, every thought." His look turned resigned. "Perry the Platypus. Camel. Pink. Jay Z. Doc McStuffins. Pizza. Enough. You're giving me a headache." He backed away to rejoin his friends. "We call ourselves immortals. In addition to our special gifts, we possess even greater speed, strength, heightened senses, and regenerative capabilities than vampires do."

Seth glanced at Wayne. "No one knows about us because we don't *want* anyone to know about us, which is why we must insist upon your silence."

"Dad," Heather said, drawing his gaze, "these immortals are good guys. They believe the commander of the vampire army that attacked the base also sent vampires to attack me."

He paled even more. "You were attacked by vampires?"

"Twice. Once, a couple of weeks ago—the same night they struck the base. Then again a few nights ago." She rubbed Ethan's arm, then slid her hand down to link her fingers with his. "Both times, Ethan was there and defeated them."

"We defeated them *together*," Ethan corrected, something like pride and admiration in the glowing eyes that met hers. "Your daughter is a valiant warrior, General Lane."

Heather's heart fluttered at his praise. "The second time they attacked, I was fatally wounded and would've died if Seth hadn't healed me. These men saved my life. And they want to save *more* lives, if—"

"Are you a vampire now?" her father interrupted. "Did they turn you?"

He had always been such a strong, commanding figure. To see him so shaken broke her heart.

"No, Dad."

"You said they healed you."

"Seth can heal with his hands."

The soldiers exchanged doubtful glances.

A split second later, Ethan released her hand, yanked the 9mm from her holster, and shot Burke.

Shouts erupted as Burke dropped to the ground. Her father and the other soldiers rushed to help him, kneeling around him and trying to stanch the flow of blood as Burke's shirt began to glisten.

Mouth falling open, Heather spun around and looked up. "What the hell did you do that for?"

Ethan shrugged. "I believed another demonstration was in order." His face darkened. "And thought I'd teach him a lesson as well: Fuck with what's mine and he'll pay the price."

"Damn it, Ethan!" Seth grumbled and strode forward.

What's mine? Heather thought some part of her should object to him referring to her as though she were some possession of his, but . . . she found she kinda liked it.

Though they were wary as hell of him, the soldiers didn't shy away at Seth's approach. All stuck by their friend, a dozen hands attempting to render aid at once.

Seth knelt beside her father. "Easy, Burke," he murmured when the injured man's eyes widened and he tried to move away. "You're going to be fine. This will only take a moment." He looked to her father. "Tell your men to release him."

Heather held her breath as her father stared into Seth's eyes.

General Lane looked to the others. "Let him go."

The men all did as ordered, but stayed close.

Seth rested a hand on the fallen soldier's chest.

Seconds later, Burke gasped. The tightness in his expression eased as Seth siphoned away his pain and healed his injury.

Seth withdrew his touch. Rising, he offered his hand to the soldier.

Staring up at him with awe, Burke took it.

Seth drew the man to his feet and clapped him on the back. "Looks like you're even. As long as you don't put Heather at risk again, Ethan won't harm you."

Burke nodded.

As Seth walked away, returning to stand beside David, Burke yanked up his shirt.

The wound in his chest, like Ethan's, had healed.

Expressions of amazement wafted from his comrades.

Heather met her father's gaze. "As I said, these are good men. They didn't know about the attack on the base until I spoke with Nick. We were at the base today, trying to find some clue that would lead them to the vampire army so they can destroy it. They aren't familiar with army bases, so they asked me to accompany them and see if anything stood out as odd. Anything that might have made that particular base seem a more attractive target."

Her father shifted his gaze to Seth. "You found it."

Seth arched a brow. "The biohazard symbol in the basement?"

"Yes. They were researching ways to counter biological weapons our troops may be exposed to. Or the American people, if terrorists should ever manage to strike that way."

"Those biological weapons were present in that facility?"

"Yes. You can't learn how to counter them if you don't have them on hand to study."

"The doors down there did not appear to be damaged. Were any of the toxins taken?"

"No. As far as we can tell, those doors were never breached. That was one of the many things that puzzled us about this. If the . . . vampires . . . attacked the base because they wanted to get their hands on the bioweapons, why leave without them?"

Heather glanced at Seth. "Could the doors have been too thick for them to break through?"

"We saw no evidence they had even tried."

She didn't remember having seen any either.

David shook his head. "Unless the walls are as thick and impenetrable as the doors, it wouldn't have mattered. The vampires would've just plowed through them. Wood, Sheetrock, and insulation would've proven no deterrent to them."

"Then what was?" she asked.

"The biohazard symbol?" Zach suggested and looked to Seth. "Perhaps you were right. Perhaps these vampires weren't told exactly what was on the island they were ordered to attack. Slaying the soldiers might have been fun to them, but most humans hold at least *some* fear of illness. If these vampires did not abandon their humanity very long ago, they may have little understanding of their new condition and may not realize that such things can no longer harm them. Laughing in the face of the common cold is one thing. Coming face-to-face with something you've been taught to fear, something that has killed thousands or hundreds of thousands—if not millions—in the past, is another."

A thoughtful silence ensued.

General Lane studied them all. "Are you saying these vampires might not have been there for the weapons? That they just killed our men for the fun of it?"

"Yes," Seth answered. "Their goal was most likely to spark an international incident, to pit you against whomever you would eventually blame for the attack."

"On whose order?"

"I can't tell you that."

"What *can* you tell me?"

"Very little, I'm afraid. We don't even know where this vampire army is consolidating. That's why we're here. That's why we didn't simply find you while you slept tonight and erase your memory of seeing us earlier. We need your help. You have access to information we do not. And your mind is, as you know, very difficult to read. Your daughter doesn't wish to see you harmed and asked us to sway you to our side instead, if we can."

Her father returned his attention to her.

"Please, Dad. This is a straight-up win-or-lose situation. Help them out and keep their secret, and they'll find this vampire army, destroy it, and prevent it from killing again. Refuse to help them or betray them and they'll erase your memory, likely causing brain damage."

He swore, as did several of his men.

"Without your help, they'll have a harder time finding

these vampires and taking them out, so—for all we know—
the vampires could attack another military base. Or even a
well-populated civilian target." She took a step forward, eyes
pleading. "I saw the base, Dad. I saw the bloodstains. I saw
the marks left behind by the soldiers who tried to claw their
way out of the vampires' grasps. The vampires who attacked
that base *enjoyed* what they did. They aren't going to just sit
back and call it a day. They're going to do it again. And again.
And again."

A long moment passed.

General Lane looked to Seth. "What do you want me
to do?"

The relief that rushed through her was so great it brought
tears to Heather's eyes. Racing forward, she threw her arms
around her father's neck.

He clamped his arms around her and hugged her back,
squeezing the stuffing out of her. "Are you really okay,
baby?" he asked in a broken whisper.

She nodded, unable to speak.

"Your eyes are red. You've been crying."

She swallowed past the lump in her throat. "Mom always
said you were stubborn as a mule. I was afraid you wouldn't
cooperate, that you wouldn't join them."

"Us," Ethan corrected. "You were afraid he wouldn't join
us. You're one of us, too, now, Heather."

Her father jerked back. His eyes lowered and squinted as
he looked at her teeth.

Heather laughed. "I'm not a vampire, Dad. A lot of
humans work with the immortals and know about them. The
immortals consider them family."

He nodded, but seemed unwilling to release her. So
Heather stayed by his side, his arm around her shoulders.

"I will need your men's vow of silence as well," Seth said.
"Should they have no wish to help us, we can simply erase

their memories of this. Because they lack your stronger mental barriers and have known about it for a shorter amount of time, the damage would be minimal and would not adversely affect their lives as it would yours."

The soldiers exchanged looks that seemed to carry as much meaning as words. These men knew each other well. Had served together for a long time.

"We're with you," Burke said.

The rest nodded.

Thank goodness.

Her father seemed as relieved and pleased as Heather was. "How can we help?"

Seth considered the question. "We need a country of origin for the vampires. Anything that may tell us where we should begin our search. We don't believe they are amassing on U.S. soil. Recent events have led us to keep a closer eye on things here. So the army must be forming elsewhere. Unfortunately, our network of contacts has found nothing so far, and the base yielded no clues."

"What should we look for?" her father asked.

"Teleporting that many vampires would've required the use of enough power for me to sense it," Seth said. "So the vampires had to have reached the island through other means."

Heather nodded. "You're probably combing through every bit of intel and chatter and every satellite feed you can get your hands on. We just need you to tell us what you come up with."

Ethan crossed to stand in front of them. "As well as what conclusions the military is drawing. We can't rule out that, as Seth suggested, this was meant to spark an international incident. Seth didn't find any evidence that would implicate another country, but you hit the scene before he did, so you might have."

The arm around Heather's shoulders tightened at Ethan's nearness.

It might take a while, she thought, for her father to adjust to her budding relationship with the immortal. Her father clearly wanted nothing more than to shove her into the Humvee and get her as far away from Ethan and the others as he could.

Oddly, she didn't think it would take *her* time to adjust to it. She didn't think she had ever felt so comfortable around a man before. So in tune with him.

She smiled up at Ethan as Seth continued to speak with her father.

Ethan caught her look and smiled back, his expression full of affection. He winked.

She grinned.

How the hell had he remained single for so long? He was such an easy man to love.

"Heather will be going home with me."

Her father's words jerked Heather out of her mushy thoughts. "Dad . . . what?"

Ethan shook his head. "She wouldn't be safe."

Ooh. Wrong thing to say.

Her father stiffened. "You think I don't know how to protect my own daughter?"

"I have no doubt, sir," Ethan said, "that you know very *well* how to protect Heather from any and every threat posed by *humans*. But with all due respect, I don't think you know how to protect her from vampires. She's been tossed into vampire battles twice so far by the one leading this army. A vampire can move faster than your eyes can follow, making it difficult to aim your weapon in time to stop him. A vampire is strong enough to pick up that Humvee behind you and throw it fifty yards with little effort. Walls, windows, even roofs cannot keep vampires at bay. You would be no match for them if they were to come for her, even if these soldiers were to remain with you and help you guard her. *I* and the other immortals, however, *would*."

Heather could almost feel the irritation that pummeled her father.

Ethan took a step closer, his eyes fixed on her father's. "Make no mistake, General, I *will* guard her with my life. Should I fall while doing so, Seth and the others will take up my sword. There is no place on Earth your daughter will be safer than she will be with us."

Heather stared up at him, knowing he meant every word. He really would give his life to protect her. What woman wouldn't melt at such a declaration?

Or fear for him?

She patted her father's chest and stepped away. "It's okay, Dad. I *want* to go with him. Ethan and I are . . ." She bit her lip and caught Ethan's gaze. "I don't know. What *are* we, Ethan?" She was going to say *dating*, but they hadn't actually been on a real date yet.

He seemed to understand what she was asking and pursed his lips thoughtfully. "Seeing each other?" he suggested.

At the same time, Zach said, "Lovers?"

General Lane sucked in a breath.

Heather's eyes widened. She gaped past Ethan at Zach. "You did *not* just say that!"

His brows drew down in a perplexed frown. "Why? I thought you were looking for a nice way of telling him that you're sleeping together."

David clapped a hand to his forehead.

"Smooth," Seth murmured.

"Zach!" Heather protested. "He's my *dad*! He does *not* want to hear about me . . . about us . . . I was going to say *dating*, that we're *dating*, but we haven't actually had a chance to . . . I mean, the whole vampire thing hasn't . . ." Growling, she spun back to her father, but avoided meeting his gaze. "We're seeing each other, Dad. Okay? Ethan and I are seeing each other and I really like him."

Utter silence.

Miserable and embarrassed, she looked up at Ethan. "How red is my face?"

"About as red as Burke's blood."

Some of the soldiers laughed.

Seth cleared his throat. "I realize this is all a lot to take in, General," he told her father, his voice kind, "but I do assure you that we will—as Ethan vowed—do everything in our power to keep your daughter safe. She is not our prisoner. Nor is she suffering from Stockholm syndrome. She is with us by choice and, though this could have been broken to you a little more delicately," he added with a cutting glare at Zach, "she and Ethan do have feelings for each other."

Her father touched a finger to her chin and nudged it up so she'd look at him. "This is what you want? You *want* to go with him? With them?"

She nodded. "Yes. It's what I want."

"I'll be able to contact you whenever I want to?"

She looked to Ethan and Seth.

Seth nodded. "I'm afraid we destroyed her cell phone after the last time you spoke with her so you wouldn't be able to locate her. I'll have another phone delivered to her within the hour and she will call you herself with the new number."

"I assume it will be untraceable?" her father said.

"Yes. We must earn one another's trust, General. Until then, I must take measures to protect all of those around her who would be at risk should you unwisely choose to betray us."

Heather would not remember later what words were spoken next. She didn't hear them, too busy thinking how hard it must be for her father to let her go. To stand there, once they wrapped up the conversation, and watch Ethan rest a hand on her lower back and guide her away. How much it must be killing her dad to climb into the Humvee with the other soldiers and watch her walk away with the immortals, fading into the darkness beyond the headlights.

Her father had always been her protector. Long after she had grown up and begun to protect herself, she had remained— in his mind—the little girl he wished to safeguard.

The Humvee's engine rumbled to life as she and the others strode into the night.

"Sir?" a voice called after them. "Excuse me, sir?"

Heather glanced back and saw one of the soldiers jogging toward them.

Tim.

Stopping, they waited for him to reach them.

He halted a few feet away, his eyes glued to Seth's face. Tim held a black cap in his hands and began to twist it again and again. He looked as if he had enough to say to fill the pages of a novel, but couldn't find the first sentence that would allow the rest to flow freely.

The quiet stretched, filled only with the sounds of crickets and other nocturnal creatures.

Seth offered Tim a gentle smile and patted his shoulder. "I'll do it tonight."

The man sagged, his face lighting with a smile as tears filled his eyes and spilled down his blackened cheeks. "Thank you," he said hoarsely. "Thank you so much. *Thank you.* If there is ever anything, *anything* I can do for you . . ."

Seth motioned to the Humvee with a lift of his chin. "They're waiting for you."

"Yes, sir." Nodding, Tim swung around and jogged back to the vehicle.

"What did he want?" Ethan asked.

"His little girl has cancer. She has already undergone two rounds of chemotherapy, and her prognosis is not good. After witnessing my abilities, he hoped I might heal her."

David clapped him on the back. "Chris and the network will have to alter her medical records so her miraculous recovery won't make the news."

Seth nodded. "And I'll have to bury a lot of memories."

"Bury?" Heather asked. "Not erase?"

He nodded. "Burying them should suffice for something like this."

The Humvee pulled a U-turn, its headlights illuminating the hills to the west, and carried General Lane and his men away.

"You're a good man, Seth," Ethan said softly.

Heather thought it sad that Seth looked as though he disagreed.

Chapter Fifteen

Ethan and Heather only stayed at David's place long enough for Darnell to give them the new phone Seth had promised. Then Zach teleported them—and Lisette—to the couple's home.

Ethan wasn't sure whether he should consider the meeting with Heather's father a win or a loss. General Lane had agreed to work with them, but it sure as hell could've gone better.

Anger rose as he catalogued the night's events.

As Zach and Lisette headed into the kitchen to get something to eat, Ethan remained with Heather in the living room and felt his fury burn brighter with every second that passed.

Heather watched the couple go, then swiveled to face him. "So, what did you think of . . . ?" The half smile on her lips vanished as she looked up at him. "Wow. You look pissed."

"*Pick* me *up*?" he growled, taking a menacing step toward her.

Eyes widening, she took a step backward.

"*Use me* as a *shield*?"

She raised her hands, palms out. "Okay. You need to calm down. Your eyes are *really* bright."

"Heather! What the hell were you thinking?" he demanded.

"I *wasn't* thinking. Or I *was*. I just—I was thinking that my dad's men wouldn't risk shooting you if I was in the way."

"Clearly, you were wrong! Burke shot me anyway and damned near shot *you* in the process!" Recalling it only made him want to shoot the man again.

"I know. I totally didn't expect that." She continued to ease backward as he advanced toward her, matching him step for step. "Look. You're upset. I understand that. You didn't want me to get hurt. But *I* didn't want *you* to get hurt either."

Her continued disregard for her own safety floored him. "I'm immortal!" he roared. "How many times do I have to tell you that to get you to stop trying to put yourself between me and danger? I'm *immortal*, Heather! A bullet won't kill me! Am I going to have to shoot myself in the head right in front of you to prove it?"

Her face paled. "Please don't do that."

"Yes," Lisette said in the kitchen. "Please, don't. If you do, Tracy will bitch and moan for weeks over having to scrub the bloodstains out of the furniture."

Heather's mouth fell open at the bland pronouncement.

"It's true," Tracy confirmed, entering from the hallway. "Bloodstains are hell to get out of fabrics."

Ethan shot her a glare.

Tracy stopped short. Swallowing hard, she said, "Yeah, I'm just going to . . . join them in the kitchen. Sorry I interrupted." She hurried into the kitchen.

Heather turned back to face Ethan, who continued to crowd her, too angry to stand still. "Okay. I get it. You're angry and . . ." She scowled. "Stop stalking me, damn it! I can't think straight while you're looking at me as if you want to strangle me."

He halted. "Now you think I want to hurt you?" he asked incredulously.

Rolling her eyes, she emitted a growl of her own. "No! Oh my *gosh*, you have a bug up your butt tonight!"

Lisette, Zach, and Tracy all burst into laughter in the kitchen.

Against his will, Ethan felt his own lips twitch as some of the fury drained from him.

"No," Heather said in more even tones, "I do *not* think you want to hurt me. You would never do anything to hurt me. I know that." She sighed. "You're angry. And I understand why. I just . . . I like you. Okay? I mean I really, really like you, Ethan. I wasn't lying when I told you I've never in my life felt this strong a connection to someone. I've never felt this *comfortable* with someone, even family, as if I could say or do *anything* . . . like complain about you having a bug up your butt when you look positively murderous."

He did smile then.

"You make me laugh," she said. "You're smart. You're fun to talk to. You make my heart race and are the best lover I've ever had." Her voice softened. "It would be so easy to fall in love with you."

His heart began to pound in his chest.

"So I panic inside whenever I think someone is going to hurt you. And I do crazy things, like try to put myself between you and the threat. I don't think, *Eh, he's immortal. He can take it.* I think, *I can't lose him. I just found him.* And"—she shrugged—"then I stop thinking altogether and . . . act."

Now *he* couldn't think. He had assumed, on some level, that most of her attraction to him stemmed from her inability to read his mind. But she hadn't even mentioned that. "You care about me," he murmured with some amazement.

"Yes. Very much." A spark of vulnerability entered her soft brown eyes.

"I feel the same for you," he told her. Resting his hands on her hips, he drew her toward him until their bodies touched. "Which is why it terrifies me and infuriates me whenever you try to sacrifice yourself for me. You can't do that, Heather."

"I told you—"

"If something happens to me," he interrupted, "you won't lose me. I can recover from anything short of having my head removed. Even excessive blood loss won't kill me, not the way it will a vampire. But *you* are mortal. If something happens to you, and Seth or Zach or one of the other healers isn't around or can't get to you fast enough, I'll lose you. And for the rest of eternity, I will have to live with the knowledge that you died needlessly, thinking you were protecting me, and will wonder what could have been."

Biting her lip, she leaned into him. "I'm sorry. This whole immortality thing is still new to me. It hasn't made it to my subconscious yet. Once it does, I'll react better in a crisis."

How he wished he could promise her there would *be* no more crises.

Ethan sighed. "I just want us to have a chance to see where this can lead, to see what we can have together."

She offered him a tentative smile. "So do I." Then she winked. "You're irresistible. I want to see if that's going to wear off in time."

"It will," Zach promised from the kitchen.

Heather laughed.

Ethan felt the tension drain from him. "How I wish I could court you properly."

Richart had managed to carry on a normal courtship with a mortal woman. For a time. How lucky he had been. None of the rest of them could seem to manage it.

He groaned. "And how I wish I could've made a better impression on your father. If he believes I would use you as a shield to protect myself . . ."

She laughed. "I don't think you have to worry about that. You bitched at me for trying to shield you, then nearly strangled Burke to death for endangering me, then when Seth wouldn't let you do *that*, you shot Burke in the chest to teach him a lesson and warned him not to endanger my life again.

Once my dad gets over the shock of the whole vampire and immortal thing, he's going to love you."

Ethan hoped she was right. He had been raised in a different time. Her father's approval was important to him. *Family* was important to him. He didn't want Heather to lose hers if she pursued a relationship with him.

"Stop worrying," she admonished and gave him a little shake.

The movement rubbed the front of her body against his, stirring an instant response.

Sending her a sly smile, he slid his hands up and down her back. "I'll worry until you do something to take my mind off things."

She smiled. "So you're saying you need a distraction?" Rising onto her toes, she pressed her hips into his.

Pleasure darted through him. "Hell yes." Ethan slid his hands down to her shapely ass and lifted her up with ease.

Laughing, Heather locked her legs around his waist. "Sounds good to me." She cupped his face in her hands and pressed soft lips to his.

Ethan thought he would never grow tired of the taste of her. Nor did he think that the sizzle of excitement that always seared him when she kissed him would ever dissipate. He parted his lips and groaned when she boldly stroked his tongue with hers.

He started down the hallway, loving the feel of her riding the rigid length behind his fly.

"Does this mean we aren't hunting tonight?" Zach asked from the kitchen.

Ethan tore his lips from Heather's long enough to say, "I'm taking the night off."

Then their mouths fused once more, hungry and aggressive.

"We aren't hunting tonight," Zach told Lisette, his tone deadpan. "Whatever shall we do with ourselves?"

"Not what you're thinking," she retorted with a laugh. "Our bedroom isn't soundproofed."

"So? We'll make a game of it. *I'll* see how many orgasms I can give you while *you* see how long you can go without making a sound."

"Zach!"

"Come on, guys," Tracy complained. "I'm standing right here."

Ethan didn't hear whatever came next. He was too caught up in the feel and taste of Heather as he carried her down to Richart's room. As soon as he kicked the door closed, he lowered her feet to the floor.

Both moaned as her legs slid down his length.

Then their hands flew into action, untucking shirts and unbuckling belts. Ethan toed off his boots and socks. He knew he could easily divest them both of their clothing in record time, but he loved the feel of her hands on him, sliding under his shirt and dragging it up over his head.

Her fingers dipped into the waistband of his pants to work the button and draw down the zipper. He sucked in a breath as she liberated the hard length of him from his silk boxers and began to stroke him.

One of her holstered weapons hit the floor with a thud.

"Being a little daring with that, don't you think?" she muttered.

"Speak for yourself," he retorted, then groaned when she laughed and gave him a squeeze, circling the sensitive tip of his cock with her thumb.

The rest of her weapons fell away as he tore open buckles and untied ties. "How many of these damned things are you wearing?"

She laughed. "You should know. You put them on me."

Her laugh ended in a gasp when he finally freed her shirt from her pants and slid one hand beneath it to nudge her lacy bra aside and caress her breast. The pink tip hardened beneath his touch. Her hand on his cock tightened when he delivered a sharp pinch to her nipple.

"I need to be naked," she moaned. "Now."

As much as Ethan wanted her hand to stay right where it was, he wanted her bare flesh against his even more. Breaking her hold, he yanked her shirt over her head and swiftly divested her of the bra beneath.

Her face flushed with pleasure. Her brown eyes glinted with need.

Ethan dropped to his knees and patted one of her shoes.

Heather placed her hands on his shoulders and raised a foot so he could tug off her boot. The other soon hit the floor beside it, as did her ankle socks. His hands seemed too big next to the small button on her pants, but he managed to unfasten it, his knuckles brushing the pale, smooth skin of her stomach. The cargo pants hung low on her hips, leaving her belly button bare. The zipper was so short he wondered why they hadn't just used a second button instead.

Tucking his fingers in the waistband of the pants, he dragged them down her lovely legs. His eyes fastened on the scrap of lace left behind.

It left little to the imagination.

"Your eyes are glowing," she whispered.

"I bet they are." He slowly drew the flimsy material down, remained still long enough for her to step out of them and kick them away, then leaned forward and buried his face in her stomach. As she raked her fingers through his hair, he nudged her legs farther apart, kissed his way down to the dark thatch of curls that tempted him, and delivered a long, slow lick to her clit.

Head falling back, Heather moaned. She clenched her fingers in Ethan's silky hair, gave it a little tug that elicited a masculine moan. His mouth was warm and wet and oh so wicked as he stroked and licked and sucked and toyed with her, driving the pleasure upward until a climax struck, fast and hard.

Her knees buckled.

Ethan rose and caught her before she could sink to the floor, then laid her on the bed.

Limp as a noodle, Heather stared up at him as he shucked his pants and boxers.

Muscles rippled with every movement. So *many* muscles. He was huge. Everywhere.

Her gaze slid to his erection, energy and need igniting within her once more.

Ethan smiled, his eyes glowing a vibrant amber. Tucking his hands beneath her knees, he slid her toward him and braced her feet on the edge of the bed. "I'm not finished with you yet."

"Really?" She arched a brow and sent him a flirty smile. "Perhaps *I'm* not finished with *you*." Sitting up, Heather nudged him back a step, then slid off the bed and sank to her knees in front of him.

If his eyes could get any brighter, they did as he stared down at her.

Heather grasped the cock straining toward her, so large her fingers wouldn't meet when she curled them around the long, hard length. Leaning forward, she delivered a long, slow lick to the velvety tip and circled it with her tongue.

Ethan hissed in a breath, then buried his fingers in her hair. Every muscle in his body flexed and tightened as Heather drew him deeper into her mouth in teasing increments, eventually taking him as deep as she could, and hummed her own pleasure.

"Shit, that feels good," he whispered.

Heather teased him with lips and tongue, eliciting more moans and praise with every stroke and pull and lick. His muscles bunched tighter and tighter as he urged her on. Her own breath grew short as she imagined him driving inside her with every rock of his hips.

Then, suddenly, he swore. Heather glanced up as Ethan drew back.

Reaching down, he lifted her to her feet and spun her around. Excitement rose as he bent her over the bed with rough hands, then found her entrance with his cock and plunged inside her.

Heather cried out. Pure pleasure.

Her hands fisting in the covers, she arched back against him, silently begging for more.

Ethan drove inside her, holding nothing back, the bed rocking and creaking and shifting with each thrust. Then she felt his warm, broad chest brushing her back. Felt his lips burrow through her hair and find her neck.

He slid a hand beneath her, still pounding into her, and clasped her breast.

Heather moaned as his grip tightened, becoming almost painful.

His sharp teeth grazed the soft skin of her neck.

Her breath caught.

He slid his other hand down and teased her clit.

She moaned.

"You like it?" he growled in her ear.

She nodded, unable to speak, her breath coming in gasps that housed moans as the pleasure built and built. The fingers of one hand worked her clit as the other kneaded her breast, pinching the hard tip. His long, hard length hit all the right spots as he continued to thrust into her. Again and again.

"You want more?" he taunted, his voice so deep and gravelly with need, she nearly came at the sound of it.

"Yes," she gasped.

The fingers stroking her clit did something marvelous at preternatural speeds.

Heather cried out as an orgasm careened through her, more

intense than any she had ever experienced before. On and on and on it went. Stealing her breath. Her body clamping down around Ethan's and squeezing him tight as ripples of pleasure struck.

Stiffening above her, Ethan shouted with his own release, his grip on her tightening until she thought she would have bruises the next day. But damn, it felt good. Unbelievably good. Those ripples of pleasure still rocked her.

Collapsing on top of her, Ethan shifted his hands to the bed on either side of her and supported the bulk of his weight on his forearms. He lowered his face to the covers beside her. His warm, short breaths fanned her hair. Those brilliant amber eyes met hers. "Did I hurt you?"

Heather shook her head and curled one hand over his, still trying to catch her breath.

Ethan kissed the back of her hand, then rose.

Heather moaned when he withdrew from her body, then frowned when he chuckled. "What?" she asked, forcing herself to straighten and stand on wobbly legs.

Grinning, he motioned to the huge, heavy bed.

Looking down, she laughed. They'd moved it two or three feet across the floor. "You're good," she said.

"You're the best," he murmured and dipped his head to claim her lips in a kiss full of affection. "Want to see if we can move it a few more feet?"

Heather grinned. "Seriously?"

He nodded, his smile so boyish and appealing that she had to steal another kiss. "Being an immortal has a lot of perks," he murmured.

As Heather became aware of the growing erection prodding her stomach, she smiled. "I think I'm going to like these perks."

* * *

Heather couldn't seem to stop smiling. She and Ethan had spent the night and most of the morning making love. Each time seemed to have meant more than the last, bringing them closer and closer together. And he was a cuddler. How awesome was that? Even now, he dozed with his body curled around hers, one arm forming her pillow, the other wrapped around her.

A knock on the door made her jump.

Ethan swore and rolled away. Slipping from the bed, he strode naked to the door.

Heather watched with both pleasure (the man's ass was just too attractive) and amusement, wondering if he intended to flash whoever was out in the hallway.

He opened the door enough to reveal his tousled head and bare chest, but kept the rest of himself behind the door. "What?"

"Put this on," Tracy said, out of sight, "and come upstairs in half an hour. Don't ask any questions. Just do it."

Ethan took something from her and closed the door. Turning to Heather, he frowned and held up a hanging clothing bag.

"What's that?" she asked.

"I have no idea."

"Maybe it's new hunting clothes." Tossing back the covers, Heather rose and padded over to him.

His eyes acquired a familiar amber glow as they roved her bare body. "It's too early to hunt. The sun won't set for several hours yet."

Laughing, she shook her head. "How can you still be turned on when we just made love I don't know how many times?"

He smiled. "You just push my buttons, beautiful."

She winked. "Push them and stroke them and—"

"Enough!" He laughed. "Or we won't find out what this is about."

Heather grasped the zipper on the bag and drew it down.

"It's a suit," she told him, puzzled. "And a dress. I think there are even shoes in the bottom." She rummaged around. "Yep. There are shoes." She drew out the dress, far fancier than anything she had ever owned. Not that she usually went places that required formal dress. "What do you suppose this is for?"

"If it means I get to see you in that dress, I don't care."

She grinned. "I wouldn't mind seeing you in that suit either."

"Let's do this then."

Fortunately, they had showered a couple of hours earlier before they had finally drifted off to sleep. So all Heather had to do was don the clothing and see if she could tame her hair.

The dress fit perfectly. Clinging to her from breasts to hips, it flared out into a looser skirt. Spaghetti straps left her shoulders and arms bare. The neckline dipped low, exposing more cleavage than she was accustomed to showing. Heather wasn't sure it suited her until she saw Ethan's reaction.

His eyes lit up like candles as he gave her a long, slow once-over.

She grinned. "Just like a mood ring."

"You look beautiful. As always."

"Thank you. You look *hot*."

The suit fit his large, muscular form as though it had been tailored to him. Silver pinstripes adorned black material whose quality, she suspected, was of the you'll-never-be-able-to-afford-this variety. A bright white shirt provided nice contrast to his naturally tan features. He had even shaved, she noticed, as he lifted his chin and reached up to adjust a black necktie.

"I mean, you look *really* hot," she repeated, straightening it for him.

His face brightened with a teasing grin. "So I clean up well?"

"Definitely."

He seemed genuinely pleased by the compliment. "Let me help you with your shoes."

Warmth filled her when he grabbed the high-heeled shoes and knelt in front of her.

Was this what it felt like to be a married couple? she wondered. Taking pleasure in even something as mundane as getting dressed together?

He guided one of her feet into the first shoe, then did the same with the other, as if he were Prince Charming and she Cinderella. Sitting back on his heels, he frowned at the sexy pumps. "How the hell do you walk in those things?"

"I may not be able to," she said with a wry smile. "It's been a while." She took a few cautious steps toward the door and back, feeling wobbly as hell. Then her legs and ankles seemed to say, *Oh yeah, I remember this crap*, and she found her stride. "Just like riding a bike."

Ethan rose, shaking his head. "I'm glad I'm not a woman."

She winked. "I am, too."

Chuckling, he slipped his own dress shoes on, then offered her his arm. "Shall we?"

She looped her arm through his. "We shall."

When they stepped out into the hallway, they found Zach and Lisette doing the same. The other couple was dressed as formally as Heather and Ethan.

Zach looked handsome as hell, but kept shifting his shoulders and reaching up to tug at his tie. Lisette was beautiful. Heather wished *she* were that pretty and glanced up to catch Ethan's response.

Her pulse skipped.

He had barely spared the others a glance. His luminous amber gaze instead continued to devour *her*.

Heather licked her lips.

His eyes brightened.

Forcing herself to look away, she greeted the other couple with a smile. "Anyone know what this is about?"

Lisette shot Zach a squinty-eyed look. "I think Zach does, but he won't tell me."

The elder immortal smiled. "I was enjoying your efforts to tease it out of me too much." In a sultry voice he said, "Please, Zach. If you tell me I'll—"

Lisette clapped a hand over his mouth and flushed bright red.

Heather and Ethan laughed.

Zach removed Lisette's hand from his mouth and pressed a kiss to her palm instead of bending over to reach her mouth.

Heather glanced up at Ethan and thought him the perfect height for her. He was tall, but not tall enough that he would have to pick her up to kiss her properly.

"Ahh," Zach said, "but picking Lisette up always puts her right where I want her—pressed up against me with her legs wrapped around my waist."

Lisette's mouth dropped open. "Zach!"

Heather didn't know whether to laugh or to complain about Zach's having read her thoughts.

Ethan settled a hand on her lower back. "I'm not even going to ask." He guided Heather forward. "Let's go see what's up before Lisette's face gets any redder."

Zach and Lisette held back to let them pass, then followed behind them.

Heather had to take the stairs slowly, unused to climbing them in such high heels.

She loved that Ethan seemed to know it and slid an arm around her for support.

Heart already pounding in her chest, she felt the most wonderful fluttery feeling in her belly, almost as if they were going out on their first . . . date.

She and Ethan stopped short upon exiting the basement stairwell. Down the hallway, Tracy and Sheldon waited for them, both garbed in tuxedos. Two tables, draped in white tablecloths, had been placed close together in the center of the living room. Tall white tapers sported flickering flames that illuminated lovely place settings.

All the other furniture had been moved to the edges of the room.

"What's this?" Lisette asked, pleasure brightening her voice as she and Zach stopped beside Heather.

"I heard what Ethan said about wishing he could court Heather properly," Tracy said, "and know that you and Zach didn't have anything *close* to a normal courtship when the two of you got together, so I thought it would be nice for you guys to have a date night. Or day. Whatever." She grinned. "Sheldon helped me put it all together."

Sheldon saluted them with a grin.

Lisette smiled up at Zach. "Is *that* why you played music all night and wouldn't let me come upstairs for a sandwich? You knew what they were doing?"

He nodded, his lips turning up in a smile. "I heard Tracy call Sheldon and enlist his aid."

Grinning, Lisette hugged him tight. "I love you so much!"

Heather looked up at Ethan, tempted to say the same.

He winked down at her, a soft smile playing about his lips.

Tracy bowed and motioned to the living room. "Your tables await."

Ethan held Heather's chair for her, then seated himself across from her.

Zach did the same for Lisette.

Sheldon approached the table with a white towel over one arm and dramatically poured each a glass of . . .

Heather raised her eyebrows. Sparkling grape juice?

He smiled as he filled her glass. "Alcohol sort of lost its appeal for immortals when they lost the ability to get a buzz from it. The virus doesn't let alcohol affect them at all."

"Oh." That was kind of a bummer.

"I was going to bring you some wine," he said as he straightened, "but figured you'd want to drink whatever they drank. And, honestly, I'm a beer kind of guy. I wouldn't have known what to buy."

She smiled back. "This is fine. Thank you, Sheldon."

Bowing low like an obsequious servant, he backed away and bumped into Zach.

Heather laughed as he straightened with a jerk and spun around.

Zach narrowed his eyes.

Sheldon smiled and shrugged. "Sorry, man."

Heather thought his steps were a little quicker, though, as he headed into the kitchen.

Ethan smiled. "I'm beginning to see why Richart keeps him around."

Lisette nodded and smiled at Heather. "Sheldon is my brother's Second and is a never-ending source of entertainment for us."

"He seems nice," Heather commented.

A groan sounded from the kitchen. "She called me nice," Sheldon complained. "That's the kiss of death to guys. Women want nice guys to be their *friends*, not their lovers." A long moment passed. "I stand corrected," he murmured, his voice deepening.

Lisette laughed, then raised her glass. "To one night of normalcy."

They all toasted and sipped the sparkling juice.

And their double date began.

At first, Ethan and Zach seemed reticent around each other. But Lisette seemed to know just what to say to lure everyone out of their shells. Conversation soon flowed freely, as did laughter. Sheldon helped a lot with the latter, alternately assuming the personas of a stereotypically staid and somber butler and a comically inept waiter.

Ethan was charming and funny and so damned appealing. Heather learned more about his past, his transformation, the century he had spent since then . . . and liked him more with every tidbit he revealed.

As the meal progressed, the certainty that Ethan was *the*

one, that he was everything she had been searching for, grew within her until she thought she might burst with the knowledge. She really did believe she could tell him anything. She felt so at ease with him—as though they had known each other since they were children—and thought they could spend every day for the rest of their lives just talking and would never grow bored or run out of things to say.

Sheldon and Tracy cleared the tables, then returned. Tracy transferred the candles to the fireplace mantel while Sheldon moved the tables to the outer edges of the room. Then Tracy picked up a small black remote and aimed it at the Bose speaker Heather hadn't noticed on the mantel. Soft music swelled.

Tracy smiled as Sheldon stepped up beside her. "We'll be upstairs if you need anything."

Winking, Sheldon followed Tracy out of the room and up the stairs.

Heather turned to face Ethan as Etta James began to sing "At Last."

Performing a gallant bow, he held his hand out to her. "May I have this dance?"

Her heart pounding at the warm affection reflected in his brown eyes, Heather nodded and placed her hand in his. "You may."

He pressed a kiss to her knuckles. Drawing her close until their bodies brushed, he slid an arm around her waist as she placed her free hand on his shoulder. Then they began to sway.

"I don't know how to dance," Heather heard Zach murmur.

"It's easy," Lisette whispered. "Just take me in your arms and let the music guide you."

Heather didn't spare them a glance. She couldn't tear her eyes from Ethan's.

This had to be love, she thought, this unbelievably wonderful feeling that seemed to permeate every cell of her body as she stared up at him and met those beautiful brown eyes.

His arm tightened, urging her closer as brown gave way to luminescent amber. His body hardened against hers, but he made no move to whisk her away to the bedroom. No, he seemed to want nothing more than to hold her, sway to the music, and enjoy the moment.

How she wished she could read his mind and know what he was thinking just then. Know if he was as swept away as she was.

And how she wished this moment would never end.

Chapter Sixteen

Ethan closed his eyes and rested his cheek on Heather's soft hair. He didn't know how long they had been dancing, but Tracy's mp3 player had cycled through several songs. All oldies she must have guessed he and Lisette would appreciate.

The current tune ended.

A big band song came on, drums thumping, trumpets blaring. "Sing, Sing, Sing." Benny Goodman.

Opening his eyes, he lifted his chin. Heather leaned back and looked up at him, her full lips quirking in a smile. They glanced over at Zach and Lisette, who looked equally surprised.

Ethan grinned down at Heather. "May as well go with it." Loosening his hold on her, he spun her away from him, then back again.

Heather laughed and stumbled against him. "This might be a good time to tell you I can't dance."

Tracy and Sheldon jogged into the room. "Sorry! Sorry!" Tracy called over the music. "I forgot that was on the playlist. Sheldon has been teaching me to swing dance."

When she reached for the remote, Ethan stayed her. "No, leave it on. It'll be fun."

Heather arched a brow. "You can swing dance?"

Tracy laughed. "Hell yeah, he can swing dance. So can Lisette. They totally rock!"

Heather grinned and stepped back. "Show me."

Ethan glanced at Lisette, not so sure that was a good idea. Heather didn't know about his past relationship with Lisette. And Zach . . . offered Lisette a resigned smile and shook his head. "Go ahead. I can see you want to."

Grinning, Lisette slipped her high-heeled shoes off and tossed them aside.

The next thing Ethan knew, they were dancing together like they had in the 40s. Ethan had been stationed in Harlem at the time, and Lisette would get Richart to teleport her there on weekends. They'd danced to music by some of the best. Had rubbed elbows with the greatest jazz musicians. And had had one hell of a time, night after night after night.

Lisette laughed as Ethan tossed her over his head, then swung her around his back and caught her on his other side. Sheldon and Tracy joined them and proved to be as schooled in the dance as Ethan and Lisette were.

Ethan spun Lisette away from him, then held his hand out to Heather.

Smiling, she shook her head. "I told you. I can't dance. Not like that."

"Sure you can," he said, wanting her back in his arms. "Take off your shoes."

Resting a hand on Zach's arm, she bent to remove the uncomfortable pumps.

As soon as her feet were bare, Ethan grabbed her hand and drew her onto the makeshift dance floor. "It's easy. Just follow my lead."

From the corner of his eye, he saw Lisette do the same with Zach.

In what seemed a very short time, both Heather and Zach had learned enough of the moves to engage in lively dance. Ethan thought both were naturals, with a great sense of rhythm and a willingness to try anything. Heather shrieked as Ethan flipped her over his shoulder to land smoothly on her feet behind him. A moment later, he lifted her, swung her around his back, then caught her coming around his other side.

Laughter and smiles abounded as the couples danced, especially when Sheldon began to spontaneously shout out 1940s jargon. The temperature in the room rose. Skin began to glisten with perspiration. Ethan hadn't had so much fun in decades.

A phone rang downstairs.

The immortals all stopped dancing.

"What's wrong?" Tracy called over the music.

Ethan grabbed the remote and turned the volume down. "Heather's phone is ringing." He dashed down to the basement to retrieve it, then sped back upstairs.

Sheldon groaned. "Don't answer it. We're having too much fun."

Ethan shook his head and handed it to Heather. "It's probably her father, checking on her. I don't want him to worry. We can crank the music up again in a minute."

Heather took the phone and answered the call. "Hello?"

Ethan smiled. The dancing had left her breathless.

"Heather, baby, are you okay?" Her father's frantic voice came over the line.

Heather's brow furrowed. "Yeah, Dad. I'm fine. What's wrong?"

Ethan heard her father mutter a quick prayer of thanks. "I was afraid . . ."

"Afraid what?" She lowered her voice. "That the immortals had harmed me? I told you, they're good guys, Dad. They—"

"No. I was afraid you might have been attacked by vampires again."

Ethan glanced at the window, surprised to see that the sun had set.

Heather shot him a concerned look. "Why would you think that?"

"Because you said you were attacked the same night vampires struck the base. And it's happening again. I think vampires are attacking another base. No, I *know* they are. It *has* to be vampires."

Ethan took the phone. "General Lane? It's Ethan. What base? What can you tell us?"

Zach closed his eyes.

Seth appeared beside him a moment later.

"It's a class-three prisoner detention facility," the general spoke quickly. "Small. Isolated like the other one. It's location classified. The bases have all been put on high alert, so we knew the moment the attack began."

Seth took the phone from Ethan and addressed the general. "Where are you now?"

"In the building Heather questioned Nick Altomari in."

"Are you alone?"

"Yes."

"Are there surveillance cameras in the room with you?"

"No."

Seth vanished.

Heather bit her lip. "What is he going to do?"

Ethan curled an arm around Heather. "See what he can learn, I guess."

Zach nodded. "This is the break we were hoping for. If the attack is happening as we speak, Seth can learn its location and we can descend upon the vampires in force, take them out, and bring this to an end."

Seth reappeared with the general.

"Dad!"

Some of the color drained from General Lane's face. Teleporting for the first time tended to do that. But the tension that tightened his features relaxed a bit when he saw his daughter. "Heather!" Lunging forward, he drew her into a tight hug. "Are you okay?"

"I'm fine, Dad. Vampires didn't attack me this time."

Zach arched a brow. "Which begs the question why."

Ethan wondered the same thing.

Seth shook his head. "We'll have to worry about that later. The base the vampires are attacking has even tighter security than the other one did."

Sheldon frowned "Seriously?"

General Lane nodded. "There are people who would pay a *lot* of money to break out the prisoners we keep there. Even more money than they would for the bioweapons."

Sheldon's eyes widened. "Who the hell are you holding there?"

"That's classified."

Seth moved forward to touch Ethan's and the general's shoulders. "Zach, bring Lisette, Sheldon, and Tracy to David's place."

The room went black.

David's living room replaced Lisette's.

David, Darnell, Marcus, and Ami played with Adira on the floor. Aidan, Chaahk, and Imhotep were present as well.

Zach appeared with Lisette, Sheldon, and Tracy.

Seth addressed Aidan. "I want all the local immortals here now. Their Seconds, too."

Nodding, Aidan vanished.

The others all stood, Ami with Adira in her arms.

"Darnell," Seth ordered, "call Chris and tell him to send a large contingent of men to guard this house, then call Richart and tell him to teleport Chris here as soon as Chris has made the arrangements."

Darnell drew out his phone and started dialing.

"And, Darnell?" Seth added. "Tell Chris to lock down the

network and let the vampires out to play. I want to cover all bases and don't want to leave the network unguarded."

Darnell nodded and turned away to murmur into his cell phone.

General Lane held on to Heather as the room erupted into activity.

Chaahk and Imhotep raced to the armory in a blur, then returned loaded down with weapons they donned and distributed to various sheaths and loops and pockets.

Aidan reappeared with Roland and Sarah, then vanished again. Bastien, Melanie, and their Second Tanner were with him when he returned. Then he disappeared again. Étienne, Krysta, and their Second Cam popped in with him next. Then Alleck and Linda.

"No," Seth said, before Aidan could disappear again. "Alleck, Linda, we have a situation. I don't expect any trouble at the network, but can't rule anything out."

Ethan frowned. "Do you think the attack on the base is a diversion? Something to draw us away from here?"

Seth shook his head. "I don't know *what* Gershom's plan is."

Linda took a step forward. "Vampires are attacking another base?"

Seth nodded. "I want you and Alleck to guard the network. Darnell is telling Chris to lock it down, then let the vampires out to provide backup."

General Lane frowned. "I thought vampires were the bad guys."

Heather patted his back. "They are, Dad. Most of them anyway, but a few good ones work for the immortals."

Aidan teleported Alleck and Linda away, returning seconds later.

The room began to fill. The mortals, having been up all afternoon taking care of business for their immortals, wore their usual black cargo pants and T-shirts. The immortals' state of dress ranged from hunting gear to hastily donned sweatpants and, in the case of Melanie and Sarah, robes that Ethan suspected concealed bare bodies.

David motioned to the hallway. "Everyone get dressed and arm yourselves." David always kept a substantial supply of clothing in his home for immortals or their Seconds to change into if they dropped by after hunting. Or for emergencies such as this.

All the immortals, except for Ethan, Seth, and David, sped from the room in a blur.

Ethan caught Heather's gaze. "You should change, too. I want you to arm yourself as heavily as the Seconds."

Heather pried herself from her father's embrace. "I'll be back in a minute, Dad. Don't worry. Everything's going to be okay."

Ethan hoped she was right.

Lisette zipped back in and took Heather's hand. "Come on. I'll show you where all the good girly stuff is."

Ethan almost laughed as the women strode from the room. The girly stuff consisted of clothing identical to the males', only in smaller sizes.

Seth rested a hand on David's shoulder. "We shall return shortly. I want to gather as much intel as we can."

The two vanished. Ethan assumed Seth returned to the building from which General Lane had called.

General Lane turned to Ethan and looked him up and down.

Awkwarrrrd.

"So . . . you two were on a date?" the general asked.

"Yes, sir. I was teaching Heather how to swing dance when you called."

His eyebrows shot up. "Heather can dance?"

"She can now," Ethan said with a smile as he began to back away. "Would you excuse me for a moment? I need to change and grab some weapons."

The general nodded.

Ethan shot away in a blur.

In record time, the Immortal Guardians donned hunting gear and piled on the weapons. Katanas. Shoto swords. Broadswords. Short swords. Daggers. Sais. Throwing knives. Throwing stars.

Ethan headed back upstairs with the others, noting the females' absence. Lisette, Melanie, Sarah, and Linda must be waiting for Heather to finish dressing and arming herself at mortal speeds so she wouldn't be left alone. He made a mental note to thank them later.

Darnell waved them all over to the dining room. "Don't forget these, gentlemen," he said, motioning to the tranquilizer guns lined up on the table next to a box full of EpiPen-like autoinjectors that contained the antidote to the only known sedative that affected immortals and vampires. "Make sure you have one of the autoinjectors in every pocket." He handed a tranq gun to Ethan, then one to Roland. "We don't know what weapons these guys will be carrying, so if you see any immortals fall, get them to a teleporter immediately so they can be transferred to the network's infirmary."

General Lane moved closer, giving the tranq guns a look. "What are those?"

Darnell eyed the general. "Until we're confident we can trust you, those are classified."

The general studied Darnell for a moment, then nodded. "Fair enough."

The women entered the room.

"Over here, ladies," Darnell called.

Ethan stared. Heather was decked out in a black T-shirt and black cargo pants with heavy boots. Her hair had been drawn back into a braid like Lisette's, ensuring it wouldn't get in her way during a skirmish. A pair of holstered Glock 18s adorned her thighs. Extra thirty-three-round mags poked out of a couple of pockets. And sheathed knives were strapped to her wrists.

Though small (at least compared to him), she looked like she could totally kick ass.

Why did that turn him on?

Zach greeted Lisette with a kiss and drew her over to the weapons table.

Ethan wished he could greet Heather with a kiss, but her father was watching, damn it.

"How do I look?" Heather asked as she stopped before Ethan and looked up at him.

"Like you can kick ass," he told her with a smile.

She grinned. "I *can* kick ass."

"Yes, I know. It's one of the many things I l-like about you." Hell. He had almost said *love*. It was too soon for that, wasn't it?

General Lane stepped up beside Ethan and cleared his throat.

Ethan sighed and made a mental note to ask Étienne how the hell he dealt with his wife Krysta's parents.

Heather winked at her father. "Bet you never thought you'd see me looking like this."

He shook his head. "You *do* look like you can kick ass."

She laughed.

Seth and David reappeared.

"Okay, gather round," Seth called.

Ethan placed a hand on Heather's back and guided her over to the living room as a circle of warriors and their Seconds formed around the eldest immortals. The other immortal males shifted to allow Ethan to maneuver Heather to the front so she could see. Zach and the other married males did the same with their petite wives.

"I have the location of the base," Seth announced. "The ⸻ k is taking place as we speak. The military doesn't know ⸻ vampires are besieging it. I've shut down the power and the backup power at the building General Lane and the others were using to monitor the situation, have locked it down so no one can enter or exit, and have disrupted their video feed and phone service. David and I buried the memories of everyone we could in the short time we were there to delay a response by America's military. Chris is working on his end to disrupt their information flow and to keep everyone else out of the loop."

General Lane pushed forward to stand beside Ethan. "You can do that?" He looked understandably appalled.

Seth nodded. "I saw the video feed, General. I saw what your men missed in the chaos because their eyes couldn't catch what mine could in the blurs of motion they watched." His gaze roved the immortals. "The vampires are wearing Russian military uniforms."

Curses erupted.

Richart appeared with Chris and Jenna.

Seth met the general's gaze. "You know what will happen if America thinks Russia has attacked two of its bases, don't you?"

General Lane nodded, looking as shaken as his daughter, who had gone pale.

Every mortal in the room paled.

"We need to shut this shit down," Seth told them. "Security at this base is tighter than the other one. It's built like a fucking bunker with most of it underground. Even with their preternatural strength, the vampires are having a hard time getting inside." He looked to General Lane. "Do you have the authority necessary to command the soldiers at that base?"

"Yes."

"Do they know you? Have you been to this base? Interacted with the higher-ups?"

"Yes."

"Then call whoever is in charge there and tell him you're on your way."

He shook his head. "I don't have the number."

"Chris?" Seth said.

Chris pulled a small spiral notebook out his pocket and shouldered his way through the throng. "I got it." Thumbing through the pages, he held the notebook out to General Lane.

A muscle in General Lane's jaw jumped. "How the hell did you get that?"

Chris shrugged. "It's what I do."

"Call it," Seth urged. "Now. We're running out of time."

General Lane drew a cell phone from his uniform pocket and dialed the number Chris showed him.

Heather turned to Ethan as her father spoke to whoever answered. "If my father's going, I'm going."

"The hell you are."

"I'm the reason he's caught up in all this. I—"

"Heather," Seth interrupted, "you're staying here." His tone brooked no argument. He turned back to her father. "General Lane, tell him to step into an empty room that has no surveillance cameras."

The general did so.

Ethan heard complaints and what-the-hells erupt on the other end of the phone.

"He's there," General Lane said.

"All right, let's do this," Seth told the group. "We don't have time to strategize, so just take out as many vampires as you can and tranq the rest. We'll—"

"Seth," Ami cut in.

He broke off, startled by the interruption.

"I should go with you," she said.

"No." He looked to the others. "As I was saying—"

"Seth," Ami interrupted again, louder. "I *have* to go with you. You and Zach may not sense Gershom's presence if
 learned to block you the way Zach has. He could be there
 lose enough for you to capture when you get there,

close enough to *harm* you or the other immortals while you're distracted by the vampires, and you wouldn't even know it. *I* would."

Marcus, who stood behind her, wrapped his arm around her and the baby, drawing her back against him. "It's too dangerous."

"And letting Gershom get away if you have an opportunity to capture him isn't?" she countered.

"She's right," Zach said. When Seth's eyes flashed golden with fury, Zach held up a hand. "I don't like it any more than you do. But this bastard is trying to start fucking World War Three. And you know what Einstein said about World War Three."

David spoke: *"I know not with what weapons World War Three will be fought. But I know that World War Four will be fought with sticks and stones."*

"Exactly," Zach said. "If Gershom is there, we need to catch him and turn him over to the Others. And Ami may be the only one who can sense him."

Ethan still wasn't sure how that worked. One of Ami's alien abilities was being able to recognize the unique energy signature of any person with whom she came into contact. Everyone had one, apparently. And once she learned it, she could always sense that person's presence if they were near. It was how she had known about Zach's clandestine visits to David's home long before Seth had. She had sensed him.

Ethan didn't know how or when she had obtained Gershom's energy signature. But if she knew it, then she really *would* know instantly if he put in an appearance at the base.

"Let me help you end this," she pleaded.

Seth hesitated.

"We're running out of time," David murmured.

Seth gave her an abrupt nod.

Marcus swore.

Ami crossed to Aidan. "Would you take Adira to the network?"

Aidan looked to Seth, then nodded.

"Marcus," Ami said, "get the diaper bag."

Marcus left the room in a blur.

"Should I stay at the network to help guard her?" Aidan asked.

Seth nodded. "Gershom seems to delight in fucking with me. I don't want him anywhere near Adira. If he shows up at the network, bring her here. If he follows you here, teleport her away and keep teleporting, over and over again until you hear from me. Every time you teleport, it will slow him down a little more and make it more difficult for him to find you."

Aidan nodded.

"And take Chaahk or Imhotep with you."

The elder immortals in question looked at each other, then did *rock, paper, scissors*.

Chaahk swore. Imhotep grinned.

"Have fun," Chaahk grumbled and joined Aidan.

Marcus raced past into the kitchen, then entered the living room, carrying a duffel bag and a big-ass diaper bag crammed full of Ethan didn't know what. He looped the straps of both over Aidan's shoulder. "I put milk, juice, and snacks in the diaper bag. This one," he said of the duffel, "contains some of her favorite books and toys."

Both parents hugged and kissed Adira, then handed her over to Aidan.

Aidan clumsily gathered the toddler against his chest. As soon as Chaahk clutched his shoulder, the three vanished.

Darnell crossed to Ami, his arms full of weapons.

She donned them quickly with his aid, all the while ignoring her husband's irate glares.

"Ami," Seth said, holding his hand out, "you're with me."

"Okay."

"Marcus, you, too." As soon as the couple reached his side,

Seth said, "Seconds, be ready. I'll send Aidan, Zach, or Richart for you if things get hairy."

The Seconds stepped back.

Ethan stole a quick kiss from Heather, then urged her to join the other mortals.

"General, step forward," Seth ordered.

General Lane snagged a couple of sidearms from the table, then joined Seth.

That he did so without balking surprised Ethan. Usually those who were most accustomed to *giving* orders weren't so great when their turn came to *take* them.

Marcus slid an arm around Ami, then rested a hand on the general's shoulder.

"Everyone else," Seth said, "grab a shoulder."

Every immortal touched the shoulder of the person on his or her right.

"Zach, be ready to teleport them on my mark."

Zach nodded.

Such would be an incredible exhibition of power. Richart, a mere two centuries old or thereabouts, could only teleport one or two people at a time and grew weary quickly if he had to do so more than once.

"General," Seth said, "is your man still waiting?"

"Yes."

Seth gave no additional warning. He just teleported the four of them away.

The room to which the cell signal guided Seth was bare. Cement walls surrounded them, reinforced with as much heavy steel as those at the network, he suspected, if vampires couldn't breach them. No paint. No furniture. No fixtures of any sort aside from the lone fluorescent bulb overhead.

A shout of surprise erupted from the room's sole occupant. The officer dropped his phone and drew his sidearm.

General Lane leapt forward and threw out a hand. "Hold your fire! Hold your fire!"

The man focused wide eyes on the general's face. "General Lane?"

"Yes. Lower your weapon, Colonel."

The man lowered his weapon and, after two tries with shaking hands, returned it to its holster. "What . . . How did you—?"

"That technology is classified," the general said, all business.

Seth silently applauded the general for finding the perfect thing to say. Unlike the media, soldiers understood that some things needed to remain classified in order to give the military an edge over those they fought. Implying that teleportation was some kind of new hush-hush technology the military was developing had been a stroke of genius.

Chris had been right. General Lane would make a strong ally.

Though the colonel's eyes still bugged and his breathing remained rapid, some of the tension left his stance.

Above, through layers of concrete and steel and soil, Seth could hear rapid gunfire. Screams. Growls and howls of glee as vampires bred chaos and visited their frustration over their inability to breach the compound upon the soldiers trapped outside it.

"Has the compound been breached?" the general asked.

"No, sir. Not yet. But I don't know how much longer it will hold."

That was all Seth needed to hear. He looked at Ami. "Is he here? Do you sense him?"

Ami squeezed her eyes shut as she concentrated on sifting through the many energy signatures on the premises.

The colonel started to speak. "Who—?"

The general cut him off with a motion of his hand.

All waited in silence.

"I don't sense him," she announced, opening her eyes.

"You two stay here and let me know if that changes," Seth ordered. He looked to the general. "If your men should harm them—"

"They won't," General Lane interrupted. "I'll see to it."

Seth nodded and teleported above.

Mayhem. Destruction. A setup not unlike the other base.

Tropical jungle outside fences strewn with razor wire. A sandy moat with craters blown in it from mines the vampires had tripped on their initial approach. A cement wall.

But far fewer structures rose around him, since most of the base lay underground.

Seth was a little surprised by how many human soldiers still lived.

A bullet tore through one shoulder. Seth swore and telepathically summoned Zach, sending him mental images of the base and directing him to the jungle.

Seth drew a katana as a vampire raced past after a fleeing soldier. One swing of the sword swept the vamp's head from his body, which did indeed bear a Russian uniform.

Another bullet struck Seth in the hip as he cut a swath to the wall and, leaping it and the fence beyond, made his way to the jungle.

The Immortal Guardians awaited him there, weapons drawn.

"The vampires haven't breached the base yet," he informed them. "They're satisfied, for the time being, with tormenting the soldiers. Avoid the sandy moat—it's full of mines—and have at 'em. Kill those you must. Tranq the others. Save as many soldiers as you can. I'll bury their memories later."

The immortals' eyes all flashed amber as they shot forward—a sea of black that rose like a tidal wave, swept over the walls, and poured inside.

More screams erupted as vampires began to fall and the rest of them realized *they* were now the ones under attack.

Seth leapt into the fray.

"The ones in black are friendlies," General Lane announced over hidden speakers. "Repeat, the ones in black are friendlies. Do *not* shoot them. They are here to help us."

Exclamations of disbelief filled the night. The soldiers no doubt had noticed the immortals' glowing eyes and fangs. But soldiers were trained to follow orders without question, and follow orders these did, doing their best to restrict their fire to vampires and swearing when they accidentally hit an immortal.

Seth grabbed a vampire that had just knocked a soldier to the ground, intent on disemboweling him. Tossing the vampire up in the air, Seth swung his katana and decapitated the vamp as he fell to the ground. The fallen soldier gaped up at him, fear bright in his eyes.

Seth knew his own likely glowed golden as he fisted a hand in the man's uniform shirt. "Grab your gun."

The soldier scrambled to grab the gun he had dropped.

Seth lifted the soldier and raced in a blur over to a small structure of unknown purpose behind which several other soldiers had hunkered down.

"Don't shoot!" the soldier screamed as his friends all turned their weapons upon them.

As one, they gaped up at Seth.

Seth released the soldier. "Aim for the chest or torso, and once they slow down enough for you to see them more clearly, hit the major arteries."

Drawing his second katana, Seth spun around and buried the blades in two vampires who raced up behind him. The vampires stopped short, then stumbled backward. Blood splattered Seth as his blades flashed again and severed major arteries.

"What the fuck *are* you?" a soldier blurted.

"A friend," Seth said and pointed his sword at the vampires as they gasped their last breath. Bloodstains spread across their Russian Spetsnaz camo uniforms. "*They* are the enemy. Take care to distinguish between the two."

He saw a dozen vampires descend upon Ethan and, without another word, raced toward him, cutting his way through vampires as he went and rescuing what soldiers he could.

Ethan swore as a vampire's blade sank into his side.

A dozen or so had converged upon him at once. Unlike the night he had fought similar numbers on Heather's front porch, he didn't have the house behind him to limit the vampires' attack. He was out in the open here, his back exposed.

As he slashed a vamp's carotid artery, another blade sliced a deep channel across his back. Pain lanced through him.

Ethan spun around to punish the fucker who had cut him and heaved a sigh of relief when Seth took two of the vampires out from behind.

"Thanks." Bolstering his energy, Ethan tore anew into the group crowding him.

With Seth at his back, it didn't take long. Damn, he loved fighting alongside Seth. He didn't often have the privilege of doing so. The eldest of them was all grace and power, his every movement smooth and delivered seemingly without effort. He was what every immortal fighting here tonight aspired to be.

"You've been watching too many chick flicks," Seth muttered, a smile in his voice.

Ethan laughed as the last vampire in the group fell.

"Safe hunting," Seth said and shot away to help Roland and Sarah.

"What the fuck?" a soldier wearing a headset whispered in the base's underground video surveillance room.

Large flat screens adorned three walls. Smaller screens

rested on desks manned by half a dozen soldiers. The action all currently displayed strained credulity.

"This isn't happening," another soldier whispered. "This isn't real. It can't be."

General Lane could only stare as the violence played out before them in high def.

The immortal Marcus and his wife Ami stood by his side. More soldiers had crowded into the room behind them.

Most were too stunned by what took place on the screens to question when and how the hell General Lane and two visitors had managed to join them. And none had seemed to put together that the general's companions were garbed like the glowing-eyed men and women in black who tore vampires apart like tissue paper topside.

General Lane's heart pounded. The vampires and immortals could move so swiftly that, at times, they became a barely discernible blur. Then the motion would cease, and he and the others would see an immortal yank his or her blade from the body of a vampire, then turn to seek another target and blur again.

"They're so fast," someone whispered.

"Shit!" someone in the back shouted. "That one just saved Conner! Did you see that?"

General Lane followed his gaze to a monitor on the left and saw Seth speaking to a small cluster of soldiers. Seth spun around all of a sudden and slew two vampires who attacked him from behind. Then the immortal leader shot away in a blur.

General Lane kept his gaze on Seth, saw him help Ethan and the others, saw him deliver three more soldiers safely to the group. Saw Ethan deliver two as well.

"I don't understand what's happening," someone murmured.

"They're saving our asses is what's happening," another said. "The ones in black are saving our asses."

"Yeah, but what the fuck are they?"

Pounding erupted on the access doors above. General Lane leaned forward to examine one of the smaller monitors and swore. Several vampires had yanked a damned tree up by its roots and were using it as a battering ram to try to break through the heavy doors and reach the men below.

Marcus pointed to the monitor. "Where is this?"

General Lane took an AK-47 from a nearby soldier, then turned to the door and started shouldering his way through the wide-eyed throng. "I'll show you."

"Bring a couple dozen men with us," Marcus ordered as he and his wife followed.

Colonel Colson, the officer who had greeted them upon their arrival, immediately began to issue orders.

Booms echoed down the hallway, a marcato accompaniment to the boots clomping rhythmically on the floor. Heavy doors that would ordinarily withstand the direct hit of a bunker-busting missile began to buckle.

The strength the vampires must be applying to it boggled the mind.

The immortal Marcus planted himself a few yards in front of the doors and turned to face them.

Gasps sounded as the soldiers in their midst got a better look at his attire and finally realized that one of the preternatural beings in black stood in their midst.

Marcus motioned to them. "Put your backs to the walls so they can only come at you from one direction."

When no one moved, General Lane commanded, "Do as he says."

The soldiers parted like the Red Sea and put their backs to the walls.

More heavily armed soldiers from the surveillance room jogged up the hallway and did the same, faces grim with determination.

Marcus accepted their presence with a nod. "Torso shots will slow them down enough for you to hit the major arteries here, here, here, and here." He pointed out all of the major arteries on his own body, then drew short swords. "General Lane, you should consider returning to the—"

"I'm staying here." He wasn't going to ask these soldiers to do anything he wasn't prepared to do himself.

"So be it. But I want you in the back, ready to issue orders should we fall and . . ." He turned to the small woman beside him. "I ask that you take Ami with you and see to her safety."

Ami drew a couple of Glock 18s. "I'm staying here with you. I can see to my own safety, husband. You've seen me in battle before."

"This is different."

She arched a brow. "Different than the two of us standing against and defeating thirty-four vampires?"

"Holy shit," a soldier whispered. "They *are* vampires."

"I'm pretty sure this guy is, too," another responded as Marcus's eyes flashed amber.

Marcus smiled at his petite wife and shook his head. "You always were too stubborn for your own good."

Grinning, she winked up at him. "Like minds."

He laughed and, dipping his head, captured her lips in a long, hot kiss.

Eyebrows shot up as soldiers exchanged looks.

Another loud thunk thundered through the hallway, followed by a groan as the doors buckled a little more beneath the pounding.

Marcus ended the kiss. "General Lane, I still want you in the back. You're too valuable to lose."

General Lane didn't know what that meant and sure as hell didn't like that Marcus made it sound as though these men's lives were somehow worth less than his own.

Do it. Seth spoke in General Lane's head. *You're the only one here who is certain we are friend and not foe. If you fall, your men may decide to disregard your orders. Trust me when*

I say you won't like what will happen to them if they start targeting my Immortal Guardians.

Though it grated, General Lane sought a position at the back of the long line of soldiers.

Marcus swiveled to face the doors, his feet braced a shoulder's width apart, short swords clutched in his hands, shoulders relaxed as though he had done this a thousand times.

And perhaps he had.

His wife, Ami, put her back to the wall at the head of one line of soldiers and knelt. She reached for a rope looped over her shoulder and removed a one-by-four board, perhaps two feet long, that the general hadn't noticed hung down her back. Six dark stripes adorned it at regular intervals. As General Lane and the other soldiers watched, she set her Glocks on the floor, drew six thirty-three-round magazines from her pockets, and attached them to the board. He frowned. By Velcro? That's what those stripes on the board were? Velcro? And the other side of the Velcro had been glued to the bases of each mag.

When she finished, she had a Glock in each hand and six full magazines standing at attention before her.

She glanced at the soldiers and, noticing their curiosity, shrugged. "For fast and easy reload. Reaching into a pocket takes time I may not be able to afford."

The soldier beside her cleared his throat. "You aren't . . . one of *them*?" His eyes went to Marcus.

"No," she said simply, "but they let me be part of the family anyway."

"Here they come," Marcus warned.

The soldiers all raised their weapons.

Tensions rose as the pounding continued.

Ami gasped.

Marcus jerked his head toward her. "What?"

She looked up at him with wide eyes. "Gershom is here."

Seth appeared beside Ami, startling them all so badly General Lane was surprised no one fired a shot.

Katanas dripping scarlet liquid on the floor, he looked down at the redhead. "Where? Show me."

Rising, she gripped his arm.

The two vanished.

Marcus swore as the first vampire clambered through the doors.

Chapter Seventeen

"Ethan!"

Ethan glanced over and saw Seth, with Ami at his side, motion to a long stairwell that led down to sunken doors.

Vampires gathering there used a huge tree trunk as a battering ram, pounding it over and over into the doors with such force that the trunk began to splinter apart. More vampires approached with a second uprooted tree, tearing away the foliage to hone their weapon.

Ethan looked to Seth. "Is General Lane down there?"

"Yes."

Ethan finished off the vampire in front of him and shot toward the battering-ram vampires. No way in hell would he let anything happen to Heather's father.

From the corner of his eye, he saw Roland and Sarah rush toward the same vampires and guessed that Marcus must be down there, too.

Ethan grunted as a vampire cut him across his middle. Lucky shot, the bastard. Ethan decapitated the vampire and pressed forward.

He, Roland, and Sarah reached the battering-ram vampires just as the doors bent enough to allow vampires to scramble inside, one or two at a time. Ethan and the others did their best to reduce those numbers, but more vampires raced up behind them as word spread that the compound had been breached.

How many damned vampires were there? This had to be the largest vampire army they had ever fought, which—considering recent events—was saying something.

Ethan had no idea how many he had slain. But he incurred so many wounds in the process that his energy began to flag, his movements to slow. He just wasn't as strong as the older immortals present, something that always grated.

Richart and Jenna appeared in the vampires' midst. Then Étienne and Lisette joined the fray.

Several vampires came at Ethan's back. Gritting his teeth against the pain of yet another stab wound, he swung around to face them only to see them fly through the air as though they were mice being tossed by a playful cat.

Imhotep saluted him.

Ethan grinned. "Thanks."

Smiling, the elder turned his blades on the other vampires bearing down on them.

Sean, Bastien, Melanie, and Krysta dove into the skirmish. They must have finally succeeded in wiping out all of the other vampires aboveground.

Seth and Zach were notably absent. But Ethan didn't have time to ponder that as he cut his way to the damaged doors and dove through the hole after the remaining vampires.

Bullets sprayed him. Pain cut through his chest like a knife. Breathing became a struggle as a lung collapsed.

"Hold your fire! Hold your fire!" Heather's father bellowed. "He's friendly!"

And damned if a human soldier didn't dart forward and drag one of Ethan's arms across his shoulders. Helping him to his feet (Ethan hadn't even realized he had sunk to his knees), the soldier guided him to one side.

Ethan let the man take his weight for a moment as the

virus within struggled to reinflate his lung. It succeeded, but the rest of Ethan's wounds ceased healing.

Straightening, he nodded to the soldier. "Thanks. I'm okay now."

The young man—he couldn't have been more than twenty-one years old—gave him a disbelieving once-over.

Ethan laughed, then winced at the pain it caused. "I know. I look like shit. But I can still fight." And fight he did, taking up a position beside Marcus and swinging his swords until the last damned vampire fell.

The human soldiers held their positions, still tucked up against the walls, none sporting injuries as far as Ethan could see.

Silence fell. At least he thought it did. His sensitive ears continued to ring from the loud gunfire even though it had ceased.

"All clear on this side," Roland said outside the door.

"All clear up above, too," Étienne added.

"All clear in here," Marcus reported and sheathed his weapons. Turning, he examined Ethan. "You okay?"

Ethan nodded, trying not to wheeze too loudly. "I'm good."

Turning his face up to the ceiling, Marcus bellowed, *"Amiiiiiii!"*

"I'm here!" she called from somewhere above.

Marcus shot through the damaged doors in a blur.

Ethan's weapons hit the floor with a clatter as his grip faltered. Unable to remain standing, he dropped to his knees and sat back on his heels. His head drooped, too heavy to hold up, his chin touching his chest. He heard his fellow immortals moving around outside the doors and tried to muster enough energy to stand and go see how he could help them.

"Hey, man," the young soldier who had helped Ethan earlier said tentatively, "you sure you're okay?"

Weak from blood loss, Ethan nodded.

Heather's father knelt beside him and touched his back. "Get a medic," he ordered someone.

Now that the adrenaline rush had ceased, Ethan could feel every one of the dozens of cuts and gashes and puncture wounds the vampires had inflicted.

"Lie back," General Lane ordered. Without waiting for a response, he eased Ethan onto his back on the floor.

Outside the door, Sarah said, "Roland, where's Seth?"

"I don't know. I don't see him."

"What about Zach?"

"I don't see him either. Why? What's up?"

"Ethan's down," she said.

"I'll heal him."

"You can't. You've lost too much blood."

"Richart!" Roland called. His ears must be ringing, too. He was talking a little louder than he normally would, as were all of the other immortals.

"Yeah?" Richart responded from a distance.

"Teleport to David's, infuse yourself, then bring Ed and some of the Seconds back with you, along with a goodly supply of blood! Ethan's down!" Roland stepped through the hole in the doors just as General Lane tore Ethan's shirt open to examine his wounds.

Gasps sounded.

Oh, come on, Ethan thought. *It can't be that bad.*

Based on Roland's grim expression as he knelt beside the general, it could. "How the hell did you manage to stay on your feet?" the dour immortal growled.

Ethan couldn't even manifest a shrug. And his head spun too much to shake it.

Shouldering the general aside, Roland rested a slick, ruby-soaked palm on Ethan's chest.

Heat flowed into Ethan, easing the pain as Roland healed the worst of the wounds: those in Ethan's chest and abdomen.

Soldiers crowded closer, whispering words of awe. A few crossed themselves.

Sarah clambered through the doors and caught Roland just as he began to sag to one side.

"Damn it," she said, cradling her husband's upper body in her arms and running a blood-streaked hand tenderly across his hair, "I told you you'd lost too much blood to heal him."

"Ethan!" Ed shouted outside.

"Down here, Ed!" Sarah yelled back.

Ed scrambled through the hole in the door, pulling a cooler in after him.

Sarah looked to the general. "Could we get some privacy, General?"

General Lane looked to the soldiers. "Turn your backs and form a wall."

The soldiers instantly did as bidden, standing shoulder to shoulder a few rows deep with their backs to them.

General Lane looked up at the camera attached to the ceiling near the doors. "Shut off the video feed!"

The red light on the camera went dark.

"Okay," he said. "Go ahead."

Ed knelt beside Ethan and opened the cooler.

Ethan thought the general's face lost a little color when Ed started lifting out bags of blood and distributing them to the immortals.

His eyes on Heather's father, Ethan raised the bag to his lips and sank his fangs into it, letting them siphon the blood into his veins. He was so depleted that he barely felt a difference after one bag, making him wonder just how much blood he had lost. Strength *did* flood Ethan's limbs, however, with further infusions, drawing a sigh of relief from him.

Sitting up, he looked to the doors as Lisette and David entered.

"Where's Seth?" Ethan asked.

Lisette swallowed. "We don't know. He and Zach disappeared after Ami showed them where to find Gershom."

A spark of worry flared. Both Seth and Zach could communicate telepathically over long distances. Surely they would have kept David and Lisette informed if they could.

"You've had no word from them at all?" he asked.

"None," David admitted, face grim.

Heather paced David's living room, unable to sit still.

An hour earlier, Richart had appeared out of nowhere, his face and form splattered with blood, and announced that Ethan was down. After ordering Ed to bring as much blood as he could carry, he had then teleported them both away. A moment later, he had returned for Tracy and Sheldon, then disappeared again.

"Ethan is okay, Heather," Darnell assured her. "We would've heard by now if he wasn't."

He and the rest of the Seconds clustered around laptops, helping Chris and the network monitor the fallout, keeping an eye on the Internet to make sure none of the soldiers at the base tried to upload images or video to YouTube, Instagram, and similar sites.

Heather's worry didn't lessen. "Is there anything I can do to help?" she asked, tucking her hands in her pockets. "The waiting is driving me crazy."

Tanner, a tall blond who was so neat and tidy he looked like an accountant, entered from the hallway. "Would you like to help me get things ready for the immortals' return?"

"Okay." She thought Tanner might be Bastien's Second.

Tanner guided her over to the dining room table, where they collected the leftover autoinjectors and returned them to a room he called the Armory.

Heather's jaw dropped. *Geez, it's a good thing the ATF doesn't know about this place.*

The extent of the weapons stored there—so many that

there were plenty left behind even with the immortals out and armed for bear—made her stare so long her eyes dried out.

Tanner laughed. "I know, right? I had the same reaction the first time I saw it."

Heather closed her gaping mouth and helped him put away the autoinjectors. "How exactly did you manage to buy so much without . . ."

"Triggering any government agency red flags?"

She nodded.

"Chris Reordon."

Heather began to think that, even though he was human, Chris Reordon might just be as scary and intimidating as the immortals. That man had his hands in *everything*.

Once they had tucked away the autoinjectors, she and Tanner returned the handful of tranq guns and other weapons that had been left behind where they belonged. They then piled neatly folded towels on the dining room table and added bowls of fruit, along with a couple of platters heaped with dozens of sandwiches they prepared together.

"Judging by Richart's appearance," Heather broached hesitantly, "the battle was . . . pretty grisly. I don't understand how they can eat after that."

"It isn't because they aren't affected by it or have become desensitized to it over the centuries," Tanner responded. "It's just the way their bodies work. They burn through calories and energy faster than we do, particularly when fighting, so they're always ravenously hungry after a battle." He grinned. "Especially Lisette."

Heather wrinkled her nose. "But won't they be covered in blood?"

"Yeah. After a battle this size, they'll pretty much look as if they went swimming in a vat of it. But they can shower it off and be back up here, ready to eat, in seconds. The towels are for their hair. None of them will take the time to dry it."

Heather applauded Tanner for thinking of everything the immortals would need upon their return, things she would have never thought of herself. But at the same time, she thought it sad that the powerful men and women had been through nights like this so often that he *would* know what they would need afterward.

Theirs was a dark and dangerous world. So contrary to the afternoon she had shared with Ethan, Lisette, Zach, Tracy, and Sheldon. The romantic dinner. The dancing. The laughter.

As she waited for Ethan to return, Heather vowed to give him many more days and nights like that in the future.

Richart and Ethan suddenly appeared.

Heather jumped. Her heart lodged itself in her throat when she saw the blood that coated Ethan and how many cuts and tears and bullet holes his clothing sported.

Tears burned the backs of her eyes as she hurried forward.

Ethan took a quick step back and raised his hands. "Let me get cleaned up first."

Stopping short, she nodded.

Ethan dashed out of the room.

Richart vanished.

Heather crossed her arms and turned to face the others.

The tapping of computer keys ceased as they all leaned back, faces grim, and waited.

Ethan returned in an amazingly short time. His fresh clothing bore a few damp patches, indicating that he hadn't taken the time to dry off properly. His hair looked as though he had just finger-combed it and slicked it back.

But he appeared undamaged, she was relieved to see. Undamaged and beyond weary.

As soon as he opened his arms, she rushed into them and hugged him tight.

"Are you okay?" she whispered.

"I'm fine. Your dad is, too." His arms tightened. "I can't

stay. I just knew you would be worried and wanted to reassure you."

"I *was* worried," she admitted, not wanting to let him go. But cold water drip-drip-dripped from his hair onto hers.

Stepping back, she reached for one of the towels on the dining table.

"Thank you." Ethan produced a tired smile as he took the towel and dried his hair.

Darnell stood. "The other immortals?"

The rest of the Seconds stood.

"All good," Ethan assured them. "Except for Seth and Zach. Gershom put in an appearance. I didn't see him myself. But Ami said he was there and showed Seth where. Both Seth and Zach took off after him, and . . . we haven't heard anything from them since."

"Has David?" Darnell asked with a frown.

"No."

"What about Ami?"

"She hasn't heard anything either. Richart is taking her and Marcus to the network to be with Adira and will have Aidan help him start teleporting the other immortals here."

"What about Lisette?" Tanner asked. "I thought she and Zach were pretty much always in contact telepathically."

Ethan shook his head, lips tight. "She tried contacting him and got no response."

"How's she holding up?"

"She's worried as hell. We all are."

"What's the body count at the base?" Darnell asked.

"I don't know yet, but it's high." Ethan looked at Heather. "Your father and David are on the phone right now, talking with Chris, trying to help him concoct a cover story the military and government will accept."

Her dad was helping them? Working with them? What an incredible relief.

"Chris has conferenced in the heads of all the Russian

branches of the network," Ethan went on, glancing at the others. "Every one of the vampires wore a Russian uniform."

Somber silence.

"Were they really Russian?" Darnell asked.

Ethan sighed. "I don't know, but whatever they spoke sounded Russian to me."

Heather didn't know how they could keep something so huge—so international—like this from hitting the news. "What about the other soldiers at the base? How are they handling it?"

"As well as can be expected. They saw us save enough of their buddies that they're cooperating and seem to be accepting us. David is having the toughest time of it, I think. He's being pulled in three directions and has to divide his time between helping Chris, listening to the soldiers' thoughts for anything that might bring more trouble, and listening for Seth. Lisette and Imhotep are helping him, but he has his hands full."

Ethan tossed his damp towel over a chair and gave Heather a look of regret. "I'm going to head back and see what I can do to help. Your dad and the other soldiers seem more comfortable around me, so . . ."

Heather didn't want him to go. She wanted to hug him tightly for at least twenty-four hours straight to assure herself he was really okay. But she understood duty. One couldn't have a father in the army without learning that very quickly.

Turning to the table, she grabbed a towel and tucked some sandwiches into it. "Here."

Ethan took it, a genuine smile dawning at last. "Thank you." Leaning down, he pressed a quick, hard kiss to her lips.

Richart appeared, Jenna in tow. Aidan appeared beside them a moment later with Étienne and Krysta. All but Aidan were coated in blood and looked exhausted.

Richart eyed Ethan. "Ready?"

Ethan nodded.

Aidan stopped Richart when the latter took a step toward Ethan. "Go get cleaned up. Infuse yourself. Get something to eat. I've got this."

Richart nodded, curling an arm around his wife. "Thank you."

Aidan crossed to Ethan. "You ready?"

Heather stole another quick kiss before the duo disappeared, and wondered how long it would be before she saw them again.

Ethan checked the clock on his phone, confirming that the sun had risen.

Aidan had teleported all of the immortals save Ethan, David, Lisette, and Imhotep to David's place. According to the latest text from Darnell, most were bunking there for the day.

Ethan glanced at Lisette. Brow furrowed, she conferred with David.

Neither one of them had heard from Seth or Zach. It scared the hell out of Ethan.

Seth must know how concerned they all would be. He wasn't one to ignore that. And Zach sure as hell wouldn't want to worry Lisette. What had happened?

They would all know it, wouldn't they, if something had . . . if the two had been . . . ?

He couldn't even finish the thought. But they would've felt *something*, right?

Unsettled, relieved that Lisette couldn't read his thoughts and the anxiety housed within them, he looked around for a distraction.

Ed, Sheldon, and Tracy had elected to remain at the base and had worked wonders as far as easing the soldiers' fears. Ethan surmised that seeing the human men and women treat the immortals the same way they did each other went a long way toward making the immortals seems less intimidating. The Seconds did a damned fine job, too, of skirting the sol- diers' questions in order to avoid disclosing information David would just have to bury later.

David went quiet and looked toward the ceiling. "The network is here."

Ethan ambled down to the surveillance room, deserted on General Lane's orders, and watched helos arrive and land within the base's walls. A massive cleanup crew disembarked, all the faces unfamiliar to Ethan. Chris Reordon's crew had been too far away, so they had enlisted the aid of the network nearest the island. Ethan recognized the network head who arrived in one of the helicopters. A tall, rugged Latino man, Alejandro bore the same air of authority and command that Chris did.

Aidan suddenly appeared in the men's midst, Chris at his side.

Lucky bastard. Because he was so old, Aidan could with- stand exposure to direct sunlight for a time. Since dark clouds had rolled in with the dawn, Aidan could probably remain outside for a couple of hours or more. And did, teleporting equipment and people in and out at the network leaders' commands.

The two network leaders worked well together. There was no butting of heads. No stepping on toes. No pissing contest. No resentment on either man's part regarding the other's presence the way Ethan expected there would've been had they instead headed different human law enforcement agencies. Ego never came into play, he was pleased to see. Efficiency reigned supreme as the two parties worked together to keep the vampire attack a secret from the rest of the world, to put a plausible cover story into play, and to ensure that the soldiers who had lost their lives would receive the honorable burials they deserved.

Ethan returned to the cafeteria or mess hall in which

everyone in the base, save the prisoners, had gathered. General Lane nodded to Ethan, then ordered the soldiers to turn in and get some much-needed rest.

For the first time, Ethan thought the soldiers would defy the general. Every man present wanted to stay and ensure their fallen friends were taken care of, the bodies handled with respect.

Then they all yawned and began to weave where they stood.

As one, they shuffled off down a hallway Ethan hadn't explored.

Even General Lane appeared surprised.

"Thank you," David said, looking at Imhotep.

The powerful telepath nodded.

General Lane looked back and forth between them. "What did he do?"

Imhotep answered. "I commanded them to sleep. It will be easier for David to alter their memories if they aren't conscious, and doing it himself would have just taxed him further."

"You really think this will work?" General Lane asked, his expression skeptical.

"It should," David said. "Chris has never failed us."

"So what's the plan?" Ethan asked. He had been so distracted helping Ed and the other Seconds put the soldiers at ease that he had missed it.

"All evidence will point to one of two theories," David said. "A terrorist cell hacked into the mainframes of both this compound and the information hub Seth shut down earlier. On this one, however, they managed to gain control over the utilities as well and sparked several natural gas explosions, killing the soldiers whose lives were lost tonight."

"Who will be blamed?" Ethan asked.

"That has yet to be decided."

"And the second explanation?"

"Hackers attacked the mainframes to prove such weaknesses exist in order to force the government to take action. The gas explosions were a repercussion they neither foresaw nor planned."

"And who will take the fall for *that* one if investigators should pursue that avenue?" Ethan asked.

"Chris has a fall guy in mind. I didn't have time to get the who and why. But I trust his judgment."

As did Ethan.

David turned to Heather's father. "General Lane, would you mind joining the men above? You know more about the military and how they will interpret things than we do, so we would appreciate your input."

The general nodded. "I'll head up there now."

"Ethan, would you go with him and introduce him to Alejandro and the others?"

"Of course."

"Once you've done that, you're free to leave if you wish. Aidan can teleport you to David's. Lisette, you, Ed, Sheldon, and Tracy can leave, too. I'm sure you're all exhausted. Imhotep will stay with me and ensure the soldiers remain asleep while I alter their memories."

Lisette nodded, face grave.

Ethan left the room with General Lane and headed through the labyrinth of hallways toward the only entry/exit. "How are you holding up?" he asked, thinking the general had done well so far.

General Lane cut him a glance. "Better now that I know my daughter's boyfriend won't die from his injuries."

Ethan smiled.

Heather's father arched a brow. "You *are* her boyfriend, aren't you? I saw the way she clung to you before the battle."

"Yes, sir. I'm her boyfriend." At least, he thought he was. He *wanted* to be.

But how odd did it sound to say that, as if they were teenagers embroiled in their first crush and he had just given Heather his letterman jacket?

"We really do appreciate all of your help, General," Ethan said. "I don't think tonight would have gone as well as it did if you hadn't taken control of things down here and backed us up." Ethan had gained a healthy respect for Heather's father. A hell of a lot had been thrown at him in the past forty-eight hours. He had handled it well.

General Lane nodded, his expression troubled. "I can't say I'm comfortable with lying about how the soldiers died tonight."

"I know. But you understand the necessity of it, don't you?"

"Yes." He sighed. "Good men and bad men can be found in every profession. The military is no exception. There are those who, if they learned the truth, would want to jump on the bandwagon and create a vampire army of their own. If they were to learn of immortals, too, and the special gifts you possess . . ." He shook his head, needing to say no more.

Light brightened the end of the corridor, where the two doors had been forced open.

Ethan squinted as they approached it. "You did a good thing, sir, protecting Heather and helping her hide her gift all these years." Just thinking of Heather made Ethan feel warmer inside. "I don't know what the future has in store for us, but . . . thank you for keeping her safe."

General Lane studied him a long moment, then nodded. "Call me Milton."

"Yes, sir," Ethan said, then grimaced. "Sorry. Habit. My mother may have had her hands full raising five boys, but she drummed good manners into every one of us."

They had nearly reached the open doors when General Lane

grabbed Ethan's arm and brought him to a halt. A couple more steps and sunlight, muted by clouds, would embrace them.

"Won't going out in daylight hurt you?" he asked.

"Yes," Ethan admitted. "The clouds will help, but I'll only be able to stay aboveground for a few minutes."

General Lane released his arm and clapped him on the back. "Then let's do this quickly."

Chapter Eighteen

Ethan jerked awake, his heart pounding.

He looked down. Heather slept soundly, curled up against him in bed, her bare flesh soft and warm.

As soon as he had returned to David's, Ethan and Heather had retired to one of the quiet rooms in David's home. He would've preferred to return to Lisette's house, but thought Seth would probably want them to have the protection of David and the other elders.

He glanced around, wondering what had startled him awake.

A sound he would not have heard had he been mortal drew his attention to the door and the doorknob that slowly turned.

Ethan reached for the dagger he had placed on the bedside table.

The door swung inward on silent hinges.

Lisette stood silhouetted in the doorway.

Returning the dagger to the table, Ethan disentangled himself from Heather as carefully as he could and slipped naked from the bed. He snagged a pair of boxer shorts from the chair in the corner and slipped them on as he crossed to the doorway. "What's up?" he whispered.

Lisette entered and closed the door behind her. She wore

a satiny robe, belted at the waist. Her neatly combed hair indicated that she hadn't slept.

As Ethan drew nearer, he noticed tears glistening in her eyes. "Oh shit. What happened? Is it Zach?"

Her lips turned up in a tremulous smile even as moisture spilled over her lashes and down her cheeks. "He's okay," she said, her voice choked. "They both are."

"Are they back?"

She shook her head. "No." Then she burst into tears, sobbing as if her heart were breaking.

Ethan wrapped his arms around her and gathered her close. "Shh. It's okay." He had never seen Lisette cry before. Not even from the pain of severe wounds. He wasn't sure what to do or say. "It's okay. It'll be okay."

Lisette buried her face in his chest, sobbing so hard she couldn't speak.

Ethan drew his hands up and down her back and kept making soft shushing noises that seemed ridiculously inadequate.

"Ethan?" Heather asked.

Maneuvering them around so Lisette's back was to the bed, he peered over her head at Heather.

Heather sat up with a frown and reached for the T-shirt he had discarded earlier. As she hastily drew it over her head and pulled it down to cover her bare body, her gaze flitted from him to Lisette and back again.

Ethan stopped rubbing Lisette's back long enough to hold his arms out, palms facing the ceiling, and mouth, *What do I do?*

She motioned him over to the bed.

"Why don't we sit down for a bit?" he murmured, guiding Lisette over to the bed and sitting beside her on the edge.

"What happened?" Heather whispered, edging forward on her knees and reaching out to touch Lisette's back.

"She must have heard something from Zach. I *think* he and Seth are both okay."

Lisette nodded and eased away from him, wiping her eyes.

Heather jumped out of bed and hurried to the bathroom. A second later, she returned with a roll of toilet paper. "I couldn't find any Kleenex."

Ethan shrugged. "We never catch colds and don't have allergies."

"Lucky you." Folding up some tissue, she handed it to Lisette. "Here."

Thanking her, Lisette dried her eyes and wiped her red nose. "I'm sorry," she said, the words ending on a hiccupped sob. "I've just been so w-worried." Her French accent thickened.

Heather sat on the other side of Lisette and touched her shoulder. "You don't have to apologize. We understand."

Ethan nodded.

"It's just . . ." Lisette shook her head. "Zach's life was so l-lacking in warmth and affection before we met. He said n-now that he's gotten a taste for it, he craves it c-constantly."

Heather nodded and offered Ethan a smile. "I can understand that."

Ethan returned the smile, falling a little more in love with her.

"I don't know w-when it started," Lisette continued, "but Zach gradually became a constant presence in my mind. N-Not necessarily listening to my thoughts, just . . . I don't know . . . being with me."

Ethan couldn't imagine that kind of closeness. To have the person you loved most always with you. To *always* feel their presence inside you. If his mind weren't wired so differently, preventing others from reading his thoughts, he could have had that with Heather.

"I didn't realize how much a part of me he had become until he v-vanished last night," Lisette said, tears welling once more, "and I couldn't feel him anymore. I thought . . . I was afraid it meant . . ."

Heather eased closer and wrapped an arm around her. "But you said he's okay, right?"

Ethan continued to caress Lisette's back in soothing strokes, relieved when she seemed to draw comfort from them both.

Lisette nodded. "He finally spoke to me. Telepathically," she added. "He said he and Seth are chasing Gershom. Apparently, Gershom is doing what Seth told Aidan to do. As soon as he arrives in one place, he teleports to another. He's been at it for hours, and it's taking all their concentration to track him. That's why Zach vanished from my mind."

The fact that the Other was powerful enough to outrun the two eldest immortals this long astounded Ethan. "Do they need blood?" Teleportation took a lot of energy.

Lowering her gaze, Lisette shook her head. "No time. They can't stop long enough for an infusion."

But Ethan sensed there was more to it than that. When Zach had been tortured last year, Lisette had refused to give him blood, believing he might be something more than a *gifted one* infected with the vampiric virus. That he might be an angel. Or a fallen angel. Or *something* along those lines, thanks to his wings.

She hadn't been right, had she?

"Seth knew everyone would be worried," Lisette told them, her breathing finally beginning to calm as the sobs retreated, "and it was distracting him, so he ordered Zach to stop and contact me, let me know they're both okay. Zach was going to contact David, too, then teleport to Seth's latest location and rejoin the hunt."

Ethan considered her words. "Do you think Aidan could help them?"

"No. Even as old as he is, I don't think Aidan could keep up."

"What about the Others?" Heather asked with a frown. "Didn't Seth say the oldest immortals—those like him and Zach—are supposed to be hunting this guy, too? Why are *they* AWOL during all of this?"

Ethan looked to Lisette. "That's a damned good question. Did Zach mention the Others joining the hunt?"

Lisette shook her head. "No."

"Then let's see if David can't send Seth and Zach reinforcements."

David raced through the forest until he was out of earshot of the Immortal Guardians resting in his home. He would have to travel a good five miles to keep Chaahk and Imhotep from hearing him, since those two remained awake and watchful.

The sun's brilliant rays blanketed the evergreens that thrived on his vast property, bouncing from leaf to leaf and winding down to dapple him with light. He felt no pain, though. David could stand outside for hours in the afternoon, particularly if trees like these partially shaded him, before discomfort would make its initial strike.

Closing his eyes, he sent out a summons.

"A little louder next time, perhaps?" a voice drawled.

David opened his eyes and watched Jared, one of the Others, step from the trees across from him. He was garbed as Zach often was: in leather pants and boots and nothing else, leaving his large, dark wings the freedom to carry him wherever he wished.

"Seth and Zach ran into Gershom last night," David said, not bothering with a greeting, "while the latter was busy attempting to start World War Three. They're hunting him as we speak, but he's leading them on quite the chase. Why are you not helping them?"

"We *are* . . . in our own way," Jared responded, all sarcasm gone.

"And how is that? By sitting on your asses and observing the way you usually do?"

Jared's lips tightened. "Tread carefully with me, David."

"I suggest you do the same. I'm a greater threat to you than you know," David advised. "Are you going to help Seth and Zach?" he pressed. "You *do* still wish to avert an apocalypse, don't you?"

"Yes," Jared gritted. He paced away, the wings folded in at his back swishing against the leaves and grass they brushed. "We knew the moment the hunt began. That much energy being expended is impossible to miss." He turned to face David once more. "The simple truth is . . . we can't keep up."

David frowned. "Gershom is that much more powerful than you?"

"Yes."

"Can he match Seth?" David's concern increased tenfold when Jared hesitated.

"Possibly. We aren't sure. But we believe he can at least match Zach."

David shook his head. "Is there nothing you can do to help them?" Hell, no wonder the Others had had no luck capturing the renegade over the past year.

"We've spread ourselves out around the globe and are following the progression of the energy flow," Jared answered. "Hopefully, the hunt will stay close enough for one of us to jump in and hold Gershom until Seth and Zach can arrive and capture him. If one of us *does* manage to latch onto him, he will summon the rest of us and we can all converge upon Gershom together."

"That's a pretty big if," David said.

"Yes. But I'm afraid it's the best we can do right now."

Unable to warn Seth of Gershom's strength without distracting him, David hoped Jared's plan would work.

* * *

Ethan returned to the room he and Heather shared.

Sitting up in bed, Heather channel surfed, her eyes on the flickering screen of the television that hung on the opposite wall. No sound broke the silence, the volume muted. Blue light brightened and faded on her pretty features as the images on the screen changed.

Ethan felt such . . .

Hmm. What *did* he feel upon finding her waiting up for him?

Relief? Gratitude? A sudden warm conviction that he could face *anything* as long as he had Heather at his side?

He closed the door behind him.

Heather glanced over at him. Setting down the remote, she left the television on to light the room for her. "Is she okay?"

Nodding, he crossed to the bed. "She's asleep. I think knowing David is going to do what he can to send Seth and Zach reinforcements helped." He settled himself on the bed beside her and touched his lips to hers. "Thank you."

"For what?"

"For calming her when she was crying. I've never seen her like that and didn't know what to do."

Heather's face lit with a wry smile. "All I did was hand her some tissue. *You're* the one who calmed her."

Ethan shook his head and took Heather's hand. Guilt dawned as he played with her slender fingers. He had yet to tell Heather about his former relationship with Lisette. He hadn't seen a need to at first. Then he had been distracted by the vampire attacks and . . .

He should have told her as soon as they had temporarily moved in with Zach and Lisette. But, damn it, he dreaded her response. Zach had wanted to kill Ethan after Seth had told *him*. Hell, Zach was *still* hostile toward Ethan, although

Ethan thought that had diminished somewhat since Zach had realized Ethan was falling hard for Heather.

And Ethan *was* falling hard.

He hadn't wanted anything to spoil his time with her. Violence had thrown them together. And their feelings had developed so swiftly that he supposed he feared those feelings might be too new to hold up to more conflict.

But he couldn't put off telling her any longer. Heather had just spent half an hour comforting his ex-lover. Wouldn't she want to know that?

He sure as hell would if their roles were reversed.

"You're quiet," she said.

He nodded. "There's something I need to tell you." That was all he managed to get out before words failed him.

"What is it? You can tell me anything," she encouraged with a gentle smile.

"The thing is," he stalled, "I don't know how you're going to react. But *I* would want to know if it were me. And—"

"Is it about my dad?" she interrupted, fear dawning in her expressive face.

"No. No—no. It's nothing like that," he promised. "Your dad is fine."

Her brow smoothed as her smile returned. "Then just tell me."

He drew in a deep breath and hoped he wasn't about to make a colossal mistake. "Lisette and I used to be lovers."

Her expression didn't change. "And?"

He frowned. "What do you mean, and?"

"I mean I already knew that. What's the big secret you want to tell me? Did the two of you have children together?"

"No," he replied, nonplussed. "Immortals can't have children."

"You can't?"

"No."

"Why not, if you don't mind my asking?"

"Immortal males' sperm die almost as soon as we ejaculate, which is why I can't infect you with the virus by having un-protected sex with you. The virus dies with the sperm."

"Geez. I didn't even think of that," she said, sobering. "I'm usually very careful, but figured you were immune to STDs. And it wasn't my fertile time, so . . . I just didn't think of that."

"I would never put you at risk, Heather, would never infect you against your will *or* risk getting you pregnant." Though the image that flashed through his mind of her pregnant with his baby was damned appealing. "Even if I *could* get you pregnant, I wouldn't because we don't know how the virus would affect a fetus or an infant."

"I don't understand. Marcus and Ami have a baby. Adira seems fine."

"That's . . . a long story," Ethan hedged, not wanting to get into the whole Ami-is-an-alien thing just then. "They're a very rare exception."

"Okay." She considered that a moment. "So, what was it you wanted to tell me?"

He frowned. "That was it, that Lisette and I used to be lovers."

"I already knew that."

He shifted on the bed so he could face her. "You did? How?"

She rolled her eyes. "It's pretty obvious, Ethan."

"*How* is it obvious?" he repeated, wondering what had given them away.

"Well, take today, for example," she said and motioned to the closed door. "When Lisette came in crying, you got out of bed naked and she didn't bat an eyelash. Clearly she has seen you naked before. Many times. She was totally comfort-able with it. And you were totally comfortable with her seeing you."

"I put on boxers," he objected.

"When you were halfway to the door. And you didn't even *attempt* to cover your family jewels before you did."

He had thought Heather asleep. "Maybe I'm an exhibitionist."

She arched a brow. "You told me yourself you're old-fashioned. If you weren't, you probably would have stripped naked in front of me the night we met, and asked me to tend *all* of your wounds, not just the one on your back."

He had to laugh at that. "So . . . today made you guess?"

She shook her head, her eyes sparkling with amusement. "No, Zach's obvious hatred of you did. The man radiates jealous fury whenever you're in the same room with Lisette. He goes out of his way to ensure you're never alone with her. And haven't you noticed the way he wraps an arm around her and pulls her close every time you're near?"

He had. But he had thought Zach simply liked touching Lisette as much as Ethan liked touching Heather. "I do the same with you," he said, and drew her attention to their clasped hands. "I love touching you, so I do it every chance I can get. How did you know Zach isn't just doing the same?"

"Because he glares at you when he does it. It didn't take me long to figure out his hatred of you was very personal. The double date just confirmed my suspicions."

"The dinner and dancing?" Ethan asked with some surprise.

She shook her head, her smile carrying a touch of sorrow. "You and Lisette know *everything* about each other, Ethan. And you danced together as if you had done it a million times."

They probably had. "I didn't know it was so obvious," he commented.

She raised one shoulder in a shrug. "Most likely it's only obvious to me and Zach."

Ethan couldn't help but notice she wasn't screaming and shouting at him. "So, you're okay with it?"

She opened her mouth, paused, then closed it. "No. I'm not. But I'm trying very hard to be, because Lisette seems like a nice person. Plus I don't want to be the kind of woman who freaks out if we happen to run into one of your old girl-friends. We're both adults. *You* didn't come to *me* a virgin. And *I* didn't come to *you* a virgin."

"Oh, but you did," he said somberly. "You swore you'd been saving yourself for me. That you had never made love before. Never kissed a man before." He squeezed her hand. "That you had never even held hands with a man before you met me."

Grinning, she patted their clasped hands. "You just keep believing that, honey."

Ethan laughed and pressed a kiss to her knuckles. "I'm sorry I didn't tell you earlier. I just . . ." He didn't want to admit he had been afraid it would turn her away from him.

"I know," she said, seeming to understand. "It's actually probably a good thing that you didn't. If I had known from the beginning that you and Lisette used to be lovers, I would have taken one look at her and run the other way."

"Why?" he asked, but already knew the answer. Knowing someone you were interested in had had lovers before you was one thing. Having to deal with one of those former lovers on a daily basis was another.

"Because she's so beautiful," Heather said, a spark of vulnerability entering her eyes. "I can't compete with that."

His jaw dropped. "You've got to be kidding."

"No."

"Heather, honey, you're gorgeous."

"No, I'm not. Lisette is taller and more slender and—"

"Lisette wasn't the woman I couldn't take my eyes off during our double date. *You* were. And *your* lovely body is the one I couldn't wait to pull closer to me when we danced." He frowned. "Actually I *always* want to pull your beautiful body closer to me. I swear, I haven't spent so many hours of every day with an erection since I was a teenager."

Heather laughed. "Really?"

He drew her attention to the hard length his boxers did little to conceal.

"Oh." Her smile turned wicked for a moment, then faded. "What?"

"Do you still love her?" she asked, looking as though she feared his answer.

"Only as a friend."

"But you loved her as more than that once?"

Ethan considered that. "I thought I did, but . . . I realize now that there was always something missing with her. Something . . . undefinable." He recalled how angry he had been when Lisette had started seeing Zach, the jealousy that had seared him when he had realized Lisette belonged with Zach in a way that she and Ethan had never belonged together. "I didn't realize it at the time, because I *couldn't* define it. Didn't even want to try. I was content with things the way they were. But now that I've found it with you . . . now that I feel that something . . . *extra* . . . something *more* . . . that crucial whatever-the-hell-it-is that makes me think, *Finally* . . . I've *finally* found it . . . I've finally found *her* . . . after all these years . . ." He gave her a little smile and shrugged. "I've finally found *you*. I know I never loved her the way Zach does. I never felt for her what I feel for you."

Heather bit her lip.

Ethan's stomach knotted. "I'm sorry. I didn't say it right. I—"

Leaning forward, she cupped his face in her free hand. "You said it fine."

His heart raced as she touched her lips to his.

Heather sat back and studied Ethan, whose brown eyes now bore a faint amber glow.

"You look troubled," he murmured, his face uncertain.

"Ethan, I want to ask you something," she confessed, already doubting the wisdom of it.

"Okay."

"I feel weird about it, though, because I always sort of cringe when I see women do this in movies and TV shows."

"Now I'm *really* curious. *And* afraid," he joked with an adorable half smile. "Ask away."

Heather drew in a deep breath. "Where exactly do you see this going?"

His brow furrowed. "I'm weary from battle, so my thoughts are coming a little slowly. What do you mean by *this*? Do you mean this conversation?"

"I mean us," she clarified. "Best-case scenario, where do you see us going?"

He stared at her.

The silence stretched.

And with every moment he didn't speak, her stomach twisted into a tighter knot. "Oh. I see."

"I don't think you do. I think I failed to make my point clearly a minute ago."

"Ethan, it's okay," she lied, striving for a lighthearted tone. "You don't have to—"

"Heather," he interrupted.

She clamped her lips shut.

"I didn't answer you because I was afraid you would freak out."

"I won't freak out," she promised, not knowing how else to respond.

"You asked me for the best-case scenario."

She nodded.

"Barring the onset of Armageddon," he said with a tired smile, "the best-case scenario, as far as I'm concerned, is this: You fall in love with me. You ask me to transform you. Then we spend the rest of eternity together."

Heather's heart began to slam against her ribs.

"But as I said, I thought telling you that might freak you out," he continued. "We haven't been together for very long.

And even though I want to spend every minute I can with you and have yet to find anything about you that I don't like—"

"I'm falling in love with you," she blurted.

His lips closed.

"I asked you because I'm falling in love with you." She sighed. "I've never felt so attached to a man before, like I could spend every waking moment with you and never grow tired of you or grow bored or lose interest or run out of things to talk about. I know that may sound a little weird and stalkerish, but—"

Ethan took her hand and pulled her toward him. His lips met hers, silencing her nervous speech.

Her heart beating faster, she drew back. "I'm falling in love with you," she professed again. "I was so afraid for you tonight. It really drove home just how strong my feelings for you have become. If this is just a temporary thing for you—"

"It isn't. Why do you think I keep trying to impress your father?"

Joy and hope rose. "Really?"

He nodded, his face lightening with a grin. "He called me your boyfriend tonight. I think he may actually be starting to like me."

She grinned. "How could he not?"

Ethan preened. "I *am* irresistible, am I not?"

Laughing, Heather shoved him.

Ethan settled back beside her. "Look, our relationship didn't have a conventional beginning. We didn't start off dating. Didn't go through the usual rigmarole of only showing each other our best sides or offering our wittiest conversation to make a good impression. We bared it all from the start . . . figuratively speaking. There was no pretense. We spoke frankly. We liked what we heard. Liked what we saw," he added with a leer that made her chuckle. "We didn't play games. And we got to know each other faster as a result."

"Plus, the whole life-threatening situation thing drew us closer."

He nodded. "You can learn a lot about a person from the way he or she faces death."

A groan escaped her. "I don't even want to know what you learned about me." She had shaken in her boots during every skirmish.

"Are you kidding? I learned that you're brave as hell. A true warrior who—"

She snorted. "I babbled like a maniac the night we met and tried to convince myself I was still asleep."

"Hell, that's better than screaming and running away or crapping your pants."

Another burst of laughter escaped her.

"You could have done either or both . . . as many humans have in the past, I might add. Instead, you stayed when the vampires struck and helped me defeat them. You allowed me to explain who and what I am. You cared for my wounds. And you haven't backed down from a fight since. Do you really not know how much I admire you for that?"

She opened her mouth to protest.

"Although we need to do something about your determination to place yourself between me and danger. Seriously, you have to cut that shit out now, Heather. I want to see where this will go, see if we can make it to that best-case scenario. I can't do that if you die."

She wanted to see if they could reach that best-case scenario, too. "I'll try."

He smiled. "So you aren't worried that things are progressing too quickly for us? I don't want to scare you off, but I haven't done this before and am sort of flying blind and just going on gut instinct."

"It *is* happening fast," she admitted. "But you've been in my dreams and my head for a year now, Ethan. And considering the fact that Gershom has targeted me for who knows what purpose and could kill either one of us at any moment, I'm okay with not taking things slowly."

He waggled his eyebrows. "Think of everything we would've missed if we had."

Heather laughed.

Ethan's corresponding laugh turned into a yawn. Poor guy.

"Still tired from the battle?" she asked, combing her fingers through his mussed hair.

"Yeah. I need to get a few more hours of healing sleep. Think you can join me?"

She nodded. All the worry of the past few days had caught up with her, leaving her as tired as though she had fought in the battle herself.

Scooting down in bed, they drew the covers up and snuggled together. Then, after sharing a tender kiss, they let sleep reclaim them.

Chapter Nineteen

Chris Reordon called a meeting at David's place shortly after sunset.

Holding Heather's hand, Ethan found his seat along with the others.

"There will be no hunting tonight," David announced as soon as everyone was settled.

Eyebrows raised.

"Why?" Ethan asked.

Chris answered. "Because every Second present called me and expressed concern about his or her immortal's safety. They know how distracted you are and worry that it may lead you to make costly mistakes if you hunt vampires as usual."

Ethan looked at Ed.

Ed shrugged, offering no denial.

"What about the vampires?" Krysta asked. "I don't feel right about letting them roam unchecked."

"Nor do I," Chris told her. "So I called in my special ops teams and have stationed snipers on the college campuses, since vampires tend to flock there. All of my men are armed with both tranq guns and automatic weapons."

"I thought humans weren't allowed to hunt vampires," Krysta countered with some confusion.

Ethan knew she had been told as much before her transformation.

"It isn't an ideal solution," David responded. "But Immortal Guardians are the world's most effective weapon against the vampire menace. We must, on occasion, break the rules in order to protect you."

Silence fell, heavy with unspoken concern.

"Has there been no word?" Sarah asked, voice hushed.

David shook his head. "Not since Zach contacted us this afternoon."

Aidan frowned. "Just how powerful *is* Gershom?"

Roland grunted. "Clearly more powerful than we suspected if he has been able to elude Seth for this long." He looked to Chris. "Isn't there anything your techno geeks can do to help Seth and Zach locate him?"

Chris shook his head. "Gershom lives completely off the grid. If he used a cell phone or the Internet or even had a damned bank account, we would have someplace to begin. But . . ."

Sheldon fidgeted. "How long can they keep this up?"

Both Seth and Zach had fought vampires at the military base and had lost quite a bit of blood before beginning the pursuit. Gershom had likely been fresh and at full strength.

"I don't know," David admitted.

Richart's brow furrowed. "I can't believe they've kept it up this long. Teleportation takes an enormous amount of energy. I would've fallen flat on my face after only an hour."

Aidan nodded. "I'm damned near three thousand years old and couldn't have kept it up nearly this long."

Sarah bit her lip. "It just feels like we should be doing something. Like we should be helping them in some way."

David sighed. "At this point—"

Seth and Zach appeared near David's chair. Zach leaned heavily against Seth, his arm draped across Seth's shoulder.

Gasps rippled through the room.

Lisette lunged to her feet.

The two eldest immortals stumbled forward a step, then sank to their knees.

David leapt up and reached Seth just as the Immortal Guardians' leader started to fall backward. Taking Seth by the shoulders, David eased him down onto his back.

Lisette did the same for Zach. "Zach?"

Ethan, Heather, and the others all crowded around.

Both warriors appeared to be in about the same shape wound-wise as they had been the last time Ethan had seen them. So they must have expended so much energy chasing Gershom that their wounds couldn't heal.

Both also appeared to be losing consciousness.

David placed a hand on Seth's chest.

Seth's eyes flew open as he drew in a sharp breath. As color returned to his pallid face, he gave his second in command a grateful look. "Thank you."

David nodded. "Aidan?"

Aidan shouldered his way through the crowd and knelt beside David. "Yes?"

David looked to Lisette. "Release Zach and sit back."

She did as ordered.

David gripped Aidan's wrist, then touched Zach's chest. A moment later, Zach gasped, his eyes opening as color returned to his face.

When David withdrew his hand and released Aidan's wrist, the Celt sagged to one side.

His Second, Brodie, caught him and braced him to keep him upright.

"Sorry," David said with a faint smile. "They were low on

energy and that was the fastest way I could replenish them both."

Ethan thought David looked ready to keel over now, too.

Aidan nodded, his head sagging a bit as if he barely had the strength to hold it up. "You'll have to show me how to do that one day."

"Me, too," Roland added.

Adira began to whimper and squirm in her mother's arms.

"It's okay, sweetie," Ami murmured. "Seth is okay. He's just resting."

Seth held a hand up to Ethan.

Ethan grasped it and tugged until Seth was sitting upright.

Seth nodded his thanks. "Let her come to me, Ami." He even *sounded* tired.

Ami lowered Adira to the floor.

The powerful immortals and their Seconds all parted to let the tiny toddler make her way through them to Seth.

A weary smile touched Seth's lips as she climbed onto his lap and wrapped her chubby little arms around him. "Well," he addressed the throng as he smoothed a large hand over Adira's soft curls, "he got away from us."

Ethan had no idea how to respond to that. Nor did anyone else, judging by the quiet that blanketed the room. Seth was . . . undefeatable. Seth had *always* been undefeatable. How could Gershom possibly be more powerful than him?

Zach sat up with Lisette's aid. "Stop panicking," he drawled. "You're all worrying that Gershom is more powerful than your illustrious leader. Well, he isn't."

Seth nodded. "Gershom knew his destination every time he teleported. We didn't. Whenever we reached a place he had been, we had to mentally trace the tendrils of energy he left behind to determine his next destination, then teleport after him. That took time."

"So he managed to get a little farther ahead of us with each teleport," Zach finished. "The farther ahead of us he got, the more time his energy trail had to fade before we encountered it and the longer it took us to trace it."

Richart studied them both, his face grim. "He must be incredibly strong to teleport so many times and for so many hours."

Zach's lip curled. "He's not as strong as you think."

Seth grunted. "When we followed him to the Himalayas, we found one of the Others down on the ground. Gershom had sensed Teman's presence and popped in behind him. Before Teman knew Gershom was there, Gershom did what you just saw David do. He sucked the energy out of Teman, bolstered his own, then resumed his flight."

David swore. "The Others were supposed to be helping you. Teman was supposed to leap into the fray and hold Gershom until you had time to catch up to him."

"Well, Ami was right. It would seem Gershom has become as adept at shielding his presence as Zach has," Seth told them. "Teman said he didn't have any inkling at all that he was no longer alone until Gershom touched him."

"Then how the hell are we going to catch him?" Roland asked.

Lisette wrapped her arm around Zach and helped him rise. "We'll have to answer that question another day. Right now these two need rest."

Ethan helped Seth stand.

Darnell did the same for David. Brodie helped Aidan.

Ami moved forward to take Adira from Seth.

Lisette caught her brother's gaze. "Can you take Seth and Zach to our place? They'll rest better there."

Richart nodded.

The fact that neither elder teleported there himself, allowing the younger immortal to do it for them, spoke volumes about their current physical state.

Richart teleported Zach and Lisette first.

Ethan kept a hand at Seth's back to steady him. He found

it unsettling to see two such immensely powerful warriors look so exhausted.

And to know that they might not be able to stop whatever Gershom planned.

Ethan reached for Heather's hand and linked his fingers through hers.

A plan that might still, in some way, involve Heather.

A few nights later, Chris circled David's large dining table, handing every man and woman a folder.

Once more, every Immortal Guardian and Second was present.

Appearing fully recovered, Seth sat at one end of the table, David at the other.

"General Lane was able to give us a lead on the vampires who attacked the second military base," Seth informed them.

Opening his folder, Ethan glanced at Heather's father, who had joined them for the meeting. "How's the cover-up going? Is our story holding up?"

He nodded. "Hundreds of hackers try to break into classified government files and systems every day. It was only a matter of time, they're saying, until one succeeded and did some real damage. Those who have been pushing for more funding to combat cyberattacks are having a field day with this."

"Which fall guy did you end up going with?" Ethan asked curiously. "Terrorists or the hacker who did it to prove the weakness existed?"

"Officially, the latter. The powers that be thought it would cause less of a panic if the story ever went public. Thus far, the military has managed to keep both attacks under wraps. But should any media outlets ever get wind of it . . ."

Ethan nodded. "And unofficially?"

"Terrorists. There was simply no way to convince them that the attacks on the two bases were unrelated."

Beside Ethan, Ed frowned. "How exactly have you kept this from going public? Even if our military manages to keep it under wraps, other countries would've seen it with their satellites, wouldn't they?"

"You can thank the network for that," Seth told them. "Network contacts worldwide disrupted the feed of the satellites trained on that location and erased all images that were captured before they could do so."

Damn, Ethan thought. Where the hell would the Immortal Guardians be without the humans who aided them?

Chris motioned to a large image he had propped on an easel. It depicted a satellite image of a string of islands and what appeared to be a large ship several miles offshore. "Thanks to General Lane's intel, we learned that the vampires hitched a ride on this freighter, then ditched it and swam to shore here." He pointed to the island with one of his trusty number two pencils.

Zach frowned. "Did the freighter know what they were carrying?"

"No," Seth responded. "They don't even remember why they swung by the island. The crew's memories of that night have been erased."

"Erased? Not buried?" Étienne asked.

"Erased," Seth confirmed.

"Did the vampires kill anyone onboard?" Lisette asked.

"No. And none of the humans exhibited the symptoms of substantial blood loss that would've indicated the vamps had fed upon them."

"Isn't that . . . odd?" Heather asked, glancing up at Ethan, then at the men and women around the table. "I mean, I didn't think vampires were known for their restraint."

"I assume they were ordered to keep their fangs to themselves," Seth surmised, "so no alarm would be sounded that might alert the base to their approach."

Roland frowned. "They all must have been newly turned to show such restraint."

Ethan agreed.

Chris removed the image of the islands and revealed a satellite image of Asia behind it. "It took some doing—I had to bring damned near every European and Asian network and their contacts into play—but we were able to backtrack the vampires' movements and locate their base or lair."

Ethan frowned. "Why didn't Gershom just teleport them all to the island? Judging by the chase he led Seth and Zach on earlier, he's clearly powerful enough to do so. Why risk the vampires leaving a trail we could follow?"

"I'm wondering the same thing," Chris said, "and worry this may be a trap."

Zach leaned forward, bracing his elbows on the table. "Not necessarily. This is Gershom's first—at least as far as we know it—interaction with vampires. It may be something as simple as him getting off on seeing others jump to do his bidding."

Seth nodded. "We have no idea what has driven him to tamper in mortal affairs in such a way, why he seems hell-bent on watching the world burn."

"Maybe he's fucking crazy," Sheldon suggested.

Seth shrugged. "Or perhaps he has developed a god complex and wants to rule over whoever rises from the ashes of the next world war."

"Like I said," Sheldon muttered, "crazy."

Zach glanced at Seth. "The god complex thing may not be too far off, if that is his particular insanity. He has watched you rule over thousands of immortals and hundreds of thousands of network humans for millennia. Perhaps he thinks it's time he carved out his own piece of the pie."

Seth's brow furrowed. "I wouldn't say I *rule* over them."

Sheldon nodded, his face somber. "Of course not, Your Highness."

Laughter erupted.

Even Seth cracked a smile before he returned his attention to Zach. "Do you really think he's jealous? Of me?"

Zach shrugged. "He does seem to be targeting you, at least in part. He has already fucked with your head once, trying to pit you against your Immortal Guardians. And his actions resulted in the deaths of two immortals. After watching you for all these years, he had to have known what a blow that would be."

A heavy silence fell.

To say that Seth had taken the losses hard would be a gross understatement. Even now, a year later, pain flashed in his eyes, adding a faint golden glow as he looked away.

"Now he's fucking with Heather and Ethan," Zach continued, "for reasons we've yet to discern. He could've sparked an apocalypse in a hundred different ways without involving you and your Immortal Guardians. I think it's safe to assume you're part of his stratagem."

Shit. Ethan had been so busy worrying over what Gershom's plans for Heather were that he hadn't considered what the bastard's plans for Seth might be.

Aidan shifted. "I don't like the sound of that."

Nor did any of the others, Ethan guessed by their expressions.

"We can't afford to lose you, Seth," Aidan continued.

"You won't," Seth announced, then turned to Chris. "Tell them what you've found."

It seemed to take Chris a moment to redirect his thoughts. Knowing how assiduously the network head protected the Immortal Guardians, Ethan guessed Chris had already begun to turn his attention toward protecting Seth.

And how odd was it to think Seth might need protection?

"We followed the surprisingly faint trail of the vampires' travel," he said, distracted at first, then more focused as he proceeded, "and found them holed up in Russia."

Swears erupted.

Chris held up a hand to forestall questions. "Anatoly and the other network heads in Russia have confirmed that neither the Russian government nor the Russian military have any knowledge of the attacks. It took a hell of a lot of work, but we were able to track the vampires to their lair here, near the border of Kazakhstan."

Ethan contemplated the map. "Then they *are* Russian?"

"That's what it looks like," Chris answered. "But as I said, the Russian government and military are *not* part of the operation and aren't even aware that this group attacked two U.S. military bases."

Roland scowled. "Who the hell *are* these vampires, then?"

Seth spoke. "Men who would profit from starting a war between the two superpowers."

"A *nuclear* war?" Tracy sputtered. "Who the hell would win in that?"

Seth smiled grimly. "No one. But Gershom can be very persuasive. And, as many of you immortals have seen in your long lifetimes, getting rich almost always triumphs over doing good. The right things don't seem so right when one can profit far more from doing wrong. The men who raised this covert vampire army for Gershom believe they stand to earn billions from World War Three."

"That's insane," Tanner gritted.

Seth shrugged. "One man's insanity is another man's profit."

"What are we going to do?" Lisette asked, brow furrowing.

"Strike the lair in much the same way we did Shadow River," Seth told her.

Ethan shifted. "Will *we* be striking it or will the immortals stationed in Russia do it?"

"I would prefer that you do it," he answered. "You've more

experience with this particular kind of battle and know the unique challenges it presents. But I will ask some of the immortals in Russia to join us so that they will be prepared if another such group should arise there in the future."

"When do we strike?" Aidan asked. As usual, the Celt seemed to anticipate the battle with peculiar eagerness.

"That depends on you," Seth informed them. "I'd like to move quickly on this. They've attacked two bases in a very short time. I'd like to take them out before they have a chance to attack a third. Would you be up for a fight in the morning?"

All voiced affirmatives.

"Then we'll attack at five a.m. our time and catch them midday. If we strike in daylight, we may have the advantage. Both of their attacks happened at night, so they may not have protective suits like yours."

The vampires Immortal Guardians had fought in the past never had.

Chris seated himself at the table. "Anatoly's network soldiers will back you the way my men did here when you descended upon Shadow River. How many of you speak Russian?"

Several raised a hand.

"Good. You can translate for the others. Seconds, you'll all remain behind. I will, too."

Protests erupted.

When Ed launched several of his own, Ethan winced.

A Second's primary duty was to protect his or her immortal so that immortal would live to fight another day. Surrendering that duty to *anyone* else, let alone a complete stranger, would not sit well with them.

"Anatoly's men can handle it," Chris told them. "And you may be needed here."

Seth held up a hand to silence the angry words. "We still don't know the extent of Gershom's plan. He put in an appearance at the last attack, but that doesn't necessarily mean he will do the same when we strike his vampire army. He may instead choose to handle unfinished business and target those he believes we have left unprotected."

Unease made Ethan's stomach churn as Seth turned his gaze upon Heather.

Heather swallowed. "You think he may come after me?"

"It's a possibility."

General Lane paled. "I can hide her. I can surround her with—"

Seth shook his head. "All Gershom would need to do is read your mind to find her. Once he did, your human soldiers would not even slow him down. Besides, we need you to go to work as usual and keep your eyes and ears open. Alert us to anything the military or other agencies you collaborate with may pick up on. Our network contacts are going to scramble all satellite signals in that area to prevent anyone from viewing the attack, but we can do little if a surveillance drone should happen by."

Ethan took Heather's hand and squeezed it. "So what should we do? How do I keep Heather safe?"

"Stay here. David's home has long been considered off-limits by the Others. Gershom could have fostered mischief here long before now, but has not. Let us see if he will stay true to that. If not, the Seconds and a virtual army of network soldiers will be stationed here to protect Heather. I'd like some immortals to remain behind as well. You, of course, Ethan. Richart and Jenna. Marcus, I want you here to protect Ami and Adira."

"I want to stay behind, too," Roland said, surprising Ethan. "To help Marcus."

Seth shook his head. "We'll need your strength and speed in Russia. Sarah's, too. Bastien, I want you, Melanie, Linda, and Alleck to guard network headquarters. If something goes down there and the vampires have to join the fray, you may be the only ones who can keep them in line."

The two couples nodded.

"I think I should go to Russia with you," Ami inserted, casting her husband a wary look.

Marcus's head snapped around. "Hell no!"

She shook her head helplessly. "I *have* to. I'm the only one who can sense Gershom's presence."

"Absolutely not," Marcus insisted, intractable. "I want you here. No, scratch that. I *don't* want you here. I want you and Adira at the network where you'll be more heavily guarded. The place is a virtual fortress. You'll have me, four other immortals, an assload of humans armed to the teeth, and—if things get bad—the vampires for protection."

"Actually," Chris said with some reluctance, "that may not be such a good idea."

"Why?" Marcus demanded. "It worked before."

"Before," Seth said, "the vampires were eager for a fight to relieve their boredom. Now . . ." He looked to Bastien.

Bastien sighed. "Cliff hasn't been himself since he suffered the break. And his behavior is beginning to affect the other vampires. I don't know if they would be up for a fight."

"Which, again," Chris said, "is why I want the Seconds to remain here at David's, along with the immortals Seth named. I suggest at least one elder immortal be added to the list if you can spare him, Seth, just in case. I know Roland wants to do it, but one who can teleport would be better."

Aidan swore. "I'm going to have to miss the battle again, aren't I?"

Seth sent him an apologetic smile. "I'm afraid so. Now that Zach has pointed out I may be a target, I can't rule out that Gershom may attempt to strike at me personally by attempting to harm my adopted daughter and her child while I'm distracted."

Ami bit her lip. "Seth, I *can't* stay here. If I don't go with you, Gershom could harm you or any of the other immortals and you would have absolutely no warning. You wouldn't even know he was there or see him coming without me there to sense him."

Zach leaned back in his chair. "He put in an appearance at the army base. I think there's good reason to suspect he will do the same in Russia, particularly if he let us find the base on purpose and now waits for us to walk into a trap."

Ethan could see the struggle their arguments precipitated in their leader. Had Seth alone been the one about to walk into a possible trap, he wouldn't have hesitated to insist Ami remain behind. But *his* life wouldn't be the only one on the line.

Marcus's face darkened. "You can't actually be considering it!"

Seth opened his mouth.

But Ami spoke first. "Marcus, honey, you know what Seth means to me." Her gaze encircled the table. "What you *all* mean to me. You're my family now. You rescued me. Took me in. Saved my sanity. Gave me purpose. Gave me a *place* in this world when I couldn't return to my own." She met her husband's distressed eyes. "I can't remain here when we all know Gershom could put in an appearance at the battle like he did last time and strike without anyone even knowing he was there. If something like that happened and he managed to . . ." She shook her head. "How could I live with myself, knowing I could have prevented it?"

Marcus's Adam's apple bobbed up and down. "I can't lose you, Ami," he declared, voice hoarse. "You know what that would do to me."

"You won't lose me," she vowed.

He shook his head. "If I could be there to protect you—"

"You can't. Adira needs you here."

Could there be anything worse, Ethan wondered, than having to choose between the safety—and perhaps the life— of your wife and that of your child?

"Marcus." Seth spoke, drawing the immortal's tormented gaze. "You know I love Ami. If I have to keep her at my side at all times to protect her during the battle, I will. I'll also ensure that more than one teleporter will be present to whisk her away at a moment's notice."

Marcus nodded, but took Ami's hand in a tight grip.

After a long moment, Chris cleared his throat. "Okay. Let's talk strategy."

When the meeting adjourned, Heather and Ethan did their best to reassure her father that all would be well. Heather hoped they didn't lie. After a hug that lasted long enough for her to understand he feared he might lose her, General Lane left.

Heather and Ethan retreated to the room they'd claimed at David's home and made love. Their touch carried an edge of desperation, a hint of good-bye that brought tears to her eyes.

"Don't," Ethan whispered. Cupping her face in his hands, he pressed a kiss to each eyelid and brushed away her tears.

"It feels like we're saying good-bye."

"We aren't. We won the battle at the second base. We'll win the one in Russia, too."

"And if the fight comes here? If *Gershom* comes here?"

"Then we'll win this fight, too," he vowed.

Heather didn't feel so confident. "He keeps tampering with my mind, Ethan."

"I know. But we'll stop him."

"If you don't . . ."

"We will. He isn't going to get near you."

She touched her fingertips to his lips. "I don't want to become a pawn like that doctor at the network."

"Dr. Whetsman?"

She nodded. "I need you to promise me that if Gershom

screws with my head again and I end up trying to hurt any of you, you'll stop me."

"Heather—"

"I mean it. I want you to do whatever you have to do to take me out of the game. Okay?"

A muscle in his jaw twitched.

"Promise me, Ethan. If Gershom made me his puppet and I hurt you or the others like that doctor did Linda, I would never forgive myself."

He sighed. "Fine. I promise . . . to *incapacitate* you, not kill you," he clarified. Then his lips turned up in a wicked smile. "But only if you'll let me kiss it and make it better afterward."

She smiled. "Kiss what?"

"Everything," he said with a leer.

Heather laughed, so glad she had found him. "It's a deal."

He touched his lips to hers in a tender kiss. "Have I told you today that I love you?"

She smiled. "Yes, but I wouldn't mind hearing it again."

"I love you, Heather."

She stroked his strong, stubbled jaw, met his luminescent amber gaze. "I love you, too."

Drawing him down to her once more, she lost herself in the passion that flared between them and pretended—at least for the moment—that the rest of the world didn't exist.

Alas, the time to get ready for battle swiftly arrived.

Heather followed Ethan up to the armory and watched Ed help him pack on the weapons. She couldn't help but stare at some of the other immortals who milled around the huge armory. Those who would fight in Russia wore odd, rubbery suits—like the one Ethan had donned the day Seth had taken her to the base—that fit their muscular forms like a diving suit.

Ready for battle, the immortals began to amble from the room, leaving the Seconds behind to arm themselves.

Ethan rested a hand on the small of Heather's back. "I want you to gear up, too. I want you armed with every weapon you know how to use and as much ammo as you can carry."

She nodded. "Absolutely." She would've insisted upon it had he not mentioned it.

"I'll take care of it," Ed said. "You go ahead with the others."

Ethan hesitated, glancing at Heather.

Ed snorted. "I've been arming your ass for thirty years. You think I can't arm someone half your size? Go. You need to familiarize yourself with where Chris's men are stationed and see if Seth has any last-minute instructions before he and the others leave."

When Ethan lingered, Heather smiled. "Go ahead. I'll be there in a few minutes."

As soon as Ethan left, Ed began to load her up with weapons.

The room emptied as everyone else finished gearing up and wandered out.

Ed cleared his throat. "Listen, if something goes down . . ."

She eyed the gruff Second curiously. Ethan had said the man was in his fifties, but damned if he didn't look thirty.

"I want you to stick close to me. Ethan told me you're good with weapons and fierce in battle. But he also said you have a propensity for trying to sacrifice yourself for him."

She grimaced. "I can't help it. When things get crazy, I forget he's hard to kill and just . . . act."

"Which is why I want you to stick close to me. Ethan has waited a long time to find you, Heather. You make him happy in a way I've never seen him before. I don't want him to lose you." He made an adjustment to her shoulder holster. "How does that feel?"

She rolled her shoulders and shifted around a bit. "Okay."

"What about the extra ammo? Does it restrict your movement?"

It was heavy as hell, weighing down her pockets, but didn't hinder motion. "No."

"Good. Let's go protect our boy."

Chapter Twenty

Ethan spent several minutes roaming the grounds around David's place, familiarizing himself with the many, *many* network special ops soldiers now stationed around the house and throughout David's property. Three even perched upon the rooftop, he noticed as he strode up the walk toward the front door.

Had his vision not been preternaturally sharp, Ethan wouldn't have seen most of them in the darkness. All were cloaked in midnight-hued clothing, their faces blackened with he-didn't-know-what. Their weapons were likewise black and failed to glint in the moonlight. Atop each man's head rested night-vision goggles or monoculars.

The soldiers guarding the front of David's home all nodded a greeting.

"Thank you all for being here," Ethan said, hoping their presence would not be needed. "We appreciate your support."

The man closest to Ethan smiled. "Here's hoping we'll all be bored off our asses."

Ethan clapped him on the shoulder and stepped inside the front door.

Immortals and their Seconds milled around. The mortals

all radiated tension, the immortals seemed as relaxed as though they were heading out to see a movie.

Except for Marcus. Ethan could understand that one's disquiet as he stuck close to his wife and toddler.

Seth strolled into the room from the hallway, accompanied by three men Ethan didn't recognize. Pausing, Seth said something to the trio that was lost amongst the cacophony of other voices. The three men nodded, then vanished.

"Who were they?" Ethan asked Sheldon, who loitered nearby.

"Three of the Russian immortals who will fight today," Sheldon replied.

"They're teleporters?"

"Yeah. Seth wanted to familiarize them with David's home so they can teleport here if the need should arise."

"Ah."

Ed and Heather entered.

Ethan felt his pulse kick into high gear.

Garbed all in black, Heather had tactical knives strapped to her thighs, sidearms in shoulder holsters, and a few small daggers in sheaths on her belt. She also carried a wicked-looking automatic rifle.

Holy shit, she made his blood heat.

Sheldon laughed and shook his head.

"What?" Ethan asked.

"Your eyes are glowing and you look like you want to devour her."

"I do. She's fucking hot."

Catching his words as she approached, Heather grinned. "I take it I pass muster?"

"Hell yes, you do."

Sarah laughed nearby. "You guys get turned on by the craziest things."

"Not really," her husband corrected. "We just adore strong women."

Beside him, Ami hugged little Adira, then handed her over to her husband.

Marcus settled the baby girl on his hip and drew Ami to him for a tight hug.

Ethan thought Marcus looked positively tormented when he let her go.

"Masks on," Seth instructed as Ami crossed to stand at his side.

The immortals who would accompany Seth to Russia— with the exception of David, Zach, Imhotep, and Chaahk— donned the rubbery masks that would protect them from sunlight.

"Everyone ready?" Seth asked.

All responded in the affirmative.

"Then let's do this. Huddle up."

The immortals formed a huddle. An instant later they disappeared.

And the long wait began.

Ethan guided Heather over to a love seat. As she sank down on the comfortable cushions, he settled beside her and wrapped an arm around her shoulders.

The others found seats as well.

Darnell, Chris, and Sheldon manned laptop computers that would keep them apprised of the battle in Russia.

No television helped the others while away the time. No music pulsed through the room. All cell phones and tablets remained tucked away.

No one wanted anything to impede the immortals' ability to hear an enemy's approach.

Even little Adira remained quiet aside from the *ih-eeh-ih-eeh-ih-eeh* sound her rubbery teething ring made as she chewed on it. Her big green eyes studied them somberly while she leaned against her father's chest.

Ethan glanced around. "Where's Aidan?"

"Downstairs," Darnell answered. "He's listening to ensure the escape tunnels won't be breached without our knowledge."

Every basement bedroom boasted a wardrobe with a false back that concealed the entrance of a tunnel that led deep into the evergreen forest that thrived on David's property. Though David's home had never been attacked en masse before, he had wanted to cover all bases just in case and ensure immortals would have a safe avenue of escape—day or night—should the need ever arise.

"Okay," Darnell murmured, staring at his computer screen. "The battle has begun."

Knees bobbed up and down as Darnell, Chris, and Sheldon fed them live insights into the fray. Shoulders tightened as minutes crept past at a snail's pace.

The *ih-eeh-ih-eeh-ih-eeh* noises ground to a halt as Adira's eyelids grew heavy and sleep claimed her.

Marcus rose, cuddling her to his chest. "I'm going to put this one to bed and give Aidan a break."

Sheldon closed his laptop and stood. "We'll come with you." Tucking the laptop under his arm, he reached back and took Tracy's hand.

Tracy rose, and the small group headed down to the basement.

A moment later, Aidan strolled into the living room.

Aidan studied Ethan and Heather.

How he envied them. Envied *him*. Ethan had only been immortal for a century and had already found a *gifted one* he loved and whom he hoped would one day transform for him.

Aidan suspected she would. He had little difficulty reading

her thoughts and knew she was already considering it. Their feelings for each other had hit them both like sledgehammers. Quick, hard, and heavy. Really the only thing holding her back was a deep-seated fear that Gershom had further plans for her and might use her against Ethan and his immortal brethren.

Aidan liked her. She was an honorable woman, willing to sacrifice her own happiness to ensure the welfare of others.

Would he ever find such a woman for himself? A woman who could love him despite the darkness that had crowded him for centuries now? A woman who could alleviate the darkness, perhaps eradicate it entirely? A *gifted one* who would transform for him so he could actually *welcome* the endless stretch of days and nights before him?

A sound reached his ears. Miles away. Too far away for Ethan to hear yet, Ethan being so much younger than Aidan.

Swearing, Aidan rose. "Here they come."

Every man and woman present leapt to his or her feet.

"Who?" Ethan demanded.

"Vampires, by the sounds of it. A hell of a lot of them. Five miles out. Chris, prepare your men."

Aidan teleported to the basement hallway just outside Marcus and Ami's bedroom.

Marcus stepped into the doorway just as Aidan appeared.

Sheldon and Tracy sat in chairs in the bedroom behind him, their eyes on Sheldon's laptop. Both glanced up at Marcus's movement.

"What is it?" Sheldon asked.

"Vampires," Aidan announced and met Marcus's gaze. "Dozens of them. I'm going to take Adira to network headquarters." Striding past Marcus, Aidan crossed to the crib.

"I go where Adira goes," Marcus said, picking up a bulging bag Aidan knew from experience was packed with toys and diapers and whatever the hell else babies needed.

Aidan reached down and carefully lifted the slumbering

toddler into his arms. "No. All is quiet at the network. She'll be safe there. And you're needed here. Badly. You'll understand that in a moment when you hear just how many vampires are headed this way."

Yanking the bag away from Marcus, Aidan teleported to the network's infirmary, the other man's curses ringing in his ears.

Melanie jumped and emitted a startled squeak at his sudden appearance. "Damn it. I'm never going to get used to that."

Bastien, Linda, and Alleck all lounged nearby.

Aidan tossed the diaper bag to Bastien, then turned to Melanie. "David's home is under attack. Too many vampires to count."

Alarm pinching her pretty features, Melanie hurried forward to take Adira.

Bastien frowned as he rose. "Do you want me to go back with you?"

Alleck stood. "I can come, too."

"No," Aidan said. "Stay here and keep your ears open. If anything—*anything*—happens, call me immediately so I can come get Adira. If we allow anyone to harm so much as a hair on that baby's head, Seth will slay us all."

Aidan teleported back to the basement of David's home.

A fist caught him in the jaw as soon as he arrived.

"Take me to my daughter!" Marcus roared.

"She's safe," Aidan gritted and drew his short swords. "As I said, all is quiet there and I told them to call me in an instant if that changes."

Rapid suppressed gunfire—a *lot* of it—disrupted the quiet outside.

"Get your head in the game," Aidan ordered, halting further protest, "and make sure none of those bastards find their way in through the tunnels. I'll help Chris's men outside."

Sheldon and Tracy armed themselves with automatic rifles and joined Marcus out in the hallway.

Aidan teleported outside, appearing between the two soldiers who guarded the front door.

Sensing movement, both men swung around.

Aidan used a telekinetic push to keep them from shooting him.

Recognition lit their features.

"I thought you could use some help," Aidan told them.

Nodding, they turned their weapons back upon the figures swarming toward them over David's lawn and opened fire.

So many vampires. Almost as many as he had slain at Shadow River. How the hell had Gershom raised such a large army without their knowledge?

The human soldiers sprayed the vampires with bullets. Some vampires stopped short and danced backward as the painful projectiles struck them. Others continued to flow forward, weapons glinting in their hands as they bared their fangs and roared with rage and pain.

Aidan gathered his energy and thrust out a hand. A strong telekinetic push yanked weapons from the hands of all the vampires in his line of sight and sent the blades flying into the dense trees behind them.

The vampires stopped and jerked around. Mouths fell open in astonishment.

Aidan took advantage of the lull and swept forward. Bullets struck him as he swung his swords and tore through the vampires. Such could not be avoided short of his ordering the humans to lay down their weapons. He moved faster than their eyes could follow, teleporting from one side of the house to the next, slashing every vamp within reach.

Richart suddenly appeared a few yards away, doing the same. "I've got this side."

Aidan nodded and teleported back to the front of the house.

Jenna darted outside and threw her blades into the mix.

Aidan gritted his teeth as more bullets struck him.

When a few of the network soldiers hesitated, realizing they'd shot him, Aidan sent them all a telepathic message: *Don't worry about shooting me. I'm an elder. I can take it. Just kill as many vampires as you can.*

And he *could* take it . . . to a point. Even three-thousand-year-old immortals had their limits. He swore silently as another bullet tore through one shoulder, and hoped Jenna and Richart would fare better.

Deflecting the blade of one of the vampires who had managed to hang on to his weapon, Aidan swung his short sword in a powerful arc that would remove the vampire's head.

Ethan backed away from the windows. "Go down to the basement," he ordered Heather.

"No. You can't take them all on by yourself."

"I'm not," he assured her as vampires began to crash through the windows and gunfire erupted. "I have a roomful of Seconds to help me."

And they were doing a hell of a job stopping the first vamps inside.

Like Ethan and Heather, the Seconds had backed toward the wall that divided the living room from the kitchen so the vampires would all come at them from the same direction and there would be less risk of shooting each other.

"Ed!" Ethan called.

"Yeah?" his Second returned, his gun spitting as many bullets as the other Seconds'.

Like the network soldiers outside, the Seconds had all attached silencers to their weapons. They really did think of everything. The deafening noise of weapons being fired inside an enclosed space mere feet away would have been as painful as a wound to immortals with preternaturally sharp hearing.

"I want you and Heather to prevent the vampires from getting downstairs. Ed, take the top of the stairs. Heather, take the bottom."

Heather shook her head. "But—"

"Aidan took Adira to the network. But if things get hairy there and he ends up having to bring her back, Marcus will need help protecting her." And Ethan needed Heather farther away from the first wave, damn it. "Just go. I'll be fine."

Reluctance to leave him pinching her features, she nodded and hurried down the hallway.

Ethan breathed a sigh of relief as Ed followed.

Leaping forward, Ethan swung his short swords.

Bastien watched his wife cuddle little Adira to her chest. Every time he saw the two together, regret that they could not have a child of their own inundated him.

The toddler slept on, oblivious to the tension around her.

Alleck and Linda sat nearby, shoulders stiff, ears peeled for any sound that would indicate the network was under attack.

"Bastien?" Melanie said.

When he met her eyes, he found fear rising in them. "What is it?"

"I'm starting to get that feeling," she told him, face full of dread.

He swore.

"What feeling?" Alleck asked.

"The same one I had the night mercenaries bombed the original network headquarters."

The German immortal swore. "You have premonitions?"

Linda paled. "Should we call Aidan?"

Bastien shook his head. "Not yet. Not until we absolutely have to. Adira may be safer here." He motioned to the baby. "Let's take her to Cliff's apartment."

Linda's brow furrowed. "I don't know that Marcus would like that."

"It doesn't matter if he likes it," Bastien replied, his eyes on his wife. "She'll be safer there if something goes down."

Melanie nodded, understanding dawning. "Those rooms are built to prevent vampires from being able to escape. They should serve just as well to keep vampires out." Turning, she headed out into the hallway and down to Cliff's apartment.

Bastien and the others followed.

"Would you swipe my key card for me, honey?" Melanie asked.

"Where is it?"

"Back right pocket." She turned away to give him better access.

A faint smile curled his lips as he slipped the long fingers of one hand into her pocket. "Can I cop a feel while I do it?"

"I was counting on it," she teased.

"Come on, guys," one of the vampires complained from his apartment down the hallway. "I can't take the lovey-dovey stuff today."

Melanie laughed.

Bastien swiped her card and entered the security code for Cliff's apartment.

When a thunk sounded, Bastien pushed the door—as heavy as that on a bank vault—inward.

Melanie entered first, Bastien on her heels.

Cliff waited inside, his face sober. "I don't think this is a good idea."

Bastien's heart ached for him. Ever since his break, the vampire had lived in constant fear that he would hurt those around him again.

"I don't think I should be around the baby," Cliff continued, confirming Bastien's thoughts.

"You won't hurt Adira," Bastien told him with utter confidence.

"Maybe you should drug me," Cliff suggested. "Or maybe I should hang out in Stuart's apartment, just to be safe."

Bastien looked over his shoulder at Linda and Alleck, who hovered in the doorway. "Linda, would you and Alleck open the doors to the other vampires' apartments? It'll save us some much-needed time if something goes down."

The two left.

Bastien crossed to stand close to Cliff, Melanie at his side.

Conversation erupted out in the hallway as the rest of the vampires were freed.

Speaking preternaturally soft so his words wouldn't carry, Bastien said, "I need you here, Cliff. I need you clearheaded."

"But—"

"David's place has been overrun with vampires. If vampires should attack the network, too, it will be up to *us* to keep this baby safe. And you're an exceptional fighter."

Melanie caught his gaze. "Are you sure we shouldn't call Aidan?"

"Aidan will only have two choices if we do: Take Adira to David's place and hope they can keep the vampires from getting to her there or teleport from place to place with her instead and hope Gershom won't catch on and pursue him. Because alone, Aidan will be no match for him."

Melanie swore.

"No vampire should be able to break through that door," Bastien told Cliff. "But if they do, I trust you to take them out."

Swallowing hard, Cliff nodded.

Bastien turned to Melanie. "Let me have the baby."

When Melanie handed the little one over, Bastien awkwardly settled the child against his broad chest. "Grab a box," he told Melanie, "and bring a shitload of tranquilizer guns loaded with darts that will drop a vampire. I don't want you to have to stop and reload, and I don't want you to have to engage any of them in battle. I know you can kick ass, but today you'll have to stick close to the baby, so I don't want vampires getting anywhere near you."

"Okay." Melanie hurried from the room.

Bastien met Cliff's gaze. "Gear up."

Accustomed to following Bastien's orders, the young vampire swiftly donned hunting togs and adorned his body with the many impressive weapons Bastien had purchased for him when Seth had given Cliff permission to hunt.

Chris Reordon would hit the roof if he ever found out Bastien let Cliff keep the weapons in his apartment.

Melanie returned, carrying a banker box full of tranq guns and darts. The hilts of two short swords poked out above the rest. "Just in case," she said.

Bastien nodded his approval. "Put them in the bedroom. Unless the vampires tunnel through fifty feet of soil and use explosives, the only way into that room is through the door."

Melanie nodded and set the box just inside the doorway.

Bastien followed. "Let's put Adira on the floor between the wall and the bed."

Melanie yanked a cover off the bed and spread it on the floor. Then Bastien laid the baby atop it.

Adira rolled onto her side with a sigh.

Bastien stood. "Does she need a blanket?" The baby girl looked so tiny and fragile.

"No, she's fine." Melanie rose.

Bastien slipped his arms around her. "Still have that feeling?"

"Yes. And it's getting stronger."

He pressed a kiss to her lips. "You have Aidan's number?"

"Yes."

"If vampires attack us, I'll do everything I can to keep them on the ground floor. But should any get past me and manage to force their way into this apartment in numbers you and Cliff can't handle, call Aidan."

"I will."

"And if you have even the *slightest* suspicion that Gershom is here, call Aidan immediately. Gershom can teleport, so even the thickest doors and most complex locks won't keep him out if he comes looking for the baby."

"Okay."

"I love you."

"I love you, too. Be careful."

Cliff caught Bastien's gaze. "I'll guard them both with my life."

"I know you will. Thank you." Bastien clasped Cliff's arm and pulled him into a hug. He never knew from day to day when Cliff might reach the point of no return.

Alleck stepped into the doorway. "What should we do with the vampires?"

Bastien strode from the apartment and closed the heavy door. "Todd," he called, heading toward the heavily armed human guards positioned in front of the elevator and the door to the stairwell.

"Yeah?" Todd asked.

"We have reason to believe an attack may be imminent."

The guards all swore.

"I want each of you to give one of your tactical knives to a vampire."

Todd looked at the others and hesitated. "What makes you think an attack is coming?"

"Melanie has a bad feeling. Lest you discount the significance of that, the last time she had a bad feeling, mercenaries bombed the hell out of the original network headquarters."

Every human guard present handed over a tactical knife. Some handed over two while Todd spoke into his walkie and gave the rest of the guards in the large building a heads-up.

"Send all of the elevators up to the first floor, then disable them. I'm going to head up to the lobby."

"Linda and I will head up to sublevel one," Alleck said.

Bastien eyed Linda doubtfully. He had never seen her in action before, so he didn't know how skilled she was with weapons.

"Don't worry," she said, guessing his thoughts. "I've trained as extensively as Melanie has. Alleck and I will do our best to keep any vampires from getting past us."

Bastien nodded and turned back to the human guards. "Melanie and the baby are in Cliff's apartment. The rest of the vampires will stay here and help you guard them."

"Yes, sir."

Surprise struck. Bastien had injured so many of the guards here during his darker days that none of them had ever spoken to him with respect before. It felt . . . good.

Nodding to Alleck and Linda, Bastien dashed up the stairs.

He had almost reached the ground floor when he heard a deep, accented voice say, "Hello, gentlemen."

An alarm blared. Curses erupted.

Bastien burst through the door that led to the lobby in time to see the guards stationed there leap to their feet and raise their weapons.

A man garbed in black pants, boots, and no shirt faced them. Standing perhaps six feet eight inches tall, with midnight hair and glowing golden eyes, he bore dark wings similar to Zach's that spanned the width of the lobby when he spread them.

Oh shit.

The Other's thin lips stretched into a cruel smile as he met Bastien's gaze.

"Gershom," Bastien snarled.

Gershom arched a brow. "So hostile."

"Call Aidan now!" Bastien bellowed, loud enough for Melanie to hear down below, and shot forward, swords drawn.

Gershom tossed something at the guards.

"Grenade!" a guard shouted.

Bastien jerked to a halt and looked back at whatever hit the floor and skidded past him.

It wasn't a single grenade. It was a cluster of them.

Grinning, Gershom disappeared.

Bastien raced over to the grenades, picked them up, and hurled them at the front of the building as the guards ducked behind the massive granite desk they manned.

Light—blindingly bright—flashed as thunder filled Bastien's ears. Shrapnel struck like a thousand knives as flames engulfed him and a wave of energy lifted him off his feet and slammed him against the wall behind the guards.

Bastien dropped to the floor.

Pain crashed through him.

"Shit!" one of the guards shouted.

Bastien tried to sit up, but his limbs were slow to respond. Glancing down, he saw numerous projectiles protruding from his body.

"Here they come!" someone shouted out of Bastien's line of sight.

John Wendleck, one of the guards on duty, helped Bastien sit up. Peering over the desk, he swung back to face Bastien and held out his wrist. "Take my blood."

Bastien shook his head.

"Do it," John urged. "I've never been bitten before, so it won't transform me. And we're about to be overrun."

Bastien sank his fangs into the man's wrists and siphoned as much blood as he dared take into his veins. Almost instantly, the virus began to push the projectiles from his body and flood him with strength.

"Thank you." Grabbing the swords he had dropped, Bastien

rose and faced the enormous hole the grenades had blown in the front of the building.

In the darkness beyond, an army of vampires sped toward them.

Melanie swore when the building's alarm began to blare.

Adira woke with a start and began to cry.

As Melanie hurried over to pick her up, she heard Bastien say Gershom's name, then yell for her to call Aidan.

Cliff swore. Backing toward Melanie, he tightened his hold on his katanas and kept his eyes trained on the door of the apartment.

A thunderous boom shook the building and assaulted their ears as something exploded on the ground floor.

Adira wailed even louder and clung to Melanie while Melanie held the baby with one arm and yanked her cell phone out of her pocket with her free hand.

"Shh. It's okay, honey," she soothed as she dialed. "It's okay."

"Yes," Aidan answered, the clash of weapons loud in the background.

Before Melanie could speak, a man as tall and imposing as Seth appeared just inside the apartment's heavy door. He was garbed much like Zach usually was—black pants, black boots, and nothing else—and radiated power. Large dark wings framed his form as he swept the room with eyes that glowed golden.

Her blood turned to ice.

Gershom.

"Come now!" Melanie cried into the phone.

Aidan instantly appeared beside her. Glimpsing Gershom, he grabbed Adira and vanished.

Gershom tilted his head to one side and regarded Melanie with cold curiosity. "Surely you don't believe you can stop me."

He started to say more, but paused. His eyes shifted to the ceiling, as though something above had drawn his attention.

Heart pounding, Melanie bent and drew the short swords from her box of tranquilizer guns.

Gershom returned his attention to her. "Interesting."

As Cliff rushed forward with a roar of fury, Gershom vanished.

Aidan tugged his coat closed around the baby wailing against his chest and teleported to Telfer, Western Australia.

"It's okay, little one," he murmured as he instantly teleported again to Svalbard, Norway. "It's okay. Uncle Aidan will keep you safe."

He took her to Motuo, China. Then to La Rinconada, Peru. Easter Island. Kosaka, Japan.

He spent mere seconds in each destination before he moved on, fearing Gershom would appear at any moment and try to tear the babe from his arms.

Aidan vowed he would die before he let the Other have her.

In McMurdo, Antarctica, he began to croon a song his mother had sung to him when he was a boy. It took them through Colmar, France. Kiffa, Mauritania. Burano, Italy. Monsanto, Portugal.

The babe ceased weeping in Bibury, England.

Her breath stopped hiccupping in Mombasa, Kenya.

Her little head began to bob with weariness in Meissen, Germany.

She fell asleep in Salta, Argentina.

And still Gershom didn't appear.

Had Melanie and the other immortals found a way to detain him at the network?

Or had Gershom simply opted to stay and wreak havoc there instead?

Aidan didn't know. But he thought it was worth the risk to

return Adira to David's home, where Gershom had not yet put in an appearance . . . as far as he knew.

At least there, Aidan would not have to battle the Other alone if Gershom caught up with him. He feared Adira's fate should such come to pass.

Heather shifted from foot to foot in David's basement, nerves jangling, as the cacophony of battle raged above her. How the hell many vampires were attacking?

At the top of the stairs, Ed fired almost continuously. "Marcus!" he yelled suddenly. "I'm about to be overrun!"

Heather glanced over her shoulder at Marcus.

Marcus looked at Sheldon. "I haven't heard any movement in the tunnels so far, but don't let your guard down."

Sheldon nodded.

Aidan abruptly appeared, Adira in his arms.

Alarm splashed across Marcus's features.

"Gershom is at the network," Aidan said. "And it's under attack. Too many vampires to count."

Marcus dropped his weapons and took the baby, cuddling her close. "Is she—?"

"Adira is fine. I teleported multiple times to throw Gershom off in case he followed me, but I haven't seen or sensed him." Aidan looked to the ceiling, then back at Marcus. "The vampires are about to make their way down here. Give the baby to Tracy, and help me end this so we can better protect Adira if Gershom makes an appearance." He disappeared.

Sheldon looked at Marcus. "Go. We'll keep her safe. I swear it."

Tracy gently pried the sleeping baby from Marcus's arms.

Adira roused, her face scrunching up with a disgruntled frown.

"Marcus!" Ed shouted.

Heather spun around and fired as a vampire made it past Ed and shot down the stairs.

She leapt backward as the vampire tumbled to the bottom of the stairs, hit the floor, and skidded several feet, leaving a trail of blood along the way. As soon as he halted, she hit him in the major arteries.

"I can do this, Marcus," Sheldon said behind her. "I'm not the screwup I was when I first started. I'll protect her. I'll keep her safe."

Another vampire zipped down the stairs in a blur.

Heather fired again until he crumpled at her feet.

Marcus raced past her and swept up the stairs.

In a brief reprieve, Ed rushed down and planted himself at Heather's side. Blood speckled his face and neck. "They were coming at me from too many directions. At least this way they'll—"

Heather fired as a blurred form sped down the stairs toward them.

The vampire hit the floor at their feet, tried to get up, then collapsed.

She looked at Ed.

"Only come at us from one direction," he finished. "Good job."

She nodded, heart slamming against her ribs, then fired again as another vampire made it past Marcus, wherever he was, and rushed them.

The same continued for so long that she and Ed both had to reload more than once.

"Incoming!" Sheldon shouted.

Heather risked a glance over her shoulder and saw two vampires emerge from a bedroom at the far end of the hallway.

"Shit!" Tracy exclaimed. "They found one of the tunnels!"

"I need to help Sheldon," Ed told Heather.

"Go," she said. "I've got this."

Another vampire shot down the stairs toward her.

Heather's gun spat fire.

As the vampire hit the basement floor hard enough to crack his skull, pain shot through Heather's thigh.

She cried out. Her right leg buckled. Hopping on her left leg until she could regain her balance, Heather glanced down.

A dagger stuck out of her thigh.

Ed returned to her side and knelt, lowering his rifle to the floor. "Keep your eyes on those stairs."

Heather gritted her teeth as he examined the wound.

"Good. He missed the femoral artery. Sorry, but this is going to hurt."

Agony sliced through her leg as he yanked out the dagger.

Heather cried out again, tears rising in her eyes.

Another vampire darkened the doorway at the top of the stairs.

She fired, stopping the vampire before he could even start down toward her.

More pain careened through her when Ed wrapped a bandage around her thigh and tied it tight enough to keep pressure on the wound.

Grabbing his rifle, he stood. "You okay?"

She nodded. Damn, it hurt. "Thank you."

He patted her back, then ran down the hallway toward Sheldon and the others.

"Seth!" Tracy spoke loudly. "David's place is under attack. The network is, too." She must have called him on her cell. "If you can spare any . . . She's here in Ami and Marcus's room . . . Okay."

Another vampire sped toward Heather.

Chapter Twenty-One

Ami swung her katanas, opening arteries in vampire after vampire after vampire. Her warm breath formed white clouds on the frigid Russian air that poured through the large hole network soldiers had blown in the front of the building.

She and Seth had planted themselves in front of the opening of what she guessed was a housing building, judging by the number of vampires the two fought.

Roland, Sarah, Étienne, and Krysta had all shot to the rear of the building and steadily worked their way back toward the front, herding whatever vampires they didn't kill toward Seth's and Ami's deadly blades.

Outside, white snow reflected bright sunlight like a mirror.

Nevertheless, vampires continued to rush toward the doors, believing they had a better chance of surviving daylight than they did the warriors who picked them off, one by one.

Ami had long since run out of ammo. The numbers here rivaled those they had fought at Shadow River. Almost all vampires with some humans thrown in. Had the Russian contingent of immortals and network soldiers not aided them, Ami didn't think she, Seth, and the others could have held the vampires off this long.

Barely audible amidst the chorus of cries and racket of

weapons clashing, Skillet's "Monster" sounded. Ami glanced at Seth as he sheathed a sword and retrieved his phone.

"What?" Seth answered, his voice clipped as he continued to combat the vampires racing toward them with one sword.

Ami ducked a vampire's fist and swung. Her blade bit deep into the vamp's arm, severing his brachial artery. Her next swing cut across a vampire's neck. Warm ruby liquid struck her in the face.

"Where's Adira?" Seth asked.

Ami's pounding heart stuttered.

"Help is on the way." He pocketed the phone. "Sascha!"

Had something happened to Marcus?

Please, not Marcus.

Ami's lapse in concentration cost her. A blade cut across her middle. Before she could recover, another blade bit into her thigh.

A large Russian immortal appeared beside her and tore into the vampires who had scored the hits. "What?" he asked Seth in heavily accented English.

"Take Ami to David's. Vampires are attacking. If you're needed there, stay and help them. You can return here as soon as the tide turns."

Sascha didn't hesitate to clutch Ami's shoulder.

Cold, snowy Russia fell away, replaced by the warmth of David's basement.

At the foot of the stairs, Heather fired an automatic rifle at vampires who raced down the stairs toward her. At the other end of the hallway, Sheldon and Ed fired at vampires who poured forth from a bedroom doorway. Roughly in the middle, several yards beyond Ami's bedroom, Tracy fired at any vampires who made it past Sheldon and Ed.

How had vampires found the escape tunnel?

Sascha swore and teleported to Sheldon's side.

Ami ran toward her bedroom, panic almost choking her. Bursting through the doorway, she halted. Relief rushed through her, so strong moisture welled in her eyes. Marcus stood beside the crib, staring down at Adira. Adira stared back up at him with somber green eyes, her favorite teether forgotten in her lap.

"Marcus," Ami breathed and smiled as he turned his head. She strode toward him, tears spilling over her lashes. "When Seth got the call, I was afraid something had happened to you."

He offered her a faint smile. "I'm fine."

She stopped short. Icy fear clawed her.

The man before her looked like Marcus and sounded like Marcus . . . but his energy signature was all wrong. This was *not* her husband.

"Who *are* you?" she forced through cold lips.

He tilted his head. "How did you know I wasn't him?"

Seth! she screamed telepathically, pouring every ounce of energy she had into the cry to try to make it reach him.

Losing his smile, the Marcus impersonator shook his head. "I wish you hadn't done that."

Ami lunged toward him, blades raised, fearing he would hurt Adira.

The man vanished.

Seth appeared beside her, his face stricken. "Is it—?" He gaze slipped past her and fell on the baby. Relief flooded his features. "What happened?"

"Someone was here," she said, hurrying over to the crib. Dropping her swords, she picked up Adira and hugged her close. "One of the Others, I think."

His face darkened with rage. "Gershom was here?"

"No. Someone I've never encountered before. He looked like Marcus. And he sounded like Marcus. But his energy signature was all off."

Zach appeared beside Seth. "What happened?"

"One of the Others was here. Not Gershom, someone else."

Zach gaped. "Are you shitting me? Gershom isn't working alone?"

"Apparently not. Can you trace the one who was here?"

Zach closed his eyes. His brow furrowed. "Yes."

"Then hunt the fucker down," Seth snarled. "When you find him, do whatever you have to to detain him, then summon me."

Face grim, Zach teleported away.

Seth nodded to the baby. "She's okay?"

Ami nodded. "I don't think he hurt her. She wasn't crying or anything."

Marcus appeared in the doorway, face and form blood-spattered.

Ami tightened her hold on Adira and took a quick step back. Then she felt Marcus's familiar energy signature and realized it really *was* her husband this time.

"What happened?" he demanded. "I heard Ami scream."

"She's okay. They both are," Seth assured him, then met Ami's gaze. "Put the babe back in her crib."

She did.

"I must return to Russia," Seth told her. He touched her shoulder. Energy flooded her in such a strong burst she gasped. "Call to me again if you need me. You'll have no difficulty reaching me now."

She nodded.

Tracy backed into view, gun firing.

"You're really okay?" Marcus asked.

Ami nodded.

Tracy glanced over her shoulder. "A little help here?"

Marcus joined the skirmish outside the bedroom.

Ami leaned down and kissed Adira's forehead. Then, retrieving the katanas she had dropped, she planted her feet just inside the doorway and prepared to protect her daughter from anyone and anything that made it past the others.

* * *

Breathing hard, Ethan backed toward the door to the basement. The number of vampires they faced had finally begun to dwindle. A fortunate thing, because he had suffered so many damned wounds that they had stopped healing.

He allowed himself a quick glance down the stairs and saw Heather staring up at him, weapon raised, her face full of determination.

Aidan and the others who were still on their feet had things under control up here. So Ethan zipped down to Heather. "Are you okay?"

She nodded.

He gave her a quick once-over and felt his stomach sink when he saw the bloody bandage wrapped around her thigh. "Your leg—"

"I'm fine. You?"

"Yeah. We've almost . . ." He trailed off as he looked beyond her.

Marcus, Richart, Sheldon, Tracy, Ed, and one of the Russian immortals Ethan had seen with Seth earlier all battled vampires who must have found their way in through at least one of the escape tunnels.

Ethan raced over to Ed's side. "Go help Heather. I've got this."

Ed backed away, weapon firing.

Ethan dove into the fray, swinging his blades despite his dwindling strength.

The Russian immortal nodded to Ethan. "I must go now," he said in heavily accented English. "They need me in Russia."

Ethan nodded and sank a blade into the nearest vamp as the Russian teleported away.

Down here, where no broken windows ushered in the

predawn breeze, the stench of blood and death and decay grew to overpowering proportions.

A second vampire he fought fell onto the pile of his moldering comrades. Then a third and a fourth.

Ethan found he had to pause to catch his breath and braced his hands, still clutching the hilts of his swords, on his knees.

Silence fell, broken only by the groans of the wounded above.

Straightening, he glanced around.

No vampires remained standing.

Heather glanced back at him over her shoulder, her brow furrowed.

All movement upstairs ceased.

Ethan had no doubt that every immortal in the house strained to hear any noise that would indicate a second wave would strike.

Several minutes passed.

He heard Chris Reordon begin to issue orders above.

Tracy met Ethan's gaze. "Is it over?"

He sighed. "I sure as hell hope so."

Bastien yanked his sword from the heart of a fallen vampire and swung around . . . to find himself, Melanie, Alleck, and Linda the only ones left standing on sublevel one.

They had successfully prevented the attacking vampire army from descending any farther.

Gershom had not returned. Nor had Aidan returned with the baby.

Bastien couldn't decide whether that was cause for concern or relief as he examined the hallway around him.

The white walls, ceiling, and floor looked as though someone has slung gallons of red paint on them. Clothing and decaying corpses littered the floor around them in such numbers it was damned near impossible to take a step without tripping.

Melanie's glowing amber eyes met his. "Is it over?"

"I think so." He sure as hell hoped so. They had all taken a beating. And every human guard on this floor was down. The few civilians who hadn't had time to evacuate to the lower floors before the vampires made it this far had fallen, too. He nodded at them. "No time to wait and see. We need to start looking for survivors and save anyone we can."

Sheathing her weapons, Melanie limped toward the first casualty.

The acrid scent of smoke stung Seth's nostrils, distracting him momentarily from the nauseating aromas of death and decay.

All movement ceased as quiet fell on the compound.

Few of the buildings remained standing. Defeating this army of vampires had taken everything the immortals had had and then some. *Then some* being an assload of explosives the Russian branch of the network had employed.

"Is it over?" Lisette asked.

Seth closed his eyes, let his preternaturally sharp senses seek anything that would indicate more human minions would take up the fight their vampire comrades had lost.

"It's over," he confirmed.

Network soldiers went to work, locating the wounded and collecting the bodies of their fallen comrades.

Eyes still closed, Seth called to Zach telepathically. *Zach? Have you found him?*

I'm on his trail. Don't distract me.

Lisette limped over to Seth's side. "Where is Zach?"

"Pursuing one of the Others who put in an appearance at David's. Ami found the Other standing over Adira's crib, bearing Marcus's appearance."

Horror filled her bloodstained features. "Is Adira all right?"

"Yes. Ami summoned me before the Other could harm her."

"It wasn't Gershom?"

"No."

"And Zach?"

"Is bitching about me distracting him, so I assume he's fine."

"Who do you think it was?"

"I don't know. We'll have to wait until Zach catches up with him."

She seemed as displeased by the notion as he.

Seth would much rather hunt down the culprit himself. But he had three battle scenes to help the network clean up and conceal from authorities. Dozens of wounded humans to heal and teleport to various network infirmaries.

Sheathing his swords, he stepped out into the crimson-stained snow.

Heather thanked Aidan as he healed her thigh, as well as the cuts a few of the vampires had managed to get in before they had collapsed.

She hadn't realized there had been so many, hadn't even felt most of them, until the battle had ended and adrenaline had ceased pumping through her veins. Then every slice the damned vampires had scored had begun to burn and throb.

Ethan availed himself of bagged blood while Aidan healed Heather's wounds. Like every other immortal present, he bore countless injuries. So much blood coated him and dampened his hair that she could barely distinguish him from the others.

"Let's go get cleaned up," he suggested.

Nodding, she dragged her weary body to her feet and shuffled down the hallway with him. Once inside the bedroom they'd claimed, Heather stood, shoulders slumped, as Ethan opened the shower door, turned on the water, and adusted the temperature. She didn't think she had ever been so exhausted in her life.

"Let me help you, honey."

She looked up as Ethan moved to stand before her and started divesting her of her various sheaths and the weapons she hadn't used.

"Are you okay?" he asked, bloody brow creased.

"Yeah. Just tired."

He nodded. "Anything else?"

She sighed. "Upset by the losses." Several of the network soldiers hadn't survived. "And . . ."

"And?"

"It's going to take me a while to get used to this. To the violence and death."

"You say that as if you feel you *have* to get used to it," he murmured, watching her intently.

Heather was too tired to tread carefully. "Won't I? If I stick around, won't this become a norm for me?"

Setting the last holster aside, he went to work on her belt. "Nothing about this was a norm, Heather. We've never been attacked on three fronts at the same time before. We've never been divided by an enemy like this in an attempt to reduce our numbers and conquer us. Hell, until now the only time *any* of David's homes have been breached by an enemy was when Bastien kidnapped Sarah. And we sure as hell have never seen a vampire army that spanned more than one continent and claimed such numbers. Even Shadow River wasn't this large."

When he untucked her shirt, she raised her arms and let him pull it over her head. "You still hunt vampires on a nightly basis."

"But *you* may not have to," he said slowly. "If you decide to join us, that is." He removed her bra, pants, and bikini panties. "You could continue doing what you're already doing." He pulled off all of his clothing in a blink. Numerous scars that would fade while he slept marred his large, muscular body. "You could be Chris's eyes and ears. Continue working with your dad."

At last she found a faint smile. "Could you maybe not mention my dad while we're both standing here naked? I mean, I know I'm too tired to do any fun stuff, but . . . still."

Laughing, he looped an arm around her and guided her into the shower. "Yeah. I didn't think that one through."

And she had evaded his question. His veiled request.

Warm water sluiced down over her, sweeping away the remains of battle as steam enveloped them. Heather reached for the soap.

Ethan stopped her. "Let me." Grabbing the soap, he lathered up a cloth she hadn't seen him grab. The tenderness with which he bathed away the splashes of blood on her bare form made her want to weep. As did the disappointment he tried to conceal behind teasing comments and soft smiles.

He had recognized her evasion for what it had been.

Heather tried to take the cloth from him once she was clean, but he would have none of it.

"You're weaving on your feet," he said just before he blurred and soap suds flew. Seconds later, he stilled and rinsed himself clean.

She found a smile. "Aren't you tired at all?"

"A little. But the blood replenished much of my energy."

Lucky him. Heather could barely keep her eyes open.

Ethan shut off the water. Helping her out of the shower, he toweled her dry, kept her upright long enough for them both to brush their teeth, then climbed into bed with her and tucked her up against his side.

"Ethan?" she murmured, sleep so tantalizingly close she let her lids drift shut.

"Yeah?"

"It isn't that I don't want to transform so we can be together."

The hand that had been stroking her arm fell still.

"It's that I'm afraid I pose a threat to you. We still don't know why Gershom messed with my head." A yawn stole her voice. "Or if he plans to do it again. Or if I would even be able to tell if he did."

"Heather . . ."

"I love you. But if I stay with you, he'll"—another yawn shook her—"always be able to use me . . . against you."

Darkness rose around her and drew her into its soundless embrace.

Ethan's heart pounded in his chest as he listened to Heather's breath deepen with sleep. It sounded as though she wished to be transformed. As if she wanted to become immortal so she could be with him. Forever.

Forever was a long damned time for immortals and could be daunting when faced alone. But Ethan would embrace it eagerly if he had Heather at his side.

He let himself imagine it for a moment. Let warmth invade his chest and excitement stir in his veins as he pictured spending a thousand lifetimes with the woman snuggled up against him.

Ethan didn't think he had ever wanted anything more.

He drew her closer.

Although perhaps he *did* want something more.

He wanted Seth and Zach to find Gershom and cut his fucking heart out so Heather could abandon her fears and feel free to become immortal.

He pursed his lips.

And so they could prevent Armageddon, of course.

Perhaps, he thought wryly, the fact that Armageddon came in second was an indication of how much he loved Heather and wanted to spend the rest of eternity with her.

Pressing a kiss to her soft, damp hair, he closed his eyes and let a deep healing sleep claim him.

* * *

Seth had thought he had his hands full shielding the three battles they had fought tonight from the public and authorities. That ended up being nothing, however, compared to trying to assuage David's fury over Gershom having sent vampires to attack his home.

David's temper didn't erupt often. But when it did, it rivaled Seth's.

Like children trying to avoid a spanking, the immortals and their Seconds had all skedaddled to their rooms, leaving Seth to try to calm his friend's ire. Not an easy task, since Seth battled his own fury over the brush with danger Ami and Adira had experienced.

He eyed the rubble around him. The house was a shambles, the furniture reduced to splinters, every window shattered. It looked even worse in the morning sunlight.

Knowing the immortals and their Seconds needed rest, Chris had told Seth he wouldn't send the full force of his cleanup crew out to right the damage until nightfall.

"My home, Seth!" David continued to rage. "My homes have *always* been off limits!"

"I know. He did it to send us a message."

"That all bets are off!" David thundered.

Seth again examined the scarlet-stained debris around him. After this, they sure as hell were.

Seth. Zach spoke in his mind.

Yes?

I think I've found him.

"Zach is summoning me," Seth told David, interrupting his tirade. "He thinks he's found the one who tried to harm Adira."

David's glowing amber eyes met his. "Bury him, Seth."

He nodded. That was the plan.

When Seth teleported to Zach's side, he found himself in a familiar place he had not expected.

The two of them stood alone in a clearing, the darkness of night replacing morning.

No clouds hid the plethora of stars above them.

And no Other occupied the clearing with them.

Frowning, Seth surveyed his surroundings.

The earth around them curved upward on all sides into rolling hills as if he and Zach stood in the center of a large, grassy bowl. No trees rose from the ground to block the light of the moon that offered them muted light. Not until one's gaze reached the tops of the hills. There, trees erupted into forest so dense that even Seth's sharp eyes couldn't penetrate it.

Something rustled in the grass that teased their knees. Some tiny nocturnal creature out looking for a snack.

Seth looked at Zach.

"He's here," Zach murmured, his brows drawn down as he scrutinized every shadow. "I know he is. I followed him here and he hasn't teleported away yet. I just can't find him."

Both he and Zach had been there before . . . under rather tense circumstances. At the time, their renewed friendship had not yet solidified. Distrust had still racked them. So much so that Zach had thought Seth intended to hand him over to the Others.

"Coincidence?" Seth asked Zach.

"I think not."

Seth agreed.

Do you sense anyone's presence? Zach asked him telepathically to prevent the Other from hearing.

Yes, but it's faint . . . as though he's trying to mask it but hasn't quite mastered that talent yet. Either that or he's too weary from his attempts to elude you to keep it up much longer. "Show yourself!" Seth bellowed, almost wishing they had Ami with them to point the way.

Zach looked at him and arched a brow.

Seth shrugged. No harm in trying the direct route.

The constant serenade of nocturnal creatures fell silent.

A disembodied voice wafted on the breeze. "I believe you once called this place neutral territory."

Again Seth and Zach shared a look.

Seth had told Zach as much the night he had brought Zach here to inform the Others that one of their own had lost his fucking mind.

"I did say that," Seth acknowledged.

"Then I trust you will not launch an attack when I show myself," the voice posed.

Do you recognize his voice? Seth asked Zach.

It's one of the Others, Zach said, *I just can't place it. I think he's altered his voice to keep me from identifying him.*

"Gentlemen?" the Other pressed.

"We shall endeavor to restrain ourselves," Zach responded, his own voice rife with sarcasm. Apparently he, too, would make no promises.

"I suppose that's as good as it's going to get," the Other muttered.

Dense foliage on the north ridge parted as a dark figure emerged from the forest.

Zach tensed.

Not yet, Seth cautioned. *It could be a trap.* The fact that they didn't sense Gershom didn't mean that one wasn't present, as well.

The Other took his time, descending the hillside and strolling toward them as if it were a lazy Sunday afternoon and he were just out for a stroll.

Testing their resolve, perhaps.

The Other stood about Seth's height—six foot eight—and wore black leather pants similar to Zach's, boots, and no shirt. Dark wings bracketed his body, their tips brushing the weeds and prairie grass and setting them into motion with each step he took.

As soon as Seth could make out his features, he swore.

"You've got to be fucking kidding me!" Zach growled and lunged forward.

Seth threw a hand out and gripped Zach's arm to keep him from tearing into the Other. *Let us ensure he is alone first. If he's in league with Gershom . . .*

Well, he and Zach would have their hands full and might have to call in reinforcements.

Zach stopped, eyes blazing a vibrant gold, every muscle tense and poised to strike.

Seth was none too pleased himself.

Jared halted a few yards away. Eyeing Zach, he arched a brow. "Hello, cousin."

"Are you fucking kidding me?" Zach roared again.

Jared was one of the Others who had tortured Zach for straying from the path and interfering in mortal affairs. For aiding Seth and his Immortal Guardians, in fact.

Seth didn't blame Zach for wanting to gut the man.

"You fucking tortured me for daring to tell Seth that his cell phone was broken and that his Immortal Guardians needed him, then tortured me again for months just for *talking* to him, then you pull the shit you did tonight?" Zach shouted. "What the fuck was that if not interfering in mortal affairs? You tried to harm Ami's baby!"

"I wasn't there to harm the baby," Jared denied placidly.

"Bullshit!" Zach took a menacing step toward the Other.

Seth kept a tight grip on Zach's arm.

Jared looked to Seth. "Can't you keep him under control better than that?"

Seth offered him a grim smile. "I'm only keeping him under control because I want to kill you myself."

That arrow hit its mark. Something flickered in Jared's

dark brown eyes. All present knew that if it came down to a battle between Seth and Jared, Seth would be the victor.

Jared shifted his stance slightly. "I wasn't there to harm the baby."

"Bullshit!"

"Zach," Seth reprimanded. He wasn't getting any deception vibes from Jared and wanted to hear what the man had to say.

Yes, Seth wanted to kick Jared's ass and was struggling to hold his own furious temper in check. But Seth had falsely accused three different immortals of betrayal the previous year. The evidence had driven him to do it, distasteful though he had found it. And the evidence had misled him. Seth had learned a hard lesson not to take things at face value.

Zach clamped his lips shut.

"I wasn't there to harm the baby," Jared repeated. "I was there to protect her. I would've stayed to protect Amiriska, too, when she arrived, but she moved to attack me and I didn't wish to restrain her."

Seth shook his head. "Ami said you were standing over Adira's crib and had cloaked yourself in Marcus's appearance."

"What better place to protect the child than in her own room?" Jared rebutted. "I assumed Marcus's appearance for two reasons. One, so if Gershom arrived he would take one look at me and discount me as a threat, giving me a better chance of attacking and holding his ass until you and the Others could join us. And two, so the babe would think me her daddy and not be afraid." Jared's brow furrowed. "Although I'm pretty sure she saw right through my ruse. She truly is an exceptional child."

Seth stared at him.

Zach looked at Seth. "Do I really need to say this is bullshit again?"

Seth agreed. "Why should we believe you?"

"Because I'm the one who brought Heather and Ethan together."

Seth stared at him. *Jared* had done that? Not Gershom? "Why?"

Jared frowned and shifted again. "That is something best explained with Heather and Ethan present."

"Not going to happen," Seth retorted.

"Trust me, cousin, when I say they'll want to hear this."

"I've no reason to trust you, *cousin*."

Jared shook his head. "Well, I'm afraid you've little choice. Their lives . . . and yours . . . and the lives of your Immortal Guardians all *depend* upon you trusting me."

Zach stopped straining against Seth's hold.

Seth released Zach's arm as all the fight seemed to leave him. *What is it?*

Zach's gaze never strayed from their visitor. "You've seen something," he said. "You've seen the future."

Seth studied Jared. He had forgotten that Jared was subject to prophetic visions. Far stronger visions than those Seth received.

"Yes," Jared confessed, his expression chilling Seth.

"What did you see?" Seth asked.

"I saw Gershom succeed," Jared told them. "I saw Armageddon unfold. And this time, when the world is wiped clean, no one is going to warn Noah to build a boat."

Shit. "You're saying—"

"No one will survive," Jared declared. "No bunker will be deep enough to protect humans. No amount of doomsday prepping will save lives. And *we*—all of us Others and your Immortal Guardians—will be destroyed as well."

Stunned silence.

"You've had this vision?" Seth asked him.

"More than once. Which is why I was at David's place during the battle." Jared met each man's gaze. "It's time to choose sides, gentlemen. And I've chosen yours."

Seth could find no response. He had been so sure he and Zach would be able to stop Gershom. *Do Jared's visions always come true?* he asked Zach.

Always. But he's never done anything before to try to alter their outcome. This is unprecedented. Whatever he saw must have scared the hell out of him.

Seth agreed. It *must* have if Jared was willing to risk all to join Zach, Seth, and the Immortal Guardians.

"What does this have to do with Heather and Ethan?" Seth asked him. "We know you've been manipulating her dreams and pitting vampires against them . . . at the very least."

"Once more I ask that you allow the couple to join us so they can hear it, too. With you two as their guard, they've nothing to fear from me."

Still no hint of deception bled into his words.

Seth looked to Zach. "Go get them."

Seriously? Zach asked, his look questioning Seth's sanity.

Yes.

You're the one who keeps saying this could be a trap.

Then be quick about it. Tell them they're welcome to come armed. But warn Ethan to keep his shit in check. I want to see where Jared is going with this and won't be able to do that if Ethan lets fury drive him to attack the moment he hears who Jared is.

Sending Jared a warning glare, Zach vanished.

Chapter Twenty-Two

"Ethan."

Heather jerked awake.

The mattress beneath her shook violently as a thud sounded.

"Ethan!"

Gasping, she raised her head and yanked the covers up to her chin.

Zach stood at the foot of the bed, scowling at the immortal still slumbering beside her. "He sleeps even harder than Lisette does," he grumbled and kicked the bed frame again. "Wake up, damn it!"

Ethan didn't so much as twitch, deeply ensconced in a healing sleep.

Sitting up, Heather touched his bare shoulder. "Ethan?"

Ethan's eyes opened. "What?" He blinked up at her. "What is it?"

She nodded to their guest.

Spying Zach, Ethan sat up. "What are *you* doing here?"

"We've found the Other who has been fucking with Heather's mind. Seth is holding him . . . in a manner of speaking . . . and would like you two to join us."

Heather's heart began to pound. They had found Gershom?

Was this it, then? Would they finally learn why he had been manipulating her dreams?

Ethan stared at Zach, wide awake now. "You've caught Gershom?"

Zach shook his head. "Different Other. Turns out Gershom isn't the one who was doing it. Get dressed while I get David up to speed."

He vanished.

Heather leapt out of bed and began yanking on hunting clothes as fast as she could.

Ethan dressed in a matter of seconds, then packed on a buttload of weapons.

As soon as Heather tugged a shirt over her mussed hair and zipped up her pants, Ethan began to load *her* up with weapons as well.

"Maybe you shouldn't go," Ethan murmured, his fear for her palpable.

"I don't think Zach is giving us a choice," she said as he fastened a holster to her thigh. "And I need to know what this Other did to me. *Why* he did it to me. To *us*. I need to know if I'm a threat to you."

Heather barely had time to drag a comb through her hair and brush her teeth before Zach returned.

"Shall we?" He didn't wait for an answer. He just gripped their shoulders and teleported them to a bowl-shaped clearing cloaked in darkness.

At least that was what Heather thought it was. She could barely see a thing.

Light bathed them as an old-fashioned lantern appeared in Seth's hand. He flattened the grass in front of them and set it on the ground.

"Thank you." Heather knew the light was for her benefit. The rest probably had no difficulty seeing each other.

Ethan wrapped an arm around her and drew her close.

Seth and Zach stood on either side of them.

A tall, bare-chested, handsome man who bore the look of an Immortal Guardian and . . . wings? . . . faced them.

Ethan glared at the stranger. "Is this the prick who fucked with Heather's dreams?"

The stranger arched a brow. "Had I not fucked with Heather's dreams, you two wouldn't be together right now."

Heather bit her lip. There was no denying that.

The stranger caught Heather's eye. "I'm Jared."

She refused to say it was a pleasure to meet him.

"As I was telling Seth and Zach, I've seen the future. Zach can confirm for you that my prophetic visions are always accurate. In the ones I began having about a year ago, I saw a future in which Gershom triumphs over you all and succeeds in sparking Armageddon."

Heather's stomach twisted into a knot.

"No one—humans, *gifted ones*, vampires, immortals, or Others—will survive."

When Heather looked at Seth and Zach, their grim countenances sent fear careening through her.

Her heart began to pound. How much time did they have?

"Why did you fuck with her dreams?" Ethan pressed.

"Because World War Three was imminent. And I knew she was the key to preventing it."

Silence fell in the wake of that bombshell.

Jared looked to Seth. "You wouldn't have found the vampires' lair in Russia before they attacked another U.S. military base. The next base they would've attacked would've been very large, very visible, and on American soil. The attack wouldn't have been hidden from the public as the first two were. It would've left no doubt that Russia was responsible. And all hell would've broken loose. You needed General Lane on your side, both to help you find the vampires before they struck again and to help you control the fallout." He shifted his attention back to Heather. "I knew *you* could make that happen."

The power to speak eluded her.

"Had I not interfered, Ethan would've fought those vampires several miles down the road from your home and the two of you would've never met. A little mind control sent the vampires veering in your direction and"—he shrugged— "the dreams lured you into their skirmish."

Seth shook his head. "Why didn't you just come to me and tell me what you'd seen? Tell me what needed to be done?"

"Because the Others are watching you like a hawk. When Zach defected, he ran straight to you and your Immortal Guardians. They assume anyone else who may begin to have doubts will do the same. I couldn't take the chance that they would capture me before I had an opportunity to speak with you. And . . ."

"And?" Ethan pressed.

"I wasn't sure anything we did would make a difference," Jared admitted. "My visions *always* come true. I've never tried to intervene and evoke a different outcome before and didn't know I could until . . ." He shifted, uneasiness creeping into his expression.

"Until?" Ethan gritted.

Jared met Heather's gaze. "Until you sacrificed yourself for Ethan in the second battle you fought together."

Ethan dropped his arm from around Heather and took a furious step forward. "You son of a bitch! She nearly died that night! And *you* sent those vampires to her home, didn't you?"

"Yes."

Zach and Seth swore.

"Why?" Heather asked.

"I knew Ethan was going to drop by that night to court you and wanted to give him added incentive to keep you close so that when your father called you in, Seth and his Immortal Guardians would learn that vampires had attacked the first base. Time was running out. I needed to get the ball rolling. I didn't know until after I implanted the impulse to attack in some local vampires that Ethan would be slain."

"I wasn't slain, asshole!" Ethan bellowed. "*She* was. Or she *would've* been if Seth hadn't reached her soon enough!"

Jared looked at each of them in turn. "And that was the confirmation I needed. That was the first time I knew absolutely that we *can* change the future. That it doesn't have to unfold as it did in my visions. Once I planted the impulse to attack in those vampires' feeble brains, I began having visions of the battle you two would fight. In every single one of them, Ethan was decapitated, then Seth teleported in and saved Heather."

Heather felt sick. Had she not thrown herself between Ethan and the vampire's blade that night, they really would have lost him. *She* would have lost him.

She looked up at Ethan, so thankful she had been forewarned.

Ethan didn't look thankful at all. He looked furious. "If you knew I was going to be destroyed, why the hell did you show Heather what would happen in her dreams?"

Jared shrugged. "I thought it best that she be prepared for battle and didn't realize she would throw herself between you and that blade. I sure as hell didn't want her to die that night. Seth and his immortals needed the connections she'd bring too much." He sent Seth a frown. "This tampering with mortal affairs thing can be trickier that I presumed."

"Welcome to my world."

"What about the other dreams?" Heather asked.

Jared frowned. "What other dreams?"

Ethan frowned, too. "You had other dreams? You didn't mention that."

Heather hesitated. She really would rather not say this in front of all of them.

"The sex dreams," Zach said.

"Damn it! Stop reading my thoughts!" Heather snapped, then turned back to Jared with a sigh. "Yes. What *he* said. The sex dreams. About Ethan." Her face heated with what no doubt was a flaming blush.

Ethan nudged her shoulder, his lips curling up in a smile. "You had sex dreams about me?"

"Yes. It's one of the reasons I felt like I'd known you for a long time when we first met."

Jared's eyebrows flew up. "I planted no such dreams in your mind."

Heather stared at him. "What do you mean? You must have. I had them for months before I met Ethan."

Seth cleared his throat. "If you dreamed of fighting vampires with Ethan every night, then thought about him during the day, it's natural that your subconscious mind would eventually begin to fabricate dreams of him on its own."

"Oh." So she had embarrassed herself for nothing. Lovely. She caught Jared's eye. "Well . . . thank you. For bringing Ethan into my life and for showing me what would happen in my dreams so I could keep the vampires from killing him."

Jared glanced at Seth and Zach, then back at Heather. "You're welcome?"

Amusement stealing away some of her embarrassment, she nodded.

Seth's expression remained grim. "Tell me again why you pretended to be Marcus and were with Adira tonight."

Heather gasped.

Ethan swore. "He what?"

Jared sighed. "You know Gershom wants to spark Armageddon. You know he wants to watch the world burn. But he also seems to bear a hell of a lot of malice toward you, Seth."

"Why?" Seth asked, his tone baffled.

"I think he resents the fact that, while the rest of us obeyed the rules and restricted ourselves to merely *observing* life, you have been *living* it all this time. I think he sees what you have, what you've done and experienced, and is bitter over having missed out on experiencing the same himself."

"Then why the hell didn't he just do what Zach did: Tell the rest of you to fuck off and join me?"

Jared shook his head. "I believe, much like the vampires you seek to exterminate, Gershom has been slowly descending into madness. It just took him thousands of years to reach the breaking point."

"And so he's targeting me?" Seth asked.

"Yes. I think he relished pitting you against your immortals last year. I think he liked manipulating one of the employees of your trusted human network into working against you. And clearly he has no desire to stop at either of those, because tonight he succeeded in dividing you."

"Divide and conquer," Zach murmured.

"Yes. He lured Seth away, then sent masses of vampires to attack both David's home and network headquarters." He stared at Seth. "We aren't stupid, you know. Every one of us is well aware of what the alien woman means to you. Every one of us knows you love her as much as you did the son and daughter you lost. What better way to strike at you than through her baby?"

Everyone present, including Heather, swore.

"Particularly," Jared added, "since you nearly kick-started Armageddon yourself when your wife, son, and daughter were slain all those years ago."

Seth had been married? And his wife and children had been killed?

Heather's heart went out to him.

"I was observing David's place when vampires attacked it," Jared continued. "Like you, I suspected Gershom might have left a trail to lure you to Russia so he could make mischief in North Carolina. When Adira was taken to the network, I followed, but concealed my presence."

"Why?" Seth asked.

"Because, as I said, the Others are watching you like a hawk. I didn't want them to see me at David's, then at the network, and drag me away, assuming I was pulling a Zach."

Heather glanced at Zach and thought the fury on his face was a little frightening.

"Shortly after the baby arrived at the network, Gershom put in an appearance and vampires attacked it. The moment Gershom heard Adira begin to cry, he went straight to the room in which she was being sheltered. The immortal Celt teleported her away—"

"Did Gershom pursue him?" Seth asked, lips tight.

"No. The moment the Celt left with the baby, I let Gershom sense my presence. He hesitated, then teleported away, taking a different path. I followed the Celt, thinking it a ruse by Gershom, that he might catch up with the two at another location. But he didn't. When the Celt returned the baby to David's home . . ." Again Jared shrugged. "I did what I felt I had to do. I pretended to be her father so I would be there to protect her *and* to throw Gershom off should he eventually follow her there to . . . do whatever he thought might hurt you most."

Seth's face paled. His throat moved in a swallow. "Did Gershom show himself at David's?"

"I didn't see him while I was there."

"Can you sense him when he's not in your sight?"

"No. I don't know he's there until he shows himself. But, unlike Gershom, I'd know him if I saw him even if he tried to camouflage his appearance."

"*Can* he camouflage his appearance in such a way? I know he can shift into animal forms, but alternate human forms *and* their personalities are more difficult to assume. Can Gershom pass himself off as one of my immortals?"

Heather held her breath, awaiting the answer.

"I don't know," Jared confessed.

Seth eyed Zach.

"I believe him," Zach said, his brow furrowed.

Seth returned his attention to Jared. "If Gershom wants to strike at me through my family, through Ami and Adira, how can I protect them?"

"By doing what you already are. Keep them close so you, Zach, or I—if you'll allow me join you—will always be on hand to guard them. David, too. Your second in command may not be as strong as *you* are, but he can give the rest of us a run for our money."

Zach's eyebrows flew up. "Really? You think David could best one of us in battle?"

Seth smirked. "Did he not warn you as much himself?"

"Yes." Zach looked thoughtful. "Perhaps I should have taken him more seriously."

"I sure as hell do," Ethan put in with a wry smile.

"Yes, but you're just a pup," Zach pointed out.

Jared cleared his throat. "So . . . where do we go from here?"

Heather slipped her hand into Ethan's.

Looking down, he gave her hand a squeeze.

"Lower your mental barriers," Seth commanded. "Let me read your thoughts."

Jared scowled and looked to Zach. "Did *you* have to do that to win his trust?"

"No. I refused."

Seth spoke before Jared could. "Zach was in love with one of my immortals, so he had a vested interest in keeping her— and the rest of my Immortal Guardians—safe. I didn't need to read his thoughts to know he wouldn't betray us."

A tense moment passed. "Fine," Jared grumbled. "Just do it. My barriers are down."

Ethan caught Heather's eye and nodded slightly toward Jared.

Really? He wanted her to read Jared's thoughts?

She hesitated. Jared had been in *her* head often enough. She supposed it was only fair that she return the favor.

Heather closed her eyes, focused on the Other's thoughts . . . and found herself caught up in the search Seth performed. Year after year of thoughts and memories and events flew past as though someone had pressed rewind. Decades passed, flowing backward. Centuries. Millennia.

A hand gripped her arm none too gently.

Eyes flying open, she looked up at Zach.

"You've seen enough," he told her. "Seth alone should see the rest."

Her stomach jumping with nerves, Heather nodded.

Ethan scowled. "Leave her alone."

Zach released her arm. "I'm doing her a favor, Ethan. There are things about the Others she can't know. If she sees any more than she already has, Seth will have to erase her memory of it."

"It's okay," Heather assured Ethan. "I've seen enough." She had seen that, like Zach, Jared questioned the path the Others had chosen. She had seen the dismay that had stricken Jared when she had been run through in the second battle with vampires he had instigated. She had seen the fear he had felt for the delicate mortal baby Seth loved when the battles had raged earlier today.

And she had felt how much Jared wished to find for himself, after thousands of years of loneliness, what Zach had found.

Seth abruptly strode forward and offered Jared his hand. "Thank you for protecting Adira. You are welcome to join us."

A faint smile curling his lips, Jared shook Seth's hand. "The Others aren't going to like this. Three defections in as many years?"

Zach joined Seth and offered his own hand. "The Others

need to follow your example and choose sides. Preferably ours."

Jared nodded.

As soon as Zach released Jared's hand, he drew back his arm and slammed his fist into the other man's face.

Heather heard bone crack as Jared flew backward a good twenty yards and hit the ground, skidding several feet and leaving a wide path in the grass.

Seth sighed and sent Zach a withering look. "Really?"

Zach shrugged. "The bastard tortured me. What did you expect?"

Somewhere in the grass and the darkness that eclipsed him, Jared groaned. "Yeah. Sorry about that, Zach."

Ethan laughed.

Heather did, too, her tense muscles relaxing.

As the words spoken in that clearing finally began to sink in, joy filled her.

She wasn't being used as a pawn by Gershom. Gershom had never even been in her head. Her dreams and thoughts *weren't* being manipulated with the intention of harming Seth and his Immortal Guardians. She was free to love Ethan now. Free to be with him without fearing she would hurt him. Free to be with him *always*, if she so chose.

Her heart began to pound.

She really *could* be with Ethan always. She could transform now and spend hundreds, if not thousands, of years with him, laughing and loving.

Yes, his was a dangerous world. But whose wasn't with Gershom out there plotting Armageddon?

Ethan glanced down at her, a frown marring his handsome features. "What's wrong? Your heart is racing."

Grinning big, she reached up, curled her free hand around his neck, and drew him down for a long, passionate kiss.

Ethan could be hers now.

All hers.

Rising onto her toes, she leaned into him.

Ethan hummed his approval and wrapped his arms around her, locking her against his hard body as the kiss went on and on.

At last, Heather broke the heated contact. Excitement filled her near to bursting. "I love you, Ethan," she professed, breathless from the kiss.

"I love you, too," he said, his eyes glowing vibrant amber.

"Enough to make me immortal?" she asked.

Grass rustled as Jared dragged himself to his feet, but Heather kept her eyes on Ethan.

He sucked in a breath. His eyes brightened. "You would do that? You would let me transform you? You would spend forever with me?" His look turned wry. "Even if Gershom succeeds and forever only ends up being a few years?"

She nodded. "However long forever lasts, Ethan, I want to spend it with you."

Ethan hugged her tight, picking her up so her feet dangled above the ground. "Thank you," he murmured, his voice hoarse. "I love you, Heather. More than I knew I *could* love another. I'm sorry so much bad shit had to happen to bring us together, but I am *so* glad we're together."

"Me, too." Over his shoulder, she saw Seth and Zach watching them. "We have an audience," she whispered in his ear.

Ethan lowered Heather until her feet touched the ground, then turned to face the elders, his arm around her shoulders, keeping her close. "She wants to be transformed," he announced.

Seth smiled. "So I heard. You may do so at your convenience. However, I ask that you do it at David's place so he can help her through the transformation."

Ethan nodded.

Heather's belly filled with butterflies, but it didn't dampen her happiness.

Jared trudged into the lantern's light, his nose and chin

bloody, and stood on Zach's other side. Scowling at Zach, he said, "I take it we're even now?"

Zach's fist shot out and struck him in the jaw. "Not quite."

Jared flew sideways out of Heather's line of sight and hit the ground with a thud.

A groan floated on the night.

Seth's face darkened with displeasure. "Damn it, Zach!"

A wicked smile curved Zach's lips. "This is going to be fun."

Aidan stared down at the list of names he had compiled. Beside it, spread out on Cliff's coffee table, was a building schematic of network headquarters.

"This one," Cliff said, pointing to a name, "you can cross off your list. She's in love with a professor at UNC and just found out she's pregnant."

"Are they married?" Aidan asked.

"No. But based on the lovey-dovey crap I hear when they call each other, they'll probably get married as soon as she tells him about the baby."

Aidan drew a line through the woman's name.

"Now, Angela might be a good fit for you." Cliff sorted through several sheaves of paper until he found the map of sublevel three. "Her office is here, just up the hallway from the cafeteria. She's single. She's pretty. She's . . . I don't know . . . maybe thirty-five. I think she might have a little girl. Is that a deal breaker?"

"No," Aidan said. "I can't give her children myself and have long wondered what it would be like to be a father."

"Well, since you're so old you can go out in daylight, you could take the kid to the park and everything."

How normal it sounded. How wonderfully beyond-his-reach normal.

"*And*," Cliff added, "she doesn't freak out when she runs into me in the cafeteria. A very good sign. If she doesn't freak out when she sees *me*, then she may not be nervous around *you* the way many of the employees here are around immortals."

Aidan smiled at the vampire. He hadn't known Cliff long, but already considered him a friend. Yet another first he had experienced since Seth had transferred him to North Carolina. Aidan would've never thought he would befriend a vampire.

He hadn't liked how solemn and restrained, though, the young man had become after his psychotic break—which Aidan had trouble thinking of as a psychotic break since Cliff had been trying to save Linda. So Aidan had decided to enlist the vampire's aid in his quest to find a *gifted one* who might love Aidan enough to transform for him and spend the rest of eternity ridding him of this aching loneliness that plagued him.

The distraction seemed to be working, at least in part. Cliff had behaved much more like his old self these last few days.

"What does she do?" Aidan asked of the woman. "Is she smart?" If he had to choose between the two, Aidan would take brains over beauty any day.

Cliff snorted. "Everyone who works for the network is smart. I think . . ." He considered it a moment. "I think she might be one of the financial geniuses that manages the network's money. I can ask Linda, if you want."

Aidan shook his head. "I'll ask this Angela myself when I bump into her. Do you know what hours she works?"

"Yeah. She—"

A knock sounded on Cliff's apartment door. A moment later, a loud thunk sounded as it swung inward.

Ethan and Heather stood in the doorway.

"Hi," Heather greeted them with a tentative smile. "Are we interrupting anything?"

"No," Cliff said and turned one of the maps upside down on the coffee table to hide what they were doing. "Come on in."

The couple entered and closed the door behind them.

"How's it going?" Cliff asked, rising.

Aidan rose as well. Ethan was staring holes in him, so Aidan suspected they weren't just dropping by to shoot the breeze.

Heather smiled at Cliff. "Good. How are the voices today?" She frowned and bit her lip. "I'm sorry. Was that insensitive? Am I not supposed to ask about that?"

Aidan looked at Cliff, uncertain.

Cliff smiled. "I'd rather you ask about it than dance around it. They haven't been as loud or persistent of late."

Her smile returned. "Good."

The room quieted.

"So?" Cliff prompted when the silence stretched into awkward territory. "Would you like to sit down? Can I get you something to drink?"

"Actually," Ethan said, "we were hoping to talk Aidan into doing us a favor."

Aidan's curiosity rose. "What can I do for you?"

Ethan took Heather's hand.

Heather looked up at him, then met Aidan's gaze. "Would you please transform me?"

Aidan stared at the couple, damned near shocked speechless. "I beg your pardon?"

"Heather would like to become immortal," Ethan said. "Seth has given his blessing. And I was thinking . . ."

Cliff gave a slow nod. "You want Aidan to transform her so she'll be as strong as he is."

"Yes," the couple replied.

Aidan frowned. "I'm not certain that's how it works."

"Roland has transformed three *gifted ones* in recent years," Ethan said.

What a shocker that was. Roland was the most antisocial immortal Aidan had met.

"All three new immortals can match him in speed, strength,

and regenerative capabilities," Ethan continued. "No one knows why, whether it's because he's so old or because he's a healer or if it's something unique to him. But if it's either of the first two things . . ."

Understanding dawned. "I'm a healer and am even older than he is, so Heather would acquire the same strength, speed, and the like that I have if I were to transform her."

"Yes." Ethan's eyes practically begged Aidan to understand. "You know the enemy we face. You know the danger he poses. I want Heather to be as strong as possible when she faces whatever Gershom throws our way."

Aidan could understand that. Vampires had launched no more mass attacks, confirming in many minds that the immortals had successfully eradicated Gershom's army and thwarted his attempt to spark World War III. But all knew it would not be his last attempt.

How would he strike next? Would Gershom again manipulate the mind of a network employee? Or perhaps impersonate an Immortal Guardian as Jared had done? None were certain Gershom could even do the latter. But both possibilities could breed frightening repercussions. And Seth, Zach, and Jared had not yet been able to locate whatever lair Gershom had fled to to regroup and plan anew.

Aidan had never transformed a mortal before. He had always assumed that when he did, it would be a *gifted one* who had chosen to spend the rest of forever with him. But he had lived three thousand years without finding that woman. There seemed little point in holding out any longer. Particularly when he could help these two.

"I'll do it."

Cliff grinned. "Awesome! Congratulations, guys." Striding forward, he shook Ethan's hand and hugged Heather. Even that showed he was returning to his old self. Cliff had been keeping a careful distance from others since his break.

"When would you like to do it?" Aidan asked.

Heather shrugged. "Are you busy now?"

"No," he responded, surprised she wanted to act so swiftly.

She offered him a sheepish smile. "I'm a little nervous, so I'd kinda like to get it out of the way."

Aidan laughed. "As you will."

Ethan looked around his living room and smiled.

The furniture from Heather's small home that had not been destroyed in the vampire attack had been fetched, cleaned, and now mixed and mingled with his own. The photographs that had hung on her home's walls now bore new frames and adorned the walls here.

He could see Heather's touch all over the house. It no longer looked like the home of two longtime bachelors. Heather hadn't added any of what he and Ed considered feminine froufrou stuff. Yet one could definitely see the influence of a woman in the place.

Ethan liked it.

No, he loved it. He loved *her*. And intended to tell her as much every day for the rest of their long, long lives.

Heather entered the living room from the kitchen. "The chicken is almost done," she announced with a smile. She had insisted on preparing it herself.

"Smells delicious," he praised.

Ed strolled in from the hallway. "All right. I'm out."

"Are you sure you don't want to stay and join us?" Heather asked.

Ethan sent her a wry smile. "He has a hot date."

"Oh."

Ed flashed her a charming grin. "A *very* hot date."

She grinned. "Well, have fun, handsome."

Ed laughed, grabbed his keys, and headed for the door.

Ethan was pleased to see Heather and his Second getting along so well. Some women would have balked at having the other man live with them. Heather hadn't batted an eyelash.

As Ed stepped out into the night, he caught Ethan's eye. "Good luck."

Ethan grimaced. He'd need it.

"Oh, come on." Heather said after Ed left. "It isn't going to be that bad."

"If you say so," he muttered.

She eyed him speculatively. "Are you nervous?"

"No. Yes. Maybe. Why do you ask?"

She laughed.

Ethan didn't know how she could face the night so casually and straightened his tie for the dozenth time. "Do I look okay?"

Her eyes lit with amber fire as she gave him a long once-over. "You look positively edible." As did she with her iridescent eyes.

Ethan drew her close and pressed a tender kiss to her lips.

She had made it through her transformation with only one hitch. As with Sarah, Melanie, and Krysta, her fever had climbed so high they had had to submerge her in an ice bath to bring it down. It had scared the hell out of Ethan, making him all the more thankful that she would never be sick again.

Fortunately, Heather remembered very little of the three days illness had claimed her.

The doorbell chimed.

His heart leapt in his chest.

Heather laughed. "You really *are* nervous."

"Yes, damn it."

She leaned up and kissed his chin. "Everything's going to be okay, Ethan."

"Your eyes are glowing," he told her.

"Oh. Hold on." Stepping back, she closed her eyes a moment. When she opened them, they were brown once more.

He smiled, relieved.

She winked. "You're cute when you're nervous."

Ethan groaned. "Don't make this more difficult for me than it already is."

"Who? Me?" she asked, the picture of innocence.

"Ah hell. I'm screwed, aren't I?"

Laughing, Heather leaned past him and opened the front door. "Hi, Dad. Come on in."

General Lane, wearing slacks and a dress shirt with the collar loose, returned Heather's smile. Stepping inside, he waited for her to close the door, then gave her a big hug. "How's my girl?"

"Excellent," she chirped.

Her father turned to Ethan and offered his hand. "Ethan."

Ethan shook his hand. "Good to see you, sir."

General Lane glanced at Heather. "Should I have worn a suit?"

"No. Ethan's nervous, so he overdressed."

Ethan stared at her. "You said I looked fine."

A teasing glint entered her eye. "Actually, I said you looked positively—"

"Don't say it!"

She laughed.

Ethan sighed. "If you'll forgive me for saying so, sir, your daughter has a mean streak."

Smiling, General Lane clapped him on the back. "I've known that for years, son. So why are you nervous?"

Heather winked at her father. "He's afraid you're going to freak out when you find out we're living together."

Ethan gaped at her. "Heather!" They were supposed to ease him into things, damn it.

She laughed. "What? You think he isn't going to recognize my furniture? He *bought* some of it."

"I thought that chair looked familiar," General Lane muttered.

Heather looped her arm through her father's and guided him into the living room. "The vampires really did a number on my place, Dad. A lot of stuff wasn't salvageable. And I'm head over heels in love with Ethan. So, instead of taking turns staying at each other's home, we just moved my stuff in here and I live here now."

Her father cut Ethan a glance.

Ethan's palms began to sweat as his last hope of making a good impression began to slip away. "I'm going to marry her," he blurted.

Heather grinned, enjoying his discomfort so much he feared her eyes would soon begin to glow with mirth.

Ethan sighed. "That's actually why we invited you over tonight, sir. We were going to provide you with a delicious dinner, maybe some wine to relax you. Then I was going to tell you how much I love Heather and ask your permission to marry her. Your approval is important to me, so I was hoping to make a good impression. But your *daughter*, it seems, would rather watch me squirm."

She shrugged, offering him an unrepentant smile. "I can't help it. I've never seen you like this before. As I said, you're cute when you're nervous."

Ethan glanced at her father to see how he was taking all of this.

General Lane looked back and forth between the two. "What about the whole mortal and immortal thing? One of you is going to age and the other isn't. Won't that be a problem?"

"Not anymore," Heather answered. "I'm immortal now."

Ethan bit back a growl and glared at Heather. "What is *wrong* with you? I thought we were going to ease him into things." Both had agreed that such would be the best way to gain both her father's acceptance *and* his approval of the changes that had taken place.

Her face scrunched up with apology. "I know. We were. But I trained hard today and I'm really hungry and that damned chicken smells good."

Ethan bit back a laugh. Fighting and training at preternatural speeds and with preternatural strength did tend to burn a lot of calories and leave one feeling famished.

She shrugged. "I was kinda hoping to get all of the gasp and swoon stuff out of the way quickly so we could eat."

Ethan did laugh then and drew her into a hug. Over her head, he smiled at her father. "She did train hard today."

General Lane stared at them. "So she's . . . like you? Heather is . . . ?"

"Immortal. Yes, sir."

Heather stepped back and grinned at her father. "Check it out." Her eyes flashed brilliant amber as her fangs descended.

How Ethan loved seeing her like that. It just made him want to pounce.

General Lane gaped.

"I know it's a shock," Ethan said tentatively. "But . . ."

He shook his head. "It isn't a shock. It's a relief." Smiling, he hugged Heather tight. Then, releasing her, he pulled Ethan into a hug, too, clapping him on the back. "Thank you."

Surprised, Ethan stared down at him as General Lane stepped back. "You aren't angry?"

Still smiling, Heather's father shook his head. "Hell no. I nearly lost her twice in one month. Three times if you count the big battle she helped you fight a few weeks ago. Now that she's immortal, there's far less chance of that ever happening."

Heather grinned, her amber eyes lighting with mischief that did not bode well. "I'm super strong now, Dad. You want to see?"

Ethan threw up his hands. "No, no, no. No demonstrations. Not until you get your strength and speed under control."

Heather bit her lip, expression chagrined. "Oh. I guess you're right."

General Lane cocked an eyebrow.

"There have been a few . . . incidents," Ethan explained. "I didn't transform Heather myself. I wanted her to be stronger than I am. So we asked Aidan, a three-thousand-year-old immortal, to do it instead. As a result, Heather has much greater speed and strength than I do."

Heather nodded. "I can even tolerate some daylight."

"She's incredibly strong," Ethan went on, "and hasn't quite learned how to harness that yet, so . . . yeah. There've been a few incidents."

Heather eyed her father sheepishly. "They had to repair the roof. Twice. And one wall."

Her father shook his head. "Well, as soon as you gain control over it, I want a demonstration."

"Done." She grinned. "And I wasn't kidding, by the way, when I said I was really hungry. Can we sit down to dinner now? Please, please, please?" She motioned toward the dining room.

Nodding, General Lane strolled toward the table.

Heather grinned up at Ethan. "You see?" she whispered. "Just like ripping off a Band-Aid. The faster, the better."

Shaking his head, Ethan kissed her smiling lips. "You're evil," he murmured.

"Am I *evil*?" she purred. "Or naughty? Perhaps you should punish me."

"Don't tempt me, minx. Your father is in the next room."

She brushed her lips against his. "You aren't really angry, are you?"

"No. I'm too busy picturing you naked and tied to the bed now."

She grinned. "I love you, Ethan."

He stole another kiss. "I love you, too."

Taking his hand, Heather backed away and tugged him after her. "Now let's go get some of that chicken."

Laughing, Ethan shook his head as he followed her.